OUTSTANDING PRAISE FOR THE
ROMANCES OF KAT MARTIN

Devil's Prize

"Kat Martin dishes up sizzling passions and true love, then she serves it with savoir faire."

—*Los Angeles Daily News*

"Kat Martin is a premier historical writer . . . and *Devil's Prize* enhances her first-class reputation."

—*Affaire de Coeur*

Bold Angel

"Sizzling with sexual tension and ripe with rich emotion, this medieval romance is a real pleasure . . . As in her past historicals, Martin keeps true to time but the romance is paramount." —*Publishers Weekly*

"Moves quickly through a bold and exciting period of history. As usual, Kat has written an excellent and entertaining novel of days gone by." —Heather Graham

"An excellent medieval romance . . . Readers will not only love this novel but clamor for a sequel."

—*Affaire de Coeur*

Sweet Vengeance

"Kat Martin gives readers enormous pleasure with this deftly plotted, stunning romance." —*Romantic Times*

"A rich read, memorable characters, a romance that fulfills every woman's fantasy." —Deana James

MIDNIGHT RIDER

KAT MARTIN

St. Martin's Paperbacks

This is a work of fiction. All of the characters, organizations, and events portrayed in this novel are either products of the author's imagination or are used fictitiously.

MIDNIGHT RIDER

Copyright © 1996 by Kat Martin.

All rights reserved.

For information address St. Martin's Press, 175 Fifth Avenue, New York, NY 10010.

ISBN: 978-1-250-04141-8

Printed in the United States of America

St. Martin's Paperbacks edition / March 1996

St. Martin's Paperbacks are published by St. Martin's Press, 175 Fifth Avenue, New York, NY 10010.

10 9 8 7 6 5 4

In memory of my uncle, Joaquin Sanchez, one of the great American cowboys, his father, Pete, and the dozens of men who were the last of the vaqueros.

A special thanks to my husband for his help on this and all of my books. I love you, honey. You are the wind beneath my wings.

What say the bells of San Juan
   to the men who pass beneath them?

No more than the wind says to the leaves
   or the current to the pebbles
   in the bottom of the stream

The chapel that houses the bells has crumbled,
   the bells gone green with lichen

Yet their echo can still be heard, the sound of time
   passing through the ages.

Spanish poem
Anonymous

Chapter One

Silver conchos. Caralee McConnell fixed her eyes on the row of shiny ornaments glinting in the torch light, the bright circles like badges of valor, arrowing down the Spaniard's long, lean leg.

Above his waist, a matching short black *charro* jacket embroidered in silver thread stretched across his broad shoulders, and at the bottom of his snug-fitting *calzonevas,* a flash of red satin flared over polished black boots, fashioned of the finest Cordovan leather.

Carly watched the tall Spanish don as he stood in the shadows at the edge of the patio, engrossed in conversation with her uncle, Fletcher Austin, and several other men. Even from the darkness beneath the massive carved oak eaves of the big adobe house, she could see the man's handsome profile, the sharp planes and valleys of his face, defined by the contrast of light and dark shadows.

Carly knew who he was, of course. Oopesh, one of the Indian serving women, had told her. And Candelaria, her little maid, seemed to swoon whenever someone mentioned his name. Don Ramon de la Guerra owned a small parcel of land adjoining Rancho del Robles, her uncle's hacienda, Carly's new home. Still, she had never met a real Spanish don and after all, the man *was* her neighbor.

She straightened the dark green satin ribbon around her throat and smoothed the front of her low-cut emerald silk gown, the skirt cut full and fashioned in the latest style. The dress was a present from her uncle, the color chosen, he said, to complement the green of her eyes and the rich auburn highlights in her hair.

It was the most beautiful dress Carly had ever owned, its rows of lace flounces showing off her tiny waist to its best advantage, although, she thought a little self-consciously, a bit too much of her high, full breasts. Still, it gave her the confidence she needed, helped her to forget that she was nothing but a Pennsylvania miner's daughter.

Carly started walking toward the men.

A man named Hollingworth was speaking, a *haciendado* from a few miles north. "I don't know about the rest of you," he said, "but I've stood for his insolence long enough. The man is an outlaw. No better than Murieta, Three-fingered Jack Garcia, or any other worthless bandit who roamed these hills. The bastard ought to be hanged."

"He will be," she heard her uncle promise. "Of that you may rest assured." Fletcher Austin stood taller than the others but shorter than the don. He was dressed in an expensive dark brown tailcoat with a wide velvet collar and an immaculate white lawn shirt with ruffles down the front.

"What do you think, Don Ramon?" The question came from Royston Wardell, the San Francisco banker who was her uncle's financier. Beside him stood a wealthy entrepreneur named William Bannister and his thirty-year-old son, Vincent. "You're an educated man, a man of culture and refinement. Surely you don't approve of this bandit's behavior, even if he is—" Wardell broke off, his neck turning red above his starched white collar.

Carly paused midstride to hear the don's reply, knowing they spoke of the outlaw, El Dragón. She had heard his name whispered among the servants. Her uncle, however, was far more condemning of the man.

"Even if he is what, Senor Wardell?" the don asked politely, but there was an edge to his words. "A man of my people? Perhaps even a man of Spanish blood?" He shook his head, firelight reflecting on his ebony hair, which was wavy and worn just slightly too long. "That he is a Californio does not make him any less guilty . . . though perhaps he feels his cause is just."

"Just?" her uncle repeated. "Is it *just* to steal what another man's hard work has earned? To ravish the innocent and murder the unwary? The man is a villain—nothing but a killer and a thief. He has raided del Robles three times already. The next time he tries it, I swear I'll see him dead."

Carly would have liked to have heard the don's reply, but her uncle had spied her approach.

"Ah, Caralee, my dear." Smiling, he ended the conversation, but not before she noticed the hard look that passed between her uncle and the don. "I wondered where you had slipped off to."

Taking a place beside him, she accepted the thick arm he offered. "I'm sorry, Uncle Fletcher. I'm afraid I'm not quite used to such late evenings. And I suppose I'm still a little tired from my journey." She tried not to look at the Spaniard, at the shiny silver conchos winking in the firelight, at the long, lean legs and narrow hips, at the shoulders nearly as wide as the ax handle the vaqueros were using to stir the flames beneath the bullock they were roasting.

"I quite understand, my dear. Five months aboard a clipper 'round the Horn—I remember only too well what a grueling voyage it is." He was a man in his early fifties, graying, but with few other signs of growing old. His jaw remained firm, his stomach taut. He was as solid as the earth beneath him, as imposing as one of the towering oaks for which his ranch was named. "Perhaps we should have waited, had the fiesta a little bit later, but I was eager for you to meet some of my friends."

Carly smiled. She had discovered she was eager to meet them, too, especially the tall, handsome don. "I'm fine now. I just needed a moment's rest."

She said nothing more, waiting for him to introduce her to the only man among the others she still did not know. He hesitated longer than he should have, then he flushed and muttered something beneath his breath.

"Excuse me, my dear. For a moment I had forgotten that you hadn't met our guest. Don Ramon de la Guerra, may I present my niece, Caralee McConnell?"

"Carly," she corrected with a smile, extending a white-gloved hand. Her uncle frowned, but the smile she received from the don was blinding, a gleaming flash of white against his swarthy skin, a smile so full of masculine appeal Carly's heart started thudding against her ribs.

"I am honored, Senorita McConnell." He raised her hand and brushed his mouth against her fingers, but his dark eyes remained on her face. A slow-burning warmth spread up her arm and seeped into her body. Carly had to work to make her voice come out even.

"*El gusto es mio,* Senor de la Guerra." The pleasure is mine, she said. She had been studying Spanish for the past four years, ever since her mother died and her mother's brother had become her legal guardian. Uncle Fletcher had arranged for her to attend Mrs. Stuart's Fashionable School for Young Ladies in New York City. She had prayed one day he would send for her, ask her to come West and join him, and on her eighteenth birthday he finally did.

The don arched a fine black brow at the correct pronunciation of her words. "I am impressed, senorita. *Se habla Español?*"

"*Muy poquito,* senor—not nearly as well as I would like."

She frowned, suddenly puzzled. "But I don't understand why your inflection sounds so different from mine."

He smiled. "That is because I was born in Spain." She could have sworn he stood a little taller. "What you hear is a slight Castilian influence. Though I was raised in Alta California, I returned to Spain for much of my schooling and attended university in Madrid."

"I see." Carly hoped *he* couldn't see that she had spent most of her life in Pennsylvania, living in a shanty near the edge of the mine patch, raised in coal dust and squalor, her father working fourteen hours a day till a methane explosion finally killed him, her mother scrubbing floors just to keep food on the table.

Determined he would not guess, she infused her voice with all the sophistication she had learned at Mrs. Stuart's school. "Europe," she drawled. "How terribly exciting. Perhaps one day, we'll have a chance to discuss it."

Something flickered in the don's dark eyes, a cool look of scrutiny or perhaps disappointment, then it was gone. "It would be my pleasure, senorita."

Her uncle cleared his throat. "Gentlemen, I'm afraid you'll have to excuse us." She felt the pressure of his hand on her arm. "I'd like a word with my niece, and there are other guests she needs to meet."

"Of course," said sandy-haired Vincent Bannister, smiling at her warmly. "Perhaps Miss McConnell will save me a dance later on."

"Of course she will," her uncle said.

Carly just nodded. Her eyes were locked with the deep brown orbs of the don.

"*Hasta luego*, senorita." He bowed just slightly and flashed one of his devastating smiles. "Until we meet again."

Her uncle's expression turned grim and his hold on her arm grew tighter. "Gentlemen . . ." Wordlessly he led her toward the majestic adobe house, through the heavy oak door leading into the *sala,* down the hall and into his study. He firmly closed the door.

At the stern expression on his face, Carly grew suddenly nervous. She began to chew her bottom lip, wondering how she might have upset him. "What is it, Uncle Fletcher? I hope I haven't done something wrong."

"Not exactly, my dear." He indicated she should have a seat in one of the carved wooden chairs in front of his huge oak desk, its thick wood darkened with age and wear. Fletcher moved behind it and sat down in a brass-studded black leather chair. Leaning forward, he opened a heavy cut-crystal humidor and pulled out a long black cigar.

"You don't mind, do you?"

"Of course not, Uncle." She didn't. She actually enjoyed the stout aroma. It reminded her of her father and the men he had worked with in the mine, and a sudden pang of loneliness slid through her. Carefully smoothing her lace-trimmed skirts, she glanced at her uncle, wondering at his change in manner, trying to imagine how she might have displeased him.

He sighed into the silence. "You're new out here, Cara-lee. You've been here only three weeks. You haven't had a chance to learn the way of things, to get used to the way things work out here. In time, of course, you will, but in the meantime . . ."

"Yes, Uncle?"

"In the meantime, you're going to have to trust me to guide you. You'll have to do exactly as I say."

"Of course, Uncle Fletcher." How could she not? She owed him everything. Her education, the beautiful clothes he had bought her, the chance for a new life out west—the very food that had filled her stomach for the past four years. With her parents gone, if it hadn't been for her uncle, she would have ended up in an orphanage—or worse.

"Try to understand, my dear. A man like myself meets a lot of different people. Some of them are business acquaintances, like Royston Wardell and William Bannister, people who do me a great many favors. Others are neighbors, like the Hollingworths, or people I value for their social connections, like Mrs. Winston and her husband, George." A couple she had met earlier in the evening. "Then there are influential Californios like the Montoyas . . . and those like Don Ramon."

"Don Ramon? Wh-What about him?"

"My acquaintance with the don is of an entirely different nature . . . more an obligation of sorts. The de la Guerra family has lived in California since the earliest days of Spanish influence. There was a time they were wealthy and powerful, when they knew every important political persona for a thousand miles around. Which means socially Don Ramon cannot be ignored."

"I see."

"Unfortunately, the fact is, the man no longer commands that sort of power. These days, he has very limited finances, and even less land. He supports his mother and an aging aunt, to say nothing of the laborers he refuses to turn away. What I am trying to say is that the man is hardly your social equal. I hoped that you would see that and behave accordingly."

"I didn't realize. . . ." But she was thinking that except for her fancy clothes and the education her uncle had bought and paid for, it was far more likely that she was not the social equal of the don.

"I'm sure you didn't." His tone grew more firm. "Fortunately, now you do. From now on, Caralee, I expect you to use that expensive education I've been providing for the last four years. I expect you to play the part of the sophisticated lady you have become, but mostly I expect you to socialize with the people I pick and choose."

He came up from his chair and leaned toward her over his desk. "Do I make myself clear?"

"Y-Yes, Uncle Fletcher."

Some of the tension drained from his heavily muscled shoulders. "I don't mean to be harsh, my dear. But after all, I am your legal guardian. It's my duty to decide what is best for you."

Perhaps it was. It was certainly her obligation to do as he wished. "I'm sorry, Uncle Fletcher. I guess I just didn't understand. I promise it won't happen again."

"Good girl. I knew I could rely upon your good judgment. You are, after all, our beloved Lucy's daughter."

Carly smiled. It was obvious her uncle and her mother had once been very close. It made things easier just knowing that.

As he walked beside her toward the sounds of the *fandango,* the strum of guitar, the smell of roasting meats, the vaqueros rowdy laughter and that of her uncle's friends, she vowed she would do whatever it took to please him, vowed she would forget the handsome Spanish don.

But when she saw his tall figure leaning with casual grace against the rough adobe wall of the hacienda, when she caught the flash of silver and found his dark eyes studying her so intensely, she realized forgetting him wouldn't be an easy thing to do.

Ramon de la Guerra took a drink of his sangria, savoring the taste of the rich red wine blended with the sweet-tart flavor of oranges and limes. Across the patio, Fletcher Austin introduced his niece to yet another group of Anglos, some of them neighbors, most of them friends who had traveled from Yerba Buena—San Francisco, it was now called.

There was no denying Austin's niece was a lovely girl, ivory-skinned and fiery-haired, with an oval face delicately boned and a small cleft on her chin—kissed by angels, he'd heard it called. She was petite but not frail, with ripe full breasts and an incredibly tiny waist.

For a moment after they had met, he'd thought she might be different than he had imagined, that she might exude a warmth and charm her uncle did not have. All too soon she had proved to be nothing but the pampered sophisticate he had expected, acting instead of feeling, cool and aloof and full of pretense.

After her return from the house, he had asked her to dance, but she had refused him, her manner carefully distant and pointedly removed. A few moments later, she had danced again with Vincent Bannister. Why not? he thought. Bannister had far more money, and money was always what a woman like that was looking for.

Ramon had known a number of such women. They came to Madrid during the season, traveling on their husbands' money, looking for excitement in a strange foreign land, easy prey for a man like him . . . or perhaps it was the other way around.

In the moonlight, Ramon caught a glimpse of flame-bright hair, saw the flash of emerald eyes the color of her gown, and thought of another such woman. Lillian Schofield. Lily, with big blue eyes and pale blond hair. Lily— the woman he had almost come to love.

He looked again at Fletcher Austin's niece. This one was younger than Lily, but in time she would turn out the same . . . if she wasn't that way already. Still, it might be interesting to bed her. She was certainly a temptation, and the small measure of revenge against her uncle would make the taking all the sweeter.

Ah, but Austin was a powerful man, and in times like these it was far too dangerous. And there were others he must consider.

He watched the girl talking to Royston Wardell, another of her uncle's wealthy friends. She smiled up at him through her long dark-auburn lashes then laughed softly at something Wardell said. Yes, she was more than tempting. Perhaps he would wait and see. . . .

"*Buenas noches,* Don Ramon."

He glanced up to see Isabel Montoya standing right beside him. It surprised him that he had not heard her approach.

"Good evening, Senorita Montoya. I hope you are enjoying the festivities."

Full red lips turned down in a pretty pout. "With *mi novio* away on business, I do not find it so much fun. It is sometimes difficult to entertain oneself, no?"

He smiled. "*Si* senorita. It is always painful when a loved one is away."

Isabel smiled softly. She was black haired and dark eyed, young but flawlessly beautiful. "I wondered . . . I thought . . . perhaps . . . since you were also alone this eve we might entertain each other."

He frowned. "I do not think your betrothed would approve of such a notion. Besides, you are hardly alone. Your father and mother, your sister and brother are also here, as well as your *duena,* Louisa."

Big dark eyes ran over his face. Beneath her white lace mantilla, she looked even younger than her sixteen years. "Surely you are not afraid of my father . . . or even Don Carlos." Her fingers moved along his lapel, brushing lightly, her eyes running over his face, unmistakable in their invitation. "I have heard it said that when it comes to the ladies, you—"

He caught her wrist, stilling her words. "You are forgetting, senorita, Don Carlos Ramirez—your betrothed—is my friend. I will do nothing to impose upon that friendship." He turned her around and gave her a gentle shove in the opposite direction. "And in the future, senorita, should I hear of such behavior as I have seen this night, you may be certain that I will inform your father. Perhaps a willow switch will entertain you well enough."

She spun to face him, her slender spine stiff and her dark eyes flashing fire. He stopped her before she could speak.

"One more word, *niña,* and I will do it now."

"You—you are *not* a gentleman."

"And you, *chica,* are hardly behaving like a lady. Go now, and next time think before you speak."

Tears gathered in her pretty dark eyes. She turned and raced away.

Ramon watched her go, thinking perhaps he should have proceeded with a little more restraint. "Women," he muttered into the darkness. He pondered Isabel's behavior and wondered if her father's friendship with a growing number of Anglos was the reason she had dared to behave so boldly.

He saw her brother, Alfredo, approaching and hoped that nothing else would go wrong. But it was not Alfredo's words that broke the silence; it was the sound of pounding hooves, thrumming hard against the earth. A rider burst through the high back gate of the sprawling hacienda, shouting and waving his dusty brown felt hat in the air.

"What is it?" Alfredo asked, starting in that direction. "What do you think has happened?"

"I do not know," Ramon said. Hurriedly, they walked toward the stable, where the man had jerked his horse to a sliding halt; and Fletcher Austin, William Bannister, and Royston Wardell fell in beside them.

"What's happened?" Austin called to the mounted man, who turned and rode toward them on his weary, lathered black horse.

"The Spanish Dragón," he said, sounding as short of breath as the horse, "that bastard El Dragón hit the Overland where it crosses the Hollingworth spread. Robbed a shipment of gold coming back this way from the San Francisco mint."

Hollingworth stepped out of the darkness beside the barn. A man in his fifties, tall and lean and weathered by his years of hard work, he recognized the rider as one of his own men.

"Christ a-mighty, Red—most a' that gold was ours. Coin I needed for payroll."

"He struck early, boss. He ain't done that before. It was just after the stage left the Beaver Creek stop, soon as it got dark. They say he come down like greased lightning. Took the gold and was halfway to the hills before they knew what hit 'em."

"Damn! The blackguard has a way a' catchin' a fella unawares. I had a bad feelin' about comin' here tonight."

The man named Red rubbed the stubble of a day's growth of beard. "He's a crafty one, all right."

"Did he shoot anybody?" Fletcher Austin broke in.

"No, him and his vi-queros just took the gold and run."

"How many of them were there?" Austin asked.

"'Bout a dozen. That's what the guard said. He's lookin' for some help to go after 'em. I figured most of the men were here."

"Get your horse, Charley," Austin said to Hollingworth. "I'll round up the rest of my men."

"I will come, too," Ramon offered, as did Alfredo Montoya.

"What's the use?" Hollingworth argued. "By now the bastard's clean away. Halfway back to whatever rock he crawled out from under."

"This time, we'll find him." Austin jerked open the heavy barn door. "We won't stop till we run the whoreson to ground."

The other men mumbled their agreement; there was quite an array of them by now. The women were standing outside the barn door, uncertain exactly what had occurred, when the men emerged leading their saddled horses. Ramon led his palomino toward them, then waited for Alfredo to join him. He turned at the sound of a woman's voice.

"What's happened, Uncle Fletcher?" Caralee McConnell caught her uncle's arm, her pretty face lined with worry, one hand clutching the cashmere shawl she had draped around her bare shoulders.

"Get back to the house, honey. This is men's business. You just see to the ladies, and the men'll take care a' the rest."

Ramon could see she wanted to press him for more information, started to, then backed off. "I'm certain Uncle Fletcher knows what's best," she said to the women. "Why don't we ladies retire to the house for a sherry? I'm sure the strain of the evening is beginning to wear on us all." With an uncertain glance at Ramon, she turned and started walking away.

The strain of the evening, he thought. He wondered how long pampered little Caralee McConnell could stand the strain of the life many of his people were forced to endure each day—all because of the treachery and greed of men like Fletcher Austin.

"Mount up, men," Austin commanded. "It's time we were away."

Ramon swung up on his palomino stallion, slid his boots into his silver-studded *tapaderos,* and followed Austin and his men at a brutal pace off toward the Hollingworth ranch.

They had no luck finding the outlaw, which set Uncle Fletcher on edge for nearly two weeks. In the evenings he paced the floor in front of the huge rock fireplace at the far end of the *sala.* Carly tried to talk to him, to comfort him in some way, but he had a formidable temper, she discovered, and he usually sent her away.

By the beginning of the third week, he was once more the man he had been. They talked during supper, though never about El Dragón. Instead Uncle Fletcher explained with pride his accomplishments on the ranch, the increases he had made in cattle and horses, and the plans he had for the future.

"Politics—that's where my destiny lies. This state needs men to look out for its best interest. Men who can see justice done. I intend to be one of those men, Caralee."

"I'm sure you'd make some fine contributions, Uncle Fletcher."

They were seated at the long oak table in the dining room, enjoying a supper of roasted meats; fresh baked tortillas; *pastel de toma,* a pie of onion, garlic, chicken, corn, tomatoes, and peppers in a corn flour crust; and *mostaza,* the Spanish name for mustard greens cooked in oil and garlic. The unusual food was delicious, as Carly had already discovered, though it had taken a while for her stomach to accept the hot, spicy flavors.

Uncle Fletcher spooned up a second serving, sending a spiral of steam up from his plate. "Perhaps an appointment to the Land's Commission would be the place to start," he said. "Bannister has influence there. Perhaps—" He broke off with that and smiled. Beneath the flickering candles in the wrought-iron chandelier, red highlights glinted in his thick, graying hair. "Young Vincent would make quite a catch. And he certainly seems taken with you."

Carly focused her thoughts on the young man she had danced with, but his image changed to one of the dark-eyed don. "Vincent . . . yes, he seems a nice enough man."

"I'm glad you like him, my dear. As a matter of fact, you'll be seeing him again quite soon."

She arched a brow. It was a two-day ride from San Francisco to Rancho del Robles. She hadn't expected the man would return so quickly. "Really? Why is that?"

"William and I are staging a horse race. Bannister's invited half the city. It'll be quite an affair, as you might imagine."

Carly leaned forward, feeling a burst of excitement. "A horse race? Here on the ranch?"

"Exactly. William has purchased an extremely splendid animal. A Thoroughbred stallion named Raja, just arrived from Australia. He'll be running against de la Guerra's Andalusian."

"You don't mean Don Ramon's palomino?" She had seen the magnificent animal that night outside the barn.

"That is indeed the one. So far the horse is unbeaten. William tried to buy him, but de la Guerra refused every offer. Bannister wouldn't give up. He challenged the don to a horse race, then searched to hell and gone till he found an animal he believes can win."

"But you said the don has very little money. Surely they must be wagering something."

He nodded. "Bannister's put up two thousand dollars against the don's Andalusian."

Carly mulled that over. If money was a problem, Don Ramon could probably use the winnings, and the thought of his losing such a beautiful horse seemed utterly unbearable. She found herself hoping he would win.

She hadn't seen the don since the night of the fiesta, though his tall, darkly handsome image had surfaced occasionally in her mind. She thought of him now and tried to tell herself the excitement coursing through her blood had only to do with the festivities ahead.

She tried—but something told her it wasn't the truth.

Chapter Two

*R*amon de la Guerra led his palomino Andalusian stallion, Rey del Sol—King of the Sun—across the dry grass toward the group of people gathered to watch the race: William Bannister's wealthy friends from San Francisco accompanied by a small number of women, Austin's Anglo neighbors, and Californio rancheros from nearby haciendas.

At least forty vaqueros were gathered near the finish line. The Montoyas were there, as well as Ramon's mother and his aunt Teresa.

Austin had gone all out, clearing a two-mile race course, building high wooden benches for his guests to sit on, decorating the starting line with red-and-blue bunting, as well as an arch at the end. The crowd was eager, laughing, and boisterous, the betting steep all around.

With thirty minutes left till time for the race to begin, Ramon paused at the finish line to speak to some of his men and saw his brother, Andreas, among them. Though he stood two inches shorter, Andreas, like Ramon, was lean, hard muscled, and swarthy. He was handsome, and if his hair had been blond, his skin more fair, perhaps almost pretty. Andreas was intelligent and far too charming.

Only longtime friends knew of their kinship. During

his years in Mexico, years he had spent feuding with his father, Andreas had changed a great deal; and with the coming of the gold rush, many of the old Spanish families had lost their lands and moved away. Except for the de la Guerras, no one knew of Andreas's return. Then their father had died and Andreas had gone into the hills, vowing to seek justice and revenge. Now to most people, he was simply a vaquero known as Perez.

"Don Ramon!" his brother called out, addressing him as if they were merely acquaintances. *"Un momento, por favor?* May I speak with you for a moment?"

Ramon just nodded. He had expected his brother to be there. At twenty-six, three years his junior, Andreas de la Guerra was impetuous, high spirited, and even a little bit reckless. He wouldn't miss this chance to see Ramon best the Anglo horse and rider. Andreas disliked the Norte Americanos even more than Ramon did. He would enjoy this chance to see them bested—he had no doubt that his brother would win.

Ramon inwardly smiled, not nearly as certain himself. But his honor had demanded he accept the wager, and Bannister's bet was a fair one.

"Buenas tardes, little brother. I am not surprised to see you, though in truth, you probably should not have come." They stood off beneath an oak tree, where they could be sure no one would hear.

Andreas smiled and clapped him affectionately on the shoulder. "I did not want to miss the race. Besides, I grow weary of confinement."

Ramon smiled. "You grow weary of having no new woman to warm your bed. I hear they have brought some into San Juan Bautista. Perhaps you should stop by the cantina, see if you can find one to your liking."

Andreas's eyes strayed toward the group of Anglos clustered down at the starting line. "I think I may not have to go so far." Ramon followed his brother's gaze to Fletcher Austin's niece, resplendent in a peppermint striped taffeta day dress and tiny matching parasol. Her fiery hair clustered in shiny ringlets on her shoulder. "I think I may be falling in love."

Ramon frowned. "Do not be a fool, little brother. That one means nothing but trouble."

"You have met her?"

"*Si*. At Austin's *fandango*. She is shallow and pretentious, not worthy of your attentions."

"Perhaps not." Andreas glanced at her one more time, and the sound of her high sweet laughter floated toward them on the wind. When it lifted the hem of her skirts, giving them a glimpse of small feet and tiny stockinged ankles, Ramon felt a tightening in his groin.

"Then again . . ." Andreas said, "perhaps the senorita is well worth whatever trouble she might bring." He grinned in that devilish way of his but this time Ramon did not smile back.

"One of these days, *hermano,* such a woman will be the death of you."

"Ah, but if a man must die, what better way to go?"

Ramon chuckled softly. The stallion danced at the end of his lead rope and tossed his beautiful head, rippling his long, pale mane. "Rey is eager to meet his opponent. It is time for me to leave."

"There is just one last thing." Andreas glanced uneasily down at his feet, and Ramon knew in an instant this was the matter his brother had come to discuss.

"Go on."

"I have only just learned that in three days time, Fletcher Austin will be bringing in a large herd of horses."

"*Si,* I know this already. His men have been rounding them up for the past several weeks."

"Then why did you not say so? We must have time to

gather the men, to make plans, preparations. We will need—"

"I did not tell you because raiding del Robles is too dangerous. We will not take the horses."

"Do not talk nonsense. Supplies are low; we need those animals very badly."

A corner of Ramon's mouth curved up. "Surely with all of the gold you stole last week—"

"You know I did not—" He broke off at the smile on his brother's face. "That is not funny."

"No, I do not suppose that it is," Ramon conceded, bothered as much as his brother by the deeds they were blamed for that they had not done. He glanced toward the group of vaqueros making wagers on the race, then returned his gaze to Andreas. "Austin will be ready. He has hired a number of extra men. The horses will be heavily guarded all the way in from the range."

Andreas grinned, etching deep grooves in his cheeks. "That is why we will wait until they reach the hacienda before we go after them."

Ramon grunted. "Your need for a woman has clouded your brain."

"Think about it, Ramon. Once the horses reach the rancho, Austin will let the extra hands go. He will not be expecting us to come after them so close to the house. We can sweep down, steal the horses, and be gone before he discovers what has hit him."

Absently patting Rey's sleek neck, Ramon mulled over his brother's words. It wasn't such a bad idea, but it would be extremely dangerous. Then again, as Andreas had said, there were hungry mouths to feed and they might not get another chance like this for a very long time.

"I have already spoken to the others," Andreas continued. "The men have all agreed. We are going after the horses, Ramon."

He stared hard at Andreas, then swore an oath beneath his breath. As head of the de la Guerra family, in most things his word was law, but he could not command his brother in this.

"If you are that determined to go, then I will be the one to lead the men."

"No. Your rancho lies too close to Austin's. It is better if you stay home."

Ramon shook his head. "You went the last time. If we are going to steal the horses, it is my turn to lead." He started walking the stallion toward the starting line, but Andreas caught his arm.

"I have a personal interest in this, Ramon. Every time we have raided del Robles, I have been the one to stay behind. I have waited long enough for my revenge. This time I am going, no matter which of us is in command."

It was as close to a compromise as he would get. *"Muy bien,"* he said, though he wasn't about to let Andreas face such danger alone. He had failed his family once. Because of it, his father was dead and his lands had been stolen. He loved his younger brother—he would do whatever it took to protect him.

He would not fail his family again.

"Then we will both ride on this one."

Andreas smiled, the tension easing from his long-limbed body. "When do we strike?"

"Just before dawn five days hence," Ramon said, starting to walk away. "We will rendezvous at the creek."

Andreas nodded, and Ramon led the stallion off toward the start of the race. Rey's thick neck bowed and his nostrils flared as they approached the noisy crowd, then a tiny brown-and-white dog not much bigger than a well-fed squirrel yapped twice and fell in step at Ramon's feet. He chuckled, reached down, and picked the animal up in the palm of his hand.

"So you have missed your friend," he said. Pausing for a moment, he set the little dog up on the saddle and immediately the stallion nickered with contentment, then began to quiet. Rey and Bajito had been born within days of each other. They had been raised together in a stall in the *establo* and had formed an odd sort of friendship.

Ramon smiled as he thought of the bewildering pair and continued walking toward the spot where Bannister's magnificent Thoroughbred, Raja, pranced impatiently near the starting line.

Carly tried to concentrate on Vincent Bannister's conversation but her glance kept straying to the Spaniard and his fiery palomino horse. With its broad chest, thick neck, long, pale mane, and even longer tail, she had never seen a more beautiful animal; nor, she secretly admitted, a man with more masculine appeal.

He wore no silver today, just a full-sleeved white lawn shirt and soft brown suede breeches that clung to his sinewy thighs. The breeches were laced up the sides, she saw, and at the bottom, flared slightly over brown leather boots. A flat-brimmed black hat hung down his broad back, secured by a thin braided lanyard around his dark throat.

She smiled to think of the powerful man, the beautiful horse, and the tiny brown-and-white dog now riding calmly on the stallion's back. She watched as the odd threesome paused and the don began speaking to a wrinkled little woman Carly presumed to be his mother. A taller, thinner woman a few years younger stood at one side, and across from them Pilar Montoya smiled at the don with undisguised warmth.

Carly had met Pilar the night of the *fandango*. She was a widow, Uncle Fletcher had told her, but her period of mourning had ended. Pilar was husband-hunting and

Ramon de la Guerra seemed the leading contender for her hand.

Carly found herself frowning at the notion, and she was afraid she knew why.

Since the moment she had seen the handsome don, she had been attracted to him. He was unlike any other man she had ever met, taller, more charming, and far more exciting. A single glance from those hot dark eyes made her insides turn to butter. Still she knew the attraction was futile. She had promised her uncle and she meant to keep her word.

Besides, as nearly as she could tell, the don had none of that same interest in her.

"They're getting ready to start," Vincent said. "We had better find our places."

"Yes. There's Uncle Fletcher now." They joined him, taking prime seats in the front row of the raised wooden dais where they could see every section of the course. William Bannister and other of her uncle's friends quickly filled the remaining spaces and still more people gathered at the starting line.

Fewer than a tenth of those attending were women. With the grueling voyage around the Horn, a trip across the Isthmus, or the prospect of a lengthy and dangerous overland journey, most of the men in California had come west alone. There were Californio women, of course, and the usual sordid array of camp followers looking for some of the loot coming out of the gold fields. But eastern women were a rarity. Carly had met only a few and none that she could call friend.

"What do you think of my father's horse?" Vincent asked as Raja was led toward the start. He was a sleek, dappled-gray gelding, long and lean of limb, more gracefully built than any horse she had ever seen.

"He looks fast enough, but the course is fairly long and not completely flat, and the ground is a little rough. Uncle

Fletcher is worried that he might not have enough stamina."

Vincent jerked as if he'd been slapped. "Raja can take any horse in California. My father paid a fortune for him, and Stan McCloskey is the best rider on the West Coast."

Though most of the hands were dressed in work clothes and the vaqueros wore open-throated white shirts and rough-cut leather breeches, Vincent sat beside her in a navy blue tailcoat and a wide white wrapped cravat tied in a bow.

"Raja will win," he said, "you may count on it."

"It may not be quite so easy," she couldn't resist putting in. "I hear Californios are among the finest horsemen in the world."

Vincent's expression turned smug. He arched a sandy eyebrow. "I would say that remains to be seen."

The riders mounted their horses, both of which were extremely high spirited, dancing sideways and tossing their magnificent heads. Gradually, the men brought each of them under control, but it must have been like trying to hold back the wind. She noticed the don rode a different saddle today, smaller, lighter, with none of the fancy silver trim.

He was a great deal larger than Stan McCloskey, a handicap to be sure. She didn't realize she was staring, admiring the way he sat his horse, till the Spaniard's dark eyes locked with hers and he flashed her a bright white smile. Carly flushed as he touched the brim of his flat black hat in a mock salute, then loosened the braided cord around his throat, removed the hat, and sailed it to one of his men.

Though she felt a considerable amount of guilt, Carly sent up a small silent prayer that he would win.

She nearly leapt out of her seat when the starting gun fired.

"They're off!" cried her uncle.

The gray got the jump on the don's palomino, but the

stallion took up a place close behind. They ran the first leg with the gray horse a full length ahead. Even from a distance, Carly could hear their pounding hooves, would have sworn her own heart pounded just as madly. The horses rounded a huge live oak that signaled the first turn and started the second leg of the course, which climbed a slightly rounded hill, a wide swath having been cleared through the dry brown grass of late summer.

There were more oaks scattered along the course, but most of the rocks had been cleared. By the time they reached the creek and leapt across it, landing with a splash on the opposite side, Rey del Sol had closed half a length, but the gray horse still held the lead position.

A light rain had fallen two days earlier; in places the ground was still damp. It sucked at the animals' hooves, taxing their muscles and draining their strength, but the more powerfully built palomino seemed not to notice. McCloskey bent over the gray, urging the animal on. The don leaned forward, too, but where the other rider surged with each of the Thoroughbred's motions, the Spaniard seemed more in tune, moving with the same fluid grace as the horse.

"They're so beautiful," Carly said, thinking she had never seen another man ride with such perfection.

"They're coming to the flat at the back of the course," Vincent said. "The gray has greater speed—this is where he'll move even farther ahead."

But Carly wasn't so sure. The gray seemed to be tiring while the Andalusian had not yet reached its peak. They flew across the long flat section at the top of the hill and started down the incline on the opposite side, the gray still half a length ahead.

Three-quarters through the third leg of the course, Vincent was frowning. According to his theory, Raja should have been far out in front.

"I've got a thousand dollars riding on that horse of

yours, William," her uncle said. "He had better not come up short."

Bannister was a tall man whose blond hair had only begun to gray. He dressed impeccably and moved with a sort of graceful precision. *Distinguished,* that was the word to describe William Bannister.

"I'm in a great deal deeper than that," he said. "Don't worry, McCloskey will come through."

As the horses rounded a large granite boulder that mapped the final turn, the crowd gasped in unison and Carly surged to her feet. The palomino had stumbled and nearly gone down, but he was back in his stride and running flat out. She could almost feel the animal's proud determination . . . or perhaps it was the don's.

Whatever it was, the pair seemed even more driven to win.

"My God," Fletcher Austin said, "that stallion of de la Guerra's is incredible."

"Yes," said Bannister, and in that moment Carly felt certain even William Bannister wanted to see the gallant horse win. "I've never seen anything so magnificent."

"The gray will be the victor," Vincent said stubbornly, but the palomino was closing fast, his strides lengthened so far out at times his nose and feet were nearly touching.

The finish line loomed ahead. Everyone was standing, shouting and cheering, including Fletcher and Carly. "You can do it," she whispered, "you can do it—I know you can!"

And they did, the magnificent palomino and its graceful rider pounding across the finish line just inches ahead of the gray. Carly was shouting with joy, laughing, her eyes suddenly stinging with tears. For a moment Vincent Bannister looked horrified, and Carly flushed with guilt.

She was afraid to look at her uncle—or worse yet William Bannister. When she did, she saw her uncle frowning, but Bannister was smiling.

"Incredible," was all he said.

"Cost me a thousand," her uncle said with a heavy sigh, "but it was damned near worth it."

"Let's go down to the finish line," Carly suggested, hoping the men would agree, and surprisingly they did. By the time they got there, Don Ramon was surrounded by dozens of joyous vaqueros, his smiling mother and aunt, the Montoyas, Herreras, Estradas, and several other Californio families.

He glanced up at their approach and the smile slid from his face.

"Congratulations, Don Ramon," Bannister said. "Once more you have proven that you ride California's most magnificent horse."

"You are very gracious, Senor Bannister. I did not expect it . . . coming from a man who tried to win by cheating."

Bannister stilled and her uncle went tense. "What are you talking about?" William demanded.

"I am speaking of this." He handed over a short-handled object with three sharp prongs on the end. The prongs held a slight trace of blood. "Your man, Senor McCloskey, used this on my horse as we rounded the final turn. Unfortunately for him, I was able to jerk it from his hand."

The crowd parted as Bannister moved toward Rey del Sol. He saw the slight puncture marks beneath the animal's ribs, the blond hair covered with a small amount of blood. He turned, stiff and red-faced, to Ramon de la Guerra.

"I give you my word as a gentleman, I knew nothing about this. I hope one day to own Rey del Sol. I would never wish to see such a fine animal injured."

The don said nothing.

"I am deeply sorry, Don Ramon," William continued. "I promise you I will deal personally with McCloskey, and I sincerely hope that you will accept my humble apology."

The Spaniard studied him for long, tense moments. "The injury is a small one. I am glad to learn you had no part in what happened. I accept your apology . . . and your two thousand dollars."

A roar went up from the crowd. The don was smiling again, that incredible blinding white smile that turned Carly's stomach all hot and liquid. Especially when he was looking at her the way he was right now.

"Congratulations, Don Ramon," she said to him softly. "Your ride was magnificent."

A bold black brow arched up. He watched her with renewed interest, realizing she was pleased that he had won. *"Muchas gracias,* senorita. You are interested in horses?"

"I have read a good deal about them on the ship as I traveled from the East. I am only just learning to ride, but yes . . . I am greatly interested in horses."

He seemed surprised at her words. It occurred to her that most fashionable ladies learned to ride very young. She flushed and hoped her small mistake would go unnoticed by the others among her uncle's wealthy friends.

"It seems most of us here have an interest in horses," William Bannister put in, handing over the winner's share, a leather pouch filled with gold coins. "I still wish to purchase your stallion. I'll pay double whatever reasonable price you name."

The don just shook his head. "Rey is among the last of my father's Andalusian horses. He must be saved for breeding." Carly had read about such horses, the same animals brought to the New World with Cortez.

"We could work out stud services. I would be happy—"

"I am sorry, Senor Bannister, Rey del Sol is not for sale."

Bannister sighed, but the don's gaze had already swung back to Carly. "Perhaps—once Senorita McConnell possesses sufficient skills—Senor Austin might be interested in one of Rey's colts. A beautiful palomino mare would make the perfect horse for a lady such as she."

Fletcher stroked his beardless chin. "Perhaps you are

right, Don Ramon. One of the stallion's colts would be a fine asset to Rancho del Robles."

As if to seal his promise, the don bent down and picked up a long-stemmed red rose, one of a half dozen the Californio women had tossed in his direction as he had crossed the finish.

"For you, senorita. In memory of this day . . . though its loveliness pales before such a beautiful woman."

Carly accepted the rose, a warm glow coloring her cheeks. She started to smile, to thank him for such a gallant gesture, then she caught her uncle's scowl. Dear God, she was doing it again, letting the handsome don charm her. Uncle Fletcher would be furious when they got home.

The smile of warmth never came, only a pasted-on version. "Thank you, Senor de la Guerra," she said formally, using her most haughty voice. She passed the rose beneath her nose, inhaling the softly fragrant scent. "Your customs are utterly charming. I'm certain that I shall remember."

Her uncle's expression relaxed. He took her hand and rested it on the broadcloth sleeve of his burgundy tail coat. "Time to go, my dear."

"Of course, Uncle." She turned away from the don, no longer willing to meet his eyes, and they began walking back toward the others.

"Very well done, my dear. Gracious, ladylike, yet putting the man in his place. I'm proud of you."

Carly felt suddenly ill. Is that what she had done? Put Don Ramon in his place? It wasn't what she had intended. She glanced one last time at the don, caught his dark look in return, then the radiant smile he flashed Pilar Montoya.

She gasped as a thorn in the blood red rose pricked her finger.

Andreas de la Guerra walked with the group of vaqueros back toward their horses. The men had come from a dozen different haciendas to see Ramon ride against the *gringo*. They had not been disappointed, and the victory each man felt was as personal as his Californio honor.

Recalling the incredible race and the Anglo's outrageous treachery, Andreas clenched his fist. His brother's daring ride had saved the day, but that didn't lessen his fury at what might have occurred.

Then again, what had he expected?

He had been fighting the *gringos* ever since his return to California, since he found his father lying on his death bed in the small hacienda, Rancho Las Almas, that was the original Rancho del Robles, abandoned when the bigger house was built.

He had been fighting them for six long months before his brother's arrival from Spain, trying to reclaim what should have rightfully belonged to them.

Ramon had joined him, though at first he was reluctant, certain that violence was not the way. Guilt had won his assistance, guilt for his father's death at the hands of the Anglos, for his mother's misery while he had been living the good life in Spain.

Andreas knew his brother could not forgive himself for not coming home sooner, for failing his family in their time of need.

It wasn't completely his fault. Diego de la Guerra had been certain he could handle the matter himself, could prove that the land was his, or fight the Anglos, if necessary, to keep it. After his death, Andreas had thought the same. It had felt good to be a man, no longer in the shadow of his brother. He was determined to set things right, to find justice with or without Anglo law.

He had started fighting back in the guise of El Dragón, and to this day he continued.

"It is time we returned to the hills, amigo." Pedro Sanchez, once his father's *segundo,* second in command, on

Rancho del Robles, rode up beside him. He was a man in his early sixties, skilled in the ways of the vaquero, wiry, hard, and tough as the leather sole of a boot.

"You go on." Andreas grinned. "I have business in San Juan Bautista."

"The same sort of business your brother wishes to have with the pretty young *gringa?*" he asked. Apparently Pedro had seen Ramon give her the rose.

"He told me she was nothing but trouble. I think she is not so much trouble for me as she is for him."

"Senor Austin will not approve of his interest. He is not a man your brother should openly oppose."

"Ramon knows that only too well. I do not think he meant to. He swore there would never be a de la Guerra Andalusian on del Robles land until we once more owned it." He shrugged. "Ah, but whether he believes it or not, my brother is only human—and the woman, she is exquisite, no?"

"She is trouble, just as Ramon has said."

"Perhaps I should save him. Perhaps if he rides with me to San Juan—"

"The widow, Pilar, can save him well enough. And there is always Miranda. She pines for him every moment he is away from the stronghold."

"*Si,* I suppose you are right." He took a last long look at the cluster of people milling like insects at the bottom of the hill. He thought he could just make out a small, auburn-haired woman beneath a pink-and-white-striped parasol.

He smiled. "On the other hand, what is life without a little trouble?"

Pedro laughed and the two men spurred their horses, riding on into the hills. At the crossroads, Andreas turned south and Pedro rode higher. Thoughts of the Americana with the pretty green eyes and pale skin, with the high, plump breasts and tiny ankles, drove Andreas on. He hoped in San Juan he would find a woman with the same full breasts who would, for a coin or two or maybe a few words of flattery, welcome him into her bed.

He wondered if his brother would go to Pilar, or if he would be patient and wait for the beautiful Anglo girl.

Chapter Three

Riding a stallion as black as the clothes he wore, Ramon de la Guerra crested the rise and looked down at the narrow creek meandering beneath the sycamore trees. Andreas was waiting, as well as a dozen of his top vaqueros who had remained loyal to the de la Guerras since the time of their fathers and their fathers before them. Two Yokuts Indians from the great central valley to the east rode at the rear of the column.

Ramon nudged the black stallion forward and began to slide down the hill leading to the boulder-strewn creek. Above his head, only a sliver of moon marked his way, and even that was shadowed by a curtain of thin gray clouds.

"Buenas noches, amigos," he called to the men, reining the horse to a halt before them. "As always, it is good to see you." Pedro Sanchez was among them, as well as Ruiz Domingo, Ignacio Juarez, Cisco Villegas, Santiago Gutierrez, and a number of others, many he had known since his childhood.

"As I have told Andreas, what we do this night is more dangerous than any of the raids we have done before. Austin and his men may be waiting. Chances are good that will not be so, that by now he will have relaxed his guard, but we cannot know this for certain. If one of you sees something amiss, you must call out a warning. We must leave the rancho, with or without the horses."

"We need those horses, Ramon," Andreas countered. "Do not make the men uneasy with talk of what may or may not happen. We can handle Fletcher Austin and his men."

Ramon swore softly. Andreas was always hotheaded. Still, he would not undermine his brother's authority in front of the men. "Just be careful. Do not underestimate Austin. If something happens, ride out as fast as you can. Get yourselves safely away."

Before Andreas could argue, Ramon spun the stallion and started off down the trail. It was more than a two-day ride from their stronghold in the mountains to Rancho del Robles, but Andreas and the others had camped in the hills close by. The horses were fresh, the men alert and well rested for the night's work ahead.

They reached the incline overlooking the rancho and reined up in a thick copse of trees. Ramon dismounted. So did Andreas and Pedro Sanchez.

"What do you think?" Andreas asked Ramon, his dark eyes scanning the sprawling hacienda, the *establo,* and granary, the bunkhouse, and *matanza*— slaughter-house—the corrals filled with horses.

"It seems to be quiet enough."

"*Si*. And look how many horses. He has built an extra corral just to hold them."

"The *gringo* buyer in Sacramento City will be pleased," Pedro said. "He does not care where the animals come from, only that there are many, and that they are sound."

Ramon watched in silence for a long moment more. Satisfied that all seemed in order, he turned and walked back to his men. "We must be sure to get the remuda." That was the saddle stock used by the ranch hands. "We do not want them coming after us."

Grasping the horn, he swung easily up into his wide

Spanish saddle, pulled his black flat-brimmed hat down over his eyes and his black bandanna up over his nose, then lightly touched his big Spanish rowels to the sides of his horse.

Carly couldn't sleep. She was still not used to the late supper hours kept by the California rancheros, or the strange night sounds of her new home: the creak of the heavy carved timbers above her bed, the crickets outside her window, the yipping of distant coyotes, and the occasional whinny of horses. The clock ticking over on the bureau read two o'clock; she could see the shiny brass hands in the thin ray of light slanting in through the shutters.

Wearily, Carly climbed out of bed. At supper, she had drunk some of the rich red wine her uncle made from grapes grown there on the rancho and now she was thirsty. She crossed the room to the porcelain pitcher sitting in the basin on the dresser but found the pitcher empty. Her uncle would expect her to awaken her little maid Candelaria, but she wasn't about to do that. Besides, she needed an excuse to move around a little. Perhaps when she returned she could finally fall asleep.

Pulling a light embroidered wrapper over her long white cotton night rail, Carly lifted the wrought-iron latch on the bedroom door and stepped out into the hallway. Built in the Spanish design, the hacienda faced a large central patio with a wide covered veranda running the length of the house on three sides. The kitchen was in a separate building a few paces off to the rear in case of fire.

Carly drew the pale blue robe a little closer around her, stepped outside into the cool night air, then crossed the yard and opened the door to the *cocina*. It was dark inside the kitchen, but she could smell the dried red peppers that hung from the ceiling, the garlic flowers and bay leaves all strung together over the huge wooden butcher-block table.

Bins of wheat, beans, lintels, dried peas, corn, and fresh vegetables lined the wall. She stepped carefully so she could avoid them. There were two six-burner iron stoves in the room, and on another wall, iron skillets, pots, pans, spoons, spatulas, and a hand-held coffee grinder dangled from the rack above the wood box.

It was usually noisy in the kitchen, alive with the slaps of tortillas being made, the chatter of the Indian serving women and the several Californio women who commanded their cooking efforts, but it was quiet now. Carly moved past the wooden butter churn to the covered barrel of water and lifted the lid. She dipped in the porcelain pitcher, filled it to the brim, then closed the lid and wiped the pitcher off with a freshly washed flour sack that served as a dish towel.

She had just reached the door when she heard it—horses pacing, snorting, their hooves thudding softly in the dirt; what might have been the creak of the corral gate swinging open. Carly walked to the window and looked out, wondering what could be going on.

At first she didn't see them, just thought the horses had somehow forced open the gate and were drifting slowly away. They moved steadily but not hurriedly, their hides a blur of color plodding past. Bays, paints, sorrels, white horses, grays, and blacks, they just kept walking through the gate until the corral was empty. Carly hurried to the door and jerked it open, but stopped dead in her tracks at the sight of the mounted men.

Dear God in heaven. The men were vaqueros; she could tell by the short jackets and flare-bottomed pants, and their low-crowned, wide-brimmed hats. But they weren't del Robles men. Dear Lord, they must be the outlaws she had heard about—men who rode with the Spanish Dragon!

Carly's hand shook on the cold wrought-iron latch as she eased the wooden door partially closed then peeked out through the crack. She needed to warn her uncle and the men in the bunkhouse, but once she stepped outside, the outlaws might see her. They might shoot her before she could sound some sort of warning.

Then her eye caught the heavy metal bell.

"That's it," she whispered to herself, straightening her spine, working to build up her courage. The bell was used as a signal for meals, for mail, for a dozen sundry communications. It was also a warning of trouble, and at this hour of the morning, no one would doubt what the ringing bell meant.

Carly checked the window to see if any of the raiders were watching the house, counted slowly to three, then jerked open the kitchen door. Bunching her nightgown in order to run left her legs bare but she hardly noticed the cold damp ground or the pebbles cutting into the bottoms of her feet.

Instead she dashed straight for the bell suspended from a stout wooden timber about twenty feet away, her long thick auburn braid flying out behind her. Carly grabbed the knotted rope and madly began to ring the bell.

Ramon jerked rein as the first harsh clang rent the air. *"Madre de Dios,"* he swore softly, his eyes searching the grounds for the source of the alarm. He spotted the small robed figure standing at the edge of the patio and knew in an instant that it was the girl.

"Andele, muchachos! Take the horses and go!"

"What about the remuda?" Andreas asked, racing up beside him, his bay horse nervously prancing. "We cannot leave without them."

"Sanchez and Domingo are rounding them up. I will help them—you go on with the others." But already Andreas had spun his horse toward the second corral and started in that direction. Ramon cursed but the words were lost in the raucous clanging, the shrilly neighing horses, and the shouting of the men. He spurred his horse and passed Andreas, shouted orders to Sanchez and Ruiz Domingo, then whirled the stallion toward the woman still fiercely ringing the bell.

By now lamps burned inside the thick-walled adobe hacienda and men streamed out of the bunkhouse in various states of undress, some of them carrying weapons. He wasn't concerned with Austin's vaqueros, since many of them were reluctant to oppose El Dragón, and most felt a certain amount of loyalty to any man of Spanish blood who opposed the *gringos*. But the Anglos were armed and already firing their rifles, Fletcher Austin among them.

The bell had gone silent; now the air hummed with the deadly roar of gunshots. Villegas returned fire, wounding two of Austin's men, but a lead ball smashed into Ignacio's arm, and Santiago's thigh ran red with blood. The girl crouched low behind a wooden watering trough. Ramon had started to rein away from her, to head back toward his men, when he realized Andreas was riding straight for her.

"Andreas!" he shouted. "Go back!" But it was already too late. A rifle shot rang out, his brother jerked as the lead ball slammed home, then slumped forward over the saddle, his shirt red-stained with blood.

Ramon felt a wave of fury like nothing he had known. He started toward his brother, but Pedro Sanchez appeared at Andreas's side and together they rode off toward the rear gate leading away from the rancho. He thought of the girl, of the havoc she had caused, of her cool demeanor and haughty eastern ways. In his mind, he saw his brother riding toward her, heard the deafening crack of the gun.

Ramon's anger surged, turning to white-hot rage. Beneath him the black horse reared. He spun the stallion, dug his heels into the horse's ribs, leaned low over the saddle, and rode hard toward the girl crouching down behind the watering trough. Lead whizzed past his ear, but he didn't slow. She screamed when she saw him racing toward her, then stood up and began to run.

It was exactly what he wanted.

As the black horse galloped up beside her, Ramon bent forward, leaned out and slid an arm around her waist, then dragged her up over his saddle. She was screaming and fighting, trying to get away, but she was no match for him. He forced her face down across the saddle, his hand pressing hard on the small of her back. He could feel her trembling as the horse picked up speed, saw her long reddish braid dangling over the horse's shoulder. She was afraid to move, he realized, now that the animal was running flat out, and felt a shot of grim satisfaction. He caught up with the others by the time they reached the trees, his vaqueros driving the herd relentlessly ahead of them.

They were moving with speed and efficiency, traveling the route that had been chosen well ahead. Rifle shots still echoed in the distance, but his men were already out of range. They moved a little farther into the trees, gaining distance from the rancho, riding out of danger and into the mountains that would insure their escape.

He stopped for a moment to secure the woman's arms behind her, to bind her feet, and gag her when she tried to scream. Then he tossed her across his horse's withers and rode on in search of his brother.

He found him slumped over the saddle, barely able to stay on his horse.

"Take the girl," he commanded a vaquero named Enriquez, who dragged her off the stallion and over to his own horse.

The stout man loaded her face down across the saddle in front of him, then swung himself up behind her. Sanchez gave Ramon a sharp look, clearly marking his disapproval that the woman had been taken, but quickly turned back to Andreas.

"How is he?" Ramon asked, worried how seriously his brother had been hurt.

"It is very bad, my friend," the older man said. "Very bad."

A chill slid through him. Not just a shoulder wound as he had thought. "We cannot stop until we reach the pass. Can he make it until then?"

When Sanchez shook his head, "I do not think so," Ramon's worry increased tenfold.

His heart began to throb dully, forcing a tightness into his chest. He turned to Ruiz Domingo. "What about the others who are wounded?" he asked the thin-faced young vaquero. "Can they make it as far as the pass?"

"*Si*, Don Ramon. The others were not injured nearly so badly."

"Ride as far as the canyon at Los Osos. There is cover there and water for the horses. Then you must separate as we planned. Martinez will take five men and head north to Sacramento City with the horses. The rest of you will wait for us at the base of the canyon. If we do not arrive by tomorrow at dawn, go on to the stronghold without us."

There was only a slight hesitation. *"Si, patron."*

Ramon just nodded, worry for Andreas overriding all other thought. As the men rode away, Ruiz in the lead, Enriquez riding with the girl, he returned to where Sanchez stood next to his brother. He was nearly unconscious, his limp form slumped over the horse. Clamping his jaw against the fear that wrenched through him, Ramon took the reins and led the animal into the cover of the trees, next to a small shallow creek.

With hands that were no longer steady, he lifted Andreas from the saddle and heard his low moan of pain. "Do not worry, little brother. Ramon is here. Everything is going to be all right."

Sanchez unfurled his bedroll and they rested Andreas

upon it. Ramon tore open his brother's linen shirt with clumsy fingers and removed the red-stained rag Pedro had stuffed into the wound to staunch the flow of blood.

"*Madre de Dios* . . ." Ramon's heart squeezed inside his chest. He clenched his jaw against the sight of his brother's torn flesh, at the shattered rib protruding through the smooth, dark skin and the frothy blood bubbling out of the hole with each of his brother's ragged breaths.

"I am . . . sorry, Ramon," Andreas said.

"Do not try to speak," Ramon whispered, a hard lump rising in his throat. He blinked back a sudden well of tears. "You must try to save your strength."

A wheezing sound rattled past his brother's bloodless lips.

Ramon smoothed back the younger man's damp black hair. "*Por Dios,* Andreas," he whispered, "why could you not have listened?"

Andreas opened his eyes. When he saw his brother's face, saw the wetness trickling down his cheeks, his own eyes moistened with tears. "Do not . . . torture yourself . . . Ramon. The raid . . . was my idea. The fault was . . . mine . . . not yours." He coughed raggedly, the motion jolting him, knifing him with so much pain that perspiration broke out on his forehead. Ramon tried to steady him, but his hands were shaking so badly, he couldn't hold on.

"Rest easy, little brother."

Andreas moved his head. "Tell . . . our mother . . . that I love her."

Ramon's throat went so tight for a moment he could not speak. He reached out and gripped his brother's hand, holding on as hard as he could, wishing it was he who lay on the bedroll, he who suffered such unbearable pain.

"And also . . . Tia Teresa," Andreas whispered.

"I will tell them." Ramon could barely force out the words. Silent tears rolled down his cheeks, dampening the front of his shirt. He wasn't prepared for this. Mother of God, he hadn't suspected his brother was wounded so badly.

"As I also love . . . you . . . Ramon."

Ramon's dark head dropped forward. He repeated the same words to his brother, words he had never spoken to another living soul.

Andreas coughed again, riddling his body with pain, and Ramon felt it as if the agony were his own. Amazingly, when his brother rested quietly once more, a corner of his mouth curved up, etching the grooves in his cheeks.

"You said . . . one day . . . a woman would be the death of me. In a way . . . I guess it was . . . the truth." Then his eyes slid closed, a last soft breath whispered past, and Andreas de la Guerra was gone.

"No. Nooo!" Ramon threw back his head and cried out into the darkness. It echoed into the stillness of the night, a terrible shriek of pain, an agony so deep it seemed it would tear him in two. The sound was primitive, savage, like the keen of a wounded wolf.

Wordlessly, Pedro Sanchez eased away from him, his eyes as wet as Ramon's. "*Vaya con Dios,* my friend," he whispered to Andreas, his deep voice rough and strained. Making the sign of the cross, he moved off toward the horses. He returned a few minutes later with a blanket, which he gently laid over Andreas's still form. Neither man spoke. There was nothing left to say.

Still it wasn't until several hours later, his heart so heavy he could not speak, that Ramon finally released his brother's lifeless hand.

Chapter Four

*T*orn between exhaustion and fear, Carly huddled beneath the branches of a tall, thick-trunked oak tree, her hands bound in front of her, her feet tied at the ankles. For the rest of that night and all through the day, they had driven the horses relentlessly, Carly now riding in front of the stout vaquero the don had called Enriquez, her body aching with every bone-jarring step his bay horse took.

They separated from the others at the bottom of a steep-walled canyon, five men and the stolen horses heading north, she and the others riding on toward a destination she could not begin to guess. When they finally stopped just as darkness began to fall, her gag had been removed and a young vaquero named Ruiz had brought her something to eat, but the plate of roast rabbit sat untouched, cold and congealing in the evening chill. A few feet away, the man called Enriquez stretched out on his bedroll, his wide sombrero pulled down to cover his broad face.

Like the others in the camp, he slept only fitfully, awakening at the slightest sound, alert for whatever danger might follow. Carly hadn't slept at all. Instead, her tired eyes searched the darkness, looking for the man who had taken her, awaiting his return, terrified of what he meant to do.

She shivered to think what that might be: torture, rape,

murder. She had heard the stories about him. She knew the kind of man he was.

She closed her eyes against the ghastly vision and finally drifted into an exhausted sleep. She awoke with a start to the crunch of pebbles underfoot in the silent graying dawn, and the knowledge that someone stood in front of her. Heart pounding madly, she jerked fully awake, her frightened gaze darting to a pair of tall, black boots. Her vision slid up long, lean legs encased in tight black breeches; narrow hips; a waist that veed to a wide, solid chest; and broad, straight, powerful shoulders. She forced her eyes upward, and stared into the face of the handsome Spanish don, Ramon de la Guerra.

Relief swept over her, so fierce it almost made her dizzy. The Spaniard had found her. Instead of being murdered she was safe!

"Don Ramon—thank God!" She pushed to her feet in front of him, staggering a little, righting herself with an effort. "I-I was so frightened. I thought . . . thank God you've come."

"Senorita McConnell," he said without the slightest hint of warmth, "how good of you to join us." The lines of his face looked stark, and grimmer than she had ever seen them. His sensuous lips were flattened into a thin, harsh line. Cold brown eyes bored into her, fathomless and unreadable, so dark they looked almost black.

An icy dread swept through her. One look in those chilling dark eyes and she knew she had never been farther from safety in her life.

"You . . . you're not . . . you're not . . ."

"Don Ramon Martinez y Barranca de la Guerra," he said with a slight, mocking bow. "At your service, senorita." The flash of his straight white teeth looked almost feral. "Or perhaps you prefer El Dragón."

Carly swayed on her feet, fear knifing through her, so

sharp it felt like a blade. She might have fallen if his long, dark hand hadn't reached out to steady her, his fingers biting like talons into the flesh of her upper arm. Carly wrenched herself free.

For a moment she couldn't speak, just stared at him as if she was seeing him for the very first time. With shaking hands, her wrists still bound, she drew her pale blue robe more closely around her. Fear warred with fury. She raised her chin and looked him straight in the eye.

"El Dragón . . ." she repeated, her voice ringing with contempt. "Such a charming imposter . . . I never would have guessed." She hoisted her chin a notch. "I actually believed you were a true Spanish noble, a man to be admired. The truth is you're nothing but a thief and a murderer."

His lips twisted harshly. "And you, senorita, are the woman responsible for the suffering and death of my men."

Carly stiffened. The edge of fear flickered its warning. It was foolish to bait him and yet she could not resist. He had made a fool of her, made a fool of them all.

"*You* are the one responsible, Don Ramon. You and your stealing, your raiding, and murder. I did nothing but warn my uncle's men. I only tried to stop you—and I would do it again!"

Black rage swept his features, turning his dark eyes to onyx and making him look like the vicious man he was. Around him the men did not stir, just glared at her with the same stark hatred she saw in the eyes of the don. The blow came swift and hard, a brutal slap that stung her cheek and sent her spinning into the dirt. He looked enormous towering above her, his body rigid with fury, his hands balled into fists.

She closed her eyes, preparing herself for the beating to come, steeling herself for the pain that was certain to follow. Instead when she opened her eyes, she saw him turn away. An older man stepped forward, reached down and cut the rope that still circled her ankles.

He spoke rapid, angry Spanish to the don, words she tried to understand but couldn't with her stomach churning and her head spinning as it was.

He took her hand and helped her to her feet. "I am Sanchez," he said, gentleness taking the edge from his voice. He was lean and hard, like the rest of the men, but age and a life spent out of doors had weathered his features, furrowing deep, craggy canyons in his face. "You must try to understand, senorita. Don Ramon is not an unkind man."

"He's a monster." A shaky hand came up to the harsh red mark on her cheek.

"He is merely a man—one who for the moment does not think clearly. He is too caught up in his grief."

"Grief? I don't understand what you mean." For an instant she thought he might not tell her, the way his shrewd old eyes continued to study her face.

He sighed and suddenly he looked even older. "In the raid last night Don Ramon's younger brother, Andreas, was killed. The don loved him very much. He would have given his own life to protect him. That was something he was not allowed to do."

Carly saw the pain that was etched in the old man's face. "Dear God." For an instant her heart went out to him, went out to them both. Then she caught herself and reined in her concern. "His brother was an outlaw. They both are. What did the don expect? Shooting was probably too good for him."

"He was a man trying to save his home, his way of life. Perhaps one day you will understand."

Carly shivered in the damp morning air. She would never understand men like these. Men who robbed and killed. Men without scruples or mercy.

"In time he will return to himself," the old vaquero said. "In the meantime, you must do nothing to anger him."

Carly looked over the old man's shoulder to see Don Ramon speaking to one of his men. He was a bandit, a murderer—and he blamed her for the death of his brother. An icy chill slid down her spine. It was followed by a pang of regret, a feeling of loss for the handsome Spanish don she had been so attracted to, a man who had never existed.

She stared at the tall, virile Spaniard, trying to fit the hard man he was into the charming man he had seemed, trying to imagine the kind of man he was inside. She had no idea what he meant to do, what cruelties he might have in store for her, but in that moment it didn't matter—Carly was determined to survive them.

He had made a fool of her once. He would not do it again.

Besides, if she could hold on long enough, her uncle would have time to find her. She didn't doubt that he would come. Fletcher Austin was every bit as hard-edged and determined as the man who called himself El Dragón.

That thought gave her a shot of strength and a tighter grip on her fear. Gathering her pale blue robe together against the cold, she backed into the shadows, and sank down in her place beneath the tree. She had faced hardship and cruelty before. Losing her sister and her father had been hard, working in the mine patch from dawn till dusk beside her mother had been hard, watching her mother die a slow, agonizing death had been even harder, but she had survived it, and she would survive this, too.

As the minutes wore on, her courage grew. By the time they were ready to leave, it wasn't Caralee McConnell, late of Mrs. Stuart's Fashionable School for Young Ladies, who awaited her captor's torment. It was Carly McConnell, Pennsylvania coal miner's daughter. A woman whose strength of will quite possibly equaled that of the don.

* * *

"This thing you have done—taking the woman—it can only come to grief." Pedro Sanchez stood in front of Ramon, his flat-brimmed hat clutched in a weathered, age-spotted hand.

"What's done is done. It is too late to change things."

"You should not have let her see your face."

Ramon ignored the censure as well as the worry in his old friend's voice. "Get the men mounted and ready. The girl can ride with Enriquez. We have wasted enough time already."

"Her uncle will follow. He will see this as a personal affront. He will not stop until he finds her."

Ramon glanced back at the girl. She was standing once more, stiff-backed and defiant, challenge burning in the depths of her big leaf-green eyes. He thought of Andreas and rage seared through him, followed by an agonizing wave of grief. He had numbed himself to it as much as he could. His men needed him, the people in the stronghold needed him, and he must not let Andreas's death be in vain.

But the pain was still there, hovering just beneath the surface, waiting for the slightest word, the merest thought to set it free. It crouched in wait like a predatory beast, ready to devour him at any moment.

He stared at the girl and his mind flashed on his brother's dying words: "You said one day a woman would be the death of me. . . ." The pain rose up, blinding in its intensity, cutting like a scythe through the numbness.

"On second thought," he said, "the woman will walk. We will see if there is more to the *gringa* than her haughty eastern manners and condescending ways." He started toward his horse, Viento Prieto, Dark Wind, but Sanchez caught his arm.

"You cannot mean that, Ramon. It is miles to Llano Mirada."

Ramon pulled free of the old vaquero's hold and kept on walking. "Enriquez!" Across the camp, the stout vaquero looked up. "Bring the girl to me."

"I beg you, Ramon, do not do something that can only bring you more regret."

"Stay out of this, Pedro." He reached the big black stallion and swung up into the saddle. Behind him, Esteban Enriquez arrived with the girl. She was wearing a soft blue robe over her white cotton nightgown, her fiery auburn hair trailing in a long, thick braid down her back. Her feet were bare, he saw, her small feet blue with the cold.

A ripple of guilt washed over him. She was so small. And as fearless as she seemed, he knew she must be frightened. Then he thought of Andreas, cold and blue beneath the blanket around his lifeless corpse, and the unwanted feeling slid away.

He untied his woven leather *reata* from his saddle, formed a loop, and settled it around her small bound wrists. He tied the other end to his wide, flat saddle horn, all the while waiting for her to beg and plead, to cry and beseech him for mercy, knowing that it would not dissuade him. Still he wanted to hear it. He would enjoy each groveling moment only the least bit more if the speaker were her uncle.

He thought of Fletcher Austin, of Rancho del Robles, of his family's stolen lands, and his brother's brutal murder. He thought of Caralee McConnell, the eastern sophisticate who considered herself above them, who thought only of money and her own self-indulgence, and his anger grew more fierce, settling like a hot stone in his belly.

"There is quite some distance to travel, senorita," he said, glancing down at her. "It is time we were on our way." He tugged on the rope, expecting to see tears, but she only lifted her chin. Eyes like green fire scorched down his body, blatantly speaking her loathing.

He clamped down hard on his temper and nudged the

stallion into a walk, ruthlessly dragging her forward. She swung into line ten feet behind the horse and started up the trail. They made their way through the small secluded valley then began to climb higher into the hills. All the while, the rope remained slack, the girl easily keeping pace with the horse.

Four hours later, she was still walking, still glaring at his back with hot, hate-filled eyes. He could almost feel them boring into him.

Occasionally he turned, unable to resist the challenge, amazed at the fact that she had not begged him to stop, or even once complained. They paused only briefly, at a stream where they watered the horses and ate a handful of *carne seca*, spicy jerked beef. When the girl refused the portion Sanchez offered, Ramon dismounted and walked to where she stood at the end of her tether.

"You will do as Pedro says." He handed her the jerky, a cold smile curving his lips. "I would not want it said we were inhospitable to a guest."

She tossed the dried beef into the dust at his feet. "I'm not hungry. And even if I were, I wouldn't eat with an animal like you."

A hot jolt of anger speared through him. He caught her arms and dragged her up on her toes. "You will not waste food while you are among us. There are those who die each day for want of what you have discarded. But you would not know of such things, would you, senorita?"

She merely raised her chin. "Why would I?"

He flashed her a ruthless half smile. "Perhaps in time you will learn to appreciate the small things in life you take so much for granted. Perhaps you will even come to beg for them."

"And maybe you will learn that I will never beg—especially not from you!"

His grip went tighter, then he let her go. Cursing beneath

his breath, he returned to Viento, mounted and started forward, the long leather *reata* tugging her into line behind him. Twice in the late afternoon, Sanchez rode up beside him, beseeching him to stop, to let the girl ride with one of the men, but each time he looked back and saw her, he heard the sharp clang of the bell, saw the lead ball explode in his brother's chest, heard the soft words Andreas had spoken as he died clutching Ramon's hand.

It was dark when they reached the place they meant to camp, the girl walking blindly, stumbling now and then, but always moving forward, by sheer will alone, it seemed to him. It angered him more than ever that she had decided to fight him, that she had not weakened as he had expected. Yet part of him was glad for it, glad to pit the rage he felt inside against someone besides himself.

She was trembling with exhaustion, he saw when he climbed down from his horse, swaying slightly though she fought to stand still. Her blue robe hung in dirty tatters, snagged on sharp rocks and thorny vines along the trail. Her hair had slipped loose from its binding. It tumbled in dark copper waves down her back and clung in damp curls to her slightly sunburned cheeks.

A knot of guilt twisted inside him. He had never been cruel to a woman. Never lifted a hand against one. But this was not just any woman. This one had murdered his brother. A bone-deep chill quelled the fires inside him. She would pay for what she had done. Her uncle would pay. He owed that much to his brother.

Then he noticed the blood on her feet.

Madre de Dios. "Sanchez!" he called out, and Pedro came running. "See to the girl." The words came out thick and strained as something squeezed painfully inside him. It mixed with the grief, stirring it up in agonizing waves, making it hard to think. "You should have said something," he told the woman darkly. "I would have seen you had something to wear for shoes."

She spit into the dirt at his feet. "There is nothing I want from you. Do you hear me? Nothing!"

She was everything he hated—he had discovered that the instant he had met her. She was grasping, hedonistic, spoiled, and self-centered.

Everything he once was himself.

Walking away, his head pounding viciously, he reached into the *bolsa* hanging behind his saddle and drew out a bottle of strong *aguardiente*. He pulled the cork and took a long, mind-numbing drink. He didn't take more than one. He did not dare. He knew if he did he would not stop. He would climb into the bottle, drink until he couldn't feel the pain.

Behind him Pedro led the girl to the stream, knelt and helped her bathe her bloody feet. A few minutes later, one of the men approached, carrying a soft pair of knee-high moccasins. The vaquero said something to the girl and though he couldn't hear it, Ramon was certain what it was.

Because as much as he hated to admit it, as much as he wished it weren't the truth, the same grudging respect his men had begun to feel for the woman had begun to blossom inside himself.

Every noise in the darkness seemed magnified a thousand times. Carly wasn't used to being out of doors. Her uncle had warned her not to go far from the house alone. The woods, he said, were dangerously overrun with wild animals: mountain lions, poisonous rattlesnakes, huge sharp-horned wild bulls, feral pigs, and worse of all, giant man-eating grizzly bears. Even now she could hear something growling in the darkness not far from camp. A second night creature howled its vicious intent just down the hill.

Carly shivered to think of it. Even if she could escape, which there seemed little hope of, she didn't know her way back home, and the animals would be prowling, just waiting to tear her in two.

And yet an even greater peril lay just a few yards across the camp.

He was stretched out on his bedroll, his black flat-brimmed hat tilted forward over his eyes. He had only just returned to the clearing, having gone off alone into the forest while the others made camp. He hadn't returned until after the men had all gone to sleep, then sat in front of the fire and stared silently into the flames. Sanchez had awakened and gone to the Spaniard's side, but he refused the meal the old vaquero had tried to coax him to eat.

As exhausted as Carly was, as frightened, as resentful of the Spaniard's brutal treatment, some small part of her felt sorry for him. She'd had a sister once, a little girl named Mary, four years younger than she was. Mary had died of a fever when Carly was nine years old. She remembered her mother weeping, remembered the terrible, hollow ache she had felt that couldn't be filled, the bitterness and sorrow of losing Mary. She could easily imagine the pain the don suffered from the loss of his brother.

Carly leaned her head against the tree and closed her eyes. She had eaten the chunk of roasted meat Sanchez had brought her and accepted the blanket he gave her even as he bound one of her ankles to the tree. Snuggling deeper into the blanket's warmth, she willed herself not to think of the don, not to think of her tired, aching muscles, scrapped shins, cut feet, or the darkening bruise on her cheek. Instead, she thought of her uncle, willing him to come, certain that he would, and finally she slid into a heavy trancelike sleep.

She awoke before dawn, to the nicker of horses and the slap of leather as the men saddled up and prepared to break camp. The young vaquero named Ruiz brought her breakfast: warmed-up tortillas, some leftover meat, and a tin cup of steaming hot coffee that tasted better than any she could ever remember drinking. She still wasn't hungry, though she forced herself to eat, and felt even more tired than she had the night before, every bone aching, every muscle sore. Her feet were blistered, scraped, and cut; her arms and legs were scratched, her lips dry and chaffed.

She heard the old vaquero pleading her case to the don, but just as before he blindly turned away.

At least she was still alive. There had been no rape, as she had feared, and except for the don, so far no one had been cruel to her. By now her uncle and his men would be hard in pursuit, and she was certain he would find her.

"It is time to leave, senorita." The words broke into her thoughts as the Spaniard strode up beside her. His features looked stark, barren. Faint purple smudges appeared beneath his cold dark eyes. He was ruthless, callous, unfeeling.

She felt a shot of loathing. "Where are we going? Where are you taking me?"

A grim smile curved his lips. "We travel far into the mountains. To Llano Mirada, a place that is sometimes my home."

"My uncle will find you wherever you go. He won't rest until he hunts you down like the animal you are."

"Better men have tried. All of them have failed. Your uncle will be no different."

"What do you want of me? What do you intend to do?"

His dark eyes raked her, bold, sensuous, unforgiving. "That remains to be seen, senorita." He dropped the braided leather loop around her wrists and drew it snug, then led her to his horse and gracefully swung into the saddle. "In the meantime, we must leave."

Anger seethed through her. And bitterness and hatred. Ignoring her ragged state of dress, her tumbled hair, and the over-sized moccasins on her feet, she flashed him a cool, cultivated smile, as haughty as she could muster. "I'm ready when you are, Senor El Dragón."

The don's face went taut and a muscle ticked in his cheek. Carly felt a jolt of satisfaction. He had meant to humble her, to see her whine and beg. He had been certain he could break her.

But each time she looked at his tall broad-shouldered figure sitting astride his night-black horse, each time she noticed the arrogant tilt of his head, she thought of the other handsome man. The one she had dreamed about, the man who had given her the rose. Ruthlessly, she forced herself to remember the dark-skinned fantasy man whose smile had charmed her and made butterflies swirl in her stomach.

The man who had been laughing at her all the while, playing her for a fool.

The stallion tossed its head and started up the trail, and Carly set out behind it. Ignoring her aching muscles, cuts, scrapes, and bruises, she fixed her eyes on the Spaniard's broad back and forced one moccasined foot in front of the other. Sanchez followed, along with the rest of the men.

By noon the sun was a fiery ball above their heads, beating down with relentless determination. The woven leather rope chafed her wrists and the blue embroidered robe weighed her down with every step. She stumbled and would have fallen if the don had not slowed. The trail was a long steep incline, sapping her strength along with her will. Her legs felt wobbly and her mouth was dry. She wasn't sure how much longer she could go on.

As if he read her thoughts, he stopped the horse, unfastened his canteen, walked back and handed it to her. She held it to her lips, savoring each long cooling drink, but it was all she could do to keep her hands from shaking.

"Llano Mirada is just there," he said, accepting the canteen and pointing toward the top of a steep ravine. "That is where we are going."

She followed his line of vision but saw nothing that looked the least bit like a camp. Just oaks and pines and manzanita, and a long rocky canyon leading up to a sheer granite cliff.

"The climb is a difficult one." His lips twisted cruelly. "If you ask me very nicely, perhaps I will give you a ride."

The canyon walls towered above her. Beneath her nightgown, her legs shook with fatigue. How could she possibly make such a difficult climb? She was dangerously close to tears, close to the point of breaking. "Go to hell."

He frowned at her, then glanced back at the steep, rock-strewn canyon with its seemingly non-existent path. For a moment he seemed uncertain. "Your pride will be your undoing, senorita."

Carly bristled. "And what of yours, Don Ramon?" Desperation drove her to taunt him. She needed her anger to carry her through. "Was it your grand Spanish pride that managed to get your brother killed? Or was it merely your greed?"

Fury blazed in his dark eyes, as hot as the tip of a flame, yet at the same time so cold she felt chilled. He turned his face away, leaving only his stark, elegant profile. Then he set his spurs to the sides of his horse and started up the grade.

They walked for a while. The trail appeared out of nowhere. It was impossible to see, she realized, and behind her the men used branches and leaves to disguise the way they had come. Her tired body sagged with defeat. Her uncle would never find the trail, and even if he did, guards were posted at intervals all along the rocky canyon wall.

Carly stumbled, hot tears burning, springing to life in her eyes. Dear God, why hadn't she asked the don for help? Why hadn't she cast aside her pride and let him be the victor he was so determined to be? What did it matter? But somehow she knew that it did. Her pride was all she had left, all that was keeping her from turning into the frightened little girl she was inside. She couldn't afford to abandon it. She brushed the tears away.

She made it more than halfway up the hill before she tripped and her legs gave way beneath her. She sprawled in the dry parched dirt beneath a thorny manzanita, several sharp barbs digging into the flesh on her leg. One of the vaqueros rode up beside her, dismounted, and carefully helped her back on her feet. He spoke softly in Spanish, words of encouragement, she thought, but with her head still spinning, she couldn't be sure.

Pedro Sanchez rode past, halting his horse beside that of the don.

"Enough, Ramon! You will let the girl go."

"No."

"You must listen to me, *hijo.* I have known you since you were a boy. Always, I have been as proud of you as if you were my own son. Do not do this thing."

"Stand away, amigo."

"I know that you are hurting. I know that it is your grief that blinds you—I beg of you to stop this terrible thing."

"I said stand away."

For a moment the old man didn't move. "Hear me now, Ramon de la Guerra. If you do this, it will be your gravest mistake, and for the first time since I have known you, you will make me feel ashamed."

The don worked a muscle in his jaw. His gaze went from Sanchez to Carly and a harsh smile curved his lips. "We will ask the girl. If it is her wish to ride, she must only say so and it will be done." He raked her with those hard brown eyes, the challenge clear in the cruel set of his jaw. "Is it your wish to ride with me, Senorita McConnell?" He was mocking her, baiting her, daring her to defy him. "If it is, you must only just ask and I will see your wish is granted."

Fresh tears threatened, burning at the back of her eyes.

Dear God, don't let him see. She stared hard at him, hating him for what he was doing, wishing she could wipe that vicious smile from his handsome face.

Wishing she could give in to defeat and say the words he wanted to hear, but knowing she could not, she glanced to the top of the trail. It didn't look all that far.

"*Si,* Senorita," he taunted, as if he read her mind, "Llano Mirada is just there." He pointed to the rise. "Not far for one so determined. What is it to be?"

"*Por Dios,* Ramon—"

Carly met his gaze squarely. With the last of her will, she straightened her shoulders. "You are in my way, senor. Lead on or remove the rope and ride off the trail so that I may pass in front of you."

Something flickered in his bold, dark eyes. He glanced to the old vaquero, who sadly shook his head. For a moment he made no move, then he nudged the big horse forward. They started up the trail at a little slower pace. When he felt a tug on the rope as she stumbled, the don eased back even more. The stallion began to prance, eager to reach his home, but the Spaniard held him firmly in check, insuring a slackness in the line, allowing her to set the pace.

Why? she wondered, when he wanted so badly to break her, to see her grovel at his feet. If she didn't know better, she would think he wanted her to make it. It was impossible, of course, and yet . . .

Carly wet her lips. The rope twisted and swung in front of her. The pale blue robe seemed to weigh a thousand pounds. She wore only her white cotton night rail beneath it, grimy now, the small pink bow torn and dangling at the base of her throat. With a show of defiance that marked her desperation, she stripped off the robe and continued up the hill. Sweat broke out on her forehead, trickled into the place between her breasts. Her breathing grew labored, her lungs on fire with each tortured breath. The blisters on her feet seared into her skin, and the top of the rise seemed to move farther away with each of her shaky steps. Still she drove herself on.

The others rode quietly behind her, none of them speaking, watching her with eyes full of pity. It didn't matter. All that mattered was reaching the top of the hill.

"It is not far now," said the don, and there was something different in his voice, a gentleness she hadn't heard since the day he had given her the rose. "Only a few more paces."

She stood beside his stirrup, she realized, having no idea when she had walked forward, yet clinging to his saddle for support. For the first time she noticed the rope was gone from around her wrists; the binding, too, had been cut and stripped away. The horse moved forward and so did Carly, one careful step at a time. The last footfall lifted her onto a wide plateau that looked out over the mountains. *Llano Mirada*, flat plain with a view.

She took two more shaky steps and stumbled. The don jerked the horse to a stop, but already her vision was spinning. She felt a hand at her waist, then the ground rushed up and she tumbled into darkness.

Ramon was off his horse in a heartbeat, but it was Pedro Sanchez who lifted the girl up in his arms.

"Stand away from her, Ramon," his friend said in a voice he hadn't heard since he was a boy. Guilt washed through him, leaving him shaken and confused, and suddenly filled with remorse. He had never been purposely cruel. He was a hard man, yes, but only because he'd had to be. He looked at the woman, saw her fiery auburn hair trailing over Sanchez's arm, saw her high full breasts rising with each of her too-rapid breaths, and a knot of regret rose painfully inside him.

Backing away, he let the older man pass, Sanchez cradling the girl as if she were a child.

But she wasn't a child, he reminded himself. She was

Fletcher Austin's niece. She was rich and spoiled, and as thirsty for power and wealth as her uncle. She was the woman who had gotten his brother killed.

He watched them and his chest felt tight. She was also courageous and proud, and she had earned a respect from him he had given to no other woman.

It did not change what she was. It did not change the way he felt. And yet . . .

Sanchez carried her into the small adobe house he and Andreas had built with their own hands, and Florentia, his housekeeper, closed the door behind them. Across the compound, the vaqueros greeted their loved ones, their families and friends in the camp. Ignacio and Santiago, the two men wounded in the raid, were helped down from their horses and led inside another small house where their women could tend them.

Ruiz Domingo, his youngest vaquero, led the pack horse that carried his brother's remains. Word had already been sent. Padre Xavier would arrive in the morning. Standing in the shade of the porch, Miranda Aguilar spoke briefly to Ruiz, then started in Ramon's direction. She was tall and graceful, her features dark and alluring. She was part Miwok Indian, part Castilian Spanish, with a smooth complexion and shiny long black hair.

"Ramon," she said, reaching out to him, her pretty dark eyes filled with tears. Her husband had ridden with Murieta, had died robbing a group of travelers ten months after Joaquin's last encounter with the law. *"Dios mio,* I am so sorry." Sliding her arms around his neck, she leaned her head against his chest.

She would go with him, he knew, take him into her soft woman's body and try to ease some of his pain. He also knew that he would not let her.

"We are all of us sorry, *querida."* He eased himself away. "Please . . . go now with the others."

"But I want to be with you. Do not send me away, Ramon."

He moved even farther from her. "I said for you to go. That is exactly what I mean."

She stood there for only a moment, head held high, long black hair streaming down to nearly her waist, then she turned and walked away. He knew she would not disobey him. Not like the Americana, the *gringa*. Still, it was that one he thought of as he made his way quietly into the forest, away from the others to a place where he could pray.

Chapter *F*ive

*T*orn between anger and pity, Pedro Sanchez watched the man who was like his own son. Ramon de la Guerra stood at the foot of his brother's grave beneath a huge live oak, holding his hat in his hands, his eyes closed, his head bent forward. It was nearly nightfall. Padre Xavier had finished the brief mass for Andreas early that morning. Since then, Ramon had returned three times to the grave.

He left there now, walking back toward the compound, though he had yet to go into his house, not even last night to sleep. Sighing into the silence, Pedro thought of leaving, of letting him continue to grieve, but his anger would not let him—that and an instinct that told him perhaps Ramon needed something besides his brother's death upon which to dwell.

He clamped his jaw. Pedro knew exactly what that something should be.

Crossing the distance between them, he walked up beside his friend. "I would speak to you, Ramon. There is something I must say."

Ramon's dark head came up. "What is it, Pedro?"

"It is about the girl."

"I do not wish to discuss the girl."

"No? Perhaps you are right. Perhaps it is better if you see your handiwork for yourself."

He shifted uncomfortably. "What are you talking about?"

"Come with me."

Wordlessly, Pedro led the way toward the house, Ramon close at his heels. They entered the small adobe building to the aroma of red peppers simmering in a heavy iron kettle suspended over the fire in the hearth, and the sound of *masa* being slapped into the flat, round shape of tortillas.

Florentia, a short stout, black-haired woman in her fifties, turned at the noise of the door closing sharply behind them. *"La comida* will soon be ready, Don Ramon," she called out. "It is time you had something to eat."

Ramon said nothing, just followed in Sanchez's wake to the door leading into the single small bedroom. The old vaquero pushed open the door and Ramon walked in.

Pedro turned to face him. "You have blamed the girl for Andreas's death. And you have blamed yourself. The girl did nothing any one of us would not have done in the same situation. You did only what it was your brother wished. You could not have stopped either one of those things from happening."

Ramon said nothing, just stared at the small figure huddled in the bed.

"It is time you forgave the girl. Perhaps even more important—it is time you forgave yourself."

She lay unconscious, her pale face bathed in sweat, the covers kicked off and her nightgown tangled up around her bare knees. The gown was clean, he saw, one Florentia must have provided, borrowed from Miranda or one of the Indian girls. The dirt was gone from her legs and feet, but not the long deep scratches. He could still see the bruise on her cheek. Occasionally, her eyelids flickered, as if the dreams she suffered were even more unpleasant than the journey that had brought her to such a state.

Ramon's mouth went dry. The air seemed to burn in his lungs. His face felt bloodless and nearly as pale as the girl's.

"If it is penance you seek, my friend," Pedro said softly, "this is the crime for which you must pay."

Ramon leaned forward, gripping the scrollwork at the foot of the old iron bed. Huddled in the center, the girl looked like an innocent child, her small hands fisted beneath her chin, her legs drawn up, her flame dark hair tousled and unkempt around her shoulders.

Ramon's chest tightened, the ache more painful with each escaping breath. *"Madre de Dios*—what have I done?"

Sanchez's tension eased as he walked up beside him. "What matters is that you care. That you are thinking clearly again. Florentia and I will see to the girl. When she is better, you can—"

"I will see to the girl. This is my fault. All of it. *Por Dios,* I cannot believe I am responsible for something like this."

"Everyone makes mistakes, my friend. Even you. A wise man learns from them."

Ramon just shook his head. "I told myself it was her fault, that she was to blame for what happened to Andreas. From the start, I knew it was not the truth, that I was the one to blame. It was wrong, what I did. Unforgivably wrong." Stripping off the black leather vest he wore, he tossed it over a chair, then sat down at the side of the bed. He leaned over and touched her forehead, which burned beneath his hand.

"Her fever is high," he said.

"Si. Florentia has tried to bring it down, but so far nothing has worked."

"Get me some water and several more clean cloths. Tell Miranda to fetch the Indian woman from the village. Tell her to take Ruiz with her and get back here as soon as she can."

Pedro smiled gently. "I will see to it, *patron.*"

Ramon looked up at the word, rarely used between the two friends. Something flickered in the old vaquero's eyes, respect, or perhaps approval.

"*Gracias,* my friend," Ramon said softly. There was a shift in the air between them, a moment that said without words what each man felt for the other. Then Sanchez nodded, backed from the room, and quietly closed the door.

Ramon sat with the girl all that night, bathing her forehead, opening her gown and bathing her shoulders, bathing her legs and feet. He would have liked to remove her clothes, to care for her more completely, but he refused to submit her to any further indignities. He knew how proud she was. How much her pride would suffer if she thought he had seen her naked.

If he hadn't felt so bad, he might have smiled. Even without breaching her modesty, he knew what a beautiful body she had. It was outlined clearly beneath her thin cotton bedclothes: the tiny waist, graceful legs, and high lush breasts. Her bottom was round and womanly, her neck pale and slender, her feet and hands small and well formed.

He took in her tumbled hair, a cinnamon brown, once alive with fiery highlights. He frowned. Like its owner, it lacked the luster it once had. Washing it would return the fire. As soon as she was better, he vowed, he would remedy that himself.

Sponging her face, he rested the cloth for a moment against her dry lips. Caralee was her name, he recalled. Carly, she had said. A pretty name, saucy and determined just as she was. As he vowed that she would be again.

Throughout the night, she tossed and turned, and in her sleep she began to speak, rousing Ramon from his thoughts as he sat beside her in the chair. At first the words were incoherent, just fever-induced, disjointed ramblings, then little by little the words began to form sentences.

"Pa? Is that you, Pa? I love you, Pa." She fisted the sheets in her small hands and tears began to slide down her cheeks. "Don't go, Ma, please don't leave me."

He smoothed the damp hair back from her forehead. "You are not alone, *nina*," he replied in the English she had slipped into. "Rest easy."

"I ain't gonna do it," she suddenly said. "I ain't gonna leave her. She's sick. She's dyin'. I don't care if'n I catch it, I ain't gonna go."

Ramon leaned forward, listening to her words, a frown of uncertainty creasing his brow. Just then Pedro walked in.

"You have been awake all night, Ramon. I will sit with the girl while you get some sleep."

"She has been talking, Pedro. I have spoken English to her on several occasions, but it sounded nothing like this. Her words were always refined, cultured. The way she speaks now sounds more like the illiterate *gringos* who come off the ships, headed for the gold fields. Something is not right here."

Pedro came closer. "What do you think it means?"

"I do not know, but I intend to find out." He shifted closer, listened to her talking again, then turned once more to his friend. "I want you to find Alberto. His cousin, Candelaria, works in the *hacienda* at Rancho del Robles. She has helped us before. Ask him to see what she can discover about our guest."

Pedro nodded. "In the meantime, I will send Florentia in to watch—"

"I am staying here."

"But you need your rest. You must—"

"Por favor, Pedro, do as I ask. Tell Alberto we need to know as quickly as we can."

Sanchez merely nodded. Arguing would do no good; Ramon intended to stay. "I will do as you wish."

Four days passed. Long, sleepless days for Ramon de la Guerra, but Carly's condition only worsened. Her breathing turned ragged, shallow, the way his brother had sounded near the end. It made the knife of remorse twist harder inside him.

The Indian woman came the second day. Trah-ush-nah, Blue Jay, was her name. The Californios called her Lena, her mission name. She was thin and dark skinned, with long straight black hair and bangs cut over her forehead, the style worn by most of the local Indians, but her features were softer, more refined. She was young, a woman in her twenties, a shaman by family tradition.

She ignored him as she worked. Using a mortar and pestle, she ground dried lemon balm leaves into powder, stirred them into a broth over the fire, then spooned them into the girl. She made a tea from birch bark, and forced her patient to drink it every few hours. She rubbed Carly's chest with an ointment made of lard, pulverized redmaid seeds, and roasted kernels of buttercup, and waved a fan made of eagle feathers over her pale face. Ramon didn't care what she did, as long as the girl got better.

By the fourth day, he had almost given up hope. The Indian woman had returned to the village, telling him she had done all she could. If Carly's condition didn't improve by the morrow, the priest was next to be called.

It was two in the morning, yet a lamp still burned on the small roughhewn table beside the old iron bed. Ramon could not sleep. He had barely been able to eat. The thought of another death on his conscience made his stomach roll with nausea. That it was a woman, that she was so young, that he was the man responsible made a hot ache rise in his throat.

Madre de Dios, he had never meant for this to happen! If only he hadn't been so caught up in his grief. If only he had been able to think, been able to block the pain.

If only he had left her at Rancho del Robles.

His heart unbearably heavy, weary clear to his bones, Ramon sat forward in his chair and rested his elbows on his knees. Lacing his long, dark fingers together, he lowered his forehead against his hands and softly began to pray.

Someone was calling her. Carly could barely hear the quietly spoken words but they were sweet and plaintive, the sound incredibly beautiful. The voice was deep, husky, melodious. It called to the Virgin Mary, it called to Saint John, it called to the heavenly angels. Please, the soft voice said, let the little one live.

She wet her dry lips and stirred, drawn to the beauty of the voice, the sensual rhythm of the words. The language was Spanish, she realized vaguely, the deep sensuous vibrations rolling through her in soft caressing waves. It moved something inside her, made her want to open her eyes, to see where the silvery, lyrical phrases came from.

She listened to the rich male cadence, demanding one moment, pleading the next, its masculine timbre a balm to her weary soul. She wanted to see the face behind such a voice, to see if it could be nearly as achingly beautiful.

Rousing herself, she opened her eyes to see a black-haired man praying softly beside the bed. His face was all that she had envisioned: perfect winged black brows, slim straight nose, high carved cheekbones, a strong jaw, and sensuous lips. Double rows of thick black lashes swept the skin beneath his tightly closed eyes. His head hung forward, his hair falling over his brow, and there were tears on his cheeks.

"Don't cry," she said in his same soft language. "You're . . . too beautiful . . . to cry."

His head snapped up. For a moment he said nothing. Then the Spanish rolled out, so rapid she didn't catch the words, but his wide bright smile made her smile at him in return.

"Chica," he said softly. "At last you have returned to us."

She studied him for long moments more, mesmerized

by the warmth and strength in his face. "I'm . . . so tired," she whispered, wetting her lips as she gazed up at him. "And I'm hungry. Could I please have something to eat?"

He stood up from his chair, tall and lean and broad-shouldered. "*Si*, of course you can. I will see to it myself." He felt her forehead, breathed a sigh of relief, then reached over and squeezed her hand. "Do not move. I promise I will only be gone for a moment."

Smiling, she snuggled down into the covers. She was glad the man was there to watch over her. When she woke up again, he was certain to have something good to fill her empty stomach.

By the time Ramon returned with a bowl of warm broth, Caralee McConnell was once more asleep. But the fever had broken. His prayers had been answered. He felt sure the girl would live.

Relief made him suddenly weary. He set the tray of food down on the dresser, settled himself in the chair and allowed himself to sleep for a while, until Pedro knocked on the door. Dawn grayed the windows. The chill of night still hovered in the room. He got up from the chair and stretched his aching muscles, then knelt to freshen the low-burning fire.

"Her fever has broken," he said as his friend walked in. "I think she is going to be fine."

Pedro crossed himself. "Thank the Blessed Virgin."

"I already did," Ramon said with a grin, the first he had allowed himself in over a week.

Pedro just sighed. "I bring news, Ramon."

"From Alberto?"

"*Si*. I am afraid you are not going to like it."

Ramon frowned. "I have not liked much of anything lately. You may as well tell me what it is."

"The girl . . . Senorita McConnell, she is not the woman you believed."

"What do you mean?"

"Alberto's cousin, Candelaria, she worked as the senorita's personal maid. She says the girl was warned by her uncle never to speak of her background, but she was so lonely, I suppose she needed a friend. She trusted Candelaria and told her the truth."

"The truth?" Ramon said.

"Si."

"And just what is this truth?"

"The girl was not wealthy as we believed. Her father was a poor, ignorant miner. He died of a lung disease when the senorita was only just ten. The girl and her mother took in laundry to earn money for food. Four years ago her mother died of the cholera. Senor Austin is her mother's brother, her only living relative. He sent her money, then arranged for a boarding school so she could finish her education and learn the proper refinements. Candelaria says the senorita wishes to repay him for all he has done. She obeys him, even when she disagrees. It was he who refused to let her dance with you. He warned her not to encourage you in any way. Candelaria said the girl felt very badly about the way she treated you the day you gave her the rose. Candelaria says it is not in the senorita's nature to be unkind to others."

Ramon felt a deep, hollow sinking in the pit of his stomach. He had made mistakes in his life more than once, but none any worse than this.

"I have wronged her badly."

"Si, that is true, but at least now you know the truth."

Ramon began to pace at the foot of the bed. "I will make it up to her. I will find a way—I swear it."

Behind them the woman stirred. Ramon reached her side just as she opened her eyes.

"You!" she shrieked, her drowsiness instantly gone, the color draining from her pretty face. "What—what are you doing in my bedroom?"

Pedro wisely remained silent and backed out the door.

Ramon smiled softly. "I am afraid this is my bedroom, *chica,* not yours."

She blanched as the truth came crashing in. A tremor moved over her small frame and her eyes flashed a moment of fear.

Inwardly, Ramon cursed. "Do not be frightened, *nina.* I will not hurt you. I give you my word."

"Your word?" She drew herself up against the headboard, the effort making her weak body tremble. "What value is there in the word of a man like you?"

"More than you might think," he said softly, "but I do not blame you for having your doubts. In the meantime, I do not wish you to tax yourself. Your illness has been long and difficult. You need time to get well and grow strong. Rest easy, little one. I will have Florentia bring you something to eat."

The Spaniard left the room and Carly stared after him in amazement. Shaking with apprehension and the weakness left by her illness, she tried to recall the scene that had just transpired with the don, but already the images seemed fuzzy and out of focus. His kindness couldn't have occurred. There was nothing kind about him. Perhaps she had imagined it.

She glanced around the small cozy room, at the bright-colored quilt on the old iron bed, at the hand-sewn carpet on the hard-packed earthen floor. There was a crude oak dresser against one wall, much like the table beside the bed, and a chipped blue porcelain bowl and pitcher sitting atop it.

Carly fought down the uncomfortable thudding of her heart and the knot in her stomach, and tried to piece together what little she knew. She was in the don's bedchamber in his small adobe house in the mountains. A place called Llano Mirada. She had been abducted from her home by El Dragón, a man who blamed her for his brother's death. Carly shivered to think of it. Dear God, what would he do?

Her hold grew tighter on the quilt. How many days had she been there? He said her illness had been long. As weak as she felt, she'd been sick for more than a day or two. She glanced at the white cotton nightgown she wore, bigger than her own, spotlessly clean and smelling of strong lye soap. Whose was it? Why had it been given to her? Who had cared for her—and why had the ruthless don bothered with her care at all?

The room felt suddenly cold and Carly pulled the quilt up to her chin. Whatever his reasons, sooner or later, she was certain to find out. Carly closed her eyes, almost wishing she hadn't awakened.

Ramon left the house feeling a lightness in his chest, though he knew it would not last long. With the girl out of danger, it was time to return to his hacienda. Already he had waited longer than he should have. He couldn't afford to arouse suspicion, stir doubts he might be involved with El Dragón.

And there were his mother and aunt to see to. A message had been sent of Andreas's death. The women would be grieving just as he was. They would need his support, and in truth it would comfort him to have theirs. It would ease their minds to know Padre Xavier had said the mass, and in time, once it was safe and the danger of discovery was past, he would see his brother's body removed to the family plot that had given Rancho Las Almas its name— Ranch of Souls. The place where generations of de la Guerras had been laid to rest, the only reason the small five-hundred-acre parcel of land remained in the de la Guerra name when the rest of their land had been taken.

Stolen, he corrected. By the *gringo*—Fletcher Austin and his band of thieves.

"You are on your way home?" Pedro asked, walking to where Ramon stood in the shade of the lean-to saddling a tall rawboned sorrel horse. Viento, the stallion ridden by El Dragón, remained at Llano Mirada. He would know only one rider now.

Ramon forced down a moment of pain. Smoothing the thick woolen blanket over the horse's back, he lifted the heavy vaquero's saddle into place atop it. "It is time I returned to Las Almas. I will come back as soon as it is safe."

"Florentia and I will see to the girl."

"I know you will. I am sure you will see she is back on her feet by the time I return." A corner of his mouth curved up. "I find myself looking forward to the challenge."

"What will you do with her, Ramon? You cannot let her go. She knows who you are and where this place is."

Footsteps sounded inside the barn, drawing the men's attention. "Perhaps you can sell her." Francisco Villegas walked toward him, a hard-faced vaquero who had joined them only a few months back. "They say the price for a pretty *gringa* runs high across the border in Nogales."

Ramon ran the cinch strap under the horse's belly, giving himself time to control the fury he hadn't expected. "The girl stays here. She belongs to me." He pulled the cinch strap snug. "I have already made that clear to the rest of the men."

Cisco Villegas grinned beneath his heavy black mustache. One of his eyeteeth was missing. The other was capped with gold. "I do not think Miranda will be pleased to hear it."

Ramon turned slowly to face him, his patience at an end. "Miranda is not your concern. Neither is the *gringa*. I would advise you to remember it." His hard look spoke its warning and Cisco backed a step away.

"*Si*, Don Ramon. Whatever you say." Turning on his heel, he walked out of the shadows, heading for the corral.

"I am not certain I like that man," Pedro said.

"Neither am I," said Ramon.

"He is a friend of your cousin Angel's, and your brother trusted him."

"*Si.* I hope he did not misplace that trust."

"I will keep an eye on him."

Ramon just nodded. Sliding the heavy Spanish bit between the horse's teeth, he settled the animal's head stall over its ears, then gathered the long braided reins. Shoving a booted foot into a leather *tapadero,* he swung up into the saddle. *"Hasta la vista, compadre."*

Pedro smiled, crinkling the lines in his weathered face. *"Hasta la vista,* my friend."

Sitting astride his big buckskin horse, Fletcher Austin lifted his dusty brown felt hat and mopped the sweat from his brow with a forearm. "Any sign of them?" he asked Cleve Sanders, his foreman, a rangy, long-boned man with curly brown hair.

"Not a trace. It's the same damn way every time we go after them. They just seem to disappear."

"Maybe Collins and Ramirez will be able to recover the stock," Fletcher said, though he didn't hold out much hope. Two days after the raid, the outlaw band had split up, the horses being driven north while most of the men continued east. Fletcher had done the same, sending a small party north in pursuit while his main body of men continued to track the larger group of men, hoping El Dragón was among them.

They had been chasing the outlaws for nearly a week. He was bone-tired and saddle sore and so were his men, but he wanted those horses. More than that, he wanted El Dragón.

The bastard had taken his niece. It was personal between them now.

"Odds are, that stock's on its way to the gold fields," he said. "There's so much demand for meat, the cattle trails are constantly in use. Collins and his men are at least a day behind them. If the bandits are smart—and so far they have been—they'll stay on the main trail till their tracks are overrun, then cut off somewhere and move up into the hills. There's no way Collins and the others are going to find them, unless they just get lucky."

"What about El Dragón?"

Fletcher fought to control a sweep of anger. "He's got Caralee. I'm not giving up until she's returned. In the meantime, we'll go back to del Robles and regroup. We'll get some of the local rancheros to join us, get more supplies, and fresh mounts for the men. Then we'll just have to hope something turns up." Fletcher clenched a meaty fist. "I swear I won't rest till I see that bastard swinging from the limb of a Rancho del Robles oak."

Fletcher smiled grimly at the thought. It wouldn't be the first time he'd hung a no-good greaser. It probably wouldn't be the last.

Chapter Six

The woman, Florentia Nunez, pushed open the heavy oak door and stepped into the bedroom. She smiled to see Carly out of bed, sitting in the straight-backed chair beside it.

"You are feeling better, no?" She carried a tray steaming with coffee and hot rolled up tortillas, and her plump cheeks held a glow of warmth.

"Yes, I am. Much better. I was wondering . . . I'd like to get dressed. I was hoping someone might loan me something to wear." It had been over a week since the don had left. The last two days Carly had prowled around the house, having regained much of her strength, but she had yet to go outside. She wasn't certain they would let her.

"*Si*, of course, senorita." The housekeeper's nod jiggled several of her beefy chins. "I have already seen to the clothes. I will just go now and get them." She set the tray down on the dresser and left the room, returning a few moments later with a long, gathered, bright yellow cotton skirt and an off-the-shoulder white peasant blouse. She set them down on the bed, along with a pair of flat leather sandals.

"I hope they will fit you. I borrowed them from Miranda Aguilar, then shortened the skirt a little and took in the waist. Pedro made the shoes."

"You and Senor Sanchez . . . you have both been very

kind." She hadn't expected it. She'd been sure she'd be treated badly. "Especially considering that I am Don Ramon's prisoner."

The rotund woman smiled. "You are Don Ramon's special guest. That is what he has said."

Special guest. That was almost funny. She wondered what the black-haired devil had in store for her when he returned. "I'd still like to thank you. You cared for me, perhaps even saved my life."

"That is not completely true. Mostly it was the don, I tended your personal needs, but it was Don Ramon who had the Indian woman brought from the village. He was the one who—"

A knock at the door interrupted what she might have said next. Waddling toward the door, the heavy woman opened it and waved in two young boys carrying buckets of steaming hot water.

Carly surveyed the water and sighed. *"Gracias,* Senora Nunez. I have never seen a more welcome sight."

"I am only just Florentia, as I have said. And a nice warm bath will do wonders."

It did. She even washed her hair. She was sitting on the bed, trying to comb out the tangles when a second knock sounded at the door. She glanced up just as the don walked in.

Carly's stomach knotted, but the Spaniard only smiled. It was a different sort of smile than she expected, the same sort he had worn the first time she had met him. An uneasy shiver slid through her.

"Senorita McConnell," he said, "I see you are feeling much better."

She looked at his handsome face and her insides twisted. She knew that face, how those handsome features could turn cold and hard, how those eyes could bore into you without an ounce of compassion. Her mind flashed with images of the night she'd been taken from Rancho del

Robles, of her brutal journey through the mountains. She imagined what a man like that might do to her next, and a tendril of fear rippled through her. The don must have seen it for the smile slid from his face.

"I am sorry. I did not come here to frighten you. What happened before . . . it was a mistake. A very bad one. You will come to no harm here. I hope you believe that."

Carly came up off the bed, angry at herself for allowing him to see her weakness, even more angry at him. "Why should I? Why should I believe anything a man like you has to say?"

"Because it is the truth."

She remembered the cold nights she'd spent in the mountains, the ruthless way he had forced her to march through the hills. Fear niggled at her insides. Carly lifted her chin. "I don't believe you. You're vile—despicable—an outlaw and probably a murderer. Whatever your reasons for seeing to my care, they only have to do with your own selfish plans."

His eyes remained fixed on her face. "If I were you, I would feel the same way. Perhaps in time, you will see that is not the way it is."

Carly pondered that. She didn't believe him, not for an instant. "If what you say is true, why the sudden change of heart? I'm still the woman I was. The woman you despise. The woman you hold responsible for the death of—"

"Do not say it, for it is not so." The skin across his high cheekbones went taut. A subtle tension moved over his tall, solid frame. "I am the one at fault," he said softly. "It is not usually my way to blame others for sins of my own making."

There was something in his eyes, something she had seen there before, a bleakness shadowed by pain, but this time it was not overridden by anger. And it seemed to be directed inward, at himself, not at her.

Carly knew what it meant to lose a loved one. The heart-break, the hollow place that would never again be filled. Her family was gone. Her sister, her father, her mother. It hurt just to think of it. It bothered her to imagine he might be feeling the same sort of pain, and a sweep of pity moved through her.

She ruthlessly forced it down. A man like the don didn't deserve her pity. He wouldn't even want it.

"Florentia says that I am your guest. If that is so, then I appreciate your generosity, Don Ramon, but I would prefer to end my stay. There is much that needs attending to back at Rancho del Robles, and I'm certain my uncle will be worried about me."

A corner of his mouth curved up. "You have never impressed me as a fool, *chica*. Surely you must know that I cannot let you leave."

Carly smiled grimly. "Then surely *you* must know that I am not your guest. I am your prisoner. There is a great deal of difference."

"Only if you make it so." He leaned back against the wall, propping a wide shoulder against it. "You will be allowed to roam the compound. There is only one way down and the trail is well guarded. I do not believe you could find your way home even if you managed to escape."

Carly said nothing.

The don regarded her closely. "I would change things, *chica,* if I could. Unfortunately, it is too late for such a thing. In the meantime, there are good people here, people who will treat you with kindness, perhaps even friendship, if that is your wish."

"Until when, Don Ramon? How long are you planning to keep me here against my will?"

The don shook his head. Glossy black hair moved against the open collar of his shirt. His neck was lean and corded with muscle, and curly black chest hair sprang up from the vee in his shirt. "I am afraid I cannot say."

"Is it money you're after? Do you mean to seek a ransom? If you do, you may discover I'm not worth as much as you think."

His hard features softened, his eyes moving over her with something that might have been pity. It made her feel exposed, naked, as if he could see inside her to the person she really was. The notion frightened her even more than the don himself.

"Ransom is not my intent," he said.

"Then let me leave. If you wish me to accept your word, then you accept mine—if I'm allowed to leave, I'll tell no one who you are or where this place is."

Soft laughter rumbled from his chest. "I am sorry, senorita, I cannot do that. Even if I were willing to accept your word, there are others here who would not."

Carly turned away from him, furious yet oddly disturbed. She didn't trust him. She knew how cold and callous he was. But there was something different about him now, something that reminded her of the man who had given her the rose.

"As your *guest*," she said tartly, "my time should be my own. If that is the case, I'd prefer that you leave."

"Whatever you say, senorita." A faint smile touched his lips. "You may spend your time here in sullen rebellion if that is your wish, or you can make the most of it, learn something about the people of the land you intend to call your home. There is much I could show you, if you would let me."

Carly eyed him warily. Why was he being so pleasant? She knew the heartless man he was, even if his charm had once again appeared. "I want to go home—Senor El Dragón. That is my wish, and the sooner the better. In the

meantime if, as you say, I am free to go outside, I would
like to see the rest of my prison."

Straightening her spine, she crossed the room toward
where he stood by the door and tried to walk past, but the
don caught her arm.

"As I said, there are good people here, but there are also
those who join our cause only because we need them, and
they can benefit from the arrangement. They are hard men,
ruthless men."

"Men like you," she put in coldly.

"Perhaps. But with me you will be safe." Taking her
arm, he led her out the door and into the small *sala* where a
couch made of willow branches sat beside a matching willow branch chair. Bright colored pillows formed the cush-
ions, and a woven rug covered the packed earthen floor.

"We will return in time for supper," the don said to Florentia, who waved in reply as he urged Carly out onto the
porch. Dressed in a full-sleeved white lawn shirt and form-
fitting black breeches that flared out at the bottom over the
toes of his shiny black boots, Ramon de la Guerra exuded
virility and strength. Whether she hated him or not, whether
he was ruthless or charming, he was the handsomest man
Carly had ever seen.

A prickle of warning slid down her spine. She did not
intend to ignore it.

Ramon walked beside the petite *Americana*, admiring the
way she looked in the simple clothes of a *paisano*. She had
been lovely that day at the races in her peppermint-striped
day dress, but in some strange way, he thought she looked
even more beautiful today. Perhaps it was the long silky
hair she had left unbound, a curtain of dark burnished copper hanging to her waist, or the way her breasts shifted
seductively beneath the blouse when she walked, a hint of
soft swells rising above the neckline.

Watching the movement of her hips, Ramon felt a tightening in his groin. He was attracted to the woman. He had been since the moment he had met her. More so now that he had seen her spirit, her courage. Now that he knew she was none of those things he had imagined.

At least not yet.

Ah, but she was still a *gringa*. Whatever he felt for her could go no farther than lust, and he would not subject her to that kind of treatment now. Not after what he had done.

Still, he could not help admiring the perfection of her features, the fine auburn brows, upturned nose, big, leaf-green eyes, and full ruby lips. Looking at her sweet, ripe beauty, it seemed impossible he could ever have treated her badly.

"Don Ramon!" Sanchez walked toward them smiling, breaking into his thoughts. "And Senorita McConnell." He glanced down at her small, sandaled feet. "I am glad the shoes fit."

"They're perfect. Thank you, Senor Sanchez."

He nodded, then turned away. "It is good to have you back, Ramon."

"I cannot stay long. Only a few days. I thought perhaps while I was here, I would show the senorita around."

"Bueno. The fresh air will do her good. And I am sure she is eager to be out of the house."

Ramon nodded. "We will join you for supper a little bit later." Turning away from Sanchez, he smiled at Carly and extended his arm. As he expected, she ignored it and simply started walking.

The encampment itself wasn't large, mostly makeshift houses among the pines at the top of the knoll. Some of the single men lived in tents. The two Yocuts Indians who rode with them had built small willow-branch huts in a clearing at one end of the camp. There was a central corral, and a couple of lean-tos. A fast-moving stream ran along the edge of the encampment, providing water and plenty of mountain trout.

"How many people live here?" Carly surveyed the women washing clothes in the stream and the children playing ball in the center of the compound. She was surprised to find the place so pleasant, with patches of grass here and there, the simple adobe houses well tended.

"About thirty-five," the don said, smiling down at a child who waddled toward him, a little girl no more than three years old. Laughing he lifted the baby up in his hard-muscled arms, kissed her chubby cheek, then handed her over to the woman hurrying toward them.

"*Gracias,* Don Ramon. My Celia is forever toddling away." The woman was no more than twenty-five, with pleasant features and soft brown eyes. She looked at Carly and gave her a tentative smile.

"Maria, this is Senorita McConnell," the don said. "She will be our guest for a while."

The baby reached toward Carly, trailed her chubby fingers through her thick dark copper hair. She found herself smiling in return. "Carly," she said to the woman. "My name is Carly."

"I am pleased to meet you." Smiling at the don, holding her baby close against her, she quietly walked away.

"I didn't realize outlaws lived with their families," Carly said, trying not to be touched by the Spaniard's easy manner with the child.

"Most of them are displaced *rancheros,* men who have lost their lands to the *gringos.* The vaqueros and others who worked for them also lost their homes. They were replaced by cheaper labor, Indian workers bought and sold by the Americanos. They are treated almost like slaves."

"That can't be true. Slavery isn't allowed in California."

"No? Indian wages are ten dollars a month, most of which goes back to the *haciendado* for room and board. If an Indian is found to be vagrant, he is auctioned to the highest bidder. The money he brings goes to the government. As I see it, my pretty *gringa,* that comes very close to slavery."

Carly said nothing to that. She had seen the Indians working around her uncle's rancho, but she had never realized how little he paid them. It bothered her to think what the don said might be true.

The sound of iron ringing against iron drew her attention toward a large wooden shed built on one side of the compound. Hand swaths, broad-bladed hoes, hammers, saws, axes, braces, bits, and planes lined one wall. Two huge horse collars hung from the ceiling, along with several saddles and other items of tack.

Walking to the rear of the shed, the don introduced her to Santiago Gutierrez, a man she remembered from the raid. Today he was working as a blacksmith, bent over a big iron anvil, his hammer ringing as he repaired a broken wagon tongue.

He glanced up, eyeing her as warily as she eyed him. "You are feeling better, I see. That is good."

Carly hid her surprise. Concern was the last thing she had expected. "I—I'm much better, thank you." He hardly looked like an outlaw, just a hard-working man with sweat on his brow, his muscles straining to his task. The don asked after his wife, Tomasina, and their two children. Santiago told him they were well.

Noticing the heavy bandage around his thigh and remembering the wound he'd received in the raid, she started to ask him how his leg was healing, but caught herself just in time. The man was a criminal. He'd been injured stealing her uncle's horses, for heaven's sake. It was hardly fitting that she be concerned for his health!

The don asked the question for her. "Your wound . . . how is it mending?"

Gutierrez lifted a glowing red piece of iron out of the

fire and dunked it in a nearby tub of water, sending up a shot of steam. "Tomasina removed the lead ball. The wound is healing very well."

"I am glad to hear it."

The blacksmith smiled and began to hammer on the still-hot iron while the don led Carly away.

"For an outlaw, he seems surprisingly pleasant," she said.

The Spaniard laughed softly and shook his head. "He is only a man. One who is fighting for what has been taken from him. To our way of thinking, none of us are outlaws."

She could certainly argue with that, but she didn't. "I'm surprised he doesn't hate me. I thought that was the way all of your men felt."

He shrugged his broad shoulders and glanced away. "Maybe they did . . . for a while. They loved Andreas just as I did." It was there again, that shadowy moment of pain. Then as quickly it was gone.

"Then why—"

"Perhaps they feel that if I can accept what you did, then they must endeavor to do so."

Carly's chin came up. "If *you* can accept what *I* did! I am the one who cannot accept what you did!" Grabbing her bright yellow skirt in one hand, Carly stalked out of the shed. She didn't go back to the house; she had been cooped up too long already. Instead she made her way down to the creek and wandered along the bank. She shouldn't make him angry. The rational part of her knew that. She was his prisoner, completely at his mercy. And yet she refused to cower. She hadn't before. She would not do it now.

He caught up with her in a quiet place where the water eddied and swirled. She sat there alone, feeling forlorn and wishing she was back at Rancho del Robles, wishing she could cry but determined that she wouldn't. Staring out over the frothy, rippling stream, she felt his presence even before she saw him.

"I am sorry," he said quietly. "That is not what I meant to say. The truth is the men have come to respect you. If you wish it, they will accept you among them."

His voice was so soft, so masculine and beautiful. It reminded her of something . . . someone. . . . She tried to recall, but the memory slid away. Carly straightened and lifted her eyes to his face.

"I wish to go home, Don Ramon. I realize the problem that poses, yet I beseech you to find a way."

The Spaniard said nothing. There was no way he could let her leave and both of them knew it. But how long could he force her to stay? And what would he do with her once he grew tired of his unwanted *guest?*

They started back to the house, Carly fighting to control the worry that bubbled up inside her, making her stomach feel queasy. Stay calm, she told herself. At least for the present you are safe. In the meantime, her uncle would be searching, and perhaps she could find some means of escape.

With that thought in mind, she surveyed the compound, noting the men, women, and children absorbed in their everyday tasks, but also the wagons and horses, and anything she might find for a weapon. She would continue to do so, to learn this place and what might be useful.

Lost in such thoughts, when they rounded the corner, she was surprised to see a beautiful black-haired woman standing on the porch. She was tall and slender, with small, pointed breasts, a narrow waist, and trim hips. The woman was elegant, not the least bit boyish, exotic, and as beautiful as any woman Carly had ever seen.

She was also angry, her black eyes snapping, her chest rising and falling with each hostile breath.

"*Buenas tardes,* Miranda," the don said pleasantly, but his features had grown taut, and it was obvious he was not pleased that she was there.

"Will you not introduce me to the woman you have brought into our camp?" she said waspishly. "The woman who killed your brother."

The don's dark eyes blazed to life. His posture grew rigid, his muscles tense, anger seeping from every pore. Carly knew that look only too well. She was glad this time she was not the object of his wrath.

"I have told you, Miranda, the woman is not responsible. For as long as I say, she is our guest. That is the way you will treat her."

For as long as I say. The words sent a ripple of fear down Carly's spine. Just how long was that? The words, combined with the hatred oozing from the black-haired woman, made Carly feel slightly sick.

"I am Miranda," the woman said with dark menace, her fiery eyes flashing a warning. "I am Don Ramon's woman. I have come here so that you will know. So that between us there will be no misunderstanding."

Standing at his side, Carly's own temper stirred. "And you, senorita—I hope *you* will not misunderstand. I have no interest in your El Dragón. As far as I am concerned he is nothing but a ruthless outlaw. If it pleases you to sleep with him, that is your misfortune. All I wish to do is return to my home."

Ramon felt the smaller woman's anger almost as hot as his own, and a corner of his mouth tugged upward in grudging respect. Ignoring them both, she swept past him into the house. He couldn't help recalling her humble beginnings and found himself admiring how well she had learned to disguise them. She was as regal as any noblewoman he had ever met, as haughty and proud as any woman of pure Spanish blood.

That thought made him uneasy. She was a *gringa*. Nothing could change that. Just as it could not change Miranda's part Indian heritage. Fortunately, he felt little more than affection for Miranda. It was all he would allow himself to feel for the saucy American girl.

Carly sat beside the don through supper. Florentia and Pedro Sanchez sat on the opposite side of the stout oak table. As he had been earlier, the Spaniard was charming and attentive, and that fact made her nervous and withdrawn. She didn't know what he was after. She only knew she hadn't forgotten the hard man he could be.

Pleading a headache, she withdrew from the table and retired to her room, but she had trouble sleeping. What were his motives? Why was he being kind when before he had been so cruel? Was he sorry for what he had done? He had never really said so, only that he'd made a mistake. Perhaps he was trying to make amends, but she couldn't seem to make herself believe it.

And even if he was, it didn't change things. She was still his prisoner, he still the master of her fate.

Lying on the mattress, staring up at the rugged hand-hewn beams above her head, she recalled the furious look he had scorched his mistress with, the woman who called herself Miranda. She was beautiful, dark-skinned and exotic. Obviously seduction wasn't the don's objective. He already had a woman to warm his bed.

In a strange way, the notion disturbed her. That even now he was probably with Miranda, kissing her, making passionate love to her. Carly knew little of such things, yet until now the notion had seemed romantic. She had hoped one day to be married, perhaps to a man as handsome as the don. One who could be just as charming.

But wasn't nearly so ruthless.

Eventually, she fell asleep, but when she did, she dreamed. Dressed all in black, the Spaniard thundered toward her astride his fierce black horse. He swept her up in his arms, flung her over his saddle, and rode away with her into the forest. Pulling the stallion to a halt, he carried her fighting and screaming to a grassy knoll beside a stream and there he began to kiss her.

Carly quit struggling. The heat of his mouth made her body go limp, made her insides grow buttery and liquid. His lips felt warm, and softer than she had expected; the arms that crushed her against him were hard as granite and utterly implacable, but he did not hurt her.

His hands swept downward, skimming lightly over her body. There was fiery possession in his touch. He wanted something from her, something more than the liberties he had taken already. His kiss demanded it, yet she wasn't sure what it was.

Part of her wanted to struggle, to free herself from his hold. The other part . . .

Carly awoke with a start, her body burning with a strange, damp, all-pervading heat. She was trembling all over, her nipples hard and tender where they pressed against the sheet.

Climbing out of bed on limbs that were painfully unsteady, she poured water into the porcelain basin, dampened a cloth, and washed her face. With a sigh, she returned to bed, but again had trouble sleeping. When she finally did doze off, it seemed only minutes till the graying of dawn began to lighten the sky outside the simple muslin curtains at the window. It would soon be morning. She wondered if the don would come.

Or if he would stay with his woman.

Miranda Aguilar raked her nails along Ramon's hard-muscled thigh. Lying beside her on the bed, he stirred with the first light of dawn and rolled onto his back. She smiled at the long, hard ridge jutting up from its nest of thick black curls, heavy and seductive against his lean flat belly.

Last night they hadn't made love. Ramon had been too angry. She shouldn't have gone to the woman. He had warned her against it, but she didn't care. She didn't care what it took—as long as the woman stayed away.

His fingers closed over her wrist, stopping the movement of her hand. "I will not tolerate your disobedience," he warned softly, reading her thoughts, his eyes dark and boring into hers. "Treat the woman with anything less than respect and you will not like the consequences, I warn you."

Her lips drew into a pout. She leaned over and kissed the head of his shaft, making it throb and quiver. "I am sorry I displeased you."

"As I said last night, I will be more than displeased should you do it again."

Ramon had a terrible temper, but he had never hurt her. Once, when she had first come to Llano Mirada, Elena Torres, the girl who was his woman then, had stolen some money from one of the men. When Ramon confronted her, demanding she give back the money, she shouted obscenities and called him vile names. Ramon tossed her over his shoulder, carried her over to the horse trough, and dumped her in the water. The woman deserved it and the dunking hadn't hurt her. Mostly her pride had been stung.

No, he had never been cruel to a woman. Except for the *gringa*. Which did nothing to ease Miranda's fears.

"Do not be angry, Ramon," she said seductively.

Bending forward, she ran her fingers lightly over his chest, bent and took his flat copper nipple into her mouth, teasing it with her tongue. Her hand strayed down to his hardened arousal. She stroked him there and the muscles of his stomach went taut. Beneath her fingers, the rhythm of his heart grew more rapid. She raised up to kiss him, but instead he gripped her shoulders and rolled her beneath him then began to suckle her breasts. His hand slid down to the folds of her sex. She was already wet and ready. Ramon spread her legs and drove himself deeply inside her.

In minutes he brought her to climax, then rapidly reached

his own. For a moment he lay quiet, staring up at the beams over his head. Then he rolled away.

"It is early yet," Miranda said softly. "The sun is only just up. For once can you not linger here for a while?"

"Not today," he said curtly. Grabbing a clean linen towel from beside the basin, he draped it around his neck, pulled on his snug black breeches, and headed out the door of the cabin, making his way upstream toward the place set aside for the men to bathe.

Miranda sighed. More and more he grew distant. She was losing him, she knew, and yet there was nothing she could do. She thought of the woman, the beautiful *Americana* with the fiery auburn hair.

Ramon had treated her badly, but he had been beside himself with grief. Still it worried Miranda, for it took great passion for such an act. Already that passion had changed from hatred to something else. She did not wish to see it change again.

Miranda slammed a slim fist down on the feather mattress. Ramon wanted the beautiful *gringa*. Miranda could see it in his eyes whenever he looked in the woman's direction.

She wondered how long it would be before he took her. She wondered as well what she could do to stop him.

Chapter Seven

Ramon crossed the compound to where Sanchez worked with the horses, most of them captured wild from the few bands left, broken to the saddle, and trained by Pedro, Ignacio, and Ruiz.

"Buenos dias, amigo," Ramon called out to his friend. The older man trotted the sleek bay mare he was riding over to the split log fence. Mostly the vaqueros rode stallions. Mares were for women and children, they believed. A real man rode a real man's horse. But here in the mountains, they took whatever they could get.

"You have decided what to do with the girl?" Pedro asked.

"I am afraid not, my friend, not yet. I did see her uncle while I was in the valley. I stopped by Rancho del Robles to pay my condolences on the abduction of his niece and to offer my assistance in helping him to find her. I told him I was sorry I was away when the trouble began."

"And?"

"He said they had scoured the high country but seen no sign of his niece or El Dragón. He is hoping there will be some sort of ransom."

"And?"

"And he declined my offer of assistance. I got the impression the help of a Californio is the last thing he wants right now."

"Lucky for you," Pedro said.

"*Si,* very lucky. Another week of hard riding with Fletcher Austin would hardly suit my purpose."

"Not when you would rather be here with the girl."

Ramon shrugged off the notion. "I owe her a debt. I cannot let her leave, but there are other things I can do to repay her."

"Like taking her to bed?"

Ramon bristled. "Do not be a fool, Pedro. I will do nothing to dishonor her. I have hurt her enough already."

"As time goes on, I hope you remember that."

Ramon said nothing. He wanted the girl, yes. But she was an innocent, and marriage was out of the question. When the time came, he would wed with a woman of pure Spanish blood just as he had vowed for the past ten years.

He owed it to his people, to his family. He owed it to himself.

Ramon sighed. He wished he knew what to do with Caralee McConnell, but until he made a decision, he would do as he had said and try to make up for the pain he had caused her. With that thought in mind, he started toward his small adobe house.

Weary from her sleepless night, Carly climbed out of bed just as Florentia came bustling in. "Don Ramon has come. He wishes you to join him for a ride. He says that you should hurry."

"Tell him to go away."

Florentia made the sign of the cross. "*Dios mio,* no! You cannot say that to the don!"

Carly's chin went up. "Maybe you can't but I can. I'll be dressed in a moment."

Ramon waited patiently in the *sala*. A few minutes later, Carly came striding in wearing her yellow skirt and white peasant blouse, her hair pulled back and secured with tortoiseshell combs.

"*Buenas dias,* senorita," he said, coming to his feet. "You are looking quite lovely this morning."

"I'm looking exactly the way I looked yesterday morning. The way I'll look every day I'm here if these are to be my only clothes."

He felt the pull of a smile. "I will see what I can do. In the meantime, since you are obviously feeling strong enough, I thought you might like to visit the Indian village."

"I think, Don Ramon, that perhaps I didn't make myself clear. Yesterday, I agreed to a walk with you around the compound. Outside of that, I don't intend to suffer your company any more than I absolutely have to."

Ramon shrugged, though he felt a hint of amusement. He liked her spirit, her fire. He would like to be the man to see her gentled and brought in hand. "That is too bad. It is quite an interesting place. And the woman, Lena, deserves your thanks. She is the one who came when you were ill."

She pondered that, studying his face with eyes the color of new spring grasses. "Senor Sanchez has been kind. Perhaps he will take me."

"I am afraid Pedro is busy. That leaves only me. There is much to learn in the village, things that would help you understand this country. But . . . if you are afraid to go with me, you can always stay here."

Her chin went up a notch higher. Spots of color tinged her pretty cheeks. "I am not afraid of you."

"No?"

"If I refuse it is only because I want nothing to do with a man like you."

She would go. She wouldn't let him best her. He would

be willing to bet his last gold *real*. He simply stood there waiting.

"Why are you doing this? The night you took me from my uncle's hacienda, you had no thought of being kind to me. Why now? What is it you want from me?"

His eyes ran the length of her body then returned to settle on her lush ruby lips. In an instant he knew what he wanted, what he had desired all along. "I would like nothing more, *querida,* than to see you settled in my bed. But I promise you that will not happen. As I told you before—with me you will be safe."

Her big green eyes went wide. She wet her soft full lips. "I-I don't know what to think of you. One day you are cruel, the next you are gallant. Today you act the rogue. Perhaps I am afraid of you after all."

"I do not think so," he said softly. "A little afraid of yourself, perhaps, but no longer afraid of me."

Carly said nothing, just stared at him as if she tried to see inside his mind. It was something he would not let her do.

"Do you ride with me, senorita?"

"Maybe I would . . . if I knew how to ride."

He grinned at that and nodded. *"Si,* I had forgotten. That is what you said the day of the horse race. Perhaps then, that is the reason you preferred to walk all the way to Llano Mirada."

At the teasing in his voice, Carly couldn't help but smile. "You're a hard man, Don Ramon, but at least you have a sense of humor."

"As do you, Senorita McConnell, I am happy to say." He captured her hand and started forward. "The village is not far. You will travel with me. As to your riding, we will begin your lessons tomorrow. You said once that you liked horses. If you wish to remain in this country, it is past the time that you should have learned to ride."

She had to admit the notion held a strong appeal—it was a necessity if she meant to escape. She had wanted to learn since her arrival at Rancho del Robles. Her uncle had promised to have someone teach her but the opportunity never seemed to present itself.

And she had seen the Spaniard ride. She had never seen a finer display of horsemanship.

"Ruiz!" the don called out when they reached the split log corral. "You have saddled Viento?"

"*Si*, Don Ramon." The young vaquero smiled. "And a gentle mare for the senorita." He was wiry, shorter than the don, but handsome, with a pleasant face and intelligent dark eyes. He had brought her food and water on the difficult journey through the mountains. Perhaps he would help her again.

Carly smiled up at him. The don saw it and frowned.

"You may put the mare away," he said brusquely. "Senorita McConnell does not yet ride. She will begin her lessons tomorrow. In the meantime, bring Viento to me."

The young man nodded and hurried to do the Spaniard's bidding. "Ruiz works with Sanchez and Ignacio. They are in charge of the remuda, the horses we keep here in the stronghold. He is the youngest of the vaqueros—which does not mean that he is a fool."

Thinking of the smile she had given him, Carly flushed. "I don't know what you mean."

"These men are loyal to me, *chica*. There is no one here who will help you."

Her spine went stiff. "The boy was kind to me in the mountains. More than I can say for you. He is pleasant to look at, and if I wish to smile at him, I will."

Ramon's frown darkened. "You are under my protection, Senorita McConnell. As long as you behave yourself, you will remain so. Seducing one of my vaqueros is not behaving—do I make myself clear?"

"Of all the gall! I suppose you consider seducing that young woman I met yesterday 'suitable behavior.' I suppose you think that is perfectly all right."

He shrugged his broad shoulders. "I am a man. It is different for me." He had the audacity to smile. It was so bright and charming it made her stomach flop over. "But I am glad to see that you are at least a little bit jealous."

Carly opened her mouth to deny it, to fling some scathing retort, but the big black stallion arrived just then, fresh and dancing at the end of its tether, tossing its beautiful head and stamping its feet. Carly took an uneasy step away.

"Do not be afraid. Viento is eager for the journey, but he will not harm you." He lifted her easily up on the saddle then gracefully swung up behind her. Feeling his arm around her waist just beneath the swell of her breast, his warm breath close beside her ear, she shivered and not with the cold.

"The sun is out," he said, "but perhaps your illness lingers." Before she could stop him, he had called for Ruiz to bring her a shawl from the house, then wrapped it protectively around her shoulders.

"Better?"

Carly simply nodded. All she could think of was the dream she'd had last night. Of riding with the don on his big black horse, of the fiery way he had kissed her, of the feel of his hands on her body. She wondered how far it was to the Indian village and suddenly wished that she had declined to go with him.

The ride was even more unnerving than she had first thought. Hard male thighs pressed against her bottom and the muscles across the Spaniard's chest flexed seductively as he handled the magnificent horse. They rode out through the guarded pass that she had come in through, but before they reached the bottom, he turned off onto a different trail and headed into a thick grove of trees.

Beneath the heavy growth of branches, the sun directly overhead, she couldn't tell north from south, east from west, and suddenly she realized that was exactly what he had planned.

She stopped trying to figure out where she was and relaxed against him, then straightened again to avoid the touch of his hard-muscled chest against her back. She was more than a little bit grateful when the don drew the stallion to a halt on a rise overlooking the village.

It sat in a clearing surrounded by pine trees, fifteen to twenty dome-shaped, mud-and-willow-branch huts interwoven with tule reeds. A larger hut partially set into the ground stood at one end, a *temescal,* the don said the Spanish called it, a sweat hut, the place the Indians also kept their weapons. Great baskets as tall as a man were nestled in the trees for the storage of acorns and seeds.

"These are Yokuts mostly," Ramon said, urging the stallion forward. "From the big central valley to the east. There are also Miwok and Mutsen—Costanoans, they are called—Coastal Indians who once ranged near the sea."

"Why do they all live together? I thought Indians lived in their own separate tribes."

"Before the time of the missions, they did. Most ranged no more than a hundred square miles. For the most part, their way of life was destroyed when the mission fathers arrived. Do not misunderstand me. The padres' intentions were good. They believed the Indians would profit by their association with the church. They would learn to grow their own food, to build small *rancherias* of their own, and their souls would be saved. Unfortunately, they never adjusted to such a life, and they were susceptible to every sort of disease. Most of them died."

She felt a wave of pity. "And these?"

"When the mission system was destroyed, the Indians were given grants of land, but eventually they lost it. They were easily cheated. They were not allowed to testify in court, which meant they had no way to defend themselves. They went to work on the ranchos but now even that way of life will not support them. The old ways have flickered to life. The different tribes have banded together in small groups like these throughout the mountains."

"I heard my uncle talking about them once. He says they raid the nearby ranchos and murder innocent people."

Sitting in front of him on the horse, she felt the bunching of muscles in his arms as he shrugged his broad shoulders. It made something flutter in her stomach.

"They are bitter," he said. "Sometimes they lash out. Just like the rest of us, they are fighting to survive."

Just like I am, Carly thought, but she said nothing more. They continued down the hill and into the center of the village, but only an old woman and two young men came forward to greet them. The men wore beards and mustaches, and something that looked like an oversized rabbit-skin diaper. They wore hair nets made of milkweed fiber, while the women wore loose-fitting chemises that came only midway to their knees.

"For thousands of years they went naked," the don said with a hint of amusement at the surprised look on her face. "The small bit of clothing they wear now is a legacy of the missions."

He leaned forward, helping Carly slide down from the horse, then he gracefully swung down himself. "Where is Lena?" he asked the stoop-shouldered old woman. "Trah-ush-nah and the others?"

She answered in the Spanish she had learned at the mission. "There is a terrible sickness. It has raged for more than a week. It kills without mercy. You should not be here."

The don's face went tense. "Smallpox?" he asked.

The woman shook her head. "The disease they call measles. It has already taken four of the old ones. All of the men and most of the women are sick. There is no one to tend them or the children."

"It is late in the year for measles. You are sure that is what it is?"

"I have seen it at the mission. I have had it myself."

A little of his tension eased. "I will return to the stronghold, see how many among my people have already had the sickness. I will send what help I can."

His hands encircled Carly's waist. He started to lift her back up in the saddle, but she pulled herself free of his grasp.

"I had the measles when I was a child. I can stay and help them."

Something flickered in the depths of his eyes. "Caring for those who are sick is not a pleasant task, *chica*."

"I'm no stranger to unpleasantness. And I've cared for sick people before."

"Si," he said softly. "I thought that perhaps you had."

She looked at him strangely, wondering how he could possibly know that she had cared for her mother and those in the mine patch who had fallen sick with the cholera. It was a terrible time, one that made her stomach churn just to think of it. She had worked until she could scarcely stay on her feet, but she hadn't been able to save her mother. Four women, two men, and three children had died, and she had been left all alone. Carly forced the memory away.

"Still," he said, "leaving you here is not a good idea. You are only just recovered from a fever yourself."

"I feel fine," she argued. "I have for days. I want to stay."

He took in her determined expression, the way her feet were planted so solidly apart, and finally gave in. *"Esta bien.* I will leave you then, but I want your word you will not try to escape. You would only get lost in the woods, and there are many dangers out there—snakes and mountain lions, huge grizzly bears big enough to track a man for prey." He tipped her chin with his fingers. "Do I have your word?"

Her eyes went wide. "Would you actually accept it?"

He smiled. *"Si,* but I also believe you are smart enough to know that without preparation you would not get far away. And as I said, your life would be in grave danger."

He was right, she knew. For a moment she had actually believed he would trust her word that she would stay. For some strange reason it would have pleased her, even if she might have considered running away.

"As you say, Don Ramon, I would be foolish to try to escape."

The don merely nodded. For a moment it seemed he had sensed her disappointment, that he understood her feelings. She didn't like the way he so easily read her thoughts. Turning away from him, Carly swung her attention to the aging Indian woman.

"Where is Lena?" she asked. "She is the healer, is she not?"

"Come. I will show you."

Carly turned to Ramon. "You had better not come back with the others. It won't help anyone if you get sick, too."

He smiled that devastating smile that made her heartbeat quicken. "I have also had the measles, *chica.* I will get what supplies we can spare and return."

Carly just stared at him. What kind of an outlaw would help a bunch of sick Indians? No matter how she tried, she couldn't seem to understand him. Wordlessly, she turned away, following the stoop-shouldered old Indian into one of the dome-shaped huts.

A few feet inside the low round door, a slender woman knelt on the woven reed carpet, dabbing some sort of paste on the stomach of a fussy child. Baskets of seeds, roots, and dried fish sat in one corner, and deer and bearskin blankets formed several more pallets on the floor.

"Lena?" Carly asked, and the slender woman turned. Her features were fine, her brows sleek and arching, her cheekbones well defined. Dark smudges of exhaustion formed hollows beneath her eyes.

"You are the Spaniard's woman from the camp," she said.

"I'm the woman you helped when I was sick," Carly corrected, ignoring an odd rush of heat. "I hope in return that I can help you. Tell me what I can do."

For the next several hours, she worked beside Lena caring for the people of the village. She spooned in life-giving liquids to fight the dehydration and used the icy water from the stream, the last of the snowpack melting in the mountains, to bathe their faces and fight the raging fevers. They suffered a dry, racking cough and a burning rash that began at the hairline and neck and spread down over their bodies.

Lena brewed a tea of dried boxwood root for the fever, and Carly held wooden bowls of the bitter brew to their lips. She helped Lena boil dried cloverleaves into a thick, sticky syrup for their coughs and made an ointment of three-leafed nightshade and lard to spread over the rash.

Ramon returned with blankets and food, with Pedro Sanchez and three of the women: Tomasina Gutierrez, the blacksmith's wife; Ramon's housekeeper, Florentia; and a busty, robust woman named Serafina Gomez. All of them worked tirelessly.

And so did Don Ramon.

They labored late into the evening, the women tending the sick, the men helping with the heavy tasks of lifting the patients, chopping wood, fueling fires, and tending the horses. Earlier in the day, they'd made forays into the woods to hunt for game, rabbits mostly, which were dressed and thrown into large iron cooking pots, along with wild onions and herbs.

Sometime during the hours after midnight, Ramon appeared in one of the huts beside her.

"You have done enough for today," he said. "You will rest now. Come with me." He caught her arm, but she pulled away and knelt once more beside the boy stretched out on the woven reed mat. He looked no more than thirteen, a gangly youth who smiled in spite of his illness.

"I can't leave yet. Lena's brother, Shaw-shuck, Two Hawks, he needs this tea to bring down his fever. He's burning up. He—"

Ramon took the wooden bowl from her weary, trembling hands. "I will see to the boy." Setting the bowl aside, he pulled her to her feet. "You need to rest . . . at least for a while."

"But—"

"I promise to see that the boy gets the tea." Drawing her out through the small, low opening of the hut, the don steadied her as she swayed against him, her legs a little shaky from kneeling for so long. He swore softly, fluently, then lifted her into his arms and started walking toward the rear of the village.

"I-I'm all right now, really I am. You can put me down."

"Hush. Do as I say and put your arms around my neck. I should not have let you stay. You are barely recovered from your own bout of sickness."

"I'm just tired, is all. Florentia and the others, they're just as tired as I am." But she did as he said, clinging to his neck to steady herself as he strode determinedly along. She tried not to notice the thick bands of muscle brushing against her breasts or the sinews in his neck that tightened at the touch of her hand.

He stopped at the edge of the woods and knelt beneath a secluded pine tree, its boughs a canopy of green above them. A few feet away, a small fire flickered in the quiet darkness, and under the tree, a bedroll had been unfurled. The don carefully placed her atop it.

"You must sleep for a while. You will be no use to anyone if you become ill."

"What about the others?"

"Pedro will see they have a place to rest."

"What about you? You've been working all day, too. Surely you're just as tired as I am."

He smiled, a flash of white reflected in the light of the fire. "As I said before, I am a man. It is different for me."

Maybe it was, but she didn't believe it. He was stronger, perhaps more determined. Whatever the case, as the moments ticked past and she lay on the bedroll, her eyelids grew heavy and she no longer cared. Soon she fell asleep but during the night she grew fitful, tossing and turning, dreaming of her mother and the ravaging, ugly death from the cholera she had battled in the mine patch. Then something warm curled around her, something solid and strong that laid her memories to rest, and finally she slept soundly.

In the morning she awoke to find herself nestled in the strong, solid arms of the don.

Carly hissed in a breath, her heart slamming hard against the wall of her chest. She tried to move, but her hair had come loose from its braid and was trapped under a broad, powerful shoulder. One of his hard-muscled thighs rode high between her legs and her bottom pressed intimately into his groin.

Dear God! Her heartbeat quickened even more, began to trip loudly in her ears. His breath fanned the back of her neck, moving tendrils of hair beside her ear. The muscles in his thigh felt rock hard where they pressed so embarrassingly against her. Carly squirmed, trying to free herself without waking him, trying to ignore the spiraling warmth in her stomach, the weakness that slid through her limbs.

"It would be better, *querida,*" he said softly, "if just now you did not move in quite such a manner."

Carly went stock still. For the first time she noticed that he was aroused, that against her bottom, the hard male ridge of his desire throbbed with purpose at the front of his breeches. Naive though she might be, she knew what that purpose was.

"I-I . . . how did we . . . why are you . . . ?"

"Hush. There is no need to be afraid. You were having trouble sleeping, that is all. Close your eyes now and go back to sleep. Morning will come soon enough."

Carly swallowed hard, squeezing her eyelids shut as he adjusted himself to a less intimate position, but his arms remained locked around her. She tried to relax, to control the tension rippling through her body, but there was no way she could possibly go to sleep.

Not with him still holding her. Not with his beautiful mouth just inches away from her ear.

The Spaniard sighed and released his hold, then tossed back his blanket and gracefully rolled to his feet. "Perhaps you are right after all. In a few more minutes the sun will be cresting the horizon. There are others to consider, and work that must be done. I will make us some coffee."

She shoved her sleep-tangled hair back from her face. "Thank you." But her mouth was so dry the words stuck in her throat and she wasn't sure he heard them.

They worked through the day and night for the next two days. Two of Carly's patients died, but the boy, Two Hawks, would live. He was twelve years old, she learned from Lena, a handsome youth with high cheekbones and coarse, straight black hair. He was a smiling boy, one the don seemed as taken with as she. Carly would never forget the sight of the tall handsome Spaniard kneeling beside the boy, the lad's head cradled in his lap as he held a bowl of broth against the boy's parched lips.

Each night she had slept beside the don, not as close as before, but near enough she could have reached out and touched him. He had been there each morning when she awakened, watching her with an oddly protective light in his eyes. Yesterday he seemed edgy and began to grow distant. Last night he hadn't joined her until late in the evening. This morning when she awakened, the Spaniard was already gone.

Ramon watched the girl walking through the camp toward the healer. Her face looked pale, her clothes were dirty and wrinkled, her hair slightly mussed, and yet she did not complain. For the past three days, she had worked ceaselessly, doing whatever was required of her, no matter how unpleasant the task. She was nothing like the woman he had once believed her to be, selfish and uncaring, concerned only with money and the luxuries it could bring.

It made him feel even worse for treating her so badly.

It made him want her more than he ever had before, more than he had wanted a woman since Lily. Perhaps even more than that.

Sleeping beside her that first night, he had dreamed of being inside her, of burying himself in her soft, wet warmth, of forgetting his responsibilities to his people, his vow to his brother to see Rancho del Robles returned to the de la Guerra name.

He imagined instead making love to her, sampling her fiery passion, the hot desire that for a time would make him forget.

No more grieving for Andreas.

No more worry about discovery, about what he would do for his people when the money from the horses ran out. At least Martinez and the rest of his men had returned to the stronghold safely. The money from the horses would last a good long while but sooner or later it would be gone.

Without Andreas, raiding as El Dragón would be far more dangerous. It wouldn't take long to discover he was missing from his rancho whenever the raids were done, that he was the man behind them.

And there was the problem of the girl. He couldn't let her go and yet he could not keep her. If he did, sooner or later, his willpower would weaken and he would take her to his bed.

Madre de Dios, he wished he knew what to do.

Ramon raked a hand through his wavy black hair then settled his flat-brimmed hat low over his forehead. He would think of something. He had to. He hoped he would think of it soon.

*C*hapter *E*ight

*S*enor Don Ramon!" Lena approached as he walked into the village, Carly right beside her. A few feet away, Florentia stood next to Tomasina and Serafina, waiting for Pedro to arrive with the heavy *carreta* that would return them home.

"The senorita says that you must leave," Lena said. She looked tired. They all did. Beneath her dark eyes, her cheeks were sunken. She appeared even thinner than she had when they arrived.

"*Si,* it is time we returned, now that your people appear to be out of danger."

"I could say words of thanks, but they would not be enough. Words cannot repay the debt my people owe."

"There is no debt. You have helped me; you saved the senorita's life. That is more than payment enough."

Lena shook her head, her straight black bangs shifting across her narrow forehead. "The white men, for years they have wished us dead. You are different. We will not forget." She turned to Carly. "May you walk with God, little Wah-suh-wi."

Carly smiled. "Thank you, Lena. Take care of Two Hawks, will you?"

"He will be running like a deer and into mischief again before the new moon rises."

Ramon smiled at the women. Working together, Lena and Carly had grown close. She, too, had befriended the boy. Ramon was also fond of Two Hawks. Each time he had come to the village, the boy had raced up to greet him. His fondest desire, he said, was to become a great vaquero. He begged Ramon to teach him, to take him to Las Almas where he could learn the skills of the Spanish horsemen.

Always Ramon had said no.

He had too many mouths to feed as it was; he didn't need another. And yet he felt sorry for the boy. The life stretching before him was dismal at best. But a vaquero was a master horseman. He had his pride to see him through, and if he was lucky, he could find work.

Carly looked up at him and he reached for her hand.

"What did she call you?" he asked as he led her toward the cart and the three other women.

"Wah-suh-wi. It is the Indian name she has given me."

"What does it mean?"

"Sunflower." She glanced away, looking a little embarrassed. "She says when I smile it's as bright as the morning sun."

Ramon felt something tug gently inside him. "And so it is," he said softly. "Exactly like the sun."

Her cheeks turned pink and her lips curved prettily. She glanced away, then down at the toes of her sandals. "They want us to return, Ramon." She looked up into his face. "They want us to feast with them. They want to thank us for our help."

"You would like that, *chica?*" But her excited look told him that she would. He liked that about her, the zest for life she nurtured inside her. The joy in living that was so much a part of his own people, but was often missing in the Americans he had known.

As his words sank in, her smile slid away and the light seemed to fade from her eyes. "Mostly I would like to go home. If you won't let me leave, then yes, I would like to return."

Ramon touched her cheek. It felt as soft as the breast of a dove. Her color heightened to a creamy pink that reminded him of roses. He thought of the night she had slept in his arms and his body went instantly hard. His heartbeat quickened, making his groin start to throb.

Damning himself—and her—he turned away. "If that is your wish," he said more harshly than he intended, "how could I not agree?"

Carly said nothing, but her smile was long gone and with it a little of the sun. She turned to Florentia who stood beside the two-wheeled cart the women had arrived in.

"Are we ready to leave?" Carly asked the housekeeper.

"*Si,* Senorita McConnell." The beefy woman motioned for her to join the others, while Ramon took Viento's reins and swung up into his saddle. "I am more than ready to go. I am looking forward to a night in my own bed."

"Strangely enough, I'll be glad to get back, too," Carly said. "If for no other reason than to wash these dirty clothes." She started to climb up in the wagon, lifting her grimy yellow skirt out of the way, and unconsciously displayed a trim bit of ankle. Ramon clamped his jaw as a second shot of heat rolled through him. Riding forward, he bent down and slid an arm around her waist, tightened his grasp and hauled her up on his lap.

"The cart is too crowded. You will ride home with me."

She stiffened against him, but he didn't care. If she was going to make him want her every hour of the day, he was suddenly determined she should suffer that same fate as well.

"You do not like to ride Viento?" he whispered in her ear, purposely brushing the small, shell-like rim with his lips.

She stiffened even more, and inside his snug-fitting breeches so did he. He cursed himself but he didn't let her go.

"I like Viento very much." She shifted to get comfortable where he held her pinned across his thighs. "It's you, senor, at times I find unbearable."

"Ah. Then I will have to remedy that." Reining the horse away from the others, he rode off into a copse of trees.

"Where are you going? What are you . . . ?" Her voice trailed off as his hand moved upward, barely brushing the underside of a breast. It was rounded and full, womanly in a way that made him ache to cup it. His fingers itched to shape it, to urge the nipple into a throbbing peak. He wondered if it would be small and tight or large and round, wondered at the exact shade of pink it might be, and heard himself groan. When he pressed his lips against the fluttery pulse at the nape of her neck, tasting the smooth white skin, a shaft of desire knifed through him.

"D-Don Ramon . . . ?" There was a hesitancy in her voice that hadn't been there before . . . and something else, something he recognized only too well for his own desire mounted with every heartbeat.

"*Si*, Cara," he whispered softly. "I am here. Do you still wish to know what it is that I want?" Reining the stallion to a halt behind an outcropping of boulders, he turned her in his arms. Her eyes had gone wide and her cheeks were flushed. Tilting her head back, he ran a finger across her soft bottom lip, bent his head, and captured her mouth in a ravaging kiss.

Carly jolted at the contact. She started to struggle, astonished at the Spaniard's boldness, determined to tear herself free, but the hard, demanding warmth of his lips, the soft white heat radiating through her body, made her clutch his shoulders instead. Her breasts crushed into the bands of muscle across his chest and waves of fire slid through her. His tongue touched the corner of her lips, coaxing her to open for him, then he took her mouth with fierce possession.

Carly moaned at the feel of his warm, slick tongue, at the tendrils of heat unfurling in her belly. The arm around her waist felt hard and male and utterly implacable. Dear God, it was just like her dream.

No, it was nothing like her dream. No dream could ever be like this!

Carly shifted in the saddle, her nipples growing hard and sensitive where they pressed against the Spaniard's solid chest. She felt his hand on her breast, kneading it softly through her blouse, making the nipple peak and distend. He cupped it, molded it, charted it with his fingers, then slid his hand upward till he touched the bare skin swelling above the low-cut neckline.

"Ramon," she whispered, "please . . ."

A deep growl erupted from his throat. He kissed her again, hot and hard, then tore himself away. He was breathing too fast, staring at her with eyes so dark they looked almost black.

She wet her kiss-swollen lips, unable to stop the small hot shivers racing through her body. "I didn't think you wanted . . . you weren't supposed to . . . you said I would be safe."

A muscle bunched in his jaw. *"Sí, querida.* You are right. I was not supposed to do this. It was a foolish, dangerous thing to do." Turning her around, he settled her in front of him in the saddle then rode wordlessly back to the women rumbling along in the cart.

"The senorita has convinced me to let her ride with you," Ramon said shortly. Bending over, he helped her slide to the ground, then backed the stallion a few steps away.

Her cheeks were flaming, she was sure, her heart still pounding so loud they could probably hear it, but she lifted her head and squared her shoulders. Walking purposely to the cart, she climbed into the back with the other women. They said nothing as the bay horse pulling the cart perked up its ears and swung once more into motion, hauling the heavy wooden conveyance along the narrow trail that served as road.

Neither did Carly. But her insides still fluttered and her heart continued its unsteady beat. When she glanced at the don, careful to be sure he wasn't watching, she saw that he rode grim-faced, his expression dark and inscrutable.

Was he angry? If he was, she hoped his fury would be short-lived. As long as she remained at Llano Mirada, Ramon de la Guerra held her life in his hands. He could set her free, or he could see her dead.

Or he could take her. Any time he wanted. Any way, anywhere. In a few short moments, he had made that perfectly clear.

A tremor ran down her spine, this one cool and not at all pleasant. She hadn't forgotten the brutal man he could be, hadn't forgotten his ruthlessness, his cruelty.

She hadn't forgotten the way she'd felt when he had kissed her.

Dear God, if she gave in to her passions, her uncle would never forgive her. She would no longer be a virgin, and Uncle Fletcher would be ashamed. He might even send her away. She had no place to go, no one to turn to. She couldn't bear the thought of more years of loneliness, yearning for a home or at least someone who cared.

More than ever before, she longed to go back to Rancho del Robles, to the safety she knew she would find there, to the new life she had started.

For the first time Carly realized how badly she needed to escape.

*　*　*

Careful that Caralee would not discover the way, Ramon saw the women safely back to the compound. Sanchez said little on the ride back home, his scowl of disapproval was enough.

"You do not need to say it," Ramon told him, once they were alone. "I meant only to teach her a lesson. Instead I learned something myself."

"Oh? And what is that?"

"That where the *gringa* is concerned I cannot trust myself. *Sangre de Christo,* Pedro, I cannot remember wanting a woman so badly."

The old vaquero just laughed. "The Americana has fire, *verdad?* She has beauty, courage, and strength. If I were twenty years younger, even I would be tempted. You must decide what to do with her, Ramon."

"If I wish to keep my freedom, there is nothing I can do—except be certain that she remains here."

"Perhaps if you explained things . . . told her the truth. There is always a chance that you might sway her."

Ramon just scoffed. "The woman is a *gringa.* She will never take the side of a Californio over her own flesh and blood."

"Perhaps you are right, I do not know. But I have seen stranger things in my many years of living. I have learned that the truth is a means of persuasion that can often pierce the boundaries of race or religion."

Ramon just shook his head. Sanchez must be getting old. To believe the woman would listen—that he could trust her to keep his secret—it was insane to even consider it.

Yet the thought began to plague him. He left the next day to return to Rancho Las Almas, determined to keep his distance from the girl. But each night he remembered what it felt like to kiss her, imagined what it might be like to make passionate love to her. And each day he remembered what his old friend had said.

If he could make her understand. If he could make her see the truth about her uncle, he could let her return to Rancho del Robles. His problem would be solved, and sooner or later, he would forget her.

Perhaps he would return to the stronghold and tell her the truth. He had nothing to lose in that.

Ramon shivered to think that he might lose his life if he was ever foolish enough to trust her completely.

The idea came from nowhere, or perhaps from the womanly instincts she'd always had but only recently begun to discover.

She had asked herself, who in the compound would most likely help her? The answer was—no one. All of them were loyal to the don. Who then had anything to gain by aiding her escape? She knew many more of them now. Some of them were mercenaries, as the don had implied when she had first arrived. They were there for a portion of the ill-gotten gains, but she had no money to pay them, and promises were worth very little.

Then it struck her. *Miranda*.

Miranda Aguilar wanted her gone from the camp.

The girl had come to the don's house that first day to make it clear that she was his woman. She wouldn't have come if she hadn't seen Carly as some sort of threat. Would Miranda be willing to help her?

Carly had learned how to ride, at least a little. The don hadn't taught her; he had left the day after their return from the Indian village. Ruiz and Sanchez had been giving her lessons. Both were fine horsemen and very good teachers, patient yet firm, determined now that they had undertaken the task to see she rode as well as any highborn Spanish woman.

They had been teaching her to sit astride, but they promised that if Don Ramon would find her a sidesaddle, they would teach her to ride that way, too. She wanted to. She knew it would please her uncle that she could ride like a fashionable lady.

For now it was enough that she could manage a horse well enough to get away.

If she could convince Miranda to help her.

Carly dressed with care that morning, brushing her hair till it shined with coppery fire, pulling it up with a pretty shell comb so that it fell seductively over one shoulder. She drew the top of her blouse down as far as she could, exposing the tops of her breasts, then made her way to Miranda's cabin and lightly knocked on the door.

Footsteps sounded, the door swung open, and the dark-haired girl stepped out on the porch. Surprise flared in her eyes for a moment, then they narrowed in dislike.

"Don Ramon is not here," she said, staring down her slender nose with contempt.

Carly just smiled. *"Buenos dias,* Miranda. A pleasant day, is it not?"

"Go away. I told you Ramon is not here."

"I didn't come to see Ramon," Carly said, purposely using the more intimate address. "I came to see you."

"Why?"

"Because I thought there might be something you could do for me . . . in exchange for something that I can do for you."

Miranda eyed her coldly, then tossed back her mane of shiny black hair and motioned for her to come in. The cabin was small, only two rooms, but the earthen floor was swept so clean it looked polished, and freshly laundered curtains hung at the window sill. Carly could smell the woman's sweet perfume.

"What makes you believe there is anything you can do for me?" Miranda said.

Carly tried not to think of how pretty she was, how lithe

and graceful, that Ramon slept in her bed. Instead she concentrated on convincing the woman that *she* was the one Ramon preferred. "Perhaps there isn't. Then again, perhaps you would be more than happy to see me gone from here. If that is the case, then maybe we can do business."

Miranda's eyes wandered over Carly's breasts, assessing their size and shape. "Ramon wants you here. Why should I disobey him?"

They stood next to a rustic table and chairs but Miranda didn't offer her a seat. "That is exactly the reason—because Ramon wants me here. Or perhaps he simply wants me."

"He does not want you, *puta*. Why should he? Already, he has me."

"If that is so, then why did he kiss me?"

Her chin jutted up, her eyes growing dark with anger but not surprise. She knew something had happened between them. The women in the cart must have guessed. Perhaps they even believed that was why the don had left the stronghold.

"Ramon is a man," Miranda said. "It is a man's desire to rut with any woman willing to please him."

Carly smiled and shrugged her shoulders, then turned toward the door as if to leave. "Well, if you don't mind sharing him . . ."

"If you were to go, Ramon would not be safe. You would turn him over to the authorities."

Carly turned to face her, leaned forward and rested her palms on the battered wooden table. "Not if we were to strike a bargain. Give me your word you'll help me escape and I'll give you mine not to turn Ramon in."

"You are a *gringa*. How could I trust you?"

"You're the don's woman. How could I trust you? You might send me in the wrong direction. You might have someone lying in wait to murder me on the trail. We will have to trust each other if we are to succeed."

Miranda chewed her lip and Carly's heart began to throb with hope inside her chest. Both of them would be taking a risk. Would the woman keep her word? The dangers Carly had mentioned were more than real. She would have to be careful, find some way to protect herself, once she was safely away.

As for herself, she would say anything to escape this place. She refused to consider whether or not she would keep her silence once she reached her home.

"I will let you know tonight," Miranda said. "Leave your window open. At midnight, I will tell you what I have decided."

Carly left the cabin afraid to hope, yet feeling for the first time as if there might be a chance. The woman clearly despised her, but Carly didn't believe she was capable of murder. She might send her off the wrong way, hoping Carly would die in the mountains, but most likely she would simply say no.

Miranda was worried for Ramon and rightly so. Carly thought that if she were his woman, she would do anything to protect him. Then again, if he really belonged to her, she might do anything to keep him from turning to another woman.

That thought was disturbing. Ramon de la Guerra was an outlaw, perhaps even a murderer as her uncle had said. She would have to turn him in—wouldn't she? She felt uneasy to think of breaking her word.

Pleading a headache, Carly ate with Pedro and Florentia then went to her bedroom early, only to wind up pacing the floor of her small room. At midnight, just as Miranda had promised, soft feminine footfalls sounded in the dirt beneath her bedroom window.

"Senorita McConnell?"

"I'm here, Miranda." She stood beside the open portal, but didn't pull back the thin muslin curtains.

"Tomorrow at dawn, there is a wagon leaving to pick up

supplies in San Juan Bautista. A vaquero named Francisco Villegas will be driving. He will do anything for a little bit of gold. I have paid him to take you down the mountain. When he nears your uncle's ranch, he will show you which way to go."

Carly closed her eyes, excitement racing through her. "I understand."

"You must be in the back of the wagon before the sun comes up. It will be sitting not far from this window."

"I'll be there."

"Do I have your word Ramon will be safe?"

Carly took a deep steadying breath. "You have my word."

"If you are lying, if you tell anyone it was I who helped you, I promise I will kill you. Do you hear me?"

Carly wet her lips. "Yes."

Gravel crunched beneath the window as the woman walked away, and Carly released a slow breath of air. She had no idea what would happen, nor what she would do once she escaped the compound. But events were set in motion. She meant to see them through.

Hours passed. Pulling the blankets off her bed, she fashioned a makeshift bedroll, stuffing the shawl the don had given her inside along with a second skirt and blouse Florentia had provided and a partially burned white tallow candle. The two-foot-long candleholder was made of heavy wrought iron. It would serve well as a weapon. She'd been hoarding food for the past two days. She rolled it up in the coarse linen towel beside the water pitcher on the dresser and tucked it in with the rest of the supplies.

Plaiting her hair into a single thick braid, she tied it with a piece of string and lay down on the bed to sleep. Instead she tossed and turned and stared up at the ceiling, praying she was doing the right thing.

At four o'clock, she gave up. She scribbled a note to Florentia, telling her not to make breakfast, that she had left at dawn with some of the women to bathe and wash her clothes in the stream. She would eat something later with Tomasina.

Anything to delay them.

It was colder than she had imagined so she took out the shawl and wrapped it around her shoulders, then pulled on her sandals and climbed out the window, makeshift bedroll in hand.

There was no one near the wagon. She climbed in the back and pulled the canvas tarpaulin over her head. Every minute dragged, turned into long, nerve-wracking hours. Finally she heard voices and the jangling of harnesses as a team of horses was hitched into their traces. The wagon creaked beneath the heavy weight of the man who climbed up on the rough wooden seat. Francisco Villegas, Miranda had said.

It was still cold outside, but a trickle of perspiration ran between her breasts. Her palms were damp, and her heart beat fiercely. As the wagon picked up speed, she slid the long wrought-iron candle stand out from inside the bedroll and hid it beneath the bundle. Then she waited, ignoring the pounding her bones were taking against the hard rough wood as they bumped along the dusty road.

For the first time it occurred to her the wagon hadn't turned toward the entrance to the compound, but rolled off in the other direction. It also dawned on her that a wagon couldn't make the steep descent down the mountain on the trail that she had traveled up.

There must be another entrance to Llano Mirada. Don Ramon had lied.

Some of her uncertainty in leaving slipped away. She couldn't trust Ramon de la Guerra, no matter how charming he pretended to be. She had trusted him before and she had wound up as his prisoner. He had promised she would be safe from his advances and then he had kissed her savagely, fondled her breasts, and perhaps meant to take even more liberties than that. Leaving—by whatever means she could—was the only choice she had.

The tarpaulin rustled, lifted at the front near the wagon seat. "Stay down and be silent," a gruff voice said. "There are guards along the trail. None of them must see you."

Carly just nodded, and the canvas fell back into place, but the image she had seen of the big, burly man with the shiny gold tooth who was driving the wagon remained.

Her fears returned full force and nothing she could think of made them go away.

Wearing a worried frown, Pedro Sanchez pulled the cinch tight on his saddle and swung himself aboard his dappled gray stallion. In the doorway of the lean-to, Florentia wrung her chubby hands.

"Where could she have gone?" she said. "None of the guards saw her leave." It was almost ten in the morning. They hadn't begun the search until nine, when the house-keeper had spotted Tomasina heading toward the stream to wash her clothes. Neither she nor any of the women had seen Carly.

"There is only one way she could have left," Pedro said grimly. "In the wagon with Cisco Villegas. He has been restless lately, eager for more spoils or a chance to spend his share of the money from the horses."

Florentia made the sign of the cross over her large plump bosom. *"Madre de Dios.* Cisco is the worst of the lot. The girl would be safer with a mountain lion."

A commotion outside the corral drew Pedro's attention. He glanced up to see Ramon de la Guerra riding toward him, astride a tall bay horse.

Relief rolled through him, mingled with regret for his failure to keep the little *gringa* safe. "I am glad to see you, Don Ramon."

"What is it, Pedro? I can see by your face that something is wrong."

Pedro sighed wearily. "The girl is missing. Villegas is the only one who could have taken her." Ramon's face went pale beneath his dark skin. "Ruiz and I are going after them. I am sorry, my friend, to have failed you, but I will see she is returned."

For a moment, Ramon said nothing, but the lines of his face looked harsh and his eyes were dark wells of anger. "The blame is not yours. I wanted her to have some measure of freedom. You could not have known Villegas would take advantage." He shoved his hat back off his head and it slid down his back, dangling from his throat by a thin braided strap. He raked a hand through his wavy, black hair. "The *bastardo* means to sell her. How long have they been gone?"

"It was his turn to go in for supplies. He left with the wagon at dawn."

Ramon swung down from his tired horse, handed the reins to Ruiz Domingo who had just walked up, and prepared to ride with Sanchez. "Saddle Viento," Ramon said to him. "Do it quickly."

"*Si*, Don Ramon."

He turned to Sanchez. "You have supplies in your saddlebags?" he asked.

"*Si*. Enough for at least three days."

"I will need them."

"I will have Florentia bring more, if you are coming with us."

Ramon shook his head. "I am riding alone. I can make better time by myself. Besides, this is between Villegas and me."

Pedro wanted to argue, to remind him what a dangerous man Cisco was, but he did not argue. He had seen the don look this implacable only one other time—the night his brother had died. The night he had taken the girl.

"I will need my weapons," Ramon said.

"I will get them for you." By the time Pedro returned to the corral, Viento was waiting saddled and ready, a bedroll tied behind the cantle, *bolas* filled with supplies, and a heavy Sharp's rifle shoved into the sheath near the horse's flanks.

Accepting the brace of pistols Pedro carried, Ramon swung aboard the big black horse. "If I am not back in three days time, take some of the men and head for Nogales. Find the girl and kill Villegas—for it is certain that he has killed me."

Chapter Nine

Carly winced at the hard jolt her body took as the horse stepped into a hole. They'd been riding for hours, no longer in the wagon but mounted now on the horses that had pulled it. For the first half of the morning, she'd stayed hidden beneath the tarp. Each time she lifted it, Villegas warned her to get back under cover. Then he pulled the wagon beneath the trees and begun to unhitch the team.

At first she hadn't noticed the saddles in the back of the wagon. Once she did, she'd been frightened, then she saw that it only made sense.

"Sooner or later the others are certain to follow," the bandit said as he tightened the cinch on the stout bay he saddled, then he boosted her up on its back. "We can make better time without the wagon."

"You aren't going back there, are you?"

He grinned, a gold eyetooth gleaming, the other one nothing but a hole. "I grow weary of Llano Mirada. It is a good time to leave."

They were heading mostly south, as they had been since early that morning. She remembered coming north the night of the raid, but the direction they had traveled then had seemed more eastly than northerly. If that was the case, they should be heading southwest, she thought with a hint of unease but forced the notion away. She didn't know these mountains, and they had left the stronghold by a completely different route than the one by which she'd arrived.

Carly rolled her head from side to side, trying to stretch the aching muscles in her neck and shoulders. Her legs ached and her thighs had been rubbed nearly raw on the stiff leather skirt of the poorly cared for saddle. She wondered how much longer Villegas would continue before making camp, wondered how much longer she could go on.

Shading her eyes, Carly stared into the late afternoon sun. It rode low on the horizon, its fierce rays turning the oaks to gold and glistening on the waters of the rocky stream they followed. A few minutes later, Villegas motioned her onto a different trail, one that turned east instead of west, and all her hidden fears shot to the surface once more.

For a while she said nothing, hoping it was just a short jog around a hill or perhaps a means of avoiding some natural boundary. When the miles began to lengthen, she bit the inside of her cheek to keep from shouting the question that hovered on her lips—Dear God, where are you taking me?

"I need to stop for a moment," she finally said, pretending to look embarrassed. "There's a stream there. While I'm . . . busy, maybe you could water the horses."

He grumbled something, but pulled his lathered animal to a halt and climbed down. Carly climbed down, too, her wobbly legs nearly folding beneath her. She walked a few paces, stretched a little, and her steps grew more steady. It was now or never. Each mile they rode ate at her strength. She would need all she possessed to confront a man like Villegas.

She turned in his direction, and as he led his horse into the creek, quietly pulled the heavy wrought-iron candlestick from where it was hidden inside her bedroll.

"You had better hurry," he said. "It will be dark very soon, and we will have to find a place to make camp."

"Yes, I can see that." Gripping the heavy iron tightly behind her, her palms so damp she feared she might drop it, she stepped closer to where he stood beside the stream. "Before we do that, however, I'd like to know exactly where you're taking me. We're heading east, not west. Why are we traveling in the wrong direction?"

"It is only a slight detour," he said matter-of-factly. "We will turn west again tomorrow. The following day you will be back at your Rancho del Robles."

He was lying; she could see it written on his ugly face. "I don't believe you. I want to know where you're taking me. And this time I want the truth."

Convince me, she thought. *Make me believe I'm wrong, that you're really taking me home.*

Francisco Villegas only grinned. "You want the truth, senorita? The truth is we travel to Nogales. You are a very beautiful woman . . . and innocent, no? The women in the stronghold, they say you are still a virgin. With that ripe little body and all of that fiery dark hair, the price for you will be a high one."

"You—you're going to sell me?" The words came out in a high-pitched squeak. Dear God, he was taking her to a brothel! He meant to make her a whore!

"Of course," he said. "Why else would I be going to all of this trouble?"

Carly wet her trembling lips, her hold growing tighter on the heavy length of iron behind her back. "I-If it's money you want, my uncle will pay you. More than you could get in Juarez."

The grin grew broader. She hated the smug look on his face. "I do not think so. Besides, there are women in No-gales. I am in need of a woman." He stepped toward her, pulled the string that held her braided hair, then ran his thick fingers through it to separate the strands. His sour breath fanned her cheek. "Perhaps the women in the stronghold

were wrong. Perhaps El Dragón has already had you. Then
I could have you too, eh?"

"They—they aren't wrong. I've never been with a man."

His hand cupped her cheek. It felt calloused and rough.
His blunt fingers stroked her, the nails broken and dirty.
"Even if I took you, you would still bring a very good
price. I think maybe it would be worth it."

Dear God! She forced herself to stand still. She would
have to hit him. There was no other way. Her fingers tightened around the weapon. "You're not going to have me—
you're not going to touch me!" Looking him straight in the
eye, she swung the heavy iron with all her strength. "I'm
going home!" It landed against his jaw and the side of his
face with such force the gold tooth erupted from his mouth
along with a bright red gusher of blood.

Shaking all over, she dropped the length of iron and
raced for her horse. Shoving her foot into the stirrup, she
swung up on its back with a strength she didn't know she
had, grabbed the reins, and dug her heels into the horse's
ribs. The animal leapt forward the same instant the bandit's arm snaked around her waist and he jerked her out of
the saddle.

She struggled for a moment, tore herself free. Carly
screamed as he slapped her, knocking her into the dirt.

"You should not have done that," he said, his breath
coming hard and fast with his anger.

She looked up at him and terror streaked through her,
making her limbs feel weak. Her cheek throbbed painfully
and the coppery taste of blood filled her mouth. Rolling to
her knees, her unbound hair tumbling around her shoulders, she frantically scanned the ground, searching for her
weapon. She spotted the length of heavy iron and dove for
it, but Villegas blocked her way. He grabbed a handful of
her hair, jerked her head up, and slapped her again.

"You dare to fight me?" Wiping the blood from his

mouth with the back of his hand, he dragged her to her feet, ripping the front of her blouse. "No man has lived who has ever gone against me—and you are only a woman."

"Then kill me," she taunted. "If you don't, I swear I'll find a way to kill you!"

He merely laughed. Cupping her breast with a thick-fingered hand, he twisted cruelly, sending a shaft of pain slicing through her. *"Puta,"* he growled. "Now you will whore for me."

Carly started to struggle, so frightened she felt dizzy, desperate to gain her freedom, but a rustling sound caught her attention and both of them went stock still.

"Let the woman go." Ramon de la Guerra stood no more than five feet away, long legs splayed, his face a cold mask of rage. His flat black hat rode low over his forehead, but still she could see the fury blazing in his midnight eyes. His jaw clamped so hard a muscle bunched in his lean, hard cheek.

Villegas quit fondling her breast. "So . . . it is you who has come for the girl. I did not think you would." He chuckled crudely. "But she is a fiery piece, no?"

"I said to let her go."

Villegas released her and Carly sank into the dirt at his feet.

"Move away from him, Cara," Ramon said softly. "He will not hurt you again."

She muffled a sob and tried to stand, but her trembling legs would not hold her up. She tried again, forced her un-steady limbs to move and crawled through the dust away from the big, burly Mexican. Her hands shook and her chest heaved. Fear tore at her insides, making it hard to breathe. Fear for herself. Fear for Ramon.

"I will kill you, *jefe*. And then I will take the girl." Villegas grinned. Two gaping holes showed where his eye-teeth should have been. "I will pleasure myself in every way I know how, then I will sell her to Ernesto. His cantina is the fanciest whorehouse in Nogales."

Ramon's control seemed to snap. Muscles bunched in his neck and shoulders as he leapt toward Villegas, grabbing him by the throat and knocking him into the dirt. The bandit broke free, but Ramon spun toward him, throwing his fist in a hard, fast punch that slammed the muscular man to the ground, his head crashing down against the hard-packed earth. Another blow followed, then another, and another.

Villegas's face was bloody, his nose flowing red down to his chin. He grabbed Ramon's shirt and rolled over, forcing his heavy weight atop him.

Ramon took several hard blows before he could free himself, then he was back on top, back in control and raining one vicious blow after another down on Villegas's thick head. The fight was almost over when Carly saw the Mexican reach for the knife that had slid out of his boot.

"Ramon!" She screamed the warning just in time. He caught the bandit's knife hand, they struggled, and for a moment, Carly feared the heavier man might win. She raced across the clearing and grabbed the heavy length of iron, then turned just in time to see Ramon sink the thin blade deep into Villegas's massive chest.

The man's big arms slowly fell away but his eyes no longer moved, just stared sightlessly toward the sky, his mouth gaping open like a dark, bloody hole. Ramon dropped the knife and came up off him, then turned to see Carly gripping the candlestick high above her shoulders, staring at Villegas and still prepared to swing.

"You can put down your weapon, *chica*," he said softly. "The man is dead. He cannot hurt you now."

She fingered the metal, finally let go, and the heavy iron slipped from her hands, landing with a thud in the powdery dust at her feet. Tears filled her eyes and began to slide down her cheeks. She saw Ramon's grim features, saw his graceful strides as he came toward her, then she was crushed against his solid chest.

"Do not cry," he whispered. "Ramon is here now."

She only sobbed harder. "I'm not crying," she said. "I never cry."

His long fingers sifted through her hair, cradling her head against his shoulder. "It is all right, *querida*. There are times we all need to cry." His hand stroked her back, soothing her gently. He whispered soft, encouraging words, but she could barely hear them. Still, they sounded sweet, his voice so gentle, so achingly beautiful. She had heard such soft sweet words before. Somewhere . . . she wished she could recall.

She glanced up at him through tear-damp lashes, and noticed for the first time that his eyes were not just brown, but ringed with flecks of gold.

"Please, Ramon," she whispered brokenly, "please don't be angry. I had to do it. I had to."

"It is not your fault that Villegas—" He held her away from him, his dark eyes fixed on her face. "You went with him willingly? You were trying to escape?"

A moment of unease slid through her. He hadn't known she was running away. Dear God, what would he do? "I-I had to go. I . . . please . . . try to understand."

He pulled her back against him, circled her tightly in his arms. "I understand, Cara. I see that this is one more thing for which I am to blame." He gently tilted her head back, his slim dark fingers lightly touching the bruise on her cheek. Then he kissed her. A feather soft kiss that said how sorry he was and for some strange reason made her want to cry again.

Then he was lifting her into his arms and striding off toward the trees where he had tied his horse.

"I was so frightened," she said, nestling her head against

his shoulder. Beneath her cheek, hard muscle bunched with each of his long-legged strides. "If you hadn't come when you did—"

Ramon flashed one of his beautiful smiles. "I saw how frightened you were, *chica*. You hit him so hard, you almost took off his head." He carried her to the place beneath a thick-leafed sycamore near where his stallion grazed, set her gently on her feet. "We will find a place to camp for the night. In the morning we will go home."

Carly fought a fresh rush of tears. She hated the thought of returning to Llano Mirada. But if it hadn't been for Ramon, her fate would have been far worse. She glanced up at the tall, handsome Spaniard. He was more man than she had ever known, stronger, braver, more beautiful. And gentle. She never would have believed he could be so gentle. The notion made something squeeze inside her heart.

"You are feeling better?"

"Yes," she said, but still he held her and neither of them moved. He stood so close she could see his heartbeat throbbing beside a muscle at the base of his throat. Her fingers pressed lightly against his chest, which rose and fell with his breathing.

His hand came up to her cheek, brushed the hair back from her temple. "Finding you gone . . . I was the one who was frightened. I could not bear the thought that you might be hurt." Through the blur of her tears, the gold in his eyes seemed to shimmer. He stared into her face as if his gaze could touch her soul. Moments passed. She was certain he meant to kiss her. Then a long weary breath escaped and he turned and walked slowly away.

Ramon crossed the clearing trying not to think of Carly and what had nearly occurred. Instead he gathered Viento's reins, led the stallion away from where he grazed, and returned to the clearing. Resting his hands on Carly's waist, he lifted her up on his saddle, setting her astride the horse, then with brisk, deliberate movements, swung himself up behind her, encircling her in his arms. He could still feel her trembling, still feel the tiny shivers running through her small body. His own heart hammered dully.

He had never been so fearful, so close to losing control, never felt such overwhelming anger as the moment he had seen her in the clearing with Villegas. He'd forced himself to wait, take the time he needed to work himself into position. Cisco stood so close to Carly he couldn't chance a shot, and somehow he had needed to end the man's life with his own hands.

It was a feeling he had never experienced. He hoped he never would again.

Holding her protectively against him, he rode back to the clearing to gather the other horse's reins, then headed deeper into the woods. He wouldn't go far. In the morning, he would return to bury Cisco's body—if the wolves didn't get to him first.

Ramon reached down to smooth Carly's silky copper hair. She was nearly asleep, he saw, exhausted by the grueling journey and the bandit's brutal assault, her small head nestled against his shoulder.

She was a virgin, she had said, and Ramon did not doubt it. It pleased him that no other man had touched her, but it angered him too, for he knew he could not be the one to claim her. He would not hurt her again, and that is all that could happen. Carly needed a husband, and Ramon was determined his children would be born of Spanish blood.

He smiled to think of the fight she had given Villegas. She was tough, this little *gringa*. A fighter. She deserved her freedom.

He wished more than ever that he could let her go.

"Why do you do it, Ramon?" They were sitting beneath a huge black oak on a ridge overlooking a small pleasant valley. The sun sat low on the western horizon, its bright yellow rays lighting the golden grasses, dry mustard, and wild oats. An eagle soared above them and quail scattered like seeds on the wind as Ramon tossed a pebble into the center of the covey.

"We fight for the return of our lands," he said. "It is as simple as that." They had been traveling slowly. Ramon must have guessed how tired she was, how her muscles ached from the newness of riding for so long.

"You're breaking the law. That makes all of you outlaws." For the first time since the night of the raid, she had begun to consider what the future would hold for Ramon and the families in the stronghold. She wouldn't have thought it could happen, but she was worried about him.

"To our way of thinking, we are not outlaws. We are just men trying to regain what is rightfully ours."

"People often make misjudgments, invest unwisely. That does not mean they've been treated unfairly."

"The government caused us to lose our land."

"How? I can't imagine they would purposely do something like that." If only she could make him see how futile his efforts were, perhaps he would stop his raiding. Then he would be safe.

She looked at him, saw a muscle clamp in his jaw.

"You do not think so? Perhaps it was not done on purpose; there is no way to know for sure. Three years ago, your government passed a number of sweeping reforms. They were supposed to settle land disputes, to ease the tension between Mexican Californios—men who had just lost a war to the *gringos*—and immigrant Americanos. But the Californios were not prepared to deal with American law."

He stared out over the valley, his painful memories etched in the lines of his face. The quail began to cluster again, to peck at the loose seeds and berries scattered across the fertile soil but another stone shooed them away.

"Go on," Carly urged gently. "I'd really like to know what happened."

Ramon sighed into the darkness. "The Californios had lived on the land for so long they took their ownership for granted. Their *disenos*—maps showing the boundaries of their grants—were often missing. The deeds that did exist were contested by the *gringos*. The grants were old, the boundaries marked by vague, indiscernible descriptions: streams that had long ago changed course, two leagues north to a skull's head on a rock, a right angle westward to the fork in a bent oak tree, that sort of thing."

"I see."

"Then the vultures swept in. Men like your uncle. They schemed and plotted with other *gringos,* found ways to steal our lands."

Carly tensed, the back of her blouse rustling against the bark of the oak. "My uncle? Surely you don't believe he'd be involved in something like that. My uncle's a highly respected member of the community. It's obvious you dislike him. What I've never understood is why? What could he possibly have done to you?"

He looked at her strangely. "You do not know? Your uncle never told you?"

"Told me what?"

"That before he came, Rancho del Robles belonged to the de la Guerras. Your uncle stole our land."

The breath seemed to *whoosh* from her lungs. It couldn't be true. Ramon was lying. Carly stiffened even more. "You can't expect me to believe that. My uncle is not that kind of man."

"You hardly know him, *chica*. You have been in California only for a very short time. But you are not a stupid woman. Soon enough you will discover that what I say is the truth."

Carly looked at him hard, hoping to see the lie in his

face. She started to argue, but Ramon came abruptly to his feet. "It is time we were off. We still have a long way to go and the day passes by."

Carly stood up, too, but inwardly she groaned. Her legs were aching and the hard leather saddle grated against the abraded skin on her thighs with every mile they rode. Ramon helped her up onto the horse, but all the while she was thinking of what he had said.

Could it possibly be true? Could her uncle be responsible for stealing the de la Guerra lands? She hadn't the slightest notion of how he had acquired the property he owned. It had never even crossed her mind. Oddly, now that she thought of it, Lena had mentioned something about Rancho del Robles when she spoke of her years at the mission. She said greed and the white man went hand in hand. That there was always a way for them to steal what they could not have.

Carly had been so tired at the time, she hadn't really listened. Now she wished she had.

They rode for two more hours and again Ramon drew up the horses. Carly winced as he lifted her down, and the don's sleek black brows drew together in a frown.

"You are that sore?"

Carly flushed with embarrassment. "It's the saddle. It rubs against my legs. The skin is—"

"Let me see," he commanded.

"Th-there's nothing you can do. Once we're back I'll be fine."

A corner of his mouth curved up. "I have seen a woman's legs before, Cara. I promise I will not lose control and ravish you."

"It isn't proper. I can't let you—"

Before she could finish, he lifted her up, carried her over to a fallen log, set her down, and jerked her bright yellow skirt up to well above her knees. Carly flushed crimson but the Spaniard merely scowled.

"You should have said something." His long fingers lightly traced the rough, red rash on the inside of her thigh and Carly felt a hot tug of fire. "You cannot go on like this." He left her a moment and returned to his horse. Taking something out of the saddlebags, he came back with a small round tin of ointment. "For the horses," he said. "For cuts and scrapes. Florentia made it. I always carry it with me."

"Horse medicine? I'm supposed to use—"

"You are supposed to be quiet while I take care of your beautiful legs."

The color in her cheeks burned brighter. Carly felt his fingers stroking over her tender skin as he applied the salve, and a rush of heat slid into her stomach. Dear God in heaven—just the sight of those long, brown fingers moving over her flesh made her mouth go dry and her palms grow damp. The scent of pine and clover rose up from the salve to mingle with Ramon's own scent of horses and leather and man.

He was finished in seconds, his movements sure and purposeful, but when he glanced up, his eyes had grown dark and a muscle throbbed in his cheek.

"Th-thank you."

For a moment he said nothing, just stared at her with those hot, dark eyes. "Do you know how much I want you?"

Carly swallowed and tried not to tremble beneath that piercing gaze. She eased her skirt down over her legs, but her eyes remained locked on his face. "You said you would not ravish me."

"No . . . I would not do that. I would make love to you. I would take you gently at first, until you grew used to my touch, then I would drive myself into you as deeply as I wish to do every time I look at you."

Carly wet her lips. Heat spiraled into her belly. She hadn't guessed how much he desired her. Not when he already had a woman as beautiful as Miranda. "I'm your prisoner. Why . . . why have you not already taken what you want?"

A hand cupped her cheek. "Because I have hurt you enough. You are an innocent. The man who takes you should be your husband, someone who can protect you. Even if I were not an outlaw, I could not offer you marriage. I have vowed to wed a woman of pure Spanish blood."

Her heart clutched, twisted painfully inside her. It shouldn't have mattered. It didn't, she told herself firmly. "Miranda?" She hoped the black-haired woman wasn't the one. She hadn't forgotten Miranda's treachery in plotting with Villegas. Ramon deserved a far better woman than that.

"Miranda is only part Spanish. She pleases me in bed, but neither of us wishes to marry. I have not yet chosen the woman I will wed."

Carly bit back a wave of relief. "That your wife is Spanish . . . is it really so important?"

"*Si*. It is a promise I have made to the Californios who are my friends. I have made such a vow to myself and to my family. The blood of Spanish royalty runs through de la Guerra veins. My children and my children's children must be of Spanish descent."

Carly couldn't help thinking of the mine patch and the lowly beginnings she had come from. The McConnells were hardly royalty, yet she would not change who she was. "You do this because you hate the *gringos* so much."

"*Si*. The *gringos* killed my brother. They have stolen my family's lands. I am a Californio. My wife and children will be Californio, too."

Carly said nothing. Her chest felt tight in a way she hadn't expected. "The salve has helped," she finally said, forcing herself to smile. "I think we should be going."

Ramon merely nodded. He moved to his horse and took a blanket from his bedroll. Placing it over her saddle, he lifted her aboard the bay, then swung himself up on his tall black stallion.

They spoke very little for the rest of the afternoon, but Ramon stopped the horses several more times. Soon it was apparent they wouldn't make it back to Llano Mirada before nightfall.

Remembering the desire she had seen in his eyes, the heat of his fingers as they skimmed over her flesh, Carly bit her bottom lip, wondering if perhaps he had planned it this way, planned all along to take her as he seemed to wish. Or if she could trust him to keep his word.

Ramon rode straight-backed in the saddle, disgruntled they had been forced to travel so slowly. They wouldn't reach the stronghold until tomorrow. He would be alone with the girl all night.

A harsh sound came from his throat. He would sleep little this night. After his tender ministrations this afternoon, his body was still hard and throbbing. Even now he could imagine Carly McConnell's smooth, white skin beneath his fingers, that if he had raised them only a few more inches, he could have touched her soft woman's flesh. He could have spread her pretty legs, opened his breeches, and buried himself inside her, eased the painful ache he felt whenever she was near.

Damn, but he had never been so driven to bed a woman.

They came to a clearing beside a marshy pond surrounded by willows, and he motioned for her to rein up. A small clear stream fed the pond, and a cluster of boulders ringed the clearing, providing a shelter of sorts. They set up camp in silence, then he rode into the woods in the hope of finding fresh game.

He didn't go far. He hadn't lied about the danger of mountain lion and grizzly. He had seen fresh bear sign just that afternoon. And wild cattle, with their long, sharp horns and vicious tempers, could often be the most deadly of all.

Still, he was able to return with a nice, plump rabbit, which Carly skinned and they roasted on a green willow bough over the flames. Afterward, he sat with his back propped against a granite boulder, watching her beside the stream, cleaning the grease from their tin utensils while he smoked a slim cheroot.

When she finished, she sat in front of the fire a few feet away, curling her shapely legs beneath her, eyeing him somewhat warily.

She picked up a small leafy branch that was lying in the dirt and began to twirl it between her fingers. "I was wondering . . ." She looked up at him, her pretty face outlined by the low-burning flames, "the night of the raid . . . why did you take me?"

He pulled the cheroot from between his teeth, trying not to notice the rich dark copper of her hair. "Because it was my brother's intention. I saw it in his eyes as he rode toward you. In that moment, just after they shot him, I felt as if I were Andreas, as if his will were mine and I was doing what he would have wanted."

"Your brother would have taken me?"

"*Si*. He had seen you the day of the horse race. He wanted you even then."

Her tongue ran nervously over her ruby lips, and Ramon's groin tightened.

"Your . . . your brother would have raped me?"

He took a draw on the slim cigar, slowly released it, and watched the smoke drift into the clear night sky. "I do not know. Never had he done such a thing . . . but then he had never been with a woman who was the niece of his most hated enemy."

She pondered that in silence, then leaned forward, the

firelight giving her smooth pale skin a rosy glow. "Would you have let him?"

Ramon looked into her lovely face, thinking how small and innocent she was, how soft and womanly, and knew he would not have let his brother touch her. "No."

Her expression shifted, subtly changed, and she smiled at him sweetly. "Perhaps I was not so wrong about you as I thought."

He smiled into the darkness, took another long draw on his cigar. "If that means you do not find me quite so despicable, I hope that is the truth."

She laughed softly, then seemed to grow more thoughtful. Shadows mingled with the firelight, forming patterns on her long, dark auburn hair. He tried not to notice when her torn blouse gaped open, exposing creamy skin and a portion of her lush, upthrusting breasts. His blood began to thicken, to pump with a heavy rhythm through his veins. Heat eddied low in his groin, strengthening his arousal, and he was glad that he sat among the shadows.

"What is it you are thinking?" he asked.

She absently twirled the leafy branch. "I was remembering what you did yesterday."

"You were thinking that I was the man who killed Villegas?"

"No. I was thinking of the way you held me, spoke to me so gently." Her eyes held his as she gazed at him across the distance between them. "Someone spoke to me that way before, on the nights that I was sick. I tried to remember. For a while I thought it was a dream. It was you, wasn't it? You were the man beside my bed."

He had wondered if she would recall. "*Si*, I was there."

"It was you who cared for me. I remember you bathing my forehead. One night I woke up and . . . you were praying."

Ramon smiled softly. *"Si, querida.* For once God heard my prayers."

Something flickered in her eyes. She looked at him as she never had before. "Thank you." It was little more than a whisper.

Ramon said nothing. For a while she watched him, studying his face as if she tried to read his thoughts, then she rose and crossed the clearing toward the bedroll she had placed some distance from his.

Tonight he was grateful she would not be sleeping so near. With each step she took, her small ankles showed beneath the hem of her simple cotton skirt and he recalled her shapely legs, the way she had shivered when his hand ran up her thigh. Her full breasts quivered against her blouse, reminding him how round and full they had felt when he had cupped them. His shaft grew harder still, and with every movement of her hips, a painful ache throbbed at the front of his breeches.

It took all his effort at control not to go to her, to drag her beneath him, push up her skirt, and drive himself inside her. She was a hunger he couldn't assuage, a fever in his blood that nothing seemed to ease. And yet he could not take her.

He felt tied in knots, mired in lust, felt the same hot roiling frustration that he had once felt for Lily. But Lily was a woman, not a girl, a vixen practiced in the ways of a woman. Finally she had come to him, welcomed him into her bed. Beneath a pale Seville moon, he'd had four glorious weeks with Lily, most of it spent between her long, white, shapely legs. He'd been nearly obsessed with Lily— until he discovered he wasn't the only young fool who shared her bed.

Chapter Ten

Sitting astride the bay, Carly surveyed the split in the trail ahead, one branch leading farther north, the other heading west, down into the oak-covered rolling hills and on into the lowlands. Wistfully, she thought of Rancho del Robles, which must lie somewhere in that direction. In front of her, Ramon paused at the top of the steep descent that led down the mountain into a small, secluded valley. She couldn't help admiring the sight of his narrow hips and broad shoulders, the easy grace with which he sat his horse.

Carly smiled. She was feeling better today, her legs growing used to the long hours on horseback. The salve Ramon had used had worked wonders. Her cheeks burned to think of the fire that had blazed from the spot where he had touched her, the gentle stroke of his long, dark fingers over her skin. He turned his horse and rode back up the trail to the place beside her, and Carly forced the memory away.

"Are we close to the stronghold?" she asked. "Surely we are. At least I fervently hope so."

Ramon ignored the question. "There is something I would know. It is important that you tell me the truth."

Her head came up at the serious note in his voice. "All right."

"The day you left the stronghold with Villegas . . . when you tried to run away . . . why did you leave?"

Carly's stomach churned. *Because you make me feel things I don't understand.* "Because I was frightened."

"Frightened? Surely you were no longer frightened of me."

Carly shifted in the saddle, looked him square in the eye. "I was your prisoner, Ramon. You could do anything you wanted with me. Anything. Of course I was afraid of you."

His dark gaze held hers, probing, searching for secrets. "And now, *chica?* Are you still afraid?"

There was something in his face, something she couldn't quite read. "Back there—in the mountains with Villegas—you saved my life. You risked your own life to do it. You promised I would be safe, and you've kept your word. No, Ramon. I'm no longer afraid of you." *I'm only afraid of myself.*

For a long, tense moment he said nothing. "The trail splits here," he said. "The path leading west would carry you to Rancho del Robles. If I could be certain you would not lead your uncle to the stronghold, I would consider letting you return to your home."

Her heart began thudding, pounding inside her chest. Dear God, he might let her go! "I have no idea where the stronghold is. I stayed under the tarp when I left there with Villegas, otherwise your guards would have seen me. Besides he went south. I don't know this country and I couldn't begin to retrace our path."

"And the night of the raid?"

"It was dark and I was frightened. I have no idea the trail you took; I was just worried about staying alive."

"That is what I thought, but I wanted to hear you say it. I could not risk the lives of my people."

She looked into his handsome face, at his long black lashes and high cheekbones. "What about you, Ramon? If you let me go, you'll be putting your life in my hands. I know who you are, that you live at Las Almas. You'd have to accept my word that I wouldn't turn you in to the authorities."

"*Si,* Cara, that is so. As you said, you know who I am. My rancho lies just miles from your uncle's hacienda. If you wish to see me dead, you need only tell him that Ramon de la Guerra is El Dragón."

Her stomach clenched, tightened at the thought of him lying in the dirt like Villegas. "El Dragón was mostly your brother. Serafina told me this was his idea to begin with. That he led more than half of the raids. She also told me El Dragón didn't rob the stage the night I met you at my uncle's *fandango.* She says there are a number of bandits who rob travelers in the gold fields, but it's El Dragón who usually gets the blame."

"As I said, you are not a stupid woman. And I have come to respect you. If you give me your word that you will not tell them who I am, then I will let you go."

Something twisted inside her. He had risked his life to save her from Villegas. He was risking it again. "Why? Why would you take such a chance?"

"There are many reasons, Cara. Perhaps it is simply that I want you and cannot have you."

Could that truly be enough? She would never know, she guessed, but it didn't really matter as long as she got home. "If everything you've told me is the truth, then I give you my word. Your secret will be safe with me, Don Ramon."

The Spaniard merely nodded. "Tell them we were moving our camp, taking you south when you escaped. Tell you were blindfolded much of the time and that you saw nothing that could help them find us. Tell them we meant to ransom you. That is the reason you were left alone, the reason El Dragón did not take you to his bed."

A warmth rose into her cheeks. "I'll tell them," she said softly. Something was squeezing inside her, pressing against her heart. For the first time she realized part of her didn't want to leave. She looked up at Ramon, and he must have sensed what she was feeling for his eyes turned smoky and dark. Bending forward, he slid a hand behind her neck and pulled her toward him. His mouth came down over hers, moving with fiery heat and an odd sort of tenderness.

She found herself reaching out for him, sliding her arms around his neck and kissing him back. Tears stung her eyes as his lips touched her forehead, her cheeks, her nose, then he returned to kissing her lips. A last hard kiss and he broke away.

"Stay on the trail," he said gruffly. "In two hours time you will reach the boundary of the ranch. Take the fork to the right and you will come to the ranch house." He whirled the big black stallion. *"Vaya con Dios, querida. El Dragón will not forget you."* And then he was gone.

Carly's hands clenched on the reins. Her insides were shaking, and her heart felt crushed inside her breast. Tears burned her eyes and began to slide down her cheeks.

"God go with you, Ramon," she whispered to his tall retreating figure as the big, black stallion picked its way back up the trail. She watched him until he disappeared. Even then she didn't ride out, just sat on the stout bay horse feeling heartsick and lonely when she should have been feeling elated.

Eventually she turned the bay and rode off down the trail toward her uncle's hacienda. She would see him again, she told herself, not that it would make any difference. Don Ramon would visit the rancho as he had done before. And he would play the gentleman. But it was El Dragón, the handsome Spaniard who had carried her away, that she would remember in her dreams.

* * *

From a ridge high above, Ramon watched Carly ride off down the trail. He followed at a distance until she reached the boundary to Rancho del Robles then turned away. He felt tired and strangely empty, as if someone had blown out a candle, leaving him alone in a darkened room.

Perhaps he was worried that the girl would break her word, but he didn't really think so. A bond had grown between them, an odd sort of kinship that had nothing to do with the desire he felt for her. It had happened the moment he had stepped into the clearing, the instant he had set for himself the task of protecting her. The bond had strengthened the moment he had seen she was equally willing to fight for him.

And if he was wrong?

Unconsciously he shrugged his shoulders. It didn't really matter. He couldn't keep her and he would not hurt her again. If she betrayed him, so be it. His life had been a full one, ripe with the company of beautiful women, the pleasures of the flesh, the taste of fine wines, dancing, and song. His only regret would be in failing his people. They needed him. His mother and his aunt Teresa needed him. And he wanted Rancho del Robles returned to the de la Guerra name.

Perhaps he had been a fool, and yet he would not change his course of action. Time would tell if the woman would keep her word.

Ramon rode back toward the compound. He would let Pedro and the others know he was safe, what he had done with the girl, and then he would return to Rancho Las Almas. In the days ahead, perhaps he would ride to Monterey. There was a girl there, Catarina Micheltorena, a direct descendant of the former governor of Alta California. She had just turned seventeen, not as old as he would have liked, but she was beautiful, and pure Castilian Spanish. She was the kind of woman who would obey his every command and bring him a host of fine strong sons. Her father believed the two of them would suit, and he was eager for the marriage.

Ramon thought of Carly. Of her courage and determination, of her innocence and womanly curves. He thought of the way she had felt in his arms, and a hollow ache rose into his chest. He nudged the stallion into a gallop.

For the first time in a long time, he realized just how lonely he was.

"Now, Caralee, my dear, let's go over this again."

Carly sighed and leaned back in her chair. "I've told you what happened a dozen times, Uncle Fletcher. I was blindfolded the night of the raid and again when the men moved their camp. I was lucky I was able to escape, that I happened on a trail that led in the right direction, that some old Indian pointed me toward Rancho del Robles. I didn't see anything that might help you find them. I wish I could help you, but I can't."

They were seated in his study, on the brown leather sofa in front of the hearth. It was still warm outside, a late September day, so the fire wasn't lit. Instead it blazed in her uncle's green eyes.

A man named Jeremy Layton sat across from them, the sheriff from San Juan Bautista. "What I can't understand, Miss McConnell, is why he didn't try to ransom you sooner. Why did he wait so long?" The sheriff was a man in his forties, lean and blond and rawboned, with a dark-tanned, slightly weathered face.

"I-I don't know. I think he wanted my uncle to worry. I gather he doesn't like him very much." It was harder to lie than she had thought, the story growing more complex with every telling.

"None of those greasers like me." Her uncle's thick hand balled into a fist. "They resent the fact they lost the war. They were too weak to keep their land, now they're taking it out on any American who happens to get in their way." He turned a hard look on Carly. "Tell me again what this bastard looked like."

Carly shuddered, thinking of Villegas, the villain she had mentally dubbed El Dragón. The ugly bandit looked as little like Ramon de la Guerra as any man she could think of. And conveniently he was dead. She rubbed her temples. She was beginning to get a headache.

"As I said, he was a big, burly man with a long, black, curling mustache. He had an eyetooth that was missing and one that was gold."

After the first stunned acceptance of her return home, after a hard, brief hug and concern for her physical welfare, her uncle had begun his endless round of questions.

"Sound like anyone you know, Sheriff Layton?" he asked.

"Not offhand, but when I get back to town, I'll go through that stack of wanted posters sitting on my desk. Could be I missed something." The sheriff had been away on business when Carly first returned. He'd only arrived at the rancho just that morning, four days after she'd gotten back home.

Four days. It felt like four weeks.

"Tell us again about the horses they stole," her uncle pressed. "You say you think he sold them?"

"Yes. I heard one of the men talking, saying that the money should last them quite a while." He was determined she had seen something that would help them find the outlaws, and the more determined he was, the more determined Carly was she would not break her word.

Fletcher sighed and leaned back against the tufted leather sofa. "I'm sorry, my dear. I know this whole ordeal has been grueling. I'm just glad you got away before that bastard . . . took liberties with your person."

She tried to keep from blushing, fought desperately not

to recall Ramon's hands cupping her breasts, her nipples straining against her blouse as they pressed against his palm, the feel of his hands on her thighs. She tried to blot out the memory of his kisses, the sweep of his tongue inside her mouth. "So am I," she said softly.

Her uncle stared at her but said nothing more. Instead he turned to the sheriff. "I'm sorry, Jeremy. I'd hoped by the time you arrived, my niece would remember something more."

"I'm sure it's been hard on her. It's got to be a painful thing to remember." He stood up from his chair and swung his gaze in her direction. "I'm sorry you had to go over all this again, miss, but I assure you it was necessary. If you think of something else, just have your uncle send word." He lifted his brown felt hat off the back of his chair and twirled it in a lean-fingered hand. "I promise you one thing— sooner or later we'll find him. When we do, he's gonna swing from the highest tree." Carly paled, but the sheriff only smiled. "Good day, Miss McConnell."

"G-good day, Sheriff Layton." She forced herself to smile. "Thank you for coming."

The lanky sheriff simply nodded. Her uncle walked him out of the house, and Carly made her way along the hallway to her room. With a sigh, she closed the door, then crossed the room and sank onto the rose satin counterpane on her bed. In a way it was good to be home. Her uncle's house was luxurious in comparison to the small adobe cabin she had occupied in the stronghold. But Ramon had once lived there, and everything about the place, the handmade bent-willow furniture, the colorful woven blankets, even the scent of his cigars that lingered throughout the cozy rooms reminded her of him, and she discovered that she missed being there.

The truth was she missed him. She couldn't afford to dwell on the fact. It would do her no good and the sooner she forgot those weeks—and him—the better off she would be. It bothered her, what Ramon had said about her uncle. Had he really stolen Rancho del Robles? She was determined to find out, but for now she meant to forget Ramon, forget what happened in the mountains, and get on with her life.

Carly sighed. She wished her uncle would forget it as well, that he would end his battery of questions and let her put the matter behind her.

Somehow she didn't believe he would.

"Well, Jeremy, what do you think?" They walked in front of the sprawling tile-roofed adobe, the sheriff leading his tall sorrel horse, Fletcher walking beside him.

"Hard to say, Mr. Austin. Could be she's still frightened. Maybe he threatened her, told her if she ever told anyone where they were, he'd come back and kill her. Maybe she's tellin' the truth and she doesn't know a damned thing that can help. You said yourself, she was new to this country. She doesn't know her way around. She was frightened, afraid they would kill her. It makes sense she wouldn't know how to go back to where they took her. Besides, from what she's said, they were headed someplace else."

Fletcher nodded. The sheriff was voicing his thoughts exactly. He'd have to give Caralee the benefit of the doubt. "What about that other? She says the bastard didn't touch her. You think that could be true?"

The sheriff lifted his sweat-stained hat and scratched his thinning blond hair. "A woman like that . . . so pretty and all . . . it's damned hard to believe. For her sake, I hope it's the truth."

Fletcher said nothing. That was one subject he intended to pursue. He had too much riding on that girl to take any chances. He had brought her west for a purpose. He wanted her married to a man who could help his political ambitions, and he knew exactly who that man was. The time to strike was at hand—he couldn't afford to find out she was carrying some outlaw's bastard.

Fletcher left the sheriff and turned back toward the house. He'd give her a chance to settle in, forget the ordeal she had been through. He'd give her some time, but he wouldn't wait long. If there was any chance Caralee was with child, he meant to do something about it.

He had to know the truth.

He wasn't about to let her ruin his plans.

The week finally passed and slid into the week after that. Carly's strong sense of will had kicked in after just a few days and she'd been able to keep thoughts of Ramon and her days in the stronghold at a manageable distance. But she couldn't still the doubts he had stirred about her uncle.

The night before, when the house had grown quiet and Uncle Fletcher and the servants were asleep, she'd slipped into his study and gone through his desk. She'd found the deed to del Robles in the small tin box in the bottom drawer. The land was sold to him by a man named Thomas Garrison. Carly had no idea who he was, but apparently the de la Guerras had already sold the land to Garrison before her uncle bought it. At the time of the sale, Ramon would have still been in Spain.

A sigh of relief whispered through her. Ramon had been wrong about her uncle. Perhaps when she saw him again, she could convince him. The unconscious thought stirred an odd rush of heat and an image of dark-fringed eyes, broad shoulders, narrow hips, and smooth dark skin. As she hurried down the hall back to her room, it took a will of iron to force the image away.

Carly slept fitfully that night, fighting hot dreams of Ramon, cursing herself for thinking of him at all. Whatever his beliefs, the man was still an outlaw, and even if he might desire her, he wanted nothing from her but a quick tumble in his bed. Fanciful thoughts of Ramon would do her no good.

Carly awoke feeling tired and out of sorts. Only the crisp fall morning with its colorful autumn leaves and dewy grasses saved her from a dismal mood. She strode from her room dressed for riding as she had done these past two days, surprisingly determined to continue with her lessons—considering the way she had suffered before.

But now she was learning to ride sidesaddle. One of her uncle's vaqueros, a pleasant older man named Jose Gonzales, had volunteered to teach her. She didn't mention the lessons Pedro Sanchez had begun, so he was more than pleased by what he called her "natural ability." And her learning to ride like a lady was obviously pleasing her uncle.

She was on her way down the hall, her sapphire blue velvet riding habit rustling as she moved, when he stepped into her path, stilling her movements.

"I'd like a word with you, my dear, if you don't mind."

"Of course, Uncle Fletcher." Curious at his mood, she followed him into his study, and he sat down behind his wide oak desk. Carly seated herself in one of the carved wooden chairs in front of it. "What is it, Uncle?"

He shifted in his seat, looking a little uncomfortable. "There is something we have to discuss, my dear. Unfortunately, it is not a pleasant topic, particularly for a young woman of your tender years. But in this you must trust me. You must tell me the truth."

A shiver of unease ran through her. "Of course, Uncle Fletcher."

He leaned forward. "I asked you before about the man who abducted you the night of the raid. You said it was El Dragón."

She steeled herself for another round of questions about Ramon. "That's right."

"You're a beautiful girl, Caralee. The man who took you is an outlaw. A ruthless, brutal criminal without the slightest hint of conscience. The fault would not be yours if such a man forced himself on you. I have to know, my dear—you didn't lie about that, did you? The man didn't rape you?"

She flushed, yet she also felt an odd sense of relief. At least in this she could tell the truth. "No, Uncle Fletcher." A faint smile curved her lips. "I guess he figured you might not pay if he stole my virtue." Then the smile slid away as a grim thought struck suddenly. "It wouldn't have mattered . . . would it, Uncle Fletcher?"

He cleared his throat. "Don't be silly. Of course it wouldn't have mattered. You're my own dear sister's child, the flesh and blood of my own kin. You don't think I would leave you at that villain's mercy?"

The smile returned, and with it a wave of relief even more vast than the first. "You might have been stuck with me if he had. I don't suppose there's much of a market these days for fallen women."

Her uncle smiled, too. "Actually that isn't the truth. You're an American. You're beautiful, and you're obviously a lady." *Thanks to me,* his look clearly said.

Carly squirmed a little in her seat. For a moment she felt as she had when Ramon said he would marry a woman of pure Spanish blood—like a ragamuffin just out of the mine patch.

"Out here," Uncle Fletcher was saying, "women like you are few and far between. Why, Vincent Bannister was devastated when he learned you'd been abducted. He offered to go after those outlaws himself, but of course I wouldn't let him. Vince is a city boy, after all. He doesn't know a thing about riding through the woods, chasing down criminals."

No he didn't. If she'd thought sandy-haired Vincent Bannister was a bit of a dandy before, now that she'd known Ramon, he seemed completely foppish.

"By the way, he'll be coming here with his father the end of next week. He's been worried about you. I sent word of your safe return, and now that you're back, he wants to see you."

"That's very kind of him, Uncle. I just hope he doesn't . . ."

His look turned slightly hard, the veins standing out in his forehead. "Doesn't what, my dear? You aren't saying you don't want to see him?"

"Vincent is a very nice boy. I just hope he doesn't think that I'm . . . interested in him."

"You're telling me you're not? Why, may I ask—and it had better not have anything to do with that bastard, El Dragón."

Carly straightened in her chair. "Of—of course not."

"If I discover you've lied to me, Caralee—if you wind up carrying that outlaw's child, I swear I'll—"

"You'll what, Uncle Fletcher?" Carly came to her feet. "Send me off someplace where you won't have to see me? Disown me? Make me fend for myself on the streets?"

Her uncle blustered and turned red in the face. "Of course not. That isn't at all what I meant." He raked a hand through his graying auburn hair. "Sit down, Caralee. We might as well get something straight right here."

She did as he said, leaning forward on the edge of her seat, her hands clenched tightly in her lap.

"What I said about men is the truth. There are a good many out there, but few of them have the breeding, the wealth and power the Bannisters have. And this little escapade will hardly enhance your reputation. Vincent Bannister wants to marry you. He's told me so in no uncertain terms."

"Vincent wants to m-marry me?"

"Of course he does. Why shouldn't he? You're a beautiful young woman. You're perfectly trained in all the social graces—I've personally seen to that. He wants to be your husband and I think it's a darned good idea."

She tried to hang on to her temper, but it wasn't easy. "Well, I think it's a dreadful idea. I hardly even know Vincent Bannister." She was crunching her skirt, she saw, mashing the soft blue velvet in a fist. She opened her fingers and smoothed the wrinkled fabric.

"I'm sorry, my dear, I didn't mean to upset you. Perhaps I should have let Vincent speak for himself, but I feel strongly that after what has happened, it would be best if you did not tarry. Marriage to Vincent will insure your entree into all the proper social circles. I want that for you, Caralee. I mean to see that you have it."

Or did he want it for himself? Carly wondered. Once he had told her he wanted an appointment to the Land's Commission. He'd said the Bannisters had a great deal of influence in that arena. She thought of what Ramon had said about him stealing Rancho del Robles and wondered if the deed from Thomas Garrison had covered up some hidden scheme.

"What if I don't wish to marry him? What if I want to marry someone I love?"

Fletcher scoffed. "Don't be a child, Caralee. There is no such thing as love. Marriages are made for the sake of expediency. If would be beneficial to both of us if you married Vincent Bannister."

"I-I'm not ready for marriage. I need time to consider. I've only just met Vincent." She couldn't seem to think. It was all happening too quickly. She had known there might be consequences to her abduction, but she hadn't thought of this one.

"I'm all you have, Caralee," her uncle said. "You must trust me to see to your best interests."

She forced herself to smile. She owed him so much. He had saved her, given her a chance for a whole new life. She had always been desperate to please him, to pay him back for the things he had done. She wanted so badly to win his acceptance, perhaps even his love.

She would do almost anything for him.

Anything but this.

"As I said, Vincent is a very nice boy. I understand your concern, but I care nothing for Vincent Bannister beyond friendship, and I'm not going to marry him," She rose stiffly, her dark blue riding skirt rustling against the legs of the carved wooden chair. "Now if you will excuse me . . ."

He didn't try to stop her, just scowled as she stalked out of the room.

Fletcher waited till she closed the door, then moved to the sideboard and poured himself a drink. He didn't usually imbibe this early, but his headstrong niece had driven him to it. His mouth curled up in a grudging half smile. Part of him admired her. She had fortitude, beauty and brains. She reminded him of his dear sister, Lucy, the only woman he had ever really respected. If he could find a woman with half his niece's spirit, he would marry her tomorrow.

Which didn't mean he intended to let her have her way.

Lifting the fine crystal snifter cradled in his hand, he took a sip of brandy, enjoying the trickle of warmth into his stomach. A little of his tension eased. Caralee was a handful, more than he had ever expected. He had seen it from the start, though she'd done her best to appear meek and mild. She needed a man to take her in hand, a man who could handle her, and it was going to be a man of Fletcher's choosing.

He took another drink. Vincent might look a little like a milksop, but Fletcher had seen him with his mistress. The boy wasn't afraid to raise a hand to her when the need arose. He wasn't one bit bashful about putting the woman in her place. And his appetite for bed sport would insure Caralee gave him sons.

At this late date, their offspring might well be the only heirs Fletcher Austin ever had.

He took another sip of his drink. At least the girl wasn't

pregnant. He was fairly sure of that. He was also certain she would marry Vincent Bannister.

Fletcher smiled. He always got what he wanted. This time would be no different. He knew exactly the way to insure that his niece and the son of his wealthy friend Bannister were married by the end of next week.

Teresa Apolonia de la Guerra loved her nephew Ramon as if he were her own son. She had no children of her own, for she had never married. Her *novio*, Esteban, had been killed in Spain's war with Napoleon, a young man only twenty. But she had never forgotten him. Only the closeness she shared with her brother Diego, his wife Anna Marie, and their two sons, Andreas and Ramon, had kept away the loneliness through the years.

Now Diego was gone. Andreas had joined him and soon would be sleeping in his rightful place beside his father in the plot up on the hill. She glanced across at Ramon, who stood staring out the window, off toward the horizon in the west.

Lifting her dark brown bombazine skirts, she silently crossed the room and rested her thin, veined hand on a muscled forearm. "What is it, Ramon? Lately you have not been yourself. I know that you still grieve for your brother, but somehow I do not think that this is what is wrong."

He turned to face her, banished the darkness from his eyes, but not before she had seen it. He was so handsome, more beautiful than any man she had ever seen . . . except perhaps for Esteban.

Ramon gently smiled. "I am sorry, Tia. It is nothing to trouble yourself about. Only that I am worried about the people in the stronghold. Without Andreas, El Dragón will not avoid capture for long."

Her hold on his arm grew tighter. "Even if your brother still lived, sooner or later, you both would be caught. You tried to tell him that in the beginning. You told him his efforts were futile. That there must be another way to regain what is ours. In your heart you still believe that is the truth."

He covered her age-spotted hand with his own strong brown one. "*Si*, that is so. But that still does not solve the problem of feeding our people."

"They are strong, Ramon. They will survive, even without your help. You cannot take care of them all."

"If I had been here when Father needed me . . . if I hadn't been in Spain—"

"It was not your fault. Your father believed the courts would uphold his title. He thought he could take care of the problem himself. By the time you knew what had happened it was already too late."

He knew all of that, but still he felt guilty. If he had been here, maybe he could have done something to save their land. Perhaps his father would not have grown ill and died of a broken heart.

"What are your plans?" Tia Teresa asked.

Ramon shook his head. "I do not know." He gazed back out the window, staring off toward the west as he had done so many times before. He had said he was worried about his people. Teresa knew that was the truth, but she believed there was something else.

"Will you go to Senor Austin's *fandango* on Saturday?" One of the del Robles vaqueros had brought the invitation that afternoon.

"I am not certain." His eyes swung toward hers. They looked troubled again. "Unless you and Mother wish to go."

"You know we are in mourning."

"We are all of us in mourning, but the Anglos do not know that and we cannot let them know. Besides, the music and laughter would be good for you both."

Something told her to say yes—for Ramon's sake—to

make an exception to the old ways, to custom and what was proper. He wanted to go. She did not know why, but she could see it in his face. Still, she thought that he would not indulge in this desire.

"Perhaps that is a good idea," she said, watching him closely. "There are few of us de la Guerras left, only the three of us and your cousins. With Maria and poor dear Angel so far away, we should do what is best for ourselves. Perhaps it would be nice to go for a while, to sit and listen to the music."

He smiled but it was tinged with a darkness she could not read. "*Bien*. If that is your wish, we will go."

Teresa patted his hand. "I will speak to your mother. I believe she will see things as I do." Not in the beginning. Anna was a stickler for propriety, and she grieved deeply for her son. Still, she loved Ramon. She would do anything for him.

Teresa meant to discover what it was at Rancho del Robles that constantly drew her nephew's attention and creased his forehead with what looked very much like pain.

*C*hapter *E*leven

*T*hey were having a *fandango*. A party was the last thing Carly wanted, but Vincent Bannister and his father had arrived three days ago and apparently her uncle intended to entertain them in style.

With an inward groan of resignation, she turned to her little Spanish maid. "Are you finished yet, Candelaria?" Sitting in front of the mirror above her carved oak dresser, Carly fidgeted while the girl put up her hair. Candelaria had gotten reasonably good at it, considering her role as lady's maid was fairly new.

"*Si*, senorita. Just a moment more and your beautiful curls will all be in place." She was a pretty girl, a little moon-faced, a tendency toward pudginess in her later years, but fair-skinned and brown-haired with big brown eyes and long thick black lashes.

Carly liked the girl. She was always pleasant and cheerful. In the beginning, Carly had been so lonely she had confided in Candelaria. Now she was embarrassed to think of the things she had told her. She had spoken of her mother and father and the life of poverty she had led in the mine patch.

Her uncle would die if he knew.

Carly sighed. She guessed it really didn't matter. In a

way, she and Candelaria were friends. Her uncle would hardly approve, but it wasn't her nature to place herself on a level above someone else.

Obviously, not a single solitary drop of royal blood ran through her veins.

Carly frowned at the thought and her stomach tightened with nerves. The de la Guerra family had been invited. She wondered if Ramon would come.

"You look very beautiful, Senorita McConnell." Candelaria stepped back to survey her handiwork, the upswept auburn curls that seemed to shimmer in the lamplight and set off the topaz gown. It was daringly low, exposing a good deal of her breasts, and her shoulders were bare as well. The skirt was cut full, slightly belled, the tiny waist V-ed in the front. Dark brown velvet trimmed the skirt, along with heavy golden lace.

"Your uncle will be waiting," Candelaria gently urged. "You do not wish to make him angry."

No, she didn't wish it, but she didn't want to spend another evening with Vincent, either.

Resignedly she stood up from her chair. Her uncle had pushed them together at every opportunity. In truth, in the beginning, she had actually tried to imagine herself as Vincent's wife. It would please Uncle Fletcher so much. She couldn't expect him to take care of her forever. Perhaps it wouldn't be so bad.

It didn't take long to discover the terrible fate being married to Vincent would be.

"I can't wait for you to come to the city," he'd said as they strolled beneath the great live oaks behind the house late one evening. "San Francisco is incredibly exciting." He sighed dramatically. "Of course it's nothing like Philadelphia." The city he had come from. "You can't find nearly the same caliber of people, or the level of sophistication, but at least you can get a decent meal. You don't have to eat those godawful tortillas and beans one has to put up with out here."

"Actually, I've grown rather fond of the food," Carly said a bit defensively. She'd tried to steer him to other topics, but he always returned to his dislike of the country, his prejudice against the Spanish landowners, or his favorite subject—himself. His interest seemed fixed on who was who among San Francisco's elite, who had the most money, and discussions of his father's business concerns.

"One of these days, the Bannisters will own San Francisco," he boasted. "The woman I marry will live like a queen." He turned her to face him, tilted her chin with his hand. "You could be that woman, Caralee. You'd be the envy of every woman in the city . . . and I'd be the envy of every man."

Then he leaned over and kissed her. Carly squeezed her eyes closed, hoping she would feel some of the scorching heat Ramon had made her feel. But she might as well have been kissing the eggplant she'd picked that morning in the garden.

It was the hand he moved up to her breast that ended the contact. She wasn't about to let him take liberties. The truth was she felt nothing for Vincent Bannister. It was only too clear that she never would.

Now, standing alone beneath the eaves of the house watching her uncle and his guests, Carly resigned herself to another evening of his unwanted company. With a silent vow to persevere, she took a deep breath and began walking toward the group of well-dressed people standing at the edge of the big wooden dance floor her uncle had ordered built for the *fandango*.

Two men played guitar and another drew his bow across a violin, evoking a bittersweet Spanish tune. Colorful paper lanterns hung from strings tied between the overhanging oak trees, and tables laden with steaming platters of food sat off to one side. A bullock turned over a spit near the edge of the gathering, its savory smell drifting through the cool evening air. A group of her uncle's vaqueros stood around it, laughing and smoking and enjoying the rhythm of the music.

Most of the guests held cups of sangria, a brew made of rich red wine, wild berries, oranges, and limes. Some of the men drank the fine imported whiskey her uncle brought in from San Francisco.

"Caralee!" Uncle Fletcher waved her toward him. "It's time you joined us. Young Vincent has been chomping at the bit."

William Bannister laughed and so did a few of the others. Vincent's face turned a little bit red.

Her uncle just grinned. "She's a sight for sore eyes, isn't she, my boy? Had that dress specially made for her. Came all the way 'round the horn from New York City." He clapped the sandy-haired man on the back, and Vincent smiled good-naturedly.

At least he had that going for him. It seemed Vincent was fairly even-tempered. "She certainly looks lovely, Mr. Austin. Your niece is a beautiful woman." His gaze flicked over to Carly. "And since that is the case, I'm hoping she'll agree to dance with me."

"Of course she will." Her uncle gave her a look that brooked no argument, and Carly forced herself to smile.

"Of course. I'd be delighted." He had that going for him, too. Vincent was a very good dancer. She let him lead her onto the dance floor and they began to move to the soft strains of a waltz. She'd been hoping for a polka or perhaps a mazurka, something lively, so they wouldn't have to talk.

"I meant what I said. You look lovely tonight, Caralee." Vincent smiled, his hazel eyes warm on her face. "Even in San Francisco, you'd be the belle of the ball."

"Thank you, Vincent, that's very flattering." But then so

was everything he said. They continued to dance. Carly was enjoying the music but couldn't manage to concentrate on Vincent's uninteresting conversation. Though she tried to will them not to, her eyes kept searching the crowd for Ramon. She recognized Sam Hollingworth and his wife, Amanda, their closest neighbors to the north; George Winston; and Royston Wardell. The Montoyas were there, and several other Californio families, but she saw no sign of the tall, dark-eyed Spaniard.

It's better this way, she told herself. Still her chest felt heavy with disappointment.

"Are you listening, Caralee?" Vincent was speaking as he led her off the dance floor. "I said I need to see you in private. There's something I want to show you."

Carly stiffened slightly against the arm he rested at her waist. Oh God, what if he proposed? "You h-have something to show me?"

"That's what I said. Meet me out in the barn in twenty minutes."

"The barn? I don't think that's a good idea, Vincent. What if someone saw us?"

"Come on, Caralee. I bet you weren't such a coward when you were tramping through the woods with the Spanish Dragon."

Carly stiffened even more. She didn't like the look that flickered in Vincent's eyes. But when she looked again, he was merely smiling. Perhaps she had only imagined it. "Why in the world does it have to be the barn? Isn't there someplace else we could go?"

"That's where the surprise is. You have to come, Caralee. I had it made especially for you. I promise you'll be pleased."

She had to admit he'd intrigued her. "All right, twenty minutes."

He grinned and squeezed her hand. "Don't keep me waiting."

Absently she nodded, but her mind had already slipped off toward the road leading into the rancho, to the carriage that had arrived while they were talking. Carly sucked in a breath at the sight of Ramon's tall figure striding along between the two elderly women who had to be his mother and aunt.

For a moment, she couldn't move. The weeks she had spent in the mountains all came rushing back as if she had never left. She could feel Ramon's mouth over hers, his kiss so hot it scorched right through her. And his hands . . . dear God, those beautiful long, brown fingers . . . the way they had kneaded her breasts, made her nipples grow hard inside her blouse. Carly swallowed as he came to a halt in front of her.

"Senorita McConnell. It is good to see you." He was dressed in his snug black *calzonevas,* the ones with the silver conchos down the side. A short, black *charro* jacket stretched across his wide shoulders, the narrow lapels embroidered in silver thread. "I do not believe you have met my mother and aunt." For their sake, he spoke to her in Spanish, smiling pleasantly, but his eyes remained locked with hers, intense in their expression, imparting a silent message. *You did as you promised. You did not break your word.*

Carly moistened her lips, which suddenly felt so dry she could barely speak. "No, we haven't met. Good evening, senoras. It is a pleasure to meet you."

His mother simply nodded. She was a robust little woman dressed in dark plum with a black fringed *rebozo* around her head and shoulders.

His aunt was taller, thinner, more frail than his mother, but her eyes were shrewd. "I am pleased to meet you, also, Senorita McConnell." She assessed Carly from head to foot, then glanced once more at Ramon, whose gaze was now carefully hooded. "Now that we have been introduced,

I remember seeing you with my nephew the day of the horse race."

Carly smiled softly. "Yes, Don Ramon was very gallant that day." She was almost afraid to look at him her heart was pounding so hard.

His aunt's keen eyes continued to assess her. Then she tilted her head toward the musicians playing at the far end of the platform. "Listen, Anna," she said to the other woman. "The music is beautiful, no?" She turned and smiled at Carly. "My nephew is an excellent dancer, just like his father, Diego, may God rest his soul. Ramon—why do you not show the senorita how a Spaniard dances the waltz?"

His fine black brows tilted into a frown. "I do not believe the senorita's uncle would find that a very good idea."

"I think it's a wonderful idea," Carly said impulsively. No matter how much it angered her uncle, she would never behave toward Ramon as she had done before.

A brow arched up, then he smiled that incredibly masculine smile she had worked so hard to forget. Her palms went damp and a trickle of perspiration seeped into the space between her breasts. Perhaps dancing with Ramon was not such a good idea after all.

He reached for her hand and brought it to his lips. "I can think of nothing I would like better, Senorita McConnell."

They left the old women beneath a red paper lantern and a bright crescent moon, and crossed to the wooden dance floor. When Ramon turned her to face him, settling a hand at her waist, it seemed to burn through the beautiful golden gown. The strains of the music rose up and he swept her along in its wake, as graceful in this as he had been astride his magnificent stallion.

He smiled down at her, the golden flecks glinting in his eyes. "So . . . I am still alive. I was not all that certain that I would be." His long sinewy legs brushed intimately between her own, sending warm little shivers racing through

her. Her fingers tingled where he clasped them, yet Ramon
seemed unaffected, every movement perfectly controlled,
his warm smile exactly in place. And he took great care to
keep the proper distance between them.

El Dragón would have scoffed at such proprieties. Carly
discovered she was slightly disappointed.

Still, when she looked up at him, she couldn't help but
smile. "You're surprised I didn't tell my uncle? I think you're
not in the least surprised. I think you knew very well that I
would not turn you in."

A smooth black brow arched up and a hint of amusement tinged his voice. "How could I possibly know?"

Carly ignored the flutter in the pit of her stomach. "I'm
not certain. Perhaps it's the number of women you've known.
Perhaps you can tell when your charm has won one of them
over."

He laughed, a mellifluous, softly rough sound. He leaned
close enough to whisper in her ear. "So it was my charm that
won your promise? Not my fiery kisses?"

A rush of heat rose into her cheeks. "You play the gentleman tonight," she teased, "but a gentleman would not remind
a lady of such a thing. Perhaps it is that Don Ramon and the
Spanish Dragon are not so different as you would like people
to believe."

Ramon's hold subtly tightened and the gold in his eyes
seemed to glow. "I assure you, Cara, in most ways we are
exactly the same." She couldn't mistake that too bold look
or the heat that blazed to life in his expression. Just as
quickly it was gone. The music ended abruptly and Ramon
released his hold on her waist.

"I hope you enjoyed the dance. I assure you that I did.
Now it is time I returned you to your friends."

She forced herself to smile. "Of course," she said, oddly
irritated by his matter-of-factness. "By now, my uncle is
certain to have discovered where I am . . . and Vincent no

doubt will be waiting." She felt a jolt of satisfaction at the scowl that darkened his face. Still, he left her in the company of some of the women and returned to his mother and aunt, standing beside the Montoyas.

Carly waited only a few more minutes, then excused herself and headed off toward the barn. She had promised Vincent she would join him, and she meant to do just that. Especially now that Ramon was dancing with the beautiful widow, Isabel Montoya.

It was dark in the shadows of the big adobe barn but moonlight shimmered in through the open windows, and Vincent had lit a lantern in one of the stalls. The smell of hay and horses drifted faintly on the cool night breeze. In the soft yellow glow of the lamp, dust motes filtered toward the hard-packed dirt floor and insects shuffled into corners.

"I was afraid you wouldn't come." He stepped closer as she approached, reaching out for her hand and pulling her toward him. The buckles on his stylish, square-toed shoes gleamed in the lamplight. His white wrapped cravat was tied in a big, puffy bow beneath his chin.

"I can't stay long," Carly said. "What is it you wanted to show me?"

He stepped back from the rough board fence that divided two of the stalls, and sitting atop the rail was the most elegant ladies' sidesaddle Carly had ever seen.

Vincent grinned appealingly. "You mentioned once before that you wanted to learn to ride. In a recent letter to my father, your uncle mentioned you'd begun your lessons. I wanted you to have the proper equipment."

She kept staring at the saddle. The leather skirt was carved in a delicate floral design, and a beige tapestry, petit-pointed in small pink roses, covered the padded seat. The saddle was exactly her size, smaller than the one she had been riding, which was an old one borrowed from one of their neighbors.

"It's beautiful, Vincent." She stepped closer, ran her fingers lovingly over the finely crafted leather. "Magnificent." She looked into his face, feeling guilty for the thoughts she'd had about him, wishing she could care for him the way her uncle wished. Her smile of pleasure faded. "Unfortunately, I can't accept it."

Vincent looked crestfallen. "You can't accept it? Why not, Caralee?"

"Because we aren't . . . because it's too expensive. I couldn't possibly—"

Vincent drew her against him. "Don't you understand, Caralee? I want you for my wife. The saddle is only the beginning. I intend to buy you jewels, clothes, everything your heart desires. I'll make you the talk of San Francisco—the queen of the city."

Inwardly Carly winced. No mention of love, nothing of feelings he might hold for her. All he ever thought of was money. He wanted her because of the way she looked, the clothes she wore, and the social graces her fancy schooling provided. He didn't care a thing about the woman she was inside. He didn't even know her.

"I can't marry you, Vincent. The truth is I don't love you. I want to marry a man I love."

He gripped her shoulders, strands of sandy hair falling over his brow. "I don't expect you to love me . . . not in the beginning. Our affection for each other will grow in time. What matters most is that we're so well suited."

"We aren't well suited, Vincent. You're nothing at all like me. I don't want to hurt your feelings, but I can't accept your gift—and I can't marry you."

The warmth slid away from his features, making him look older than he usually did. In the light of the lamp, there was an odd set to his jaw and his lips appeared grayish and thin. "Your uncle said you wouldn't agree. But the fact is, Caralee, you're going to be my wife." He looked so determined for a moment she wanted to laugh. There was no way she would ever marry Vincent.

"I have to get back to our guests. I've been gone too long already." She turned away from him, but he caught her wrist and dragged her into his arms.

"You can't leave yet, Caralee."

"Let go of me, Vincent. My uncle—"

"In time you'll understand this has happened for the best. Someday you'll even thank me for it." A clumsy kiss followed. She tried to break his hold, but his arms were like vises around her. His wet tongue slid across her lips, and a wave of fury broke over her. Damn him! Who the devil did he think he was? She kicked him hard in the shins, eliciting a yelp of pain, but he didn't let her go. Instead, he covered her mouth with his hand and forced her backward onto a thick pile of straw.

"I'll try to be gentle," he said, beginning to fumble with his clothes. "I promise it'll be better the next time."

The next time? Rage swept through her. He meant to force her, to take her virginity and *make* her marry him. The length he was willing to go to get his way told her exactly the kind of man he was. She tried to cry for help, but he was stronger than he looked, and he pinned her easily with his body.

His hands shook as he fondled her breasts, and a fresh wave of anger blazed through her. She struggled against him, scattering the pins from her hair and tumbling it down around her shoulders, then succeeded in whacking him squarely in the chin. Vincent swore foully. The gown made a ripping sound. She realized he was shoving up her skirts, once more groping at the front of his breeches. Anger made her strong. She fought against his heavy weight—and then it was gone, lifted off her as easily as if he were a child instead of a full-grown man.

Ramon de la Guerra stood a few yards away, his long

legs splayed, his hands balled into fists. Vincent Bannister sprawled in the hay at his feet.

"Stay out of this, de la Guerra." He sat up to face Ramon. "This is none of your business."

"Perhaps I am making it my business."

Carly could have hugged him. Vincent rolled to his feet and came at Ramon with more strength than she would have guessed. Vincent took the first blow, but Ramon took the second. They tied up and started swinging again, but torch light streaming in through the windows stayed the battle.

Her uncle strode into the barn, followed by Sam Hollister and his wife, Amanda, George Winston, Royce Wardell, and what appeared to be nearly half the guests from the *fandango,* including Vincent's father.

Dear God! Carly clutched her ruined clothes, her face going hot with embarrassment. With a shaky hand, she plucked at the stems of straw in her tumbled down hair. God in heaven, what would they think? Vincent straightened to face her uncle, feigning a look of contrition, while Ramon remained in the shadows.

"What is the meaning of this? What's going on here, Vincent?" Torch light lit her uncle's stout features. She'd expected to see outrage. Instead he appeared oddly calm.

"You have my most sincere apologies, Mr. Austin. Caralee is not in the least to blame. I invited her out here to give her a gift, which only arrived just this morning." He smiled charmingly, almost boyishly. Carly wanted to kick him. "She looked so beautiful, I simply lost my head."

Her uncle merely frowned. "These things happen among young people your age. You understand the consequences, of course."

Carly's mind spun. *These things happen?* Surely she hadn't heard Uncle Fletcher correctly. Then she saw it. The gleam of triumph in his cool green eyes she could not possibly mistake. Carly's gaze swung to Vincent, who also looked slightly triumphant. She stared at them both in growing horror. They had planned this from the start! Vincent had meant for them to be caught, perhaps in the embarrassing act itself.

Her face flamed even brighter, and her anger swelled until she could barely breathe. *How could they?* Frantic at what was to come, she searched out Ramon, saw his hard dark features outlined in the glow of the lamp. She could tell by his expression he realized what was happening just as she did. There was anger in the sharp planes of his face, pity in his eyes, and something else she could not name.

There would be no help from him, she realized dully. Ramon had left her to her fate and she had no choice but to accept it.

Well, she wasn't going to do it!

One of the women said something. Carly's eyes strayed toward Amanda Hollister and the other ladies in the crowd. If she didn't marry Vincent, they would no longer welcome her among them. She'd be an outcast, an embarrassment to her neighbors and the few friends she had only begun to make. Fury at her uncle swept over her, making her hands begin to shake. It was followed by a wave of defeat. Her shoulders sagged and her stomach twisted.

Good Lord, was there nothing she could do?

Vincent was speaking expansively, begging her uncle's forgiveness, asking for her hand, and insuring him he would make a good husband. They could be married, he said, before his return to the city.

Carly felt sick at the thought. She glanced again at Ramon, who stood so stoically silent, and the means of her salvation struck her like the answer to a prayer.

It was so simple, so obvious she felt giddy, lightheaded with relief. Her mind churned, fleshing the notion out, looking for pitfalls. It wasn't perfect, she admitted, but she had no other choice. And the lesson it would teach her uncle would be worth it. She could hardly wait to see his face.

Carly bit her lip against a wild impulse to giggle. Ramon would be furious, but once they were alone, she could explain things, make him understand.

She took a step toward the crowd and conjured her sweetest smile. "This has gone far enough, Vincent. You've been more than kind, in fact you've been incredibly chivalrous, but I just can't let you do it."

"What? What are you talking about?" He looked at her as if she had lost her mind. In truth she had just regained her wits in the nick of time.

"I'm thanking you, Vincent, for trying to be noble. I know you want to help me and I appreciate it more than I can say, but I see no reason for you to accept the blame for something that you didn't do."

The crowd made an audible gasp. Carly turned and stared directly at Ramon. "And since that is the case, and Senor de la Guerra is an equally honorable man, I'm certain he is also equally willing to do the right thing." Her smile held determination, a look that said he owed her this, and a silent reminder that she held his life in her hands. "Isn't that so, Don Ramon?"

For a moment he said nothing, just stared at her as if he couldn't believe what she had just done. But Carly felt certain he would speak up soon enough. The man was El Dragón. Caralee McConnell knew it. The Spaniard had no choice.

He stepped out of the shadows and into the light of the torches. His features looked harsh and grim, the skin stretched taut over his high cheekbones. "I apologize to the senorita for the liberties I have taken." A cold, unrepentant smile curved his lips. "And of course to you, Senor Austin. It is my fondest wish to make your niece my wife."

"W-why that's absurd!" Her uncle surged forward like an angry bear. "There is no way I could possibly allow my niece to marry—"

"I'm sorry we've displeased you, Uncle," Carly interrupted, "but as you said, these things happen among young people our age." He had succeeded in forcing her to marry— there was no way around it. But Ramon was by far the better choice. At least he would be, once he understood her intentions.

The don worked a muscle in his lean hard cheek. "There is, of course, the problem of our different religions." A last possible means of escape. His eyes were dark with warning. *End this foolishness now,* they said. *Before it is too late.*

This time it was Carly whose smile was triumphant. "My father was Irish. I was raised in the Catholic faith." True, she hadn't been to church since she'd arrived in California, but that didn't alter the fact that her religion was the same as Ramon's. "The priest will not object to the marriage."

"Say something, Vincent. Speak up, my boy."

"What—what are you trying to do, Caralee? How can you possibly marry this—"

"The marriage will take place on Sunday," Ramon put in coldly, his tall, hard body radiating with barely leashed fury. "Under the circumstances, I am sure Padre Xavier will waive the bans." By now the Montoyas had arrived. They were wealthy and powerful, one of the last few Californio families in a strong position of influence. Her uncle sagged at the sight of them, knowing he couldn't refuse Ramon's proposal without also insulting them.

Carly knew she had won.

"I will speak to the priest tomorrow," the don said curtly, his dark eyes still glinting with fire and a promise of retribution that sent shivers down Carly's spine. She hadn't seen that look since the morning after the raid when she'd awakened to the sight of his tall, black boots. She brushed the unsettling notion away. Once she explained, Ramon would understand.

"Caralee?" Vincent turned pleading hazel eyes in her direction, their depths still clouded with disbelief. "Are you really going to marry this—"

"I'm afraid so, Vincent." She smiled at him even more sweetly. "After all, it's the only decent thing to do."

*C*hapter *T*welve

*H*ad it only been three days? It seemed like a lifetime—and it seemed only minutes. Uncle Fletcher had ranted and raved and forbidden her to leave the house, but Carly hadn't relented. Vincent and his father had returned to San Francisco, the younger Bannister even more furious than Ramon had been.

Everyone was mad at her, but Carly didn't care.

Once again she was fighting for her life.

She glanced out her bedroom window. Flat, gray clouds threatened rain, and a stiff wind whipped through the heavy branches of the towering oak trees surrounding the house. Absently she wondered when the storm would arrive and whether it would slow their morning's journey.

They were leaving within the hour, traveling into town, meeting Ramon this afternoon at the mission. Today she would be married.

Well, sort of married.

Standing in front of the cheval glass mirror, Carly surveyed her image. She had chosen a gown of pearl gray silk, high-necked and long-sleeved with tiny tucks down the front, and a row of small pearl buttons. There were bands of magenta around the skirt, and the waist-length matching cape was lined with magenta silk.

She loved this dress. It was simple yet beautiful. She felt good when she wore it and she needed to feel good today. She needed all the confidence she could get.

Carly shivered, but she wasn't cold.

She had hoped to speak to Ramon before the day of the wedding. She was sure he would help her, once he understood it would only be a marriage of convenience. And only for a few short months.

Unfortunately, her uncle had forbidden her to see him. Now she would have to face those furious dark eyes, try not to wither at the hard set of his jaw. He wanted a wife of pure Spanish blood, not some poor half-Irish mongrel from a Pennsylvania mine patch. Ramon would believe she had trapped him into an unwanted marriage, and on the surface it was true.

"You are ready, Senorita McConnell?" Candelaria stood by the door.

"Almost. I just have to put on my bonnet." She scooped it off of the bed, but the younger girl caught her arm.

"Perhaps instead you will wear this." She held up a beautiful white lace *mantilla*. "It was my mother's. I would like you to have it. And I believe it would please Don Ramon."

Carly's fingers closed over the fine Spanish lace and a hard lump swelled in her throat. At least she had made one friend. "It's beautiful, Candelaria. I'd love to wear it." Her uncle wouldn't like it, but perhaps Ramon would approve.

Or perhaps it would only remind him of the true Spanish woman he wished to wed.

A painful knot tightened inside her, a foolish sort of ache she shouldn't have felt. It settled in her stomach, brought an ache to her chest. Carly forced herself to ignore it. She had done what she had to. In time Ramon would be free to marry whatever woman he might wish.

She forced herself to smile and raised the *mantilla* above her head.

"Here . . . you will also need this." The younger girl held out a tall, carved tortoiseshell comb. "You can return it to me later." Staking the comb into Carly's hair, she draped the beautiful lace over Carly's head and shoulders, then stepped back to survey her work and flashed a satisfied smile.

"Now you look like a Californio bride."

"Thank you, Candelaria. It's a beautiful wedding present." Swallowing past the ache in her throat, Carly left the bedroom and walked down the hall to the huge high-ceilinged room where her uncle stood waiting.

He took in her appearance and clamped hard on his jaw. "I see you're already learning the part."

Carly ignored his sarcastic jibe. "I know I've displeased you, Uncle. But perhaps in time you'll understand why I had to do what I did." Already she had forgiven him. He was trying to do what he thought best. In time, maybe he would come to understand why she couldn't marry Vincent. Maybe when this was over, he would even welcome her home. Carly hoped so. Her uncle was her only family now.

Still, if he didn't want her, she would find some way to survive on her own.

The drive into town was tensely silent. It was late in the afternoon, a yellow sun hovering above the red tile roofs, when they arrived in San Juan Bautista, a bustling little village nestled at the base of the Gabilan Mountains. Rolling golden hills beneath massive spreading oaks peered down on the city, which began as a mission site then grew with the discovery of gold. The initial boom was past, but along with its Californio inhabitants, a small influx of settlers continued to roll into the town. Still, it retained its

Spanish appearance, mostly adobe-walled structures, some so old they continued to sport hide-covered windows.

The streets were crowded: a freight wagon hauling ore from the recently discovered New Idria quicksilver mine, a Wells, Fargo & Co. stage just boarding in front of the fancy new Plaza Hotel, a broken-down *carreta* drawn by a sleepy-eyed oxen, the dark-skinned driver burning the animal's ears with Spanish curses.

The mission sat on an open grassy plaza surrounded by graceful olive trees and colorful blooming flowers. It formed the hub of the city and was the center of most of its activities. The church was built in 1797, the largest of the California missions, Carly learned as Padre Xavier showed them around. The main building stood two stories high with a long arched wing built off to the side. It was fashioned of whitewashed adobe, the impressive interior lined with wooden pews and arching columns, and painted throughout in amazingly brilliant colors: blues, reds, purples, yellows, and greens. Huge wrought-iron chandeliers hung from the ceiling, their dozens of candles illuminating the room with a golden glow.

Carly smiled at the stout little priest who gave them the tour of the church. He was balding but his work-hardened hands looked as strong as his muscled forearms, and his stomach appeared flat beneath his dark brown robes.

"Ramon tells me you are Catholic," the priest said. "How is it we have not seen you here in church?"

Carly nervously chewed her lip. "I'm sorry, Father, but I haven't been in California all that long, and as you know, my uncle is not of the faith." She tried to concentrate on what the priest was saying, but her eyes kept straying toward the door in search of Ramon. It was past the time set for the wedding. Perhaps he would not come.

Carly's stomach tightened. She would be disgraced, her uncle horribly embarrassed—not that he didn't deserve it.

Still, she had believed Ramon would come, if for no other reason than to insure she would not betray his secret.

Then again, if he didn't appear, she couldn't really blame him. And the truth was she would never turn him in just because he wouldn't help her.

Time ticked past. The priest shuffled nervously, and her uncle cleared his throat. The men were worried, too.

Another ten minutes passed. Her palms grew damp and her heart thudded uncomfortably against her ribs. He had guessed her threat wasn't real. Ramon was not going to come.

Carly stared at the door, fighting an urge to cry. She should be angry her plan had failed, but the heaviness in her heart felt more like disappointment.

"Well, Caralee, are you satisfied?" Her uncle's hard gaze burned right through her. "It's obvious de la Guerra isn't going to show. You've ruined your reputation, ruined your chances with Vincent, and now you'll be the laughingstock of the county."

Carly swallowed past the lump in her throat. She didn't bother to remind him that *he* was the one who had ruined her reputation. She merely had gambled to win a life of her own—unfortunately, she had lost. She'd foolishly believed she could save her reputation and not have to marry Vincent. But the plan had failed. Ramon had seen to that.

She tried to smile, but her bottom lip trembled. "Perhaps it's time we went back home," she said softly.

Her uncle merely nodded. His face was as red as the alcoves of the saints behind the altar at the end of the church.

"I am sorry," the padre said. "Perhaps something unforeseen has happened. It is not like Don Ramon to break his word."

Carly clung to the excuse, then let it slip away. He hadn't actually broken his word; he had never really promised he would come. They started up the aisle toward the huge carved wooden doors at the entrance, but just as they arrived, the heavy doors began to creak open.

When Ramon walked in, Carly's heartbeat seemed to stop. She noticed his snug black *calzonevas,* but there were no festive decorations down the side. A simple full-sleeved white shirt and a pair of high black boots—the occasion, his garments said, wasn't one of celebration.

A painful jolt ran through her, but she simply lifted her chin. His eyes were hard as he waited for his mother and aunt, who walked in seconds later with Pedro Sanchez. Ramon's gaze scanned her briefly, taking in her elegant pearl gray gown and the white lace mantilla that covered her head. Something flickered in the cool brown depths then it was gone.

"I am sorry I am late . . . *mi amor.*" A thin smile curved his lips. "I hope you were not inconvenienced." But there was nothing of regret in his dark features. He had been late on purpose. He meant to punish her for forcing the marriage. How could she have forgotten that this too was a side of Ramon?

"You've made your point, de la Guerra." Uncle Fletcher met his hard gaze squarely. "Is there going to be a wedding or not?"

A slight nod of his head. "But of course. That is why we are here, is it not?"

Carly said nothing as he reached out and took her hand, his grip as hard as his eyes and totally unrelenting.

"I-I was hoping I might speak to you first," Carly said. "There are things I need to explain."

"There will be time for talk later. We have kept the priest waiting long enough."

Carly didn't mention it was he who had been late. Gauging the black mood he was in, she thought it best to say nothing at all.

The ceremony was a brief one, not the High Mass spoken at the altar, an act of celebration in front of friends and family as Ramon would have wanted if his bride had been a woman of his choosing.

For the first time since all this had happened, a niggle of guilt crept down her spine. She hadn't been fair to Ramon. Then again, he hadn't been fair to her the night of the raid, when he had dragged her off on his horse and forced her to march through the mountains.

Carly straightened her spine. To hell with Ramon. In the end things would work out. In the meantime, she would just ignore him.

Staring straight ahead, she let him take her hand, heard his soft vows of marriage, repeated the words herself. He slid something onto her finger. She looked down to see a heavy gold ring, blood red stones surrounding the de la Guerra crest. Then all too soon the ceremony ended.

"In the name of the Father, the Son, and the Holy Ghost," the priest said, "I pronounce that you are man and wife. You may kiss your bride, Don Ramon."

A cynical smile curled his lips. He pulled her hard against him and covered her mouth with a hot, steamy kiss. Carly gasped at the cruel invasion of his tongue, at the anger that shuddered through his tall lean body.

Dear God, he was madder than she thought. He released her so suddenly she had to grip his shoulders to keep herself from falling. "Ramon, please, if we could only have a moment to speak."

Hard brown eyes bored into her. "The afternoon grows late. A storm threatens and it will be dark before we reach home. There will be time to talk once we arrive at Las Almas."

"But—"

Taking her arm, he thanked the priest for his service, dropped some coins into the offering box, and started down the aisle toward the wide double doors, Carly running along beside him. Pedro Sanchez followed in their wake, escorting the two older women, his craggy face creased with lines of worry.

Her uncle strode along at the rear, exiting the doors and coming to a stop when he reached Ramon's carriage. He took her hand and gave it a surprisingly gentle squeeze.

"Good-bye, my dear." He stared at the stone-faced don. "I hope to God you know what you're doing."

So did she. Dear Lord, she hadn't counted on any of this. "I-I'll be fine." Impulsively, she reached over and hugged him. "I'm sorry it turned out this way."

He faltered a moment at the unexpected gesture. "My fault," he muttered gruffly. "Damn, but I wish you had let me guide you in this."

Carly just nodded. Right now she wished she had. Even marriage to Vincent seemed preferable to the Spaniard's mounting fury.

She glanced in his direction, watched him help his aging mother and aunt climb aboard the once-grand carriage. Now a faded, weathered black, its red leather seats were spider-webbed with cracks of age and the floorboards creaked beneath the old women's weight. Standing a few feet away, Pedro Sanchez came toward her, holding his hat in his hands.

"I wish only the best for you," he said gravely.

"He's so angry, Pedro. If he would just let me explain—"

His callused hand came up to her cheek. "You have suffered his temper before, *pequeña*. You should not have done this thing." He looked over at Ramon, took in his angry features and released a weary breath. "Then again, perhaps God has had a hand in this and in the end, it will all turn out as He has planned."

"It isn't as it seems, Pedro. If he would only listen."

The old vaquero just nodded. "In time, his temper will

cool. You will have your chance to explain." But he didn't really look as if it would matter.

Carly felt a churning in her stomach. She had underestimated Ramon when she had first met him. She prayed she hadn't done it again.

The women spoke little on the ride back to Rancho Las Almas, just a cursory welcome to the family and best wishes on her marriage. Ramon spoke not at all. Pedro rode beside them on his high-spirited dapple gray stallion. By the time they reached Ramon's small rancho, a light rain pattered on the roof of the carriage, and darkness hid the burgeoning clouds. Still there was enough light to see it, nestled in a grove of sycamores, a bubbling, willow-lined creek meandering off to one side. The buildings were mostly of adobe: a barn, an outdoor kitchen, a smoke house, and several sturdy corrals.

"I hope you are not disappointed," Ramon said coolly, reaching up to lift her down. "There are only five hundred acres—not the twenty thousand of Rancho del Robles. But I suppose in time you will get used to it."

"It's lovely here, Ramon." Unwilling to endure his condemning expression, she glanced away from him toward the two old women who had made no move to leave the carriage.

"Pedro will take care of them," he said. The aging vaquero had dismounted from the stallion and tied his horse behind the carriage. As Sanchez took his place in the driver's seat, Ramon's lips parted in a chilling half smile.

"My mother and aunt will be staying with friends for the next few days . . . so the newly married couple can get to know each other."

A queasy ripple slid into Carly's stomach. This had gone far enough. Beyond far enough. "We have to talk, Ramon. This won't wait a moment longer."

A sleek black brow arched up, followed by a slight curl of his lips. "As you wish . . . *mi amor.*"

"And damnit, Ramon, please stop calling me that!"

For the first time his look held something other than fury, then it was gone. "Come. We will speak inside the house."

Thank God. Her limbs went weak with relief. At last they could talk things over, straighten things out. She let him lead her inside the small adobe dwelling, which was warmed by a fire and lit with soft oil lamps. The smell of burning cedar drifted toward them from the hearth, and a light repast of bread, cold meats, and cheeses sat beside a flagon of wine on the table in front of the sofa.

Ramon closed the door, which shut with a thud of finality that set Carly's nerves on edge even more. The minute he turned to face her, she started talking, the words tumbling out as fast as she could force them past her lips.

"I know you're angry, Ramon, and I don't blame you. I-I had hoped we could talk about this the night of the *fandango,* but unfortunately we didn't get the chance. I'm sorry for what has occurred, but I had to do what I did. I wasn't about to marry that . . . that peabrain, Vincent Bannister—I don't care how much money his family has. And after what he did to me in the barn, I had to marry someone. Surely you can see that. I would have been ruined. This way—in time—it will all be forgotten. We can get an annulment and you can marry whomever you wish. My reputation will of course be somewhat tarnished, but it won't be completely destroyed. I'm hoping my uncle will take me back, that by then he'll have realized he can't force me to do his bidding. If I can't go back to del Robles, then I'll do something else. I can go to San Francisco. There's bound to be some sort of work there, even for a woman." She glanced up, her face blushing a bit. "Respectable work, I mean. I'm very resilient. I can take care of myself. I've done it—"

She broke off then. She had almost told him she had taken in laundry in the mine patch. Good heavens, she couldn't possibly tell him *that.*

"You are finished?"

"Yes . . . well, I suppose I am. Except to tell you how sorry I am to involve you in all of this and to say that I really appreciate your help . . . grudgingly given as it may be."

"Now you are finished?"

Why was he still so angry? "You understand what it is I'm trying to say?"

A subtle turbulence moved across his features, shifted in the depths of his eyes. "You are saying you do not mean to honor the marriage. That this was only a means to rid yourself of Bannister."

"Of course. I'll be free of Vincent and in time, you'll be free of me. I'll go back to my uncle, or get a job in the—"

He gripped her shoulders and jerked her against his chest. "I think it is you who does not understand."

"What . . . what are talking about?"

"You have had your say, now I will have mine. What *I* am telling *you* is that we are married. I have taken you for my wife in front of God and a priest. I have given my solemn word and I do not mean to break it. And neither . . . *querida* . . . will you."

For the longest time, Carly just stared at him. "You—you can't be serious. We have to get an annulment. You don't want to marry me. You want a Spanish wife. You want your children to be Spanish. You've taken a vow, promised your family and friends."

A corner of his mouth curved up, but his smile was far from pleasant. "*Si, chica.* I believe I made that clear."

"Then why can't we simply—"

"I have told you why. Because we have spoken the vows. Because we have pledged ourselves before the sacred altar in the church."

"But—"

His face grew harder still, cutting off her words. "Our

bedroom is there." He pointed out to the patio to a heavy oaken door opening off the central courtyard. "Go. Make yourself ready. Prepare yourself to accept your husband."

Carly's mouth went dry. She stared into Ramon's dark features. "You can't mean to . . . you can't possibly expect me to—to—"

"I expect you to do exactly what you have pledged to do in the Holy Mother church. Now go!"

Carly bit hard on her trembling lip, a cry of stark terror lodged in her throat. This wasn't Ramon. This was the cruel, ruthless man she had known on her journey through the mountains. This man was the Spanish Dragon.

It took every ounce of her courage to lift her head and walk from the room with at least a semblance of dignity. Moving as if her legs were made of wood, she headed out the door leading onto the courtyard, then turned down the covered hallway that lead to the door Ramon had shown her.

Lifting the heavy wrought-iron latch with trembling hands, she swung it open and stepped into the lamp-lit interior. The room was small and neat and reminded her a little of Ramon's room in the simple adobe cabin in the mountains, except the furniture was finer, dark carved pieces from Spain. There was very little of it, just a heavy bureau with a mirror on top, a large carved armoire, a night stand, and an overstuffed horsehair-covered chair.

A pair of boots, fashioned of fine black leather, sat neatly beside the bed, silver spurs with big Spanish rowels strapped to the heels. One of his flat-crowned, wide-brimmed hats hung on the back of the door by a long, finely braided length of leather.

Carly moved farther into the room toward the bed, her heart thudding dully. A beautiful white silk nightgown, embroidered with snowy white flowers across the yoke, had been carefully laid atop the quilt, among the fragrant pink petals of a rose. Seeing it made her stomach tighten, and suddenly she felt dizzy. Dear God, everyone believed this marriage was real!

Ramon believed it. That was the reason he was so angry. He didn't want her for his wife, yet she had forced him to wed her, heedless of his feelings, thinking only of herself. She had thought he would understand, that he would be willing to help her.

Instead of a dandy like Vincent, she had a husband who despised her for ruining his life.

Carly pressed a hand against her lips to hold back her tears but the ache of them scalded her throat. She wouldn't cry, she wouldn't! She hadn't broken down when he had marched her through the mountains, she wouldn't allow herself to do it now. But dear Lord, she was frightened.

She remembered his cruelty the night of the raid, how cold and heartless he once was. She knew little of what occurred between a man and a woman—she was terrified to think what Ramon might do to her in his anger.

She lifted the beautiful white silk nightgown with trembling fingers, felt the coolness of the fabric as it slid through her hands. Then a faint knock sounded, jerking her attention in that direction. It was a timid knock, she realized, definitely not Ramon.

Forcing her feet to move, she crossed the room, and pulled open the heavy wooden door. A small, slightly bent Indian woman stood in the opening. She smiled, creasing her weathered face as she walked in.

"*Buenas noches,* Senora de la Guerra. My name is Blue Blanket. Don Ramon sent me to help you prepare for bed."

Just the word *bed* made the heat roar into her cheeks. Her insides knotted and her palms went damp. She pressed them against her gray silk skirt to keep them from shaking so badly. Fighting a sudden urge to flee, she glanced toward the window. Running would be futile; she had no money and no place to go. She wouldn't even know how to get there if she did. Besides, she had brought this on herself, set this whole crazy plan into motion. There was no hope for it now but to face what she had done.

"Thank you, Blue Blanket," she said softly.

"You may call me Blue. That will be enough."

Sick with dread, her body taut with nerves, Carly let the woman unfasten the row of buttons down the back of her pearl gray day dress. Blue helped her out of it and out of her layers of petticoats, then untied and removed her corset. At the woman's gentle urging, she pulled off her chemise and stepped out of her pantalets, then stood stiffly as the stoop-shouldered old Indian slid the white silk gown over her head. Blue took down Carly's hair and carefully ran a bristle brush through it, then the old woman's mouth pulled into a smile that showed gums full of missing teeth.

"I will tell Don Ramon that you are ready." Backing away, she silently slipped from the room, leaving Carly alone in the silence that rang louder than a death knell.

Ramon lifted his heavy crystal snifter, a family heirloom brought to the New World from Spain, tilted his head back, and drained the last of his brandy. Fury still pumped through him, as it had for the last three days.

He couldn't believe he was married. That he had been trapped like a naive schoolboy. Mostly he couldn't believe that the woman who had done it was Caralee McConnell, Fletcher Austin's niece. Worse yet, she was a *gringa*.

He felt like wringing her soft white neck.

His smile felt cold and bitter. At least she would finally warm his bed. He meant to take her as he had wanted to since the moment he had met her, hard and deep, pounding into her until his lust was sated. His loins swelled to think of it. His arousal pulsed stiffly against the front of his breeches, his blood pumping, growing thick and heavy, pooling low in his belly.

Carly had forced this marriage. She had meant to use him to save herself. Well now she was his wife, and he would be the one who used her.

He set the snifter down on the table, hardly aware of the driving rain that had begun to fall, and jerked open the door leading out to the patio. A cold wind knifed through his clothes, but he was too angry, his body too aroused to feel it. He didn't knock when he reached his room, just lifted the wrought-iron latch and jerked open the heavy oak door.

She was standing beside the bed, wearing the white silk nightgown his aunt had fashioned as a wedding gift. Her hair was down, gleaming like burnished copper in the light of the lamp on the dresser. A faint tremor rolled through her as he stepped through the door, and her big green eyes swung up to his face.

She looked so beautiful his breath caught, seemed to freeze inside his chest. Something warm slid through him, softening the barrier around his heart. He had seen the white silk gown when his aunt had sewn it. He knew it was exquisite, but he couldn't have imagined how beautiful Carly would look when she wore it. He couldn't have guessed the way her hair would shimmer across her shoulders, how the white of the gown would illuminate the paleness of her skin and the emerald of her eyes.

He couldn't have known the way her soft ruby lips would tremble with uncertainty, even though she kept her chin held high.

An odd pain rippled through him, a tightness that expanded and made his throat feel dry. He didn't like the feeling, didn't like the fact that just looking at Caralee could affect him in such a manner.

He forced his gaze downward, over her womanly curves.

He paused at the dark aureoles at the tips of her breasts and the swelling in his groin began to throb. He assessed her tiny waist, the shadowy triangle of down between her legs, and the throbbing grew more intense, the blood pulsing thickly through his veins.

"I see that you have accepted what is to be. That is good." She said nothing as he unbuttoned his shirt and stripped it off, nothing as he sat down on the chair and pulled off his boots. The rain thrummed hard on the red tile roof, but it seemed no louder than the pounding of his heart.

He came to his feet and started on the buttons down his fly.

"Ramon?"

His fingers stilled. Just the echo of his name on her lips sent desire blazing through him. It was stoked by the heat of his anger . . . and his unwanted emotions.

"The time for talking is past." He popped the final button at the front of his breeches but didn't take them off, just crossed to the place before her. "It is not words I now wish to hear, but the sound of your small woman's cries as I drive myself inside you."

A soft sob rose in her throat. It sounded so fearful, so totally out of character, his gaze swung up to her face. Her bottom lip quivered and her eyes were glazed with tears.

"I'm sorry, Ramon. I wish I could change what has happened."

"I told you, I do not wish—"

"I know how angry you are . . . and that the fault is mine." She blinked and the wetness began to roll down her cheeks. He remembered how much she hated to cry. "I have suffered your anger," she said softly, the sadness in her eyes touching him as nothing else could. "I have also known your gentleness. I beg you, Ramon. Show me that gentleness now."

His heart squeezed, clenched inside his chest. One moment the anger was there, fighting to break free, threatening to overwhelm him, the next it was gone. In its place were all the feelings he felt for her he had forced himself to ignore. His hand began to tremble as he wiped the tears from her cheeks. Her skin felt like silk beneath his fingers.

"Do not cry, *querida*." He pressed his lips against her temple, felt the faint tremors running through her. "Even should I wish it, I could not hurt you again."

"I'm sorry, Ramon. So sorry."

He tilted her chin with his fingers, stared into those sorrowful eyes, bent his head and brushed her lips with a kiss. "I am the one who should be sorry. We have all of us made mistakes. I am the last one who should forget it." He cupped her cheek in his hand, stroked his thumb gently along her jaw. Leaning forward, he captured her mouth, tasted the soft lips quivering under his.

"Do not be frightened," he whispered, his fingers gently coaxing, easing away her fears. "I have wanted you since the first moment I saw you. Now you are my wife. You must trust me in this as you trusted me once before."

Carly stared at him, swallowing back the tears. There was tenderness in his expression and something more, something that made her heart expand inside her. She reached for him, slid her arms around his neck.

"I do trust you." This was her Ramon. The man who had saved her life. He had returned to her and she was no longer afraid.

Lightning flashed outside the window as his mouth skimmed over her cheek and along her throat, his lips insistent and so incredibly warm. His tongue flicked over her skin, making it tingle, and her body seemed to melt into his tall hard frame. Through the sheer white silk gown, his bare chest pressed against her breasts and her nipples strained toward the heat of his skin.

He took her lips in a ravaging kiss that sent spirals of heat lancing through her. His tongue swept into her mouth while his hands slid inside her gown to cradle a breast. He teased the nipple with his finger, plucked it into a hard, taut bud, and a tide of fire blazed through her. Unconsciously, she leaned toward him, her hand moving down his shoulders, irresistibly drawn to the curly black hair on his chest. It felt soft and springy, seductive against her skin. She traced a pattern in it, felt the thick bands of muscle bunching at her touch, and heard him groan.

He kissed her again as he slid the gown from her shoulders, leaving her naked, the white silk pooling around her feet. He paused for a moment, drawing back to look at her, standing naked before him.

"So beautiful," he said gruffly. "But then I always knew that you were."

Outside the window, the wind whipped through the trees, and the sky opened up, the rain coming down in a thunderous roar. His fingers encircled her waist, pulling her against him, letting her feel the hard ridge of his need. His mouth ravaged hers, his lips hard-soft and burning with heat, his tongue thrusting deeply, rhythmically, igniting sparks of flame that licked through her body. He slanted his lips over hers, kissing her fiercely, the hand on her breast molding it gently, making it tighten and swell.

Lightning flashed and thunder roared, as if he were the one to command it. She gripped his shoulders, ran her hands along the muscles across his back. She felt the heavy cords tighten, move sinuously beneath his skin. His hands skimmed over her flesh, ringed her navel, then spread over the flat spot below. Long slim fingers laced through the burnished hair at the juncture of her thighs, eased her legs apart and slipped inside.

Carly moaned.

"Easy, Cara." He brushed her mouth with a fiery kiss.

Moving his finger in and out, he nudged the swollen bud in the folds of her sex, sending hot damp shivers along her spine. She moaned and arched upward against his hand.

"You like this, no?"

"Y-Yes." She should have been embarrassed, but all she could think of were the sweetly burning sensations, the pleasure sweeping through her, and the deep plunging rhythm of his hand. Then he was lifting her up, resting her in the center of his bed, pausing only long enough to strip off his breeches. She could hear the howl of the wind, feel the coolness of the petals on the mattress beneath her, pressing against the hotness of her skin.

Trembling all over, she watched in fascination as he joined her on the bed, all sleek muscle and smooth, dark skin. Below his navel, a thick, hard ridge rose up against his flat belly. She had seen men naked when she had helped to nurse them in the mine patch, but they had looked nothing like this.

"Ramon?"

The windows shuddered against a rush of wind. He angled his body over hers, took her mouth in a savage kiss. He nibbled the side of her neck, gently sucked on the lobe of her ear. *"Si, querida?"*

"You're so . . . big."

A soft chuckle came from his throat. "All men are this way, Cara, when they are making love."

"All of them? All of them are so big?"

Another soft chuckle. "Well, perhaps not quite so big. But we will fit together . . . you will see."

Fit together? She wasn't exactly sure what he meant. For the first time it occurred to her exactly how little she knew of such things. "How will you—how will we . . . ?"

"Hush, *querida*. No more talking. I will show you how it is done."

His hand stroked over her breast, making the hard bud

throb and quiver. Then his lips followed his hand, taking her nipple into his mouth, and Carly forgot her uncertainties, thought of nothing but the flames shooting through her body. Heat skittered over her flesh, seared through her veins, sent a wave of dampness into her core.

Ramon's long fingers were stroking her again, sliding deep inside her, making her arch up off the bed. Lightning speared across the sky; the crack of thunder shook the room, and the lamp beside the bed flickered and dimmed. Carly whimpered softly, began to toss her head. Ramon's mouth seared her lips, his hands scorched her flesh, making her burn out of control. He cradled a breast, laved it with his tongue, bit gently on the nipple, and a hot flood of desire washed over her.

"Ramon . . ." she whispered, trashing wildly, dragging a hand through his hair. It felt like black satin against her skin.

A second long finger slid in, stretching her, gently preparing her, sending shivers of heat running through her. Tiny ripples of flame licked over her flesh and she squirmed on the bed, her body silently pleading for something she could not name.

Then he was looming above her, easing her legs apart with his knee, stroking her even more deeply. Her body shuddered, tightened, drew into a hard, hot coil that begged to be sprung.

His fingers slid away, replaced by his long, hard shaft. Then he was easing himself inside, stretching her, filling her with his thick, heavy length.

Dear God, she couldn't have imagined . . .

For a moment he paused, his breathing fast and ragged, then he bent his head and took her mouth in a deep, tongue-thrusting kiss. Carly arched upward at the same moment Ramon drove forward. Something tore loose, she gasped at the pain that shot through her, and Ramon's whole body went still.

"I am sorry, Cara. In a moment your first time will be over."

She could feel his powerful muscles straining, shaking with his effort at control. "But I don't want it to be over. I want . . ."

A corner of his sensuous mouth curved up. "*Si,* I know what you want, Cara. I was worried that I might have hurt you." He started to move very slowly. "Let us see if I can give you what you want." His hardness slid in, then gently eased out, rubbing against the part of her that he had touched before. He started moving faster, thrusting deeper, setting up a rhythm that made her trembling grow more fierce. The small house shuddered with a heavy gust of wind, the storm's fury building like the fires that raged inside her. The driving rhythm increased, his narrow buttocks flexing, forcing him deeper, pounding faster and harder, matching the tempest outside.

The tightness sprang to life, the coil of tension that had been there before, knotting low in her belly. Her nails dug into the muscles across his shoulders as the spiral of heat coiled tighter, making the blood roar through her veins. The tension mounted; a sheen of perspiration covered her skin.

Then the hot, tight coil snapped free, flinging her violently out of control. She was soaring, soaring, gliding on silver wings to a place of incredible sweetness, a world of pleasure unlike anything she had known.

"Ramon!" she cried out, her body arching upward, taking him deeper inside while golden pin dots flashed behind her eyes. Pleasure rushed through her, liquid heat and spirals of delight so sweet she could taste them on her tongue.

Ramon's body tensed. Pumping into her hard and deep, he threw back his head and groaned out his release, telling her he traveled to the same place she had been. Carly clung to him as if she might not find her way back without him.

She felt his lips on her forehead. He kissed her eyes, her nose, her mouth. Outside the wind seemed to have lessened. The rain on the roof became a steady patter, the wind a soothing rush among the trees. Rolling onto his side, he pulled her against his chest, his body still melded with hers.

Gently he smoothed back locks of her hair. "I am sorry I hurt you. But the pain comes only once."

She smiled at him softly. "You didn't hurt me. There was just one instant of discomfort. I would gladly pay the cost again."

A flicker of movement where his body still joined hers. His eyes turned dark and his hand returned to her breast, skimming over the roundness, urging her nipple to life. The hardness returned to the length of him still inside her, and a fresh round of heat slid through her limbs.

"Ramon . . . ?" she whispered.

He eased her onto her back and came up over her, their bodies still deeply joined. "I will not take you again if you are sore."

She smiled into his handsome dark face. "I feel wonderful."

He nodded. "Good. I am in need of you again. I have been too long without a woman."

A flicker of hurt rolled through her. He had made her feel so special, so cared for. But he would have been the same with someone else. Carly blinked against the sudden sting of tears at the back of her throat.

It was only that he needed a woman.

And now he had a wife.

Then Ramon was kissing her again, beginning to move inside her, and the sadness slipped away. In seconds she was writhing beneath him, gripping his shoulders, crying out in passion. Again she reached the sweet place he had taken her before, then Ramon's hard body shuddered and stilled.

He moved off her, pulled her against him, cocooning her in his warmth, his long dark fingers sliding gently through her hair.

"Ramon?"

"Go to sleep, Cara. The day has been a long one and tomorrow you will be sore."

She flushed a little at that. For the first time it occurred to her exactly what they had done and how boldly she had behaved. She wanted to ask if he was pleased, but his eyes were closed and he seemed to be thinking of something else. Perhaps men were always that way after they made love. She knew so little about it.

Carly closed her eyes, but she couldn't fall asleep. Instead she listened to the rain and the wind and tried not to think of all that had happened. Still, again and again, her thoughts returned to the wedding she had forced, the unwanted bride she was—and that her husband was an outlaw, a man whose life was in constant peril.

Lying in the darkness, she wondered what Ramon was thinking, but she didn't dare disturb him. She had caused him enough grief already.

Curling against his side, she finally drifted to sleep.

In the morning when she awakened, she found Ramon had gone.

Chapter Thirteen

Ramon turned the big bay stallion toward Llano Mirada. He was riding up out of the valley, moving deeper into the low rolling hills. A bright sun shone overhead, drying the rain-drenched earth. A small herd of deer, a buck and six does, grazed in the meadow, and a golden eagle soared above the trees, its brown-speckled feathers gilded by the sun's warming rays.

He had left the house at dawn, driven by a desperate need to escape. He needed the fresh, cold air of the mountains to clear his head and help him understand what had happened.

He rubbed a hand over his night's growth of beard, lifted his hat, then settled it lower across his forehead. He should have stayed at Las Almas. He should have faced his obligations, his newly acquired responsibilities as a husband. Instead he had left his bride a short, impersonal note and ridden off into the hills.

He'd had to do it. He'd had to escape his disgust at himself for the way he had behaved. In the cold light of dawn, he'd been forced to face the truth of what had happened the night of the *fandango* and in the long days since.

For the second time since he had known Caralee Mc-Connell, the anger he directed at her should have been directed at himself.

Ramon swore bitterly. The fact was, Carly hadn't forced him to marry her. There wasn't a woman on this earth who could do that if he didn't want her. He had lied to himself, just as he had before.

That night in the barn, when she had looked at him so pleadingly, silently begging for his help, it had taken all his will not to pound Vincent Bannister into the hard dirt floor and carry her away with him. Her clever scheme had been his salvation. In the next few minutes, God only knew what he might have done.

At the time he'd been so confused by his emotions that his anger had surfaced in defense. It had ridden him hard for the next three days, been riding him still when he had gone last night to her room.

But the bitter truth was he wanted Caralee McConnell. So much he had broken the vows he had made. He had ignored his pledge to his family and the men who depended on him. Worse than that, now that he had taken her to his bed, he wanted her more than ever. Despite the fact she was Fletcher Austin's niece. Despite the fact she was an Anglo.

He urged the bay horse over a ridge, leaving the muddy trail behind, but his mind remained on Carly and the overwhelming desire he felt for her. His brother had wanted her too. So badly he had gotten himself killed.

It wasn't Carly's fault. Nothing that had happened since the day he had met her had really been her fault, yet he wondered how his aunt and his mother would feel if they discovered she was the woman who had sounded the alarm the night of the raid. He prayed they wouldn't find out.

He thought of the way he had taunted her at the wedding, thought of the cruel things he had said to her last night, and guilt welled up inside him, so strong it made the sweat break out on his forehead. He had treated her badly, had let his uncertainties drive him to say things, do things he didn't really mean.

Yet in a way he'd had no choice. He couldn't afford to feel the things she made him feel, couldn't understand his driving need to protect her. He didn't like the jealousy he experienced when a man simply looked in her direction, the warmth he felt inside whenever she was near.

Ramon reined up on the crest of a hill and looked back over the valley. Las Almas was long out of sight, but he still could see the western boundary of the twenty thousand acres of Rancho del Robles. Land that should have been his. Land he had sworn to regain for his family—the de la Guerra grant that now belonged to Fletcher Austin, his Anglo wife's only living relative.

He should have stayed, he thought again, wondering what she would think when she discovered he had left her the day after their wedding. At least he had taken her gently. Deep down he knew that no matter how he raged, no matter what he threatened, he would have done that all along.

He recalled her fiery passion, the incredible desire she aroused in him, hotter than he had ever felt for a woman. Not even Lily could make his blood heat up the way his little wife could. Yet he'd let her believe she was just like any other woman he had taken to his bed.

It wasn't the truth. He wanted her with a need that bordered on obsession, but he didn't dare let her know. She was a *gringa*. They thought differently of marriage than Spanish women. Cuckolding a husband meant nothing; sleeping with a dozen different men meant nothing. They took their pleasure wherever they could find it.

In Spain, he had moved in the circles frequented by the traveling rich, mostly Americans, English, and French. That was where he met Lily, at a close friend's villa in Seville. At first he'd been enthralled with Lily. In the next few years, he bedded a dozen more just like her.

Perhaps Caralee would be different. He prayed it was so, but he couldn't be sure.

In many ways he trusted her, but not with the keys to his heart.

He kicked the stallion into a gallop, flinging clumps of damp earth out behind the animal's hooves. There were matters he needed to attend in the stronghold and a few days away from Carly would give him time to regain control. Until his return, Sanchez and the vaqueros would keep her safe. In three days time, his mother and aunt would return from their visit with his cousins, and she would no longer be alone.

Ramon ignored a twinge of regret at the loss of three full days in the arms of his fiery little bride.

He'd left her a note on the mantel. It said he had business in the stronghold, but Carly knew better. Last night Ramon had taken her because he had needed a woman, but she had failed to please him. In fact, she had driven him away.

Her chest felt tight and a hard lump rose in her throat. She paced the floor of the warm, cozy *sala,* hardly aware of the dark carved overhead beams or the crackle of the low-burning fire in the big rock fireplace. Paintings of Ramon's father and mother, his aunt and his brother, hung on the whitewashed adobe walls; and white lace doilies draped over the back of the sofa and brightened the dark oak tables. Carly barely noticed. She was too caught up in her guilt and her terrible sense of failure.

Pedro Sanchez had come to her earlier that morning. He wanted her to know she would be safe while Ramon was away. The vaqueros had been instructed to watch after her, he said. Ramon had spoken to them before he left that morning. Blue was there to cook and clean; surely Carly would be fine until her husband returned from the stronghold.

Surely she would be fine.

But she didn't feel fine at all.

Thinking of the beautiful woman waiting for Ramon at

Llano Mirada, Carly felt sick to her stomach. If only she'd had a little more time, she could have learned how to please him.

She wanted that, Carly realized, she wanted to please Ramon more than anything else in the world.

She wanted to—because she was in love with him.

A jagged pain knifed through her as she sank down on the horsehair sofa. Why hadn't she seen it? How could she have hidden the truth from herself for so long? She was in love with Ramon, had been since the night he had saved her from Villegas, perhaps even before that.

Maybe she had loved him from the moment she had opened her eyes and seen him praying at the side of her bed.

And if she loved him, perhaps that was the reason she had forced the marriage. At the time, she hadn't considered it. She'd been certain it was necessary, her only way out of a bad situation. But maybe deep down, in a place she refused to acknowledge, she wanted Ramon so much she was willing to do anything to get him. If that was the case, she was no better than Vincent Bannister. Carly's heart wrenched at the thought.

Three days passed. At first she was embarrassed. Ramon had left right after their wedding night, and Pedro, the vaqueros, and everyone else at Las Almas knew it. She occupied the hours wandering through the house, then thankfully made a new friend out in the barn—little Bajito, the tiny brown and white spotted dog that had perched on Rey del Sol's back the day of the horse race.

The dog slept in one of the stalls near his big palomino friend, but he loved to play, and Carly had lured him outside easily for a game of fetch the stick. After that, she had come to the barn every day, carrying a bite of sugar for Rey and some scraps from supper for Bajito.

Then one day as she was sitting on the floor of the barn playing tug-of-war with the scruffy little mutt, Carly clutching one end of a rag while Bajito clung to the other, she overheard a group of vaqueros speaking outside the window of one of the stalls.

Pancho Fernandez, one of the Las Almas vaqueros, had been at del Robles the night of the *fandango*. He had heard what happened in the barn, how Don Ramon had been trapped into marriage, and carried the tale to the men. Ramon didn't really want her, he said. That was the reason he had left her alone.

Carly's throat closed up. It was the truth, but it hurt to hear him say it.

"I do not believe it," another man said as she started to creep away before any of them could see her. "What sane man would not want her, eh? Besides, I have seen the way he looks at her. There is something in his eyes I have never seen there before."

Hearing those words, a tiny ray of hope began to glow inside her, a spark that had been all but snuffed out. Perhaps she could learn to please him, somehow win his love. The hope continued to grow, brightening a little every day. Surprisingly, it strengthened when his aunt and mother returned, amazed to find Ramon had gone.

"He—he had to leave on business," Carly stammered, the color high in her cheeks. "I'm certain he'll be back as soon as he can."

His mother frowned, but his frail maiden aunt smiled brightly. "Do not worry, *niña*. My nephew is new at being a husband. He chafes a little at the bit, but in time, he will come around."

Carly's heart swelled with gratitude at the older woman's kind words. Over the next few days, they spoke often, though his mother practically ignored her. Tia Teresa had a way of sweeping aside the barriers between them. She reminded Carly of her grandmother, an Irish woman who had lived with the McConnell family in the mine patch, a woman of courage and warmth. Carly had loved everything about her, the stories she told of the grueling journey from her homeland, the feel of her gnarled old hands as they gently braided her hair, even the hint of Irish whiskey that occasionally clung to her breath.

Granny McConnell was gone now, but in a few short days she felt nearly that close to Tia Teresa, a closeness she hadn't shared with a woman since her mother died.

"Are you busy, Tia?" Carly approached the frail old woman late one evening, after Mother de la Guerra had gone to bed. The older woman was sitting in the *sala* embroidering, her veined hands working with a skill that denied her years. Carly had come in from outside in the kitchen, where she'd been helping Blue with the supper dishes.

She didn't have to help. In fact, Ramon's mother frowned at the notion of a de la Guerra woman doing such menial tasks, but Blue was old, and Carly didn't mind. Keeping busy helped distract her.

Tia Teresa set aside her embroidery, resting it carefully beside her on the couch. "What is it, *niña?* You are worried about Ramon, no?"

"Yes, I suppose I am." She worried about him every day, prayed that he and his men hadn't gone off on some dangerous mission. "But that isn't what I wanted to ask you about."

"No? Then what is it?"

A spot of warmth crept into her cheeks. "It's about the night we were married. I-It's rather embarrassing, but I . . ." She took a breath to fortify her courage. "You see I didn't know exactly what to do. Ramon was . . ." *magnificent, incredible, wonderful.* "At any rate, I think I might have done something wrong, something to displease him."

"You believe that is the reason he left?"

"Yes. . . ."

"It is the man's place to know these things. What could you possibly have done to displease him?"

"I don't know. I-I was wondering . . . how would a Spanish lady behave on her wedding night?"

The old woman smiled, making her wrinkled face look less brittle. "I can only tell you what my mother once told me, and what other women have said. I cannot speak for myself."

"I know." Ramon's aunt had mentioned her *novio,* a young man named Esteban. She said that he had been killed, and that she had never married. It was obvious that even after a lifetime without him, Tia Teresa still grieved. In a way, Carly envied her. How fierce their love must have been to survive after all these years.

The old woman picked up her embroidery, her bony fingers moving in rhythm, the needle skimming through the fabric without conscious thought. "When a Spanish man and woman marry, there is always a grand fiesta. The music and dancing begin right after the wedding, and the feasting goes on all night, sometimes as long as a week. Often the bride and groom do not consummate the marriage for several days."

Carly hated to ask such an intimate question, but there was no one else who could help her. "And when that time finally comes?"

Tia glanced up from her work. "The bride is very nervous, and of course very shy. She awaits her husband in their bed and when he finally joins her, she allows him the husbandly rights she has agreed to by the marriage contract."

"How . . . how does that happen?"

The old woman rolled her eyes as if she wondered at the endless naiveté of the young, then she smiled. "She will snuff out the candle beside the bed, lift her nightgown, and allow her husband's body to come inside her."

"H-her nightgown? She goes to bed in her nightgown?"

"*Si*. Usually it is cotton but I thought the silk would be prettier. Ramon has always liked pretty things."

"It—it's lovely." But she hadn't kept it on. Vaguely she remembered Ramon's hands sliding it off her shoulders, but perhaps that was only because she hadn't been waiting for him in bed. Maybe he would have simply raised it to her waist. She couldn't imagine it, not after the things he had done. She couldn't imagine anything between them but hot, sweat-slick skin and moist, fiery kisses.

An odd memory struck her. Carly suddenly straightened, the awful thought nearly sending her to her knees. Dear God! She leaned forward in the chair across from Tia Teresa. "In the morning, when I was"—*stripping the feather mattress to launder the blood from the sheets*—"making the bed, I-I noticed the oddest thing. There was a hole in the sheet on top. It was embroidered in the prettiest white thread, a lovely bouquet of flowers that formed a wreath around the hole. I'd forgotten all about it until now. Surely . . ."

Carly nervously wet her lips, praying she was wrong. "Surely the woman doesn't lie beneath the . . . surely the man doesn't . . ." But when she looked at Tia Teresa, bright spots of color tinted the old woman's cheeks.

She nodded sagely. "It has long been used to protect the woman's modesty. Surely my nephew . . . showed you how it is done?"

Carly's face felt on fire. "I think we accomplished the same thing, Tia, but not exactly in that way."

Tia Teresa reached over and patted her hand. "I am certain you did just fine. Besides, a man should understand if you are shy your very first time."

Shy? The flush in her face suffused her whole body. A memory arose of her begging Ramon not to stop, of her body arching beneath him, of her nails digging into his hard-muscled shoulders.

Her stomach began a nervous roll. Obviously wearing a white lace *mantilla* wasn't enough to make her a real Spanish lady. If she wanted to please Ramon, if she wanted to keep him out of the arms of his beautiful mistress, she would have to learn to behave like the kind of woman he had wanted to marry.

"You must not worry, *niña*. It is not so difficult a thing to endure. You must simply lie there and let him have his way. It is a burden the woman must carry. When I imagine such a thing with my Esteban, I know that I wouldn't have minded it so much."

Carly's head began to pound with an agonizing beat. Minded? She had craved Ramon's touch, burned for it, not simply endured it. Her body had been on fire for him; it was even now, whenever she thought of the way he had made her feel. What kind of a woman behaved that way? Obviously not a woman of pure Spanish blood.

Dear God, no wonder he had ridden away.

"Thank you, Tia," Carly finally said, her voice a little strained. "I'm sorry to bother you about such things, but there was no one else I could ask."

The old woman waved her hand as if it didn't matter in the least. "I am glad to be of help." She smiled. "Ramon will return soon, and this time, you will know what he expects."

"Yes. . . ." Carly glanced away, fighting a fresh tide of embarrassment. Until this moment, she hadn't been the least embarrassed about what had happened between them. She had only prayed it would happen again.

Now that she realized how brazenly she had acted, she was appalled by her behavior. Dear God, how would she ever be able to face him?

"It's getting late." Carly stood up from the chair. "I think I'll be going to bed."

Tia Teresa just nodded. "It is time I went to bed, too."

They left the room together, then parted and went to their own separate quarters along the corridor around the patio. All Carly could think of was the embroidered hole in the sheets Ramon was supposed to use when they made love.

She hated herself for a tingle of disappointment that if he made love to her again, she wouldn't feel the heat of his smooth dark skin against her naked body.

Ten days had passed. Ramon urged the tall bay stallion down the hill toward Rancho Las Almas. He was eager to be home. Eager to see his bride. Eager to return to her bed.

In the days since his wedding, he had come to terms with his feelings for her. His vow had been broken, but he was as much at fault as she was, and there was no sense in regret. The truth was he had wanted Carly McConnell from the start. Now she was his wife and though he had never intended to marry her, he couldn't really say he was sorry.

Fletcher Austin posed a problem, and the fact that Ramon was just as determined as ever to get back his land. But now that Andreas was gone, perhaps the raiding they'd been part of could eventually come to an end. From the beginning, Ramon had argued to find a legal remedy for their troubles, but Andreas had refused to listen. He was blind with rage at his father's needless death and the loss of the de la Guerra lands.

By the time Ramon had arrived from Spain, El Dragón was already raiding. He felt obliged to assist his brother's campaign. Andreas had, after all, assumed the responsibility of protecting the family—Ramon's responsibility—while he had been lounging unawares in a villa in Seville.

Now Andreas was dead. Ramon was the head of the family, and if there was a peaceful way to regain their land, he meant to find it. He would deal with his wife's objections when the time came.

He touched his spurs to the tall bay's ribs and the stallion picked up its pace down the hill. He wished he was riding Rey del Sol, but the big palomino was too easy to spot, just like the magnificent black stallion ridden by El Dragón. At least the bay was well trained—Pedro had seen to that.

As he had been seeing after Ramon's family and his woman.

His woman, he silently repeated. His wife. His loins went hard just thinking about the evening ahead. He could almost feel Carly's lips clinging to his, taste the sweetness of desire on her breath. In the eye of his mind, he saw her naked, the white silk gown pooled around her slender ankles, her ripe breasts quivering, the small pink tips rising up, stiff and proud against his hand.

The heat of his loins grew more fierce, blades of hot desire knifing through him. There were a dozen ways he wanted to take her, a hundred soft places he wanted to kiss. He knew she would be angry that he had left her, but perhaps there was a way he might explain. Or perhaps just kissing her would be enough to let her know how much he missed her.

Ramon pulled his hat down low across his forehead, set his spurs to the stallion's sides, and sent the animal into a gallop. It would be dark when he got home.

Ramon could hardly wait.

"He is coming! Ramon is coming!"

Carly's heart started thudding, knocking against her ribs. She ran up beside Mother de la Guerra, who stood before the window, gazing out into the night.

"Where? I don't see him."

"There—" She pointed toward the place where the trail heading east crossed the stream at the side of the house. "Can you not see? Even now he fords the creek." It was the first time Carly had seen the senora so excited. Mostly she sat rocking, or staring out the window. Carly had come to pity her. At first she hadn't realized how deeply the old woman grieved for her youngest son.

As always, the thought brought a pang of regret. Perhaps if she hadn't rung the bell. Perhaps if Andreas hadn't tried to steal her away. . . . But she had and he had and now he was dead.

Carly shoved the unpleasant memory aside. Fate had played its roll and what had happened was past. Even Ramon had set it away.

Ramon. She watched him riding toward her, straight and tall in the saddle, all easy grace and supple strength, he and the horse moving with an elegance she had never witnessed in another rider.

"He will be hungry." Tia Teresa walked up beside her. "Why do you not see what Blue has left over from supper?"

Carly smiled. "Yes. Yes, I'll do that right away." She raced out to the kitchen, gave orders to the ancient Indian woman to heat whatever she had left to feed Ramon, then ran back into the living room. She wanted to greet him out in front, to tell him she was sorry that she had behaved as wickedly as she had, that tonight it would be different, but she didn't know what he might be thinking. And she wanted to appear the proper lady.

She thought she had learned to do that at Mrs. Stuart's School for Fashionable Young Ladies, but there had been no lessons on what to do on one's wedding night. Carly flushed a little to think of it, and just then Ramon walked in, his eyes swinging to hers the instant he entered the room.

He took off his hat and hung it on the rack beside the door, turned and hugged his mother. He kissed her hand and then her cheek, a gesture of love and respect among his people, then hugged and kissed his aunt. But his eyes drifted over their heads to where she stood beside the sofa, and there was a glow in the velvet brown depths.

"*Buenas tardes,* Caracita." A hint of warmth she hadn't expected tinged his voice. "I have missed you these past few days." Perhaps he had decided to forgive her embarrassing behavior. Perhaps he was going to give her a second chance. She thought of Miranda, felt a flicker of pain, wondered how Miranda had behaved in his bed, but forced the thought away. He was her husband, not Miranda's. He belonged here with her, and this time she would be the one to please him.

"It's good to see you, Ramon." She smiled at him, and a glimmer of heat slid into his gaze. "Are—are you hungry?"

Yes, his eyes said, but not for food. "*Si.* I have not eaten since this morning."

She went outside to the kitchen, glad for the time to calm her pounding heart, then returned with a hot plate of *cocido,* a dish of beef and sausage, chiles, carrots, and beans, along with a bowl of pumpkin soup, hot tortillas, and a goblet of rich red wine.

"Will you join me?" he said, glancing up from the steaming plates of food. His eyes took in her simple brown dress, then returned to settle on her lips.

Carly wet them nervously. "No, I . . . we've already eaten." She wished she'd had time to change into something pretty and fix her hair, instead of wearing it coiled at the nape of her neck.

"Come, then, sit with me until I finish."

"All right."

"Mother?" He motioned the old woman forward. "I would hear what you and Tia have been doing to keep my bride entertained while I have been gone."

His mother smiled faintly. "Your wife works too much," she said gruffly, but there was a spark of affection in her voice Carly had never heard. "She helps that useless old Indian, Blue. I have told her she is a de la Guerra. De la Guerra women do not work like slaves, but she does not listen. Perhaps now that her husband is home, she will listen to you."

Ramon laughed softly. "She has never listened to me before. I cannot think she will do so now."

Carly flushed. She could hear the affection in his voice and so could everyone else. Inside her heart, the ray of hope blossomed into a bright-burning flame. A surge of love for him welled up, and a small lump formed in her throat. Tonight she would please him, show him she could be the kind of woman he wanted.

She waited patiently while he ate, listening as he spoke with his mother and aunt, then started to clear his dishes when he finished and shoved back his chair.

Ramon caught her hand. "The hour grows late. Why do you not leave this for Blue and return instead to our room? I will join you there in a minute." His hot look made her dizzy. Dear God, she knew what he was thinking. She was thinking about it, too!

"Yes . . ." she whispered, her mouth gone dry, the color high in her cheeks. "I'll wait for you there."

*C*hapter *F*ourteen

*C*arly couldn't look at the women, couldn't face their knowing expressions, no matter the kind thoughts that went with them. Instead she made her way out the door and down the corridor to their bedroom, grateful that the walls of the house were eighteen inches thick. Inside she hurriedly stripped off her clothes, the simple brown day dress with its round white piquet collar, her stockings and shoes. Upper-class Californio women dressed in the European fashion, the same style American women wore. Only the *paisanos* dressed as she had in the mountains.

She'd been properly clothed, yet she wished she had been wearing something else, the saffron yellow that hung in the closet, or perhaps the woolen of forest green. For the first time in a long while, she was glad for the clothes her uncle had bought her.

Jerking open the drawer of the heavy oak bureau that had been brought for her use, she reached for a soft cotton nightgown. Not the sheer white silk. She couldn't wear the silk without remembering the way her skin had tingled when Ramon had looked at her in it. The way his dark eyes seemed to burn right through it, making her flesh grow damp and hot.

Instead she pulled the plain high-necked, long-sleeved white cotton night rail over her head and hurriedly fastened the tiny row of buttons up the front. She uncoiled her hair from the nape of her neck, brushed it out, quickly plaited it into a single thick braid, then rushed across the room to the bed. Turning back the colorful quilt, she climbed in between the sheets, careful to position herself beneath the elaborately embroidered hole.

Part of her felt silly. Ramon had already seen her naked. But the other part said she knew nothing of Spanish custom, and if this would please him, she was more than willing to oblige.

She reached for the lamp, turned it down as low as it would burn, then settled in to wait. It didn't take long. Heavy footfalls sounded in the corridor outside, the door swung open, and Ramon walked in. His shoulders were so broad they filled the opening. He was all lean muscle and supple strength, his long legs encased in snug black breeches, his hard male features beautifully chiseled in a face bronzed by the sun.

Once he closed the door, blocking out the moonlight, she could barely see his face, the lamplight was so dim, but she noticed his momentary pause. Perhaps he had thought she would be waiting as she had before, that she would embarrass him by acting like a wanton.

He said nothing as he stripped off his clothes, and she tried not to notice the ridges of muscle bunching across his chest, his firm flat belly, the narrow rounded buttocks that flexed when he moved. She tried not to feel the shafts of heat slicing through her, wished she could control the telltale dampness collecting between her legs.

The bed shifted beneath his weight. He reached for her, dragged her into his arms. "I have missed you, Cara. I was a fool to leave." He kissed her before she could reply, a hot, searing, soul-drugging kiss that made her heart slide into her stomach. Dear God, this was going to be harder than she thought.

She kissed him back, allowed the sweep of his tongue, but didn't touch it with her own. Her hands rested lightly on his shoulders but she didn't cling to him as she had done before, as her wicked body urged her to do again.

His hand touched her hair and he paused once more. "I like it better down," he growled, pulling the ribbon loose at the end. He sifted his long dark fingers through it, then spread the heavy mass around her shoulders.

Carly swallowed against the heat she felt where his hands brushed her skin. Instead she lay back against the pillow and stared up at the ceiling, counting the heavy oak beams to control her pounding heart. Ramon bent over her, cupped her breasts and began to stroke them through her nightgown, sending little tongues of fire shooting through her. He teased her nipple into a hard tight bud, bent forward and bit it gently, dampening the fabric with his lips.

Dear God. Carly blinked and focused hard on the ceiling, trying to force her mind to something else. But her body felt on fire and the blood roared in her ears.

"I want you out of that nightgown," her husband said sternly, beginning to work the tiny buttons up the front. "I want to see you naked."

"But . . ." This wasn't supposed to happen. He was treating her like a *gringa*. He wouldn't say that to a true Spanish woman. His words sent a sliver of hurt trickling through her, told her exactly the way he felt. He kissed her again, his tongue gliding over her lips, then plunging inside her mouth. Warm tremors skittered beneath the surface of her skin. She thought of the *cocida* they'd had for supper, about the complicated recipe Blue had shown her that afternoon—anything but him.

The gown ripped down the front, the harsh sound jerking her from her thoughts. "I said I want you naked." There was a hard note in his voice. And not an ounce of the respect he would have shown a true Spanish woman. Another stab of hurt tore through her, along with a jolt of determination.

"I think it would be better if we left the gown on," she said with quiet dignity. "I'll be happy to lift it up for you, if that is your wish." She started to demand he use the hole in the sheet, but something warned her not to. Still, she was determined to behave the way a Spanish lady would. She wanted to please him—and she wanted his respect.

In the dim light of the lamp, she couldn't see much of his face. She caught a flicker of unease, one of uncertainty, then his features turned dark with rage.

He jerked her up by the shoulders. "I should have known. I thought you were different, but you are just like the rest." He made a harsh sound in his throat. "I am a little surprised you have tired of me so soon—ah, but then you are a *gringa*. Some of them only pretend to enjoy it. Others need a dozen different men to find their pleasure."

He let go of her shoulders, swung away to the edge of the bed. "Whichever you are, it matters little to me, for I will not be sharing your bed."

Carly stared at him in horror. Dear God, what had she done? "Ramon, please . . . where are you going?"

But he didn't answer, just jerked on his breeches and boots and strode bare-chested out the door.

God in heaven! Tears burned her eyes and began to slide down her cheeks. Again she had failed. She had thought it was important she behave as a proper Spanish lady. But all she had accomplished was to once more drive him away.

Carly climbed out of bed on shaking limbs and drew on her quilted dark blue wrapper. Perhaps she could find him, try to explain. She thought of Miranda, waiting for him at the stronghold. Had he left already, set off again to see his mistress at Llano Mirada? How did Mirada behave in his bed? Like a vixen or a lady? Whatever she was doing, she seemed to be doing it right.

She hurried across the carpet that covered the earthen floor and opened the door. A full moon showered bright rays against the earth, lit the fields with a silvery glow. Across the yard, she saw Ramon standing beside the corral, his elbow resting on one of the fence posts. Staring out into the darkness, a thin cigar clamped between his teeth, he took a steady draw, then released a plume of smoke into the star-clustered sky.

Carly continued toward him, heedless of the cold damp ground beneath her bare feet. All she could think of was Ramon and how she continued to fail him. His back went stiff when he saw her approach. He tossed the cigar away, making an arc of red among the shadows. He stared at her but made no effort to speak.

Carly looked at him and her pounding heart thrummed in her ears. She was hurting so badly and yet her chin went up. "You left me once before . . . the morning after our wedding. Pedro said you went to Llano Mirada. Did you go to her?" She swallowed past the lump that had risen in her throat. "Did you go to Miranda?"

His eyes bored into her, hard, cold, implacable. "Why would you care?"

"Did you?"

He watched her a moment and then he shook his head, tumbling strands of black hair across his forehead. "No. I saw her in the stronghold, but I did not take her to my bed."

Carly bit hard on her lip. "I'm sorry about tonight. I know you don't believe it, but I only wanted to please you."

He scoffed, a bitter sound rolling up from his throat, but he did not speak.

"I-I thought if I behaved like a true Spanish lady it would make you happy. I thought you might think of me as a wife, instead of just another woman to warm your bed. The last time we were together, I behaved very badly and you went away. I hoped this time . . . you would stay."

Ramon just stared, his dark eyes fixed on her face. "You thought that was the reason that I left? You thought that you had done something wrong?"

Her face flushed scarlet in the moonlight. "I begged you not to stop. I let you touch me . . . everywhere. Surely a lady wouldn't act like—"

He cut off her words by reaching for her, dragging her into his arms and crushing her against him. "*Santos de Christo.* How could you believe such a thing?"

"Tia Teresa said—"

"Tia Teresa has never been with a man." He tilted her chin with his hand and she could feel it shaking. "Since the moment I left here, I have thought of nothing but making love to you. I remembered every touch, every kiss. I burned to touch you that way again." He brushed her mouth with his lips. "I should have told you how much you pleased me. What I said to you that night . . . it was only that I was angry . . . and it wasn't the truth. I was confused, uncertain about my feelings. I didn't make love to you that night because I needed a woman. The truth was, I needed you."

Tears stung her eyes. She blinked but they rolled down her cheeks. "Ramon . . ." Her arms slid around his neck and she clung to him.

"Forgive me, *querida.* I have had little experience with innocence such as yours. *Por Dios,* how can a man be such a fool?" He kissed her then, a bold, hot, ravaging kiss that sent a shower of heat through her body.

This time Carly didn't fight it. She wanted to please him. She loved him.

She kissed him back, mated her tongue with his, and heard him groan. She didn't stop kissing him until he pulled away and lifted her into his arms.

"Ramon?" She clung to his powerful neck as he strode back toward the house.

"Si, querida?"

"What . . . what about the hole?"

"What hole?"

"You know, the one embroidered in the sheets."

Ramon stopped on the path, a rumble of laughter erupting from his wide chest. "My tia has a good heart, but she knows little of men. I do not think there is a Spanish man born who has ever made use of the hole sewn into the sheets."

Carly started laughing, too. She felt giddy with relief and once more was burning with hope. He hadn't gone to Miranda; he had come back to her. She wanted to tell him she loved him, but if she did, he might remember that she had forced the marriage. He might believe she had meant to trap him all along, and she didn't want to face any more of his anger. She only wanted him to make love to her.

Their laughter died away as they approached the house. Ramon nudged open the heavy oak door with the toe of his boot, strode in, and settled her on the bed.

"Whatever happens between us is no cause for shame," he said, cupping her face in his hands. "Promise me you will remember."

"I'll remember."

He reached for her nightgown, pulled it over her head. "There is no need for this. We will sleep together as God made us." She flushed, but the thought of his smooth dark skin, his hard male body wrapped around her each night, sounded so wonderful, a wave of pleasure rolled through her.

She watched him undress, enjoying the ripple of muscle beneath his skin. He came to her naked and Carly welcomed him with open arms—and with all the love she felt for him that she could no longer deny.

He kissed her fiercely, then gentled the kiss, teasing her senses into tingling awareness. He took her passionately, filling her and making her cry out his name. Then he took her gently, wooing her with soft Spanish words and tender caresses. This time when they finished making love, she knew that she had pleased him. Perhaps in time, he would even come to love her.

They slept for a while, then he took her again, and once more just before dawn. Her lips were slightly bruised from his kisses, her body gently battered and wonderfully sated. She felt content as she never had before.

Then she thought of the obstacles that still lay between them: his hatred of her uncle, his vow to regain Rancho del Robles, the danger he faced as the outlaw El Dragón. Perhaps most important, she recalled the fact she wasn't the woman he had wanted to marry.

Even nestled snugly in his arms, Carly found it difficult to sleep.

"I can't believe she's actually gone and married him. She doesn't even know him." Vincent Bannister sat across from Fletcher Austin at the Stockman's Club in San Francisco.

Fletcher had come to the city for the annual fall meeting with his attorney, Mitchell Webster, and his friend and financial advisor, William Bannister, to discuss the distribution of profits at the end of the fall *matanza,* the slaughtering of cattle for hides and tallow, as well as the sale of several thousand head driven north to the gold fields.

The meeting had gone as planned. Webster had left, but William had accompanied him to the posh Stockman's Club, and young Bannister had joined them. From the moment of his arrival the younger man had talked of nothing but Caralee.

"How could she do it?" he continued, speaking more to himself than to Fletcher. "I thought she cared for me at least a little."

"Yes, well, obviously we pushed her too hard." A waiter arrived, carrying crystal tumblers filled with fine Irish whiskey and branch water. The man set them down on the polished rosewood table in front of them, then quietly slipped away.

Fletcher shook his head. "I should have known better. I should have known she would rebel . . . after all, she is her mother's daughter." This last was said with an odd pang of pride. Lucy Austin was a woman unlike any he had known, beautiful, talented, intelligent. She had wasted herself on that no-account miner she had met in Philadelphia. True, the family had been poor then, and Lucy hadn't believed her older brother when he said one day he would be rich, wealthy enough to take care of them both.

Marrying Patrick McConnell had been a stupid thing to do, even if he was blue-eyed and handsome. Lucy had paid, of course, with a lifetime of drudgery. But in the dozens of letters he had received through the years, his sister had never complained.

In the overstuffed chair across from him, William spoke up, breaking into his thoughts. The taller man uncrossed his long legs, which were encased in perfectly tailored brown wool slacks. "It was definitely an odd turn of events," he said. "As you can see, my son has not yet recovered from the loss. It appears he held Caralee in extremely high regard."

"I'm sorry, my boy. Part of the blame belongs to me. I don't believe she would have acted as she did if we had given her a bit more time."

Vincent leaned forward. "You think she did it just to spite you? That she might have cared for me after all?" He eased back in his chair, his hazel eyes lit with a glow of satisfaction. "Yes, that must be it. As I said before, she hardly even knew the man. God only knows the misery she must be suffering. Unfortunate for both of us, I suspect."

Vincent rattled on for the next few minutes about the sad state of affairs Carly had gotten herself into, but Fletcher's mind had suddenly swung in another direction.

"Excuse me, Vincent. What was it you said before . . . something about her hardly even knowing him?"

"That's right."

Absently, he rubbed his chin. "Perhaps she knew him better than we believed."

"What do you mean?"

"Maybe Ramon de la Guerra is somehow connected with this outlaw, El Dragón. Maybe he and Caralee were together while she was being held in the mountains."

"I cannot imagine there is any truth to that," William argued. "The de la Guerra family is highly respected. Besides, Don Ramon was with us at del Robles the night the Spanish Dragon robbed the stage."

"True, but maybe he was somehow involved. If that is the case, it's possible de la Guerra may have ordered the abduction. The bad blood between us runs deep. It would suit him well to usurp something of mine . . . perhaps even my niece. If the bastard took her virtue, Carly would have felt obliged to marry him."

"If that is the case," Vincent put in, "why would she have kept his secret after she escaped?" It was obvious the boy preferred the first scenario, but Fletcher had begun to believe he might have stumbled onto the truth.

"I don't know." He leaned back against the green brocade settee, a thick finger drumming against the side of his glass. "But as soon as I return to del Robles, I'm going to try very hard to find out."

A week had passed since Ramon's return. A week of passionate kisses and sultry nights, of making love and learning the secrets of her husband's hard-muscled body. Once they traveled to a place on del Robles land, a secluded spot where Ramon had come as a boy. A narrow creek tumbled from a high ledge into a shallow pond surrounded by pine trees. They made love in the soft green grass beside the pond.

Carly smiled as she thought of it again this morning, then she swung her legs to the side of the bed and came to her feet. Ramon was already up and gone, off to work with the men to finish the fall *matanza*. They had all been working hard, rounding up cattle, branding calves, sorting the strays from the herd, and separating those that were being slaughtered from ones being sold on the hoof.

Carly stretched and yawned, her back a little stiff from the hours she had spent working over the tallow pots, huge iron cauldrons used to heat the fat taken from the slaughtered steers. It was melted into lard, some of it kept, some of it sold, and some of the tallow stored for later use in making soap and candles.

Even Ramon's mother and Aunt Teresa pitched in, and obviously were pleased that Carly felt no hesitation in doing the same.

Dressed in a simple gray cotton skirt and white cotton blouse, she grabbed a shawl and left the house. Outside, the rancho buzzed with activity, the vaqueros busy saddling their horses, the kitchen humming with the voices of men finishing the last of their morning meal. Old Blue had been up for some time, shuffling about, clanging pots and pans, setting tin plates on the table. Even on this small rancho, the cook was awake long before dawn, tending the fires, making coffee and thick pots of cocoa, frying tortillas and meat.

Carly helped for a while, enjoying the robust smells and simple good cheer of the women. But as the sun crept higher above the mountains, bathing the fields in a haze of bright gold, it beckoned her out of the *cocina,* and she went in search of Ramon. The walk would do her good, she reasoned, help to stretch her weary muscles; and the day was warm, the sky overhead as blue as a jay on the wing.

Carly made her way out through the sycamore grove. He wasn't with his vaqueros, she discovered, who were busy lassoing cattle in an open field the animals had been driven into. Still, for a moment she stopped to watch, marveling at the men's skill with the long, braided length of leather they called a *reata*. Once a steer was cut out of the herd, one rider roped its head while another caught the heels, bringing the animal to the ground.

The slaughter was quick and efficient, but the sight drove Carly back toward the house. Then she spotted several men in one of the distant pastures and set off in that direction instead. Emerging from a dense thicket, she stood beside the wide trunk of an oak, searching the grassy fields for Ramon. Rey del Sol was there, she saw, his snowy mane shimmering as he bowed his magnificent thick-muscled neck. Snorting and stamping his feet, he nuzzled a pretty little palomino mare, and for the first time it occurred to her exactly what he was about to do.

Her cheeks suffused with color, but she did not move away, just stood there staring, mesmerized by the sight of the beautiful golden stallion mounting its equally beautiful mate. So much power, she thought, such raw untamed desire. The animals nickered and snorted, whinnied and pawed the earth. The stallion bared its teeth, then used them to subdue the mare by a firm hold on her neck.

He surged up over her, balancing his hooves on her back. Then he buried his huge length deep inside her, mastering her with ease, taking what nature meant for him to have, and Carly felt an odd rush of heat. When the stallion began to move, plunging into its mate with one powerful thrust after another, a hot tingling shiver ran down her spine. Her mouth went dry, and the palm that rested on the trunk of the oak began to grow damp.

She didn't hear Ramon's silent approach, just felt his warm breath on the side of her face.

"It is a great sight, no? The stallion mounting his mare. It is a tribute to life, I think."

She licked her dry lips, suddenly conscience that Ramon's hard body pressed the length of her. He was aroused, she realized, his thick sex hard against her bottom.

"Yes. In a way it's very beautiful."

"*Si* . . . I believe that is the truth." His hand stroked over her breast, found her nipple hard and distended. The brush of his fingers made it stiffen even more. Against her cheek, his softly spoken words held the same gentle caress. "Can you feel it, Cara? Can you feel his hunger, the strength of his desire for her? Do you see how he dominates her, takes what he wants and makes her accept it?"

She nodded, her heart pulsing faster with each of his words, each purposeful stroke of his fingers.

"It happens only because the mare wants it too. She needs to know her mate is strong enough to protect her. How can she obey him if she cannot feel his strength?" His long, dark hand molded a breast, kneaded it softly through her blouse, working her tightly puckered nipple. "When he takes her as he does now, driving himself so deeply inside her, she knows that he is stronger than she . . . and that he will keep her safe."

He drew her back a little, till they were hidden out of sight behind the tree. Carly's fingers bit into the rough bark of the trunk and she leaned her forehead against it. Ramon's hand skimmed down her side, then moved lower to lift her skirts and bunch them around her waist. She felt his palm gliding over her bottom, searching for then finding the split in her pantalets. Carly gasped as his hand caressed her skin, smoothed over the roundness, then a finger eased between the globes and finally slipped inside her, probing gently, deeply, moving with ease against the slickness that had collected as she'd watched the animals mate.

"A woman is the same," he said softly. "She must know her man is strong." He bit her neck, hard enough to cause a shot of pleasure-pain. He unbuttoned the front of her blouse and began to massage her breasts. A second finger slid in, began to ease in and out, and a sweet ache throbbed between her legs. "She must know that he has the power to dominate her, if that is his wish." His mouth moved along her throat, trailing hot damp kisses. Then his hand left her breast; she felt him unbuttoning his breeches, freeing his long straining length, and she felt his hardness against her.

"Part your legs, *querida*," he whispered in her ear, his tongue darting out to tease the rim. "Do it for me." Tiny shivers raced through her, sent another rush of heat to her slick, damp core.

Her legs moved, slid silently apart for him. It never occurred to her to stop him. Just like the mare, she found herself wanting him to take her, to show her the power of his rough male strength.

Ramon complied with her unspoken wishes, spreading the folds of her sex and easing himself inside. She could feel the hotness of his loins pressed against her buttocks as he rested his hands on her waist, firmly gripping her hips, then with a single deep thrust, he buried himself to the hilt.

Carly bit back a cry of pleasure at the overwhelming heat that surged through her. Instead she clutched the tree, hung on for dear life as Ramon thrust into her again and again. Deeper, harder, slowly at first, grinding himself against her, then moving faster, with greater domination. In her mind's eye, she saw the stallion driving into the mare, its long, deep strokes claiming her, enforcing its male possession. Then Ramon's face appeared, along with his hard-muscled body, and the images meshed together, the tall broad-shouldered Spaniard and the long, deep thrusts of the stallion pounding into its mate.

A powerful climax shook her, tightening the muscles that sheathed Ramon's hardness and wrenching a groan from his lips. Two more hard, deep strokes and he too reached release, groaning again as he gripped her hips, pumping into her fiercely, spewing his hot, wet seed.

"Por Dios," he whispered as the shudders wracking his body began to subside. "If the stallion feels as I do, it is the mare who has proven her strength."

Carly laughed softly, her head falling back against his shoulder. *I love you, Ramon,* she thought, but she didn't say it. Instead she felt him easing away and her skirt falling back into place. He finished buttoning up his breeches, turned her to face him, and kissed her softly on the lips. Then he reached for her hand, lifted it and kissed the palm.

"Shall I walk with you back to the house?"

Carly shook her head. "They might think we were . . ."

"Doing what it is that we were doing?"

She grinned. "Yes."

Ramon laughed softly. "Aye, *querida,* how did I ever find such a one as you?"

Carly wasn't sure what to make of his words, but she liked the way he looked when he said them. And she liked the way that soft look made her feel.

Ignoring her earlier protest, he took her hand and they started walking toward his small adobe hacienda. He smiled at her as they drew near, and turned her toward him for a soft farewell kiss, then his gaze slid away over her head and Carly turned to see a small slender figure emerging from a grove of sycamore trees, walking toward them through the tall brown grasses. He passed the orchard and melon patch before she could tell who it was.

"It's Two Hawks!" She started running toward him, grinning hugely, eager to see the boy who had gained a special place in her affections. She stopped when he drew near, his wary, troubled expression warning her that something was wrong.

"What is it, Two Hawks? What's happened?" The slender boy's oddly fashioned breach cloth, all he had on, was dirty and covered with rust-colored blood. Long, deep scratches ran over his face and arms. One eye was black, and his upper lip was swollen and dark with crusted blood.

He stared down at the ground but didn't seem to see it. "The soldiers . . . the militia . . . they came to the village. At first we were only surprised that they were able to find us, since we were so deep in the mountains. Then they started shooting at us."

Carly's heart clenched, twisted hard inside her. When the boy looked up at her, a sheen of moisture reflected in his tar-black eyes.

"First they aimed at the men," he said, "killing any they could see, then they started on the others . . . the women, even old One Horse and the children. We ran into the woods, but they came after us. I fought with one—killed him with his own knife. I drove it into his skinny chest and I am glad." His hard expression slid away, turning bleak and forlorn. "But Lena is dead . . . and many of the others."

"Dear Lord," Carly whispered.

"I did not know what to do. I wandered through the mountains for a while . . . then I came here."

"Oh, Two Hawks, I'm so sorry." She reached for his hand, which was cold and limp, without the slightest spark of life.

"You did right in coming here," Ramon said, walking up beside her. "You are welcome to stay for as long as you wish."

The boy did not answer, just swallowed hard and nodded. If he was surprised to find Carly at Las Almas, he didn't show it. But then his sister had always believed Caralee was Don Ramon's woman.

Ramon surveyed the boy's clothes, his battered face and dazed expression. "You will have to work, of course. You can bunk in with the vaqueros." With those words, the first hint of life came into the young boy's eyes.

Two Hawks looked up at Ramon. "I will work hard. You will see. Two Hawks will take nothing he has not earned."

Ramon clamped a hand on the youth's thin shoulder and gave it a gentle, reassuring squeeze. "I will make certain you earn your keep. There will be tallow to make into candles, hoeing and weeding to be done in the garden, hogs to butcher . . . but perhaps later on," he said, knowing exactly what would lift the boy's broken spirits, "Mariano can find time to teach you something of the horses."

The man was Ramon's *segundo* now that Pedro had returned to the stronghold. "You would like that, no? To learn the ways of the vaquero?"

Two Hawks's expression changed, shone with a glimmer of hope. "*Si,* Don Ramon. I would like that very much."

"In the meantime," Carly said, "you can come with me." She forced a bolstering smile, her heart aching at the loss of the friend she had made in the village and the pain the young boy suffered. "You'll need something to wear, and I'll find you something to eat." With a glance at Ramon, she led him off toward the outdoor kitchen, certain Blue Blanket would have enough left from breakfast to feed him while she searched out proper clothes.

Along with the food, she also hoped Blue might be of some comfort. That Two Hawks was a Yocuts while Blue was a Mutsen seemed of little importance. The tragedies their people shared made them one as nothing else could.

Leaving the boy in the old woman's care, she went about her tasks, then returned with the clothes and waited while he went down to the stream to bathe and change.

She smiled as he came walking toward her. Though the clothes were a little too large for his thin frame, he looked like a different person. Dressed in buckskin breeches and a white muslin shirt, a pair of scuffed leather boots on his feet, he had washed his coal black hair and bound it behind his neck with a thin leather thong.

"I am ready to work," he said simply.

"You've been through a terrible ordeal, Two Hawks.

Why don't you rest for a while? You can start work in the morning."

His shoulders sagged and the corners of his mouth sagged down. He forced his head up at Ramon's approach.

"There is work to do in the corral," Ramon said. "Mariano is waiting to show you." He was the vaquero who had spoken up for her the day she'd heard the men talking about the don's unwanted marriage. Carly had a soft spot in her heart for the big rugged man. Still, the boy was young, and he was grieving.

"I think he should rest," Carly said. "I told him to—"

"That is your wish, *muchacho?*" Her husband's gaze swung to the boy, who looked at him and smiled, the first Carly had seen.

"I wish to work, senor."

Ramon simply nodded. "Go then. There is much to do. When you have finished, I will take you to meet Bajito. I think perhaps the two of you will get along."

"Bajito?"

"*Si,* but not until later. Now go."

The boy raced off with a spring in his step, his swatch of long black hair bobbing against his back. Carly gazed up at Ramon and realized he had been right.

"He needed to work," he said with a shrug of his wide shoulders. "It will help him to forget."

"Yes . . . and Bajito will be good for him, too. I'm glad you came when you did."

But she was always glad to see Ramon. Lately he had seemed equally glad to see her. It made her heart swell with love and hope, yet there was always a part of him that he held back. He didn't love her, but he cared for her.

It was as much as she ever would have had with Vincent. Somehow with Ramon it wasn't enough.

*C*hapter *F*ifteen

*C*arly watched Ramon walk away, wondering at his thoughts, thinking about how much she had come to love him. He'd been good with the boy, but then she had seen him with children before. How would he feel about the children she might bear him? Would he love them as much as if they were born of pure Spanish blood?

It was an unsettling thought, one that haunted her as she worked beside his mother and aunt that afternoon. They were melting the last of the steer fat into tallow, finishing with the final remnants of slaughtered beef. It was hard, sweaty work, but at last they were done, and Carly left them, meandering down to where the stream emerged from the trees. She sat down on a big granite boulder, picked up a handful of shiny black pebbles and began tossing them into the creek.

That was where Ramon found her, staring off into the water, her thoughts more troubled as the day wore on.

He sat down on the rock beside her. "What are you thinking, Cara, that has made you so forlorn?"

She looked up at him. "I was thinking of Two Hawks and Lena. How could such a terrible thing have happened? Why would the soldiers want to kill them?"

Ramon leaned back, propping his shoulders against the

trunk of an alder tree. "I spoke to the boy about it. He says two of the young men from the village went raiding. They stole half a dozen horses from a rancho at the base of the San Juan Grade. The man who owns the place was shot, wounded in the shoulder, and the militia was called in to help him. Unfortunately, they trailed the young men back to the village."

"His people must have needed those horses very badly. I saw only a few when we were in their camp."

A corner of Ramon's mouth curved up. "That, *querida,* is because they eat them."

"What!"

He nodded. "For many years, horses have been the main source of food in the Yocuts's diet. In the old days, tens of thousands of wild horses roamed these hills and the great valley beyond. It is where most of our own horses come from."

"They actually . . . eat them?"

"*Si.* They also eat gophers—they roast them hair, fleas, and all. Grasshoppers are a delicacy eaten in the spring. They boil big fat grub worms, and eat the larvae of wasps. They roast lizards, snakes, moles—"

"All right!" she said, cutting him off. "I can see their diet is far . . . broader than our own." She swallowed down the queasiness that had risen in her throat.

"You are lucky we brought our own food with us to the village."

"And I wanted to go to one of their feasts," she mumbled, making Ramon chuckle softly.

"They are different than we are. That is why there is so much prejudice against them. And they can be vicious at times. They fought with deadly skill against the early rancheros, murdered a number, and occasionally still raid and kill."

"But shooting women and children . . . it just isn't right."

"No, *chica,* it is not right. I am sorry about Lena but I am glad Two Hawks is safe."

So was Carly. If the boy reached his potential, if he worked hard and learned what he could from Ramon and the vaqueros, he would grow into a strong, intelligent man.

"It was kind of you to help him," Carly said.

Ramon just smiled. "Perhaps I did it just to please you."

She shook her head, moving a tendril of hair at her cheek that had come loose from her braid. "I don't think so. I think you would help anyone who asked you. It's just the way you are."

Ramon said nothing but his dark eyes glinted with pleasure that she would think so. He took her hand and they started walking back toward the house.

"I was speaking to your mother this afternoon," she said, broaching a subject Ramon had not mentioned. "She told me you're leaving in a couple of days . . . that you have business in Monterey." She prayed it was nothing to do with El Dragón.

"*Si,* that is so." A moment of unease flickered in his eyes, and Carly's chest went tight.

"How long will you be gone?"

"A little less than a week." His gaze came up to her face. "I thought perhaps . . . you might wish to join me."

"You want to take me with you?"

"It is not a difficult journey. I thought I could accomplish my business and afterward, we could spend some time together. There is a good hotel in Monterey. A few days to ourselves is not too much to ask for a man and his new bride."

"Oh, Ramon!" She threw her arms around his neck and he held her tightly against him.

"If I had known you would be so pleased, I would have planned such a journey long ago."

She laughed with pleasure, then thought of Two Hawks

and suddenly felt guilty. "Maybe I should stay . . . help Two Hawks get settled. He's suffered a terrible loss."

"Mariano will see to the boy. It is Two Hawks's greatest wish to be a vaquero. Your interference will not help him accomplish that goal."

She mulled that over. She had seen the truth of that earlier in the day. Still, he was bound to be feeling alone. "I-I don't know. He's so young and—"

"You will have time to mother the boy before we go. After that your attention belongs to me."

Carly grinned. "When do we leave?"

"Day after tomorrow. Two Hawks should be settled by then, and this is a matter of some importance."

"What is it?"

His glance grew a little bit wary, darkening the gold in his eyes. "Nothing to concern yourself about. De la Guerra business, that is all."

She ignored an unwelcome pang. *I'm a de la Guerra now,* she wanted to say, but in her husband's mind, she probably never would be. "I think I'll go on ahead," she said, her smile a little less bright. "Blue is making *carne asada* for supper. I'd like her to show me how to cook it."

Ramon caught her arm as she turned to leave. "There was a time we had three serving women to prepare each meal. Perhaps that time will come again."

Carly eased away. "It doesn't matter to me, Ramon. As long as you are here, that is all I need to make me happy."

Ramon's dark head came up, surprise flaring in the ink black pupils of his eyes. Surely he knew how she felt. Then again perhaps he didn't. If that was so, in a way she was glad. She had seen him with Isabel Montoya and Miranda Aguilar. Both of them were beautiful and obviously in love with him. It was just as obvious he didn't love them back.

She was Ramon's wife—but not by choice. Whatever feelings he held for her did not include love.

A soft ache rolled through her, making her heart tilt painfully inside her chest. What *did* Ramon feel for her? He wanted her, there was no doubt of that. But he had wanted other women too. He had always had a number of mistresses. How would she feel if he left her for someone else, or went back to Miranda or Isabel Montoya? Why should she believe there would never be anyone else?

Carly's stomach knotted. There was a time she might have endured it. Now she knew that part of her would die inside, leave her less than the whole woman she had become since she had met Ramon.

For the first time it occurred to her the terrible risk she had taken in giving Ramon her heart.

The smile on her lips turned falsely bright. "You mustn't worry about me," she said. "I don't mind a little hard work. You treat me well, and sleeping with you is certainly better than sleeping with Vincent Bannister." With those cool words she left him, her stomach tied in knots, her heart aching with painful uncertainty.

But her smile remained in place. In a single instant, she had come to a decision. As much as she loved Ramon, as much as that love grew deeper every day, she couldn't let him know. Not until she was certain she could win his love in return. Perhaps in Monterey, they would grow closer.

But in her heart, she wasn't sure he would ever let that happen. She wasn't sure any woman could win Ramon's love.

Especially not a woman who wasn't of pure Spanish blood.

For the next two days, Carly shoved her fears aside and immersed herself in preparing for the journey. She had never been to the old Spanish settlement of Monterey. To be traveling there with Ramon, to be alone with him for almost a week, seemed the height of self-indulgence. She was a little bit worried about Two Hawks, but the boy seemed to be adjusting as well as could be expected and getting along with the men. Blue Blanket hovered over him like a hen with her chick, and there were several other Indians on the rancho; one even worked as a vaquero.

Still, Two Hawks was different here than he had been in his village. He was quiet and withdrawn most of the time. Except for the moments he spent with little Bajito, he wasn't at all the happy carefree child he had been in the mountains. Though he was just as endearing. He was always there to lend a hand when it was needed—and he was always hungry. She wondered how long he had gone without eating on his journey from the village for it seemed the boy could never get enough to fill him up.

Which was why she wasn't surprised when one of Tia Teresa's wild blackberry pies came up missing.

"I cannot imagine what could have happened," Tia said fretfully to Anna. "One minute it was sitting on the window sill out in the *cocina,* the next it was gone."

"What was gone?" Carly asked, carrying one of Ramon's white shirts into the *sala,* along with a needle and thread.

"My pie," Tia said. She didn't cook often, but her pies were a specialty, a rare and delicious treat. "At first I believed some wild animal must have stolen it, then I found these little round stones sitting up on the sill. I cannot think what they could be."

Carly eyed the polished round stones thoughtfully. "I have no idea. Perhaps Ramon will know." But already she was thinking that she knew where the pie must have gone. She just hoped Tia wouldn't see the blackberry stains on Two Hawks's slim brown hands.

Two days later, they set off on their journey to Monterey. Sitting astride his silver-trimmed saddle, Ramon ducked his head beneath an overhanging branch, a bronzed leaf fluttering down as he held it aside so Carly could ride underneath. The morning had dawned clear and bright, a lemon yellow sun and a vibrant azure sky. He smiled to himself and thanked the Blessed Virgin for the gift of such a day for his bride.

They were traveling horseback. Ramon had suggested the carriage, but his wife had surprised him by refusing.

"I'm riding better with each of my lessons," she said. "And it would be faster if we traveled cross-country. You said there was a shortcut through the hills—we could take it if we didn't have to stay on the road." She smiled at him prettily. "Besides, I need the practice."

His hand came up to her cheek. "Aye, *querida,* when you smile that way, how could any man refuse?" It was only a two-day journey, and he was proud that she wanted her horsemanship skills to improve.

She had surprised him again when she joined him that morning perched atop his aunt's heavy old sidesaddle. At least the skirt of the saddle was no longer stiff and curling. Someone had lovingly worked it over, softening the leather, rubbing it to a glossy sheen, and cleaning the silver fittings. He had a strong suspicion his wife was the one who had taken such care.

"You are sure about this, Cara?"

"I started using a woman's saddle when I got back to del Robles. I wanted to learn to ride like a lady."

"But the saddle is too big for you. You are sure you will be able to manage?"

"I can do it, Ramon. I learned on a saddle this size."

He smiled. "All right then, the sun begins to climb. It is time we are off on our journey."

She looked so lovely in her sapphire blue velvet riding habit, her fiery hair curled in ringlets that nestled against her shoulders. It made his blood begin to thicken, made him hungry to take her again, though they had just made love that morning.

Ramon bit back a silent groan of frustration. The woman set a torch to his blood every time he looked at her. He had hoped his need for her would lessen. Instead it seemed to strengthen with each passing day. *Madre de Dios*, it wasn't like him. He wished he knew what to do.

"You are certain you have brought enough clothes?" Only one satchel was draped across the back of the mule they had packed with their bedrolls and supplies.

The journey was meant to be a pleasant one so Ramon had indulged himself. Their saddle bags held food for the trail: apples from the orchard, *pinole, carne seca*—dried beef jerky—tortillas, coffee, and Yerba Buena tea. The mule was packed with freshly roasted chicken for the evening meal, bean pies, cheese, and sweetbreads. The animal even carried a thin feather mattress for the nights they would spend sleeping on the ground.

"The satchel holds more than you think," Carly told him, her eyes a light emerald green and sparkling with excitement. "You said to bring something pretty, so I did. The dresses will be fine once they're aired out and pressed."

He could only imagine the assortment of clothes Isabel Montoya would have had to bring along. It would have taken three mules just to carry them. Then again, there would have been no use for a mule. Isabel would have insisted on traveling in the carriage.

Both his mother and Tia Teresa came out to see them off. Two Hawks was working in the barn with Mariano, where he went every evening as soon as his tasks were done.

"Have a safe journey, my son," his mother said. She turned to smile at Carly. "You, also . . . my daughter."

A film of moisture darkened the green of his wife's pretty eyes. She was smiling at his mother with such affection that something softened inside him. He had hoped his mother and aunt would accept her. He had never imagined they would come to love her as he did.

Ramon's gloved hand went taut on the reins, making Rey del Sol start to prance and toss his head. He couldn't have said that, not even in his mind. He couldn't allow himself even to think it.

He knew the danger. *Por Dios,* he knew exactly the way it felt to have a woman trample on his heart.

"Vaya con Dios," his aunt called after them. Go with God, she said. "Enjoy yourselves—and Ramon, be sure to give our best to your cousins." A letter had come. Maria de la Guerra would be visiting Monterey with her daughter.

"I will convince them to come for a visit," he said.

"Take care of yourselves," Carly called out to them.

Ramon waved a final good-bye and lightly touched his spurs to his horse's ribs. Carly rode up beside him, perched atop a well-schooled, little white mare.

"They're very dear," she said, glancing back toward the two figures fading into the distance, raising her hand to wave one last time. "I've come to care for them very much."

Ramon said nothing. He was still grappling with the notion that he was falling in love with Caralee McConnell. He could stop it from happening, he assured himself. He could distance himself from her soft looks and gentle smiles, keep himself aloof from her laughter and the passion they shared in bed.

He admired her, yes. He appreciated a woman with courage, one who wasn't afraid to stand up for herself, or to him. Respect was a good thing in a marriage. That and friendship, along with a good dose of lust, was all he needed.

He would keep it at that, he assured himself. He wouldn't let her get any closer to him than she was already.

Then he glanced across at her, saw her bright, excited smile as she pointed at a beautiful goshawk soaring among the clouds above them. Smiling in return, he felt his heart expanding inside him and knew he was already in far deeper than he had wished.

* * *

Sheriff Jeremy Layton rode his tall bay gelding up in front of the de la Guerra hacienda but didn't get down from his horse. It was the custom among the rancheros not to dismount unless you were invited. He hadn't been, and at this point, Jeremy had no reason to behave inhospitably toward Ramon de la Guerra or anyone in his family, who were, after all, highly respected members of the community.

Still . . . Fletcher Austin had begun to have suspicions the don might be involved with El Dragón. Austin was a lot of things: hard-nosed, ruthless, even a little bit greedy.

But no one ever said he was a fool.

A stout, dark-skinned man walked toward him, mid-thirties, thick-chested with a bushy handlebar mustache.

"*Buenas tardes,* Senor Sheriff. You are looking for Don Ramon?"

His name was Mariano, Jeremy recalled. One of the don's top vaqueros. "I thought I might have a word with him. He around?"

"No, senor. The don is not here."

"Then perhaps I could speak to his wife."

"Again, I am sorry. If you would like to speak to the senora . . . or perhaps to Don Ramon's aunt . . ."

"Would you mind telling me where the don and his bride have gone?"

He hesitated only a moment, then he grinned. "A wedding trip, senor. A young bride is often shy, no? There are things the don may wish to teach her . . . things that are best learned away from the knowing looks of family and friends."

Or perhaps the don had already taught her those things in the mountains, as Fletcher Austin believed. "Be sure to give them my congratulations," Jeremy said. "Tell them I'll be dropping by to see them again very soon."

"*Si,* I will tell them, Sheriff Layton."

He scanned the house and grounds, but saw nothing out of the ordinary. "Mind if I water my horse before I go?"

"No, no, of course not. It was rude of me not to suggest it. Perhaps I can get you something as well . . . coffee or chocolate . . . or maybe something to eat?"

"No thanks. Just the water for my horse."

Mariano nodded and led the way to a moss-covered watering trough. Jeremy let the horse drink deeply, sucking the cool water into his muzzle, then backed him away and settled more deeply into the saddle. As he touched the brim of his hat in farewell, he caught the shimmer of curtains moving inside the house, but no one came to the door. Not very friendly.

Then again, with the don away the two old women might have second thoughts about talking to a man they didn't know.

At the top of the rise, he paused to look back down on the hacienda. The stout vaquero spoke to a dark-skinned Indian boy, then boosted him up on the saddle of a slightly swaybacked horse. A little spotted dog yapped at the animal's feet but it didn't seem disturbed. Around the pair, work continued, several men repairing a downed length of fence, while two other vaqueros sat in the shade, braiding long thin leather *reatas.* Nothing suspicious here.

Still, he would like to talk once more to the girl. And also to Don Ramon. On Sunday, some of the men would be attending mass at the mission. He could speak to some of them then.

At least El Dragón had not been raiding.

Perhaps the man who supplied him with information had been too busy making love to his fiery new bride.

Pueblo Monterey, once the capital of Alta California, seemed very little changed from what it must have been in the early days of Spanish rule. A sleepy little village, it nestled on a gentle, pine-covered slope over-looking the bay. An American flag floated above the fort on the bluff, and on the government buildings in town, and a neat yellow stone building served as town hall. Off to one side, Carly noticed a cluster of houses, sturdily built, some of adobe, others of wood; and in the bright blue waters of the bay, a dozen vessels bobbed at anchor.

"It's beautiful, Ramon."

"*Si,* Cara. The Presidio has always been a beautiful little town." But he frowned as he leaned forward, resting an elbow on his wide, flat saddle horn to stare down at the scene below. "It has changed since the Anglos have come. There are many more cantinas. And there is much more gambling. The men play billiards from morning to night; they gamble at cards and monte. The places do not close, not even on Sunday."

He smiled, but it looked a little bit forced. "Ah, but there is also now a decent hotel. Come, I will show you. The day grows late and I am sure you will be glad for the chance to rest."

True, but she wasn't really that tired and surprisingly she wasn't even sore. And the ride from Las Almas with Ramon had been a joy she would never forget.

He helped her down from her mare and they checked into the Cypress Hotel, a lovely old tile-roofed adobe that overlooked the bay. It was once a residence of the governor, Ramon said. Lately, the place had been purchased by a group of Americans, who'd had it painted and put in good repair. The *sala,* now the lobby, stood two stories high, with stained glass windows, massive wooden beams, and a fireplace at one end large enough for a man to walk into.

Their room was small but well furnished, with a sturdy oak bed, pale blue counterpane, and white lace curtains at the windows. A balcony overlooked the blue Pacific Ocean.

"It's wonderful, Ramon," Carly said as her husband closed the heavy wooden door.

"It is not so grand as I would like, but it is comfortable." A corner of his sensuous mouth curved up. "Perhaps after supper, we will see if the bed is as comfortable as the rest of the room." Eyes tinged with gold ran over her, pausing at the curve of her breast. He reached for her, slid an arm around her waist, and pulled her against him. "Or perhaps we should find out now."

He kissed her deeply, a long, searing kiss that made her dizzy and had her gripping his shoulders. She felt him grow hard against her, thought of that hardness inside her, and vaguely considered missing the meal altogether.

Instead Ramon pulled away. "Aye, *querida,* you make a man lose his head. There will be plenty of time for making love later. In the meantime, I have ordered a bath sent up. There is something I must see to, then I will visit the bath house for a haircut and a shave. We will dine when I return."

"All right," she agreed, still a little breathless. He gave her a last hard kiss, gathered a change of clothes, and left her.

By the time he returned, she was dressed in a low-cut mauve silk gown an Indian serving woman had pressed for her, while Ramon wore snug gray *calzonevas* piped in black that clung to his long hard thighs then flared out over his boots. A matching charro jacket stretched across his broad shoulders, covering his ruffled white silk shirt.

"Where are we going to eat?" Carly asked as he propelled her toward the door.

"My cousin Maria is in town from Santa Barbara. She wished us to join her and her daughter, Carlotta, and several other guests at the home of Ricardo Micheltorena, where she is staying during her visit." He smiled at her wickedly. "Unfortunately, I told them we would have to decline their generous invitation . . . at least for tonight. This night I would have you to myself."

A little shimmer of pleasure ran through her. "I'd really like to meet them, but I can't say I'm sorry it won't be tonight."

"You will have a chance later on."

They ate in the hotel dining room, a simple fare: an *asada* of chicken and red peppers, cucumbers, corn, and a *guisado* of beef and potatoes. Yet all of it was cooked to perfection.

They spoke of their trip from Las Almas and Carly told him how much she had enjoyed the journey through the rolling California hills. They spoke of Two Hawks and how excited he was to be learning the skills of a vaquero.

"The life he's led must have been a hard one," Carly said with a hint of sadness. "Until he came to Las Almas, I don't think he ever had quite enough to eat."

"In the early days game was plentiful. The Indians never had to worry. Now, with so many miners still working the hills, the meat hunters have come. They kill whatever game crosses their path, though much of it is wasted. And many of the younger braves have left the villages to find work. The older people, the women and children are left to fend for themselves."

Carly nodded gravely. Then she thought of the boy and the missing blackberry pie, and found herself smiling again. "I think Two Hawks stole one of Tia's pies. Knowing how he is about food, I didn't have the heart to confront him."

"He didn't steal it," Ramon corrected. "Two Hawks is far too honorable for that. He bought it."

"Bought it? But how could he—" She broke off with a grin. "The stones he left on the window sill."

Ramon smiled softly. "Trading stones. Among his people, they are used as barter. To him, they are the same as money."

Carly laughed. "I believe Two Hawks may teach us as much as we teach him."

Ramon just nodded. They finished their meal and returned to their room, undressed, and made love to the sound of the wind in the trees and the distant lap of water against the rocky shore.

In the morning Ramon left for the meeting that had brought him to Monterey. Carly's single regret was that he carefully avoided any mention of what that meeting was about.

"*Buenas tardes,* Don Ramon, please come in." Alejandro de Estrada, a distinguished graying man in his early fifties, motioned the tall Spaniard in. Alejandro had written the don sometime back and been eager to meet the son of his old *compadre,* Diego de la Guerra, a man he had known and respected since his earliest days in California.

"*Gracias,* Don Alejandro, I have looked forward to this occasion for some time."

"As have I, Don Ramon." He smiled. "Before we begin would you care for some coffee, or perhaps a cup of cocoa?"

"Coffee would suit me well." A short, robust serving woman brought the refreshments into his small, tidy office. The walls were whitewashed adobe, adorned only with a painting that had been done by an artist who owed him money and the diplomas that signified he was qualified to practice law in the State of California.

Alejandro sat down at his small oak writing desk, moving aside the stack of letters he had been reading, and Ramon de la Guerra took a seat in the leather-bottomed chair across from him.

"You are here to discuss Rancho del Robles," Alejandro said. "I am well aware of your troubles. Your father came to me in the beginning. He hoped I would somehow be able to prevent the loss of his land, but at the time, I am sorry to say, I was not able to help him." He sighed deeply, thinking of the tragic death of his good friend. "I only wish I could have."

"You were his *abogado* for many years, Don Alejandro. In your letter, you said you may have stumbled onto something that could change things."

"*Si,* that is correct. The record of your father's title to Rancho del Robles was destroyed in the fire here in Monterey over twenty years ago, and the land descriptions in his original *diseño* were so vague the courts refused to accept it without a second means of verification."

The don leaned forward. "And now you have found such a means?"

"After your father's case was lost, another case was opened. The *haciendado* who owned the land, Don Hernando Seville, introduced church records to verify his claim—records of births and deaths that showed four generations of Sevilles had owned the property. At first the Lands Commission wouldn't accept it, since they have always been suspicious of the Catholic church, but in the end, Don Hernando won. His claim was ratified and Rancho Las Palmas remained in his family's hands."

"If such records exist, could they not also prove the de la Guerra claim?"

Alejandro nodded. "It is possible. Unfortunately, the priest who would know is preparing even now to leave for Los Angeles. Unless you can reach him today, it will be many months before he will return—perhaps never, should he journey on to Mexico."

The don came up from his chair. "Where is he?"

"At a small church about thirty miles south of here. I learned of his departure through the priest at the mission in Carmelo. The man you wish to see, Padre Renaldo, is very old. For a while he lived at the mission in San Juan Bautista."

"*Si* . . . I believe I remember him from when I was a boy."

"The records are not there, but if they still exist, he will know where to find them."

"Then I must go to him . . . speak to him before he leaves."

Alejandro shoved back his chair and came to his feet. "It is a long, grueling ride, but I can think of no other way. And even if you find the documents, I cannot guarantee the Land Commission will overturn its decision."

"I understand. Still, it is more hope than I have had in some time."

Alejandro rounded his desk and extended a hand to the tall, imposing don. "God go with you, my son."

"*Gracias,* Don Alejandro. My family and I are grateful for your help." He started for the door, lifted the latch and drew it open.

"Oh, and by the way"—Alejandro smiled—"my most hearty felicitations on your marriage."

For a moment, the younger man's hard look softened. "*Gracias.* I will relay your kind words to my bride." Then the lines of his face grew grim once more. Long, purposeful strides carried him into the quiet dirt street and Alejandro closed the door.

"I am sorry, *chica.* I hate to leave you like this, but I cannot take you with me. Perhaps I should speak to my cousin . . . see if there is room for you at Casa Micheltorena."

"Don't be silly. If this is as important as you say, then of course you must go. I'll be fine while you are away, and you'll be back by tomorrow night. After that, we can be together."

He bent his head and kissed her. "Monterey is a peaceful town, but it is not so safe as it used to be. Promise me you will stay inside the hotel and be sure to lock the door before you go to sleep."

"I told you, I'll be fine."

"Promise me."

"All right, I promise."

Ramon smiled, thinking how lovely she was and how much he hated to leave her. "I will be counting the hours until my return." He collected his saddle bags and turned toward the door.

"Ramon?"

"Si, querida?"

"Are you certain you won't tell me what this is about?"

A moment of unease filtered through him. He wished he could tell her the truth, make her understand that the land belonged to his family, had for generations, and he intended to do everything in his power to see it returned. But the man he opposed was her uncle. He couldn't be certain how she would feel if she knew.

"Perhaps when I come back." He pulled her against him, took her mouth in a hard, possessive kiss that said she was his and that she shouldn't forget it. *"Hasta mañana, my lovely wife. I will return as quickly as I can."*

"Good luck, Ramon."

The unease returned. Her uncle was a subject they hadn't discussed since their days in the stronghold. It was as if each of them was afraid to broach a topic that was bound to set them at odds. He wondered if she would still wish him luck if she understood what it was that he planned to do.

"Gracias, querida. Take care of yourself until my return."

Chapter Sixteen

She meant to stay in the hotel, she really did, but the day was so lovely and she had never been to Monterey.

Determined she would take only a short walk around, get a look at the sleepy little village Ramon had promised to show her, she wandered down the main street, looking through the tiny panes of glass in the shop windows. From there she strolled down to the harbor, stopping to watch a small, twin-masted brig whose white canvas sails lufted out as it arrived in the bay.

"That ship that's coming in," she said to a craggy old fisherman with long gray hair and a foot-long pointed beard who sat on a rocky edge of the bay, holding a willow branch fishing pole, "it looks like they're towing something. What are they doing?" Beside him a stringer of carp flashed silver in the sunlight, their bodies half in, half out of the water.

"That's a Boston whaler, lassie. They be bringin' in their cargo—'bout an eighty-foot gray, I'd say. She'll give up nearly a hundred barrels of oil."

"They bring whales into Monterey?"

"Aye, that they do. Once they're done wi' 'em, they tow 'em out into the bay. Beach southeast o' here is white with hundreds o' dry, bleached bones."

"I see." She watched the ship for a while, then her gaze swung away, focused on a different section of the water. Not too distant from the shore, a small brown, fur-covered animal drifted on its back atop the waves.

"Sea otter, lassie. Cute little devil, ain't he?"

"What's he doing?"

"Crackin' open his dinner. They eat oysters, ya see. Use an empty shell to bust 'em open. They float on their back like that and sun themselves. Got a damned fine life, ya ask me." A flush rose into his ruddy, bearded cheeks. "Beg pardon, lass. Haven't done much talkin' to a lady, not since I left Aberdeen."

"That's all right, mister . . . ?"

"MacDugal. Most folks just call me Mac."

Carly smiled. "It's nice to meet you, Mac. I'm Carly de la Guerra."

"Pleasure, Miss . . . de la Guerra, ya say?"

"That's right. Why? Do you know my husband?"

"His name Angel? Real handsome lad, lanky built with curly black hair?"

"My husband's name is Ramon."

"Different fellow." He shook his head, waving his long gray beard. "Can't say as I'm sorry to hear it. That one was drinkin' and whorin' over to Conchita's Cantina all night. Not the kinda man a lassie like you needs for a husband."

Definitely not. Still, Carly wondered if Angel and Ramon were related. He had said his cousins were in town, though he hadn't mentioned anyone but Maria and her daughter.

"It's getting kind of late," Carly said. "I suppose I should be going. I really enjoyed our conversation, Mac."

"So did I, lassie. You take care now, ya hear?"

Carly nodded and started back toward the hotel, still wondering about Angel de la Guerra, but mostly thinking of Ramon and how lonely the evening would be without him.

* * *

Leaning against the side of a building beneath a covered porch, his knee bent and propped against the wall, Angelo de la Guerra watched the pretty *Americana* walk away. He had been following her all afternoon, been watching the hotel since he had seen his cousin leave then ride out from the stable. Angel had been curious about his cousin's new wife from the moment he had overheard him talking to his sister about her last night.

He took a long draw on his hand-rolled *cigarillo,* let the smoke curl out through his slim, straight nose.

So this was Ramon's blushing bride.

Not bad . . . for a *gringa.* But then his cousin had always had good taste in women.

And he had been enjoying them freely for the last five years while Angel had been rotting in an Arizona prison. He thought of how many times he had wanted a woman only to have that woman choose his cousin over him. They had always been competitive, even as children. And even in the early days, Ramon had bested him in everything they'd done.

Angel scoffed. Why not? Diego de la Guerra was richer, more powerful than his own father was. Ramon was better educated. He was taller, and by far the better horseman. Women were drawn to his good looks and charm even as they scoffed at Angel's less skilled attempts to woo them. When it came to Ramon de la Guerra, Angel had always come out second best.

Even Yolanda, his childhood sweetheart, had secretly pined for Ramon. She had told him so once, that she couldn't marry him because she was in love with someone else. The fact Ramon didn't want her hadn't changed the fact that she wanted him.

Angel took a last draw on his *cigarillo* and tossed it into the street, sending up a small puff of dust that extinguished the flame. He thought of the copper-haired woman and felt himself grow hard inside his buckskin breeches. He wasn't the same callow boy he had been the last time Ramon had seen him. The last five years had seen to that.

He wanted the woman. He was a free man again and he meant to take what he wanted. It was time he evened the score.

Carly borrowed a leather-bound book, *Pilgrim's Progress,* from a shelf in the hotel lobby, then returned upstairs to her room. She had meant to eat supper there, but the minutes seemed to drag and finally she gave in to the urge and went downstairs. The dining room wasn't large, just a single long table down the middle with benches on each side and a few small tables around it, each with two spindly-legged chairs. She sat down in the one nearest the corner, and a buxom, smiling Mexican woman appeared.

"Senora de la Guerra. Your husband said you might join us. He said that we should take very good care of you while he is away."

Carly smiled. "I know I should probably eat upstairs, but I . . . well, I thought it might be more interesting down here."

"Of course, senora. Why should such a beautiful woman lock herself away in an empty room?"

Carly's smile broadened at the encouragement.

"You are hungry, senora?" The buxom woman wiped her thick-fingered hands on the apron she wore over her robust hips.

"I'm starving. The walk I took earlier must have stirred up my appetite."

"We will fix that, you will see. How would you like some nice *chilena* pie? The corn crust is golden, baked exactly right. I promise you it is delicious."

"Thank you, that sounds wonderful."

The woman scurried off to ready the meal while Carly

surveyed the rest of the people in the room. Four of them were Spanish, a man and his wife and their two children; two were dressed as miners, in canvas breeches and flannel shirts, Americans down from the gold fields. Several men wore tail coats, businessmen or government officials. At a small table near the door, a lean, tough-looking man with wavy black hair and dark eyes sat with his back to the wall. She noticed he was watching her.

He smiled when her eyes caught his. Then he lazily came to his feet and began to walk toward her, his long strides easy and sure. He looked enough like Ramon that it took only a moment for her to realize exactly who he was.

"Senora?"

"Yes?"

"I am your husband's cousin, Angelo. Do you mind if I sit down?"

"Why . . . no . . . of course not. I had heard some of his family was in town. I'm very glad to meet you."

He pulled out a chair and sat down. He was shorter than Ramon, a little more slender, but wide-shouldered and hard-muscled, obviously well built. As Mac had said, the man was handsome, in a different, more austere way than Ramon, but attractive just the same.

"My cousin has left you here alone? It is not like Ramon to leave such a beautiful woman to fend for herself . . . especially not one who is his wife."

"Something came up. He had to leave rather unexpectedly. I told him I'd be all right while he was gone."

Angel smiled, his teeth flashing white, but it didn't hold the kind of warmth Ramon's smile did. "I am sorry I missed him. I only just arrived in town this afternoon."

That wasn't the impression she'd gotten from Mac. "Then your sister doesn't know that you're here?"

"Not yet. There was some business I needed to attend to first."

Like drinking and whoring at Conchita's Cantina, she thought, almost wishing she had eaten in her room after all. There was something about Angelo de la Guerra, something she couldn't quite pin down, yet it bothered her just the same.

She forced herself to smile. "Will . . . will you join me?"

"I am afraid I have already eaten. And there is a matter of some importance I must see to." He rose from his chair, took her hand and brought it to his lips. They felt cool and dry, not the least bit pleasant. "It has been a pleasure meeting you . . . ?"

"Caralee," she supplied, oddly wishing she didn't have to tell him her name at all. But the man was her husband's cousin. She really had no choice.

"It has been a pleasure, Cousin Caralee. Be sure to give Ramon my regards."

Carly only nodded. She watched him leave, his gait more a swagger than a walk. When the plump Mexican woman brought the meal, Carly discovered she was no longer hungry.

Instead she picked at the food, forcing herself to eat at least a portion of it, then returned upstairs to read. Several times her mind strayed to Angel de la Guerra and the uncomfortable feeling she had experienced in his presence. Eventually, the pages in the book began to blur and she set the text on the bedside table. Wearily she blew out the lamp and slid more deeply between the covers. Surprisingly it didn't take long to fall asleep.

She dreamed of Ramon, a pleasant dream, filled with warmth and love and hope for the future. She wondered if Ramon dreamed of her.

Angel de la Guerra slipped silently down the hallway, moving with the stealth of a man who knew how to handle himself. It was a confidence he had lacked until his years in prison . . . perhaps until he had killed his first man.

In the lobby below, a grandfather clock ticked softly, breaking into the quiet. It was well past midnight. No light filtered beneath the closed doors; the hotel guests were sleeping. Listening for the sound of footfalls but hearing none, he pulled a long, thin piece of wire from the waistband of his buckskin breeches, eased it into the lock on the door, flicked it one way and then the other, and heard the satisfying sound of the lock beginning to turn.

Removing the wire, he quietly turned the knob and shoved open the door, then stepped soundlessly into the room.

He stopped at the foot of the bed. Caralee de la Guerra lay sleeping, her long dark copper hair fanned out across her pillow. She wore a beautifully embroidered white silk nightgown so sheer he could see the rose aureoles at the crest of her high full breasts. The sheet and blanket had been shoved down haphazardly past her waist. He noticed how tiny it was above the gentle flaring of her hips.

He was hard already just knowing what he intended, had been since before he had opened the door. Now his shaft was stiff and pulsing, his palms beginning to sweat as he imagined himself pumping into her ripe little body, the taking even sweeter for the fact she belonged to Ramon.

She was sleeping soundly. He quietly stripped off his clothes then eased back the covers and climbed into the bed beside her. She had only stirred once. Now she rolled toward him, resting a small hand on his chest, and in her sleep she smiled.

Angel smiled, too. Easing the nightgown off her shoulder, he bared a pale upturned breast, cupped it with his hand and began to tease the nipple. Just as it puckered into hardness, her eyes snapped open and she came up off the bed. He caught her scream in his mouth, slanting his lips over hers as he gripped her wrists and forced her back down on the mattress. Only the sixth sense he had developed in prison enabled him to hear the door as it swung wide.

He turned in time to see his cousin silhouetted in the frame, his face a black mask of rage. Angel steeled himself. He wouldn't be bested again.

"Ramon . . . what are you doing here?"

The bigger man did not move, just stood riveted in the doorway. "I think the question is better asked of you."

"Ramon . . ." Carly whispered.

Angel just looked down at her. He released his bruising grip on her wrists. "I am sorry, cousin. I did not know the little whore belonged to you."

A muscle bunched in Ramon's hard jaw. "The *little whore* is my wife."

Angel swore softly, fluently. "*Dios mio,* I did not know." He swung his legs to the side of the bed. "I saw her in the dining room. We spoke briefly and she invited me here. If I had known who she was . . . *por Dios,* Ramon—"

"Get out," he said.

"What . . . what is he saying?" Carly stared from Ramon to Angel, her body still trembling with anger and fear. "That—that isn't what happened."

"I am sorry, cousin." Angel grabbed his breeches, slid them on, then grabbed his shirt and boots, and started for the door.

"You don't believe him?" Carly said, finally gathering her wits enough to speak. "He came in here and tried to . . . tried to . . . and you're just going to let him leave?"

Angel closed the door, and Ramon's dark eyes swung to her face. Fury hardened his features, made him look like the ruthless, brutal man she knew he could be. "Perhaps you would prefer I leave instead, since you and my cousin seemed to be so thoroughly enjoying each other."

"What!"

"At least have the decency to cover yourself. You may

be certain that I am no longer interested in your somewhat tarnished charms—no matter how appealing they might be."

Carly glanced down, saw that Angel had exposed one of her breasts, and her face flushed crimson. With hands that shook, she hastily pulled her nightgown into place.

"Ramon, please . . . you can't possibly believe that what he told you is the truth. I don't even know how he got in here."

"But you do know who he is? You met him as he says, downstairs in the dining room?"

"I-I spoke to him only briefly. I didn't invite him here—how can you possibly believe I would?"

"I am not blind, Cara, as you seem determined to believe. I saw you with him, remember? He was kissing you, caressing your beautiful breasts." He reached over and jerked the sheet off, leaving her sitting disheveled in the bed, her body trembling, her nightgown riding up to the middle of her thighs.

"Get dressed," he said roughly. "We are leaving."

She started to shake even harder. Tears stung her eyes, began to clog her throat. It was only beginning to hit her, what had occurred, and she still couldn't make herself believe it. "We c-can't leave now. You've been riding all night. You have to get some s-sleep."

He grabbed her arm and yanked her up from the bed. "Do what I tell you!" Black rage pumped through him. It was there in every hard line of his face. His eyes were as dark as the paths leading to hell. "I promised you once I would never hurt you again. At this moment, it is a difficult promise to keep." He let go of her then, and she reeled backward till she fell across the bed.

"Do as I say. Pack your things and prepare to leave."

Carly just stared at him. Her wrists still throbbed where Angel had trapped them. Her lips were bruised from the pressure of his hard, dry lips. Her throat ached with tears and her heart hurt so badly she thought it must surely break in two.

"Why? Why is it so easy for you to believe him and so hard for you to believe me?"

Ramon didn't answer, just grabbed a handful of her clothes from the wardrobe and tossed them at her on the bed. "Get dressed, my little *puta*. I should never have brought you here in the first place. I should have known the temptation would be too much for a *gringa* like you."

A *gringa* like me, Carly thought, fresh pain knifing through her. An Anglo woman, a woman whose word could never stand against that of a de la Guerra. She blinked and hot salty tears began to roll down her cheeks. "You and Angel . . . I thought you were as different as the sun and the moon. Perhaps you are not so different as I believed."

Ramon said nothing. Just turned away as she dressed in her riding habit and shakily plaited her hair into a long, thick braid. Leaving several gold *reals* on the dresser in payment for their room, he hauled her out into the hallway and down the back stairs. She waited in the alley, the cold air slicing through her, while he went to the stable for their horses.

The white mare was saddled and ready, but he was leading Rey del Sol, the stallion obviously weary from the grueling ride Ramon had just made. Instead his big Spanish saddle rested atop a big bay gelding.

"Wh-what about the mule?" Carly asked.

"I traded it for the saddle horse. Rey needs time to recover his strength, and we will be traveling lighter this time." He smiled bitterly. "I find I am eager to be home." His hands bit into her waist as he lifted her up, set her down hard on the sidesaddle. He said nothing as he swung himself up in his heavy silver-trimmed saddle, nothing as they rode out through the empty dirt streets, nothing as they started into the hills.

He pushed hard all morning, stopped to water the horses, then they rode on. Carly didn't eat and neither did Ramon. She could only imagine how exhausted he must be. By nightfall, she felt that same exhaustion herself, coupled with the sickening knowledge that in a single long night in Monterey, she had lost her husband forever.

She tried not to cry, but in the long hours of darkness, she couldn't stop the tears from falling. She had loved him so much. She would have done anything for him. Anything. She had foolishly believed that someday he might love her in return.

Instead he had called her his whore, believed her guilty of sleeping with his cousin. Angel might be a de la Guerra, might be pure Castilian Spanish, but Carly wouldn't spit on a man like Angel. In fact, if she'd had a gun in her room last night, she probably would have shot him.

And what of Ramon? She had come to admire him. Now she saw what she hadn't seen before. The prejudice he loathed in the Anglos, his hatred of people who persecuted those who were different, was as strong in Ramon as it was in the men he opposed. It made her heartsick to think it, to know she could never come up to his expectations, never gain his trust because her heritage wasn't the same as his.

She had known it. He had made it clear from the start, but she hadn't really believed it. She hadn't allowed herself to believe it because she loved him too much.

Lying on her bedroll, Carly curled into a tight ball of misery and buried her head in her arms. Her body shook with the tears that poured from her eyes and soaked into her blanket. She didn't care if Ramon heard her crying. She didn't care about anything anymore. She only knew her life was over, that her heart was broken, that the love she felt for him had begun to seep out of her like water through a piece of broken glass.

She cried until her tears were spent, then lay there staring at the stars. She didn't really see them. Her pain was too deep, her heart too full of despair. Before the sun came up, she crossed the clearing to where the horses had been hobbled, saddled her mare, tied her bedroll on behind, climbed up on a rock, and levered herself into the sidesaddle.

She would have ridden off if Ramon hadn't stepped forward and caught her horse's bridle.

"Where do you think you are going?"

She smiled at him bitterly. "Back where I came from. I won't say home because I no longer have one. I'm returning to Rancho del Robles. If my uncle won't have me, I'll go somewhere else. I don't need you to show me the way."

A muscle jerked in his cheek. "Nevertheless, you will travel with me," he said tersely. "If del Robles is your wish, I will see that you get there." His mouth curved grimly. "Perhaps things have worked out exactly as you planned all along. If you can find a way, you can have your annulment, as you wished from the start. I am sure there are any number of men willing to pleasure you as I have, some of them in ways far beyond what I had only begun to teach you."

Her hand lashed out, slapped him hard across the face. For a moment she thought he might drag her down from the horse, the rage in his face was so great. Then it was gone, replaced by a look of sadness and utter despair. Against her will, she found herself drawn to that look, wanting desperately to ease it away.

"I didn't do the things your cousin said. I know you don't believe me, but it's the truth."

A cold, ruthless smile twisted his lips. "You chose the wrong man . . . *mi amor* . . . when you tried to seduce a de la Guerra. Angel and I, we were raised together as children. He is more like a brother than a cousin."

"He is also a liar, but maybe that doesn't matter."

Ramon's head came up.

"I trapped you into this marriage. You wanted a Spanish woman, instead you got me. Perhaps I did it on purpose—to tell you the truth, I'm no longer sure. Maybe I loved you so much I would have done anything to have you. I only know that if I did, I'm sorry." The little mare danced sideways, and Carly drew back on the reins. "Now you have a second chance. Perhaps this time you'll find a woman who can make you happy." She dug her heels into the horse's ribs and the animal leapt forward, carrying her away from him up the trail.

For long slow seconds, Ramon stared after her. Then he swung up on Rey del Sol's back and thundered up the path in her wake. His jaw was set, his expression grim. Inside his chest, his heart beat dully, numb with pain and an ache so fierce his hands shook where they held the reins.

He had known this would happen. He had seen it time and again. He knew she was an Anglo, knew better than to trust her. He knew she would only break his heart.

And yet he had let it happen. Against all his warnings, all his vows not to let her get too close. Had he loved her so much then? Had he been willing to risk the pain he knew a woman like Caralee would surely bring?

The answer came swift and hard, scorchingly bitter in his mouth. Yes, he had loved her. More than his own life. Even now he risked himself, knowing she might well go to her uncle. She very likely would, since she had been discarded.

He did not care.

Nothing mattered anymore, not since the moment he had walked into that room and seen her lying half naked in the arms of his cousin. If he hadn't changed his plans, if he hadn't rented an extra horse on the chance he might be able to return to her, if he hadn't ridden like a madman, wanting to see her so badly, he wouldn't have caught her with Angel.

He would have been duped as easily as he had been before.

Por Dies, he was a fool.

And he was paying for his foolishness with every aching beat of his heart.

They rode throughout the day, stopping only briefly to rest and water the horses. By late afternoon, they had reached the fork in the trail, one path leading to Rancho del Robles, the other to Las Almas and the lands beyond. Carly reined up at the fork.

"Is—is this the way to my uncle's?"

"*Si*. It is only a mile to the north. I will take you there."

She only shook her head. "No. I want to go alone." She turned a little and a ray of sunlight, shafting through the branches of an oak, lit her hair. The beauty of her face seemed to burn into his mind and the trembling of her lips made his own heart tremble.

Ramon said nothing, just watched her sitting so proudly astride her horse. Inside his chest, his heart was splitting, trying to twist in two. He shouldn't be feeling like this, he shouldn't be thinking of the way she had cried all night, of the soft, soul-wrenching sobs that had drifted across the camp, of the will it had taken not to go to her, to forgive her and beg her not to leave him. He shouldn't be recalling the look of hurt and disbelief he had seen on her face when he had called her his whore, the pain in her eyes when she had said that she loved him.

It wasn't the truth. If she loved him, she wouldn't have betrayed him.

"Ramon?"

"*Si*, Cara?"

"We were friends once, maybe more. Remember the way it was then, will you? Pretend that Monterey never happened. Remember the things we did, the pleasure we shared, remember the good times, not the bad. Will you do that for me?"

His throat constricted. "*Si,* Cara, I will try." His leather-gloved hands were shaking, and his chest squeezed with each of the breaths he forced from his lungs. He started to rein the stallion away.

"One more thing."

He turned toward her, saw the tears that sparkled on her cheeks. "You mustn't feel too badly about what has happened. If you had loved me, you would have recognized the truth even if your eyes said it was a lie. Find a woman you can love, Ramon. Don't settle for anything less."

His heart clenched, seemed to crumble inside him. His throat burned and he could not swallow past the hot ache that rode there. "Cara, please . . . I cannot . . ."

He didn't say more and neither did she, but her eyes remained on his face, as if she were memorizing each of his features.

Moments passed. Long, immeasurable seconds that marked the end of all that had been between them, the shifting winds that altered each of their lives. The oneness they had shared was a thing of the past. They would never do the things he had hoped for, the things he had begun to let himself dream. There would be no future for the two of them, no children they would raise to be proud and strong.

His mind fought a surging wave of pain. Carly spun the little mare, quirted its rump and began to gallop up the trail. *If you loved me,* she had said, but she was wrong. He did love her. So much that losing her was the most painful thing he had ever suffered. Watching her ride away was like seeing the light go out of his life, leaving him in darkness.

His hand shook against the pommel of his saddle, his insides felt leaden. How could he love her and at the same time hate her so much? How could he hate her and still want her?

Ramon closed his eyes, trying not to see the image of his cousin's naked body, his slim dark fingers roaming over his wife's bare breast. If another man had touched her, by now he would be dead. But Angel was family. He was a de la Guerra. He had been duped just as Ramon had been.

He reined the stallion away, the saddle horse trailing behind. At the top of the hill, he paused, watching to be certain Caralee made it safely to the rancho. She was crying, he thought, but he couldn't be sure. Perhaps in her own way, she had loved him after all.

Her horse picked its way down into the valley, Caralee sitting straight in the saddle, her chin held high and her shoulders squared. He wondered what she was thinking, wondered if she regretted what she had done. He wondered if she wished she were returning to Las Almas as much as he wished he were taking her home.

He watched her for several more moments, ignoring the dull ache in his chest, his desire to turn back time until the days before their journey to Monterey. If only he could do things over, perhaps she could have come to love him enough that she never would have strayed.

He watched till her small figure dropped over the rise, then sat back in his saddle and wheeled the stallion away. Several yards up the canyon, he paused, listening to the fading sound of her little mare's footfalls on the rocky trail as she rode farther away.

When the hoofbeats had thinned to silence and the only sound left was the wind soughing softly through the trees, he steeled himself against his aching loss and resigned himself to accepting what must be.

The past was over and done. Like his brother Andreas, Caralee was dead to him, no longer a part of his life. Yesterday he had spoken to Padre Renaldo, the old man he had ridden so far to see. The priest had told him the documents he needed were probably in a vault at the mission in Santa Barbara. Once he had retrieved them, there was a chance he could finally win back his family's land.

For the first time since the deaths of his father and brother, Ramon did not care.

Chapter Seventeen

*I*sn't that my niece riding into the rancho?" Fletcher Austin stood at a window in the *sala,* looking out toward the valley of high brown grasses and covering of oaks. He spoke to Rita Salazar, a woman who had come to the rancho looking for work just before Caralee's wedding.

"*Si,* Senor Fletcher. That is her, I think." Rita was part Spanish, part Miwok Indian. Fletcher had liked her ripe figure, long glossy black hair, and full lips. He had hired her to work in the kitchen, but he wasn't displeased when she'd wound up warming his bed.

Absently patting Rita's round behind, he studied Caralee's small figure as she rode closer, concern for her warring with an unexpected feeling of warmth. He didn't know why Caralee had come. Perhaps it was merely for a visit, as he had meant to visit her to be sure she was all right. Then again, maybe she had learned her lesson and wanted to come home.

Strangely he hoped so. He'd discovered that he missed her once she was gone.

Still, even if she did return, he wouldn't give up the woman. His niece was no longer an innocent. Ramon de la Guerra had a wicked reputation. By now his niece had been well schooled in the art of pleasuring a man, just as Rita had learned to pleasure him. He hadn't been with a woman in years, had steeled himself against the need for any sort of softness in his life. But his niece's feminine presence had begun to make him yearn for a woman's gentle touch. He was grateful Rita had come along when she did.

He motioned the buxom woman toward the kitchen with a brisk nod of his head then walked from the window and pulled open the heavy front door.

"Caralee, my dear. It's good to see you." He smiled. "I was beginning to worry. A few more days without word, and I'd have been forced to travel to Las Almas myself, to be sure that you were all right."

She looked tired, he saw, as one of the vaqueros hurried forward to help her dismount, her eyes bleak and puffed as if she had been crying.

"I'm sorry, Uncle Fletcher. I should have sent a letter. I meant to, but I never knew exactly what to say."

He studied her pale face and the lines of fatigue around her eyes. Perhaps Vincent had been right after all. Perhaps she had been miserable with the don and finally realized the mistake she had made in marrying him.

"I hope things have worked out as you planned," he said, never meaning anything less.

She walked toward him, came up to where he stood on the porch. "Not exactly. In fact not even close. The truth is you were right, Uncle Fletcher. I should have married Vincent. I should have done exactly as you said."

She looked so forlorn, he found himself reaching out to her, gathering her small frame into his arms. "There, there, my dear. It can't be as bad as all that."

"Yes, I'm afraid it can." She started to cry then, soft little mews that turned into deep wracking sobs and made his throat go tight.

"It's all right, Caralee. You're home now, back with your family where you belong."

Her head came up from his shoulder. "You mean I can stay? You'll forgive me for the things I've done?"

"There is nothing to forgive, and of course you can stay." He brushed damp burnished hair back from her cheeks. "We all make mistakes. Not all of us are brave enough to admit them."

Caralee simply nodded. For a moment more she clung to him, then she sniffed back her tears and turned away.

"Better?" he asked, handing her his handkerchief.

She blew her nose and wiped her eyes. "Much. Thank you, Uncle Fletcher."

He took the sachel the vaquero had removed from behind her saddle, escorted her into the house and down the hall to her old room. "Are you hungry? Shall I have Candelaria bring you something to eat?"

"I'm not hungry." She dragged in a shaky breath, fighting hard not to cry again.

"Don't look so down-hearted," he said, giving her hand a gentle squeeze. "We'll make this all work out, you'll see. If there's one thing your uncle is a master at it's turning a situation to his advantage." He tipped her chin. "You're still a beautiful woman—never forget that. The right man will appreciate what he's got."

Caralee forced a smile. "Thank you, Uncle Fletcher. I'm sorry for all of the trouble I've caused."

"Let's not worry about that now. Why don't you rest for a while? Your things are just as you left them. You still have plenty of clothes and if there is anything else you need—"

"No. I have everything I need in my valise."

He nodded and handed it over. "You can nap for a while, then bathe and change. Later if you want, you can tell me what this is about."

She dabbed a last tear from her cheek. "I'd rather just forget it, if you don't mind. What matters is that the marriage is over. If there is a way to make that official, then that's what I want to do."

He smiled. "Never you fear, my child. Just leave everything to me. In the meantime, try not to worry and try to get some rest."

He waited till she stepped inside her room and closed the door, his mind beginning to whirl with possibilities. He assessed a few, discarded several others, then looked over those remaining. Fletcher smiled to himself. As usual, things had a way of working out. Caralee was home and the odds were good that sooner or later, Vincent Bannister would forgive her. A marriage between them might still work.

Vincent would be in his debt and so would his father. Once he was allied with a family as powerful as the Bannisters, there was no end to what he might achieve. He hoped Caralee wasn't carrying the Spaniard's babe, but even if she was, if they acted quick enough, that could be handled, too.

Which reminded him that he also had some questions for his niece regarding the Spanish Dragon and Ramon de la Guerra's possible involvement in the outlaw's criminal activities. Fletcher walked into his study and closed the door, went to the sideboard and poured himself a brandy.

Time was all he needed, and time was on his side, now that Caralee was home. Fletcher smiled with satisfaction, lifted the glass, and tossed back his drink.

Ramon buried himself in his work. From dawn till dusk he labored, working till exhaustion overtook him, even then he wasn't able to sleep. A stillness lay over the rancho, a quiet despair that seeped from him into the men he worked with and hung like a pallor over his mother and aunt.

He'd told no one what had happened, merely said he and Caralee had decided to end the marriage. His mother had railed at him, told him such a thing could not occur. She had begged him to tell her what had happened between them until he finally lost his temper and shouted at her not to interfere.

His aunt had used more tact, speaking of Caralee whenever he was around, talking about his wife with such affection he had finally stormed out of the house. He meant to travel to Santa Barbara to search for the documents that might help him regain Rancho del Robles, but in the end sent Mariano in his stead. He was afraid his cousin might be there, that Angel might have returned to his family's small hacienda, and Ramon did not trust himself to be so lenient with his cousin again.

For the last two weeks he had been living at the stronghold. Oddly, he was glad that Miranda was not there, that Pedro had taken her to visit her late husband's family in the great central valley. Ramon wasn't ready for a woman. Any woman. Just the thought of making love reminded him of Angel and Caralee, and the bile rose up in his throat.

It had taken some time, but he had finally brought his feelings under control. As he had done in the past, he let his anger bury the pain. He nurtured it as he would a living thing, then fed on it to keep the heartache away. In the daytime he forced himself to remember the moment he had found them together in his room, to suffer again the hot, painful ache that had lanced through his heart like a blade. He thought of her with Villegas, tried to tell himself perhaps she had wanted him, too, that if he hadn't come when he did, she would have enjoyed the man's rough treatment.

It was only at night that he could not make himself believe. *Remember me the way you thought of me before . . . pretend Monterey never happened. Remember the things we did, the pleasures we shared, remember the good times, not the bad.*

And in his dreams he did. He remembered how beautiful she looked on their wedding night, remembered the way she had begged him to be gentle. He remembered her courage as she battled her way through the mountains, determined to fight him and in the long run, gaining his respect. He remembered how hard she had worked to better herself, how far she had come from a life of poverty and grief in the mine patch to a woman of grace and beauty who could move in society's most prominent circles.

He remembered the long hours she had worked beside Lena tending the sick in the village, how much she had come to care for Two Hawks, how sad she had been at the loss of his sister.

He thought of the day they had watched the horses mate, the overwhelming need he had felt for her . . . the same hot need she had seemed to feel for him. In the hours of the night in the hazy outline of his dreams, he asked himself how she could have betrayed him.

Perhaps if she had understood the depth of his feelings for her . . .

Then he would awaken, and he would have to face the truth. She was an Anglo. Just like Lily. Just like her uncle. Just as ruthless, just as cruel.

But day or night, he still hungered for her, even thought of forcing her return to his bed. She was his wife, he reasoned. She belonged to him—he could do with her as he wished. But even if he took her, salved his anger on her ripe little body, it was he who would suffer, he who would remember the way she had betrayed him every time he held her in his arms.

Instead he banished her from his mind as best he could and fixed his thoughts on the problems he faced in the stronghold. The money from the horses would soon run out. It was fall and the *gringos* would be selling their cattle and horses. The stages would be laden with gold; it was time once more for El Dragón.

For the first time since he had begun to raid with his brother, Ramon looked forward to the chance to rain his fury on the Anglos who had caused him so much pain.

"We need to talk, Caralee."

"I'm sorry, Uncle. . . . what did you say?" She was standing at the rear of the house, looking out the window toward the mountains to the southeast. Out toward Rancho Las Almas.

"I said we need to talk."

She smiled absently. "Of course, whatever you say."

He led her down the hall to his study, then firmly closed the door.

Carly turned to face him. "What is it, Uncle Fletcher?"

"To put it simply, my dear—it's that bastard, El Dragón. He hit the San Felipe stage, took two thousand dollars in payroll money headed for the New Idria mine."

Carly wet her lips. For the past three weeks, she'd felt nothing. Allowed herself to feel nothing. Now her heart started to pound and a ringing began in her ears.

"D-did they catch him?"

"No. The whoreson got away. They've formed a vigilante party. I'm taking some of the men. We'll be joining them later this afternoon." His eyes searched her face. "I was hoping there might be something you could tell us that would help."

Her fingers curled into the skirt of her fashionable plum silk day dress. "If I knew anything at all, I would tell you. Surely you know that."

"I wish I could believe it, Caralee." He came forward and took her hands, which had suddenly gone cold. "I know your loyalties must be torn. After all, Don Ramon—"

"Don Ramon? What—what does Ramon have to do with this?"

"I was hoping you could tell me."

Her head came up, but inside she was shaking. "Ramon

has nothing at all to do with the Spanish Dragon. He's very well respected. You know that as well as I do."

"The man is out for vengeance, Caralee. He believes I stole his lands. I wouldn't be surprised if he ordered your abduction just to get back at me."

Dear God. It was far too close to the truth. "Did you?" she asked. "Did you steal his lands?"

"Don't be absurd. I bought them from a man named Thomas Garrison."

The name she had seen on the deed. "Where did Garrison get them?"

Her uncle cleared his throat. "Why he . . . he bought them when they came up for sale. Diego de la Guerra couldn't prove his claim. The Lands Commission confiscated the property and ordered it sold. It was all very legal, I assure you."

She sagged down into a chair, weakened by a towering sense of relief. "I'm sorry, Uncle Fletcher. This whole thing just has me so upset."

"I understand, my dear. I shouldn't have pressed you. I only hoped . . . ah, well, perhaps this time we'll be successful. We've hired the same Indian scouts we used to track those two renegades back to their village in the high country. They're the best I've ever seen."

The blood slowly drained from her face. "You—you don't mean you were with the militia when . . . when they went into the Yocuts's village?"

"The guard needed their ranks reinforced. This country has to be protected—of course I went along."

She slowly came to her feet, then gripped the back of the chair next to hers to keep her legs from shaking. "You helped them wipe out an entire Indian village? You killed innocent women and children?"

"There was no other choice, my dear. They had to be dealt with—they're murderers, the lot of them."

"Tell me it isn't the truth. Tell me you wouldn't be a party to something as awful as that."

Her uncle's jaw went taut. His hands reached out to grip her shoulders. "You don't understand this country, Caralee. It's kill or be killed. The strongest over the weakest. Those Indians had to be stopped and so does this bandit, El Dragón. Only when we find him, death won't come as easy as it did for those poor, dumb savages."

Carly jerked free of his hold, her body shaking all over. "Ramon de la Guerra isn't in any way connected with the Spanish Dragon. Now if you'll excuse me . . ." She brushed past him, her full skirts rustling against his pant legs as she walked out the door and closed it loudly behind her. She was trembling as she entered her bedroom and leaned against the wall, squeezing her eyes closed at the thought of her uncle killing Lena and the others in the village.

She didn't come out of her room when her uncle rode off to join the vigilantes, didn't come out for supper, just picked at the tray of food Candelaria brought her to eat.

Late the next morning after a night of restless sleep, she drew on a rust-colored riding habit and her button-up ankle-high boots, and headed out the door. She needed to get away from the house, away from thoughts of her uncle, and uncertainties about what might happen to Ramon.

Heading to the barn, she asked the tall, lean vaquero named Jose to saddle her a horse. She hadn't ridden since her return to the rancho, now she couldn't imagine how she had spent so much time indoors.

"I have readied Chimara for you," the lanky Californio said, leading a small sorrel gelding from the stable.

"Thank you, Jose." The tall vaquero lifted her easily into the sidesaddle. She positioned her knee in its proper place and her foot in the stirrup. Only then did she notice the saddle wasn't the old battered one she had ridden before, but the one Vincent had given her the night of the *fandango*.

"I'm sorry, Jose, but this isn't my saddle. This one belongs to Senor Bannister."

"No, senora. Your uncle told us the day of your return that from now on this was the saddle you should use. He said he had it made especially for you. That it came all the way from San Francisco."

Her uncle had bought it, not Vincent. How like him. He had used it to try to manipulate her, and yet it was his thoughtfulness that had moved him to buy it in the first place. She would never understand him, never condone the things he did, yet in his own way she cared for him. He was good to her and he was family, all that she had left. Despite the horror of what had happened in the village, despite all her doubts and uncertainties, the affection she felt for him remained.

"Thank you for telling me, Jose."

"The saddle, it is beautiful, no?"

"Yes, very beautiful." She ran her hands lovingly over the exquisite hand-carved leather, and a hard lump rose in her throat. How could he be so kind in some ways and so cruel in others?

Taking the reins in her leather-gloved hands, she nudged the sorrel forward. As soon as the barn was out of sight, she leaned over the animal's neck and urged the horse into a gallop, desperate for the feel of the wind on her cheeks. She didn't know exactly where she was going, only that she had to get away. She had to find a ray of light in the darkness that mired her spirit and threatened to bury her in grief.

Perhaps that was the reason she rode toward the shallow pool at the base of the creek running off of the mountain. She had been happy there. She had basked in the warmth of her husband's touch, felt safe and secure and alive as she never had before. Perhaps a little of that brightness remained and would somehow reach her, help to lift the darkness from her aching heart.

Carly fervently hoped so. For the past three weeks she
had grieved for Ramon even as she tried to forget him. Her
insides felt as crushed as the dry fall leaves beneath her
horse's feet, her spirit lost and drifting. After the words
she'd had with her uncle, the pain of losing Ramon she had
kept so carefully controlled had once again torn free, and
now it threatened to overwhelm her.

She found the stream, though she hadn't been sure she
could, dismounted from the horse, and followed it to the
pool, then tied the animal beneath a nearby sycamore tree.
A soft breeze sifted through the branches, but the day was
warm for this time of year and she found herself perspiring.
Or perhaps it wasn't the warmth, but thoughts of Ramon and
the way he had taken her, there in the soft, green grasses.

Her heart ached to think of him. Perhaps she shouldn't
have come.

She knelt beside the pool, ran her fingers through the water, then opened the buttons at her throat and let the cooling
liquid trickle slowly between her breasts. She looked at the
shimmering surface of the pond, remembered the day had
been cooler so they had not gone into the water.

It wasn't cool now and suddenly she needed the cleansing water to wash away the sadness that seemed to surround
her. She unbuttoned the rust-colored riding habit, sat down
and pulled off her boots. She rolled down her stockings and
slipped them off, then began to work the laces on her corset.

A gentle rustling snapped her head up. She was dressed
in only the corset, her thin pantalettes, and chemise when
she spotted her husband sitting on a rock at the edge of the
pool. He was chewing a long stem of straw, watching her
with eyes that were dark and unreadable, as handsome as
the first time she had seen him.

"*Buenas tardes . . . mi amor.*" Bitterness rang in his
tone, dripped like venom from his words.

"What are you doing here?"

He shrugged his wide shoulders. "Same as you, I suppose. Looking for a respite from the heat." He tossed the golden stem away, came up from the rock and started walking toward her, his movements lean and graceful, as purposeful as a mountain cat after its prey.

Unconsciously, she backed a step away. "This is del Robles land. You're trespassing."

"Ah, *querida* . . . surely you do not begrudge your husband a chance to visit a place he holds dear from his boyhood." He kept on striding toward her, didn't stop till his tall hard body towered above her, forcing her to tilt her head back just to meet his gaze.

Carly wet her lips, which suddenly felt so dry she could barely speak. "I-I'm not dressed. The least you can do is turn around so that I may put on my clothes."

A corner of his mouth curved up. "Why would I wish to do that?"

"Certainly not because you are a gentleman."

He laughed at that, a bitter, sardonic sound. "No, certainly not because of that."

Her heart was pounding, throbbing inside her breast. Still, she lifted her chin and met his dark look head on. "I think that you should leave."

He laughed again, a little less harshly. "I had forgotten what a tiger you can be when you are angry."

"And I had forgotten how infuriating you can be." She reached for her riding habit, carefully folded and resting atop a rock. Ramon reached for it, too, pulled it from her slightly shaking hand.

"You will not need clothes . . . at least not yet."

A wave of heat rolled through her. *Dear God.* She looked into those hot dark eyes, saw the hunger he made no attempt to disguise, and a tingling warmth filtered into her stomach. God in heaven, she still wanted him. Perhaps more in that moment than she ever had before.

He must have read her thoughts for his mouth curved wickedly. "So . . . you feel it, too. I had wondered. . . ."

She turned away from him, trying desperately to control the quaking that had started in her limbs. "Get away from me, Ramon."

He simply caught her arm, turned her around to face him. "I do not think so." He dragged her hard against him, took her mouth in a savage kiss. Carly broke free, drew back a hand and swung it wildly toward his cheek.

He caught her wrist before the blow connected. "Once I allowed that to happen. Perhaps I wished to feel the pain. That time is past." He kissed her again, roughly, brutally, his mouth slanting hotly over hers, his tongue thrusting deeply between her teeth.

She meant to fight him. She knew what would happen if she didn't. Inside her head, her mind screamed a warning: *Don't do this! Think of the pain! After he's gone, it will be unbearable!* Her palms pressed flat against the muscles across his chest, pushing him away even as her lips clung to his, begging him to continue.

A small sound seeped from her throat, a sound of pain and surrender. She wanted Ramon, she loved him as she never would another. Her fingers curled into the front of his white lawn shirt. Her lips softened beneath his bruising kiss and her tongue slid gently into his mouth.

Carly heard him groan. His long brown fingers pulled the ribbon at the front off her chemise and her breasts spilled forward into his waiting hands. He massaged the heavy roundness, molded them, plucked hard at her nipples, making them throb and distend. He pulled the string on her pantalets and shoved them down over her hips, then his fingers were caressing her, kneading the curve of her waist, moving lower, smoothing over her buttocks then sliding between their bodies, lacing through the burnished hair at the apex of her thighs, and stroking the folds of her sex.

He eased her back a step, until she felt the rough bark of a tree against her shoulders. Her head fell back, exposing her throat to the onslaught of his kisses. His lips moved hotly across her shoulders. He lowered the straps on her chemise to bare her breasts and began to suckle there, drawing her deeply into his mouth.

"Ramon . . ." she whispered, his name a cry of agony, a well of sorrow, and a fissure of erupting heat. He lavished hot kisses on her other bare breast, took it deeply into his mouth, then bit the crest until it throbbed with pleasure. Carly arched against him, her body on fire and shaking all over, the core of her burning with slick, damp heat. Then he was unbuttoning his breeches, freeing his long hard length. Lifting her up, he wrapped her legs around his waist, his slim dark fingers gliding over her pale flesh, sliding deep inside her.

"You know you want this, Cara. Put your arms around my neck." Mindlessly she obeyed. He was spreading her wide for him, positioning his rock-hard length between the plump wet folds at her core. He teased her deliciously, then his hold grew more firm and he plunged deeply, burying himself to the hilt.

Carly bit her lip to keep from crying out as his hands gripped her bottom, lifting her and filling her, impaling her again and again. Wildly, he drove himself inside her, thrusting deeply, pounding, pounding until she couldn't think for the fiery heat coursing through her and the clatter of her heart against her ribs.

"Te quiero," he whispered. *I want you.*

"Yes . . ." she whispered. "I want you so much." So much she was certain she would die of it. And in a way she did. For the tightness coiling low in her belly exploded into light and stars that were not of this world. Carly whimpered at the pleasure raging through her, at the hot, bright sweetness that ran through her veins like melted honey.

"Ramon!" she cried out softly.

"*Si, Cara* . . . I am here . . . buried deep inside you."

He held her a moment, suspended in pleasure, then plunged fiercely, once, twice, faster, harder, deeper. Her body ignited, erupting once more into fiery delight, spinning out of control. Ramon's body stiffened as he reached his own release and his hot seed spilled into her core. Unconsciously her arms went tighter around his neck and she rested her head between his neck and shoulders. Tears burned her eyes and started to slide down her cheeks.

"Ramon," she whispered. "I love you so much."

His body went still. For a moment, he did not breathe. He was shaking as he eased himself away from her, letting her legs slide gently to the ground. He looked at the tears on her cheeks, then glanced off over her head. For seconds he just stood there. Then he started to unbutton his shirt.

Carly watched him strip it away, bend to pull off his boots and breeches. She made no move to leave, just watched him undress, caught up in the movement of muscle beneath his dark skin and wanting to reach out and touch him. Naked he drew her toward him, began to remove the balance of her clothes.

Carly said nothing as he pulled the pins from her hair, letting the heavy dark copper coil fall free, sifting his long fingers through it. Bending down, he lifted her up and she slid her arms around his neck. Kissing her softly, he waded into the water and lowered himself into the pool, taking her with him below the surface of the pond. In a shower of cool, misty spray, they came back up, entwined in each other's arms, his black hair glistening like jet in the afternoon sunlight.

He took her again, there on the bank of the pool, and

afterward smoothed strands of wet auburn hair from her cheeks, trailing cold fat droplets over her heated skin.

"I heard about the raid," she said softly after a time. "I was worried about you and the others. My uncle searches for you even now."

"He will find nothing. Unless you decide to tell him who I am."

"You know I won't do that."

"Why?"

"Because I care about you and the others . . . no matter what you believe."

Ramon said nothing for the longest time, just watched her in that dark, pensive way of his, a look that reached clear to her soul. Finally he came up on an elbow. "The hour grows late. It is time for me to leave."

Her throat went tight. She knew he would go, and yet she had hoped . . . prayed . . .

"You wanted me. I thought . . . hoped that perhaps it was more."

Something flickered in his eyes. "Always I have wanted you, Cara. Always. Even your betrayal has not cooled the fire I feel inside me."

Her heart twisted, seemed to cleave in two. Was there nothing that would make him believe her? Carly watched as he rolled to his feet, all lean grace and supple strength, and began to pull on his clothes.

"You are my weakness, Cara," he said. "Nothing I do makes me forget you. Not even the memory of you lying with my cousin."

She stiffened, anger flashing through her, helping to override the pain. How easily he accused her, how ready he was to believe the worst. "You think you're different, but you're not. You're exactly like my uncle. Your hatred is the same, your predjudice. . . . It blinds you as surely as it does the Anglos you despise."

His shoulders went rigid. He forcibly relaxed them and continued to pull on his clothes.

"You think you can come here and take what you want," she continued, "that you can use me and throw me away. Well, you're wrong, Ramon. My pride is as great as yours . . . and so is my honor. If you walk away from me now, if you continue to believe as you do, I'll never let you near me again."

For a moment, he stood stock still. When he turned to face her, anger hardened his features once more. "You are my wife. As long as that is so, you belong to me. I will take you whenever I wish it. I will use you as my cousin would have done."

Carly swallowed past the hot tears clogging her throat. "You're a ruthless, brutal man, Ramon. Time and again I have seen it, but each time you make me forget." She watched him walk toward his horse, slide a boot into the stirrup and swing gracefully up onto the stallion's back.

"I very much enjoyed the afternoon," he said. "Perhaps I will come for you, take you to Llano Mirada. Now that Miranda is gone, I have need of a whore."

The angry tears surfaced, began a scalding path down her cheeks. "Step one foot on my uncle's land and if he doesn't kill you, I swear to you I will!"

His mouth twisted up. "Perhaps it would not matter. Perhaps I am already dead." His face seemed carved in granite, his eyes a dull lackluster brown that held none of their earlier fire. For the first time Carly realized he was hurting as badly as she.

"And perhaps one day you'll see the truth," she said softly. "Unfortunately by then it will be too late."

Ramon said nothing more, just stared at her for long, tension-filled moments. Then he settled his flat-crowned, black felt hat down over his forehead, spun his horse, and thundered away.

The minute he was gone, Carly dissolved into tears. If she thought the pool might soothe her, she had been sorely mistaken. The pain was back, knifing through her insides, calling her ten kinds of a fool. She wished she could ride away and never look back, that she could forget the heartache of loving Ramon and the hurt she suffered whenever he was near.

Instead she climbed up on her horse and started back toward the house, grateful her uncle was gone, that the tears on her cheeks would go unnoticed, that the pain in her heart was a pain she would suffer alone.

*C*hapter *E*ighteen

*R*amon didn't return to Llano Mirada. He would have liked to—there his thoughts did not stray so often to Caralee. But they had just completed a raid and he must remain at home in order to allay suspicion. He rode the stallion hard all the way back to Las Almas, craving the demands that mastering the powerful animal exerted on his strength, and the cleansing of the sun and the wind.

He didn't want to think of Carly and the powerful yearning he had suffered the moment he had seen her by the pond. He didn't want to recall the way he'd been drawn to her almost against his will. Just seeing her there, in the place where they had made such beautiful love, made his blood heat up, seethe like molten lava beneath his skin. The need to touch her, drive himself inside her, had been nearly overwhelming.

He had done it to punish her, he told himself. And simply because he wanted her. He was her husband, no matter how many men she might lie with. She belonged to him and he could do with her as he wished. He told himself he had needed a woman. She was there and taking her would please him. He gave himself a dozen different excuses but none of them was the truth. He had gone to her because he had no other choice.

She had said she loved him. Again and again she had told him that. He hated her for it. For making him still want her. For making him still love her.

Ramon leaned forward over the saddle and topped the ridge at a gallop, the stallion raising dust as its sleek, golden body stretched to the task, white mane and tail flying out behind. Finally he pulled back on the reins, slowing the animal to a high-stepping walk. Rey was lathered and beginning to tire, and so was he. Thinking of the past did no good. Whatever he felt for Caralee was over and done. He had other problems to consider. His mother had been feeling poorly and he was worried about her.

And he was worried about the boy.

He could still remember the terrible look on Two Hawks's face when the young boy had approached him about Caralee.

"Don Ramon?"

He was out in the barn, currying Rey del Sol, who stood placidly in his stall while little Bajito slept in the straw at his feet. "*Si, muchacho,* what is it?"

"Mariano says the senora will not return."

Ramon's long fingers curled tighter over the brush that stilled halfway down Rey's muscular neck. "*Si,* that is so."

"Why, senor? I thought she liked it here. She told me she was happy."

He dragged the brush over the stallion's powerful shoulder. "Sometimes such things just happen."

"But she is your wife. Among my people, a wife must stay with her husband. Is it not the same with your people?"

Ramon ignored the knot balling hard in his stomach. "*Si,* but . . . there are times when things do not work as we plan."

Big dark eyes stared up at him. "She did not leave because of me? Because of what happened in the village . . . because I killed a white man?"

Ramon shook his head. "No, Two Hawks. You did only what any man would have done. You were trying to protect your loved ones. The senora understood that. Her leaving had nothing to do with you."

But Two Hawks didn't seem to believe it, and in the weeks Caralee had been gone, the boy had become even more distant and brooding. It worried Ramon, though he didn't know what to do to help him.

It wasn't until six days after his return from the pond that the notion struck him, six days of trying not to think of Caralee. Yet it was seeing her again that had finally given him the idea of what he might do about the boy. It was early in the morning when he went to the corral in search of him.

"You wished to see me, Don Ramon?" Two Hawks approached at a run, his slim face covered by a sheen of perspiration.

"There is something I need you to do, *muchacho*. There is a bundle of the senora's things sitting on the couch in the *sala*. I want you to take them to her at Rancho del Robles."

He blinked and the blood seemed to drain from his face. "You wish me to go to the senora?"

"*Si,* that is right."

"Wh-what if she does not wish to see me?"

Ramon put a hand on the youth's slender shoulder. "She will wish it, Two Hawks. Whatever has happened between my wife and me has nothing to do with you. I promise she will be glad to see you."

He still looked uncertain, but nodded with resignation. He had cut his black hair a little shorter, but still pulled it back in a thong at the nape of his neck. Already it seemed he had grown several inches, but the truth was, with the proper food and care, he had simply begun to fill out.

"Do you know the way to del Robles?" Ramon asked.

"*Si,* I was there once with my sister."

"Then go. See the senora gets her things. I am certain she will be grateful."

He watched the boy leave, knowing whatever Carly had done, she cared for the boy. She would recognize his fears, and the warmth of her greeting would lay them to rest.

Ramon ignored a twinge of jealousy that it was the boy who would receive her warm smiles and fond caresses and not him.

Two Hawks returned from the barn, leading the slightly swaybacked gelding Mariano had been teaching him to ride. Already he sat straight in the saddle, at ease on the animal as if he had been born to it. He would make a fine vaquero one day, Ramon thought. He carried himself as proudly as the great Andalusians he was only just learning to handle.

With a wave over his shoulder, Two Hawks rode out through the gate, passing a rider coming in the opposite direction. Ramon shaded his eyes toward the man who sat so rigidly in his saddle, as if he were on guard for whatever might come.

Ramon's mouth twisted, a bitter smile coming to his face. Perhaps his cousin was right to be on guard. Even now it was all Ramon could do to keep from dragging Angel down from his horse and pounding him into the dirt. Instead he forced his balled hands to relax and returned his cousin's greeting if not with a smile, at least with a semblance of civility.

"Angel. You are the last person I expected to see."

"I am certain that is so, cousin. Nevertheless, I am here."

"So I see. There is something that you want?" The question came out curtly though he tried to keep the tension from his voice.

"I will not be staying, if that is your concern. I am certain your—wife—has seen to it that I am no longer welcome."

Some of the anger drained from Ramon's stiff posture. What happened wasn't Angel's fault any more than it was his own. "I am sorry, cousin. Of course you are welcome. As for my wife, she is no longer here."

Angel relaxed a little at that and simply nodded. "We did not have a chance to speak in Monterey. I only just discovered that Andreas is dead."

"Si." A dull ache rose at the mention of his brother's name. Usually he could keep the pain at bay, but it was always there inside him, more pronounced since Carly had been gone. "Your sister must have told you. His death is not common knowledge. There are only a few of us who knew he was in the country."

"I am sorry, cousin. Your brother was a good man." Angel smiled thinly. "And also a good leader, I am told."

Ramon tensed once more, but Angel didn't seem to notice.

"There are few secrets among family, Ramon. I know of this *bandito,* El Dragón. I know Andreas was that man. Now your brother is dead, but another man leads the band and the outlaws continue to raid against the Anglos. I wish to join them, Ramon. I believe you can tell me where to find them."

In times past he would not have hesitated to tell his cousin the whole grim story. Now he simply said, "They are camped at Llano Mirada. You remember it from when we were children? The high plateau we found the first summer we went hunting on our own." Soon enough Angel would discover Ramon's involvement but not yet.

"Si, I remember." Angel smiled, making him look younger and more handsome than he had before. Ramon wondered bitterly if it was that kind of smile that had urged his wife to invite him to her bed.

"There are two ways in," Ramon continued. "Both are heavily guarded. Tell them you are Andreas's cousin." He

slid the heavy gold and ruby ring with the de la Guerra
family crest off his finger, the ring he had given to Caralee
the day of their wedding. He had found it in his saddlebag
when he had gotten back from Monterey.

"Show them this and tell them it is I who have sent
you." He handed the ring to Angel, ignoring the odd sense
of irony that his cousin should wind up with the ring he
had used to wed Caralee.

"Gracias, amigo."

"I did not know they had let you out of prison," Ramon
said.

"They did not exactly let me out. It was more like I escaped." Angel began to back his horse away. "Again I am
sorry about what happened in Monterey."

"So am I," Ramon said. "And I would advise you it is a
subject best not mentioned again."

Angel's mouth flattened abruptly. "As you wish," he
said. "I am grateful for the information." Whirling his
horse, he dug his big silver rowels into the animal's ribs
harder than he should have, and pounded away back down
the road.

Ramon stared after him until the dust of his leaving
settled into the high brown grasses. The thought of seeing
his cousin each time he rode into Llano Mirada made a
hard knot ball in his stomach. Then again, perhaps very
soon it would not matter. Mariano had returned from Santa
Barbara, and even now, safely inside a chest in the house,
Ramon held the documents that might return Rancho del
Robles to its rightful owners. He had written to Alejandro
de Estrada in Monterey and tomorrow he would forward
the lawyer the papers.

Once the case was reopened, the rancho would be returned and his raiding could end. As there was before,
there would be wealth enough for his family, work and a
home for his people.

As much as he yearned for such a thing, deep inside he knew it would not be the same without Caralee there to share it. Ramon pushed the painful notion away and started back toward the house.

Carly paced the floor of her bedroom. Her uncle had returned late last night, bone-tired, his long canvas duster covered with the grime of the trail, and angry that they had once more failed to capture El Dragón. They were not giving up, he said grimly. The Indian scouts would continue their meticulous, inch by inch tracking, combing the Gabilan Mountains and on into the Diablo Range.

Captain Harry Love, the man who had apprehended the infamous bandit, Joaquin Murieta, led the vigilantes, and he had every belief that this time they would find the Spanish Dragon and his men.

Carly continued her pacing. She was worried about Ramon, as well as Pedro, Florentia, Tomasina, and the others in the stronghold. She didn't want them winding up the way Lena and the people of the Yocuts's village had.

She had to speak to Ramon, convince him to stop his raiding before it was too late. But she wasn't even sure where he was, and considering the way things stood between them, going to him at Las Almas might seem highly strange. She didn't want to raise her uncle's suspicions any more than they already were.

Carly made a sharp turn, swirling her saffron silk faile skirts, and started back the opposite direction. Besides her worry for Ramon, something else was bothering her. Boredom. Until her return to del Robles, she hadn't realized how much she'd enjoyed the work she had done at Las Almas. They were building something there. That it was smaller than Rancho del Robles didn't matter.

They were accomplishing something, and she had been a part of that accomplishment.

Unlike her life at del Robles.

Certainly it was easier. Here she was waited on hand and foot, with nothing expected of her but a ladylike smile and an hour or two of polite supper conversation. Unfortunately, she wasn't the type to sit all day in the *sala,* tatting away the afternoon as her uncle expected. She couldn't entertain herself practicing for hours on the pianoforte. Reading occupied her time for a while, but the truth was, Carly had spent too many years out of doors. She liked hard work, liked the results it produced, and though at Las Almas she had never been expected to work her fingers to the bone, even Ramon seemed to approve of her involvement.

Perhaps he had recognized her need and bowed to it, or simple believed that since she wasn't a Spanish woman, she wasn't truly a lady—laboring was all right for a *gringa* like her. That thought wasn't encouraging, but whatever the case, she needed to be a part of what was happening on the rancho.

Or perhaps what she needed was a home of her own, as her uncle had once said.

Her heart squeezed at the thought. She'd had her own home . . . once. A real home, she had believed. She'd had a husband, people who cared about her, a mother-in-law and aunt she had grown to love. Did all of them believe as Ramon did? Did they think her capable of such a bitter betrayal? What had he told them? she wondered. What had Angel said to his sister Maria?

Tears burned her eyes, but her hands clenched into fists. Ramon believed his cousin because he was a de la Guerra. He was also a liar, but there was no way to prove it. And even if she could, she would still be a *gringa,* not the Spanish woman her husband wanted for a wife.

Carly sighed. What did it matter? Ramon had banished her from his life as if she had never existed and nothing was going to change that. He had left a void that would never be filled, but surely there was some way she could be happy. Perhaps Uncle Fletcher was right and she should marry Vincent. Already he had sent his regards. A letter had arrived by messenger just yesterday afternoon. Apparently her uncle had been quick to inform her ex-suitor of her return. Obviously Uncle Fletcher hadn't learned a thing from the trouble he had caused by his manipulations.

Then again, if Vincent still wanted her, perhaps he really did love her. Maybe she should marry him and get on with the rest of her life. Carly had no doubt her uncle would somehow arrange the annulment. He wanted her to marry Vincent. If she had done as he wished in the first place, she wouldn't be feeling the terrible pain she suffered now.

She started to pace again, then glanced out the window and stopped so short she stumbled and nearly fell. Carly stared in horror, blinked and tried to tell herself what she was seeing wasn't real.

"Dear God!" Whirling toward the door, she jerked it open and raced out into the hallway. Heart thundering, her feet flying, she slammed through the back door and out into the work yard. "Stop this! What are you doing? You've got to stop this minute!"

But the lash fell again, slicing into the small brown back that already sported several long welts and three thin trails of blood. Carly stumbled forward, racing toward the boy just as the lash whistled through the air again. Ducking her head, she rushed between him and the whip, threw her arms around his narrow shoulders and bent over him, shielding his small frame and taking the wicked blow herself.

She gasped at the sting of the vicious piece of leather,

her heart nearly breaking for the pain the boy had already endured.

"For godsakes, man, hold up!" her uncle shouted, though the man with the lash had already realized his mistake.

"Sorry, Miss McConnell." Cleve Sanders, her uncle's rawboned foreman, stepped back as he recoiled the whip. "I hope I didn't hurt you."

The thin strip of leather had cut through her dress and left a welt on her skin. It stung like fire, but other than that she was fine. "It's the boy you should be worrying about, not me."

Two Hawks just stared straight ahead, his jaw set against the pain in his back, his black eyes mutinous. His arms were stretched above his head, tied to the low-hanging branch of a tree. His back was bare, his oversized breeches hanging low on the bones of his thin brown hips. "Cut him loose," Carly demanded.

When the men made no move to free him, just shuffled from side to side looking angry and beginning to mutter among themselves, her attention swung toward her uncle, who approached from a few feet away.

"I'm sorry, Caralee, but you shouldn't be out here. This is man's business. You had better get back to the house."

"What's going on here, Uncle Fletcher? What could a boy his age possibly have done to deserve a beating like this?"

"The boy's a thief, Caralee. Like it or not, I won't have a thieving savage stealing del Robles property."

"Two Hawks isn't a thief. What is it he's supposed to have taken?"

"Stole a chicken, Miss," Sanders put in. "Damn heathens is all alike."

"A chicken? Where is it? Why on earth would he come here to steal a hen?"

"Not a live chicken, Miss. A dead one. Cook's roastin' a

whole mess of 'em, gettin' 'em ready for supper tonight. Boy reached in through the window. Stole it right off the spit."

Carly swung to the boy, her chest squeezing painfully. "Did you pay for the chicken, Two Hawks?"

He nodded stiffly. "A dozen trading beads . . . more than the tough old bird was worth."

Carly's heart turned over. She glared at Sanders, her mouth thinning into a determined line. "There, you see? He didn't steal the chicken, he bought it. Now cut him down!"

Her uncle started to argue, saw the implacable set of her jaw, and nodded his head. "Cut the boy down." The tall lean foreman who had wielded the whip took a knife to the rope around the tree limb, then cut the binding on Two Hawks's wrists. He stumbled as he fought to stay on his feet and Carly caught him beneath the arms.

"Can you make it as far as the kitchen?" she whispered so that only he could hear.

His spine went straighter and he steadied himself on his feet. "One day I will be a great vaquero. I can do whatever I must."

Knowing how proud he was, she didn't try to help him, just walked beside him while he made his way to the kitchen on his own. Once inside, she set him carefully down in a stout oak chair and turned to the buxom woman working over a thick roll of tortillas.

"Your name is Rita, isn't it?"

"*Si*, senora."

"I need something for his back, Rita. Can you tell me what I might use?"

"*Si*, I have just the thing. We keep it here for the vaqueros, for burns and scrapes and the bite of insects." She handed Carly a salve that smelled of lard and camomile.

"Thank you."

Two Hawks winced as she washed the several long thin slashes and spread the salve over the welts, but he didn't make a sound of complaint.

"I'm sorry this happened, Two Hawks," Carly said when they were finished. "I wish I had gotten there sooner."

For the first time, he smiled. "You were very brave, Sunflower. Don Ramon will not find another wife so courageous as you."

A sudden mist of tears sprang into her eyes. Carly blinked hard to push them away. "How is he, Two Hawks?" she asked softly.

"He is different now that you are gone. He does not smile as he used to. I think he wishes for you to come home."

Oh, God. "You're wrong, Two Hawks. That is the last thing Don Ramon wants."

The boy started to argue, but Carly pressed a finger to his lips and shook her head. "Where is your shirt?"

"Those men tore it off." He scowled. "It was a very fine shirt."

Carly almost smiled. "Well, this certainly won't be the first time you've gone without one. Don Ramon will see you get another once you get home."

"He sent me with some of your things, but I think he only wanted me to know that you were not angry with me."

Carly reached over and took his hand. "Is that what you thought? That I was angry with you?"

He nodded. "Because of what happened in the village . . . what I did to the white man."

It was all she could do not to clamp a hand over his mouth. Good Lord, if her uncle knew he had killed one of the men who had slaughtered his people, the boy wouldn't live another day.

"You did what you had to. I'm only just beginning to understand how difficult life out here really is." She forced herself to smile. "Now, tell me where the things are you have brought me so that I can go and get them."

He started to rise, but she gently pushed him back down. "I'll get them. You just stay here."

"I am all right now, senora. I will get your things."

She wanted to argue, but he was young and strong and she didn't want to insult him. Standing in the doorway, she waited while he fetched the bundle Ramon had sent, along with the swaybacked horse he had ridden to the ranch.

"I want you to wait for me here," Carly told him. "I'm going to go in and change, then we'll ride back to Las Almas together . . . at least part of the way."

He merely nodded. A few minutes later, she returned in her rust-colored riding habit, led him out to the barn, and ordered one of the men to saddle her a horse. They spoke little on the ride back to the rancho. She knew his back must be hurting from the stiff way he sat in the saddle, and because the welt on her own back still stung.

At the top of the ridge leading into the valley where the hacienda stood, she drew rein on her small sorrel horse.

"Tell Don Ramon what happened at del Robles. Show him your back and he'll see it's properly tended. Tell him . . . tell him I said I was sorry for the way my uncle and his men behaved."

Two Hawks nodded. "I will tell him. I will also tell him he is not the only one who is no longer happy."

"No! Two Hawks, you can't—" but already the boy had whirled his horse and begun to gallop away. Carly dragged in a breath, surprised to find her hands were shaking and tears burned the back of her eyes. What did it matter if Ramon knew how she felt?

He hadn't cared about her feelings when he believed her guilty of lying with his cousin, when he'd accused her of being a whore. Still her pride stung to think of it almost as much as the thin line of fire that burned down her back.

Turning the sorrel horse back toward Rancho del Robles, Carly vowed anew to forget Ramon, to put that episode of her life behind her. But living with her uncle didn't seem to be the answer either. Not when each day proved even more clearly how ruthless Fletcher Austin really was.

And with each passing day, she had begun to suspect more strongly that somehow her uncle truly had stolen the de la Guerra lands.

Ramon brought the axe down hard, splitting the two-foot length of oak neatly down the center. He tossed it into the growing pile and mopped the sweat from his brow with the back of a hand.

Three days had passed since Two Hawks's return with his back on fire and his incredible tale of the stolen chicken—and the fact that Caralee had taken a stinging blow herself in order to protect him. She had faced her uncle's wrath and braved the tempers of the men.

"Wah-suh-wi is very brave," the boy said. "You will not find another wife as brave as your Sunflower."

Just thinking about it made his mouth go dry. He wanted to wrap his hands around Fletcher Austin's thick neck and squeeze till the life slipped out of him. He hated to think what might have happened to the boy if Carly hadn't stood up to him. He didn't doubt the boy's story or his wife's courage. But in the weeks since he had lost Caralee, he had begun to doubt something else.

Ramon brought the axe down hard, his naked torso straining, his sweat-slick muscles rippling with the effort. He needed the exertion, needed to relieve the tension that had gripped his body since Two Hawks's return from del Robles.

He couldn't allow the anger he felt at Fletcher Austin to govern his next moves. Nor succumb to the soft ache the boy's words stirred in his heart for Caralee.

What if you are wrong? He had never allowed himself to think it. Not for a single solitary moment. He couldn't afford the chance that he might forgive her.

If he did and she duped him again, he wasn't sure he could survive it.

That was how much he loved her—so much he ached with it every time he took a breath. How had she done it? How had she stolen his heart so completely? *Por Dios,* he had fought it every inch of the way, and still she had become the most important thing in his world.

What if you are wrong? He should never have let the thought seep into his mind, for now that he had, it festered like an open wound. He wasn't wrong. He had seen them together. Angel was like a brother, had been since they were children. He was a de la Guerra. De la Guerras did not lie.

What if you are wrong? The axe handle slipped, nearly flew from his hands. It hit the heavy length of wood sideways, sent the piece of oak careening into a nearby tree. *Santo de Christo*—he wasn't wrong. Carly knew it and so did he. But the words she'd said that day at the pool would not leave him. *You're exactly like my uncle. Your hatred is the same, your prejudice. . . . It blinds you as surely as it does the Anglos you despise.*

The heavy axe rang as it severed the last piece of oak in the pile, and Ramon sank the blade deep into the top of the tree stump he had been using to position the wood. Still thinking of Carly, he looked back toward the house and was surprised to see Pedro Sanchez riding through the gate on his big dapple gray stallion.

Blotting the sweat from his neck and shoulders with a coarse linen towel, Ramon grabbed his white lawn shirt and started walking toward him.

"It is good to see you, my friend," Ramon called out.

Pedro had not yet returned from his trip to the valley when Ramon and the others had made their last raid. It had been almost two months since Ramon had seen him.

"It is good to see you, too, Don Ramon." The old vaquero reined up, then dismounted with casual ease from the saddle. "I am sorry to be so late in returning to the stronghold, but I heard the raid went well."

"*Si,* very well. But winter is near. We may need to strike one more time while the pickings are so plentiful."

Pedro mulled that over as they walked side by side to the corral and he began to unsaddle his horse. "Now that Andreas is gone, each time you ride, the threat of discovery is greater."

"*Si,* that is so. Mariano says Sheriff Layton was here while I was in Monterey. Mariano believes he grows suspicious."

"And still you mean to continue?"

"Only as long as I have to."

Pedro said nothing, just loosened the cinch and lifted the heavy vaquero saddle off of the stallion's back. Steam rose up from the damp patch of hair beneath the brightly woven blanket.

"How was your journey?" Ramon asked.

"I would have been back sooner, but Miranda's visit with her in-laws did not go exactly as planned. She decided to return to the stronghold. By then she was resigned to the loss of your attentions . . . now I learn that she may not have lost you after all."

Ramon just shrugged, but a subtle tension crept into his shoulders. "My wife is no longer here, if that is what you mean. Things did not work out between us."

"So I heard." He loosened the bridle, slid a halter on over the stallion's soft muzzle, and fastened it behind the animal's ears.

"It is hardly a secret. Caralee has returned to her uncle."

"Because you found your cousin in her bed."

Surprise flared inside him. His jaw clamped so hard he had to force himself to relax it in order to speak. "How did you learn of this? I have told no one."

"How do you think I learned? Your cousin Angel was bragging about it . . . until Ignacio split his lip like a ripe piece of melon. He has not mentioned it since."

"I cannot believe he would do such a thing."

"No?" Pedro rounded the horse and came to stand in front of him. "You did not find it difficult to believe the tale he told about your wife."

"Even if he should have kept silent, he did not lie. I found him in her bed."

"That he was there does not mean your wife betrayed you. How can you be so sure your cousin was telling the truth?"

"Angel is a de la Guerra. He is my own flesh and blood. Why should I not believe him?"

"Angel swears your wife wanted him to come to her—so of course it must be true. I have known him as many years as you have. Has there ever been a woman who did not throw herself at Angel's feet?"

Ramon grunted at the memory conjured by Pedro's words, images of Angel bragging about the whores who waited for him in every town between San Juan and the border. "Not according to Angel."

"Whores are not ladies, my friend, and I do not believe there were even so many of those."

Ramon mulled that over. "Perhaps not."

"And what of the woman in Santa Fe?"

"What woman?"

"The one who claimed he raped her the night he was arrested for robbery and murder."

An uneasy feeling began to churn in his stomach. "Surely the charge was false. A lie trumped up by the *gringos* to bolster their other false charges."

"Was it a lie?" Pedro's eyes held his. "Or would your wife have been another helpless victim if you had not arrived when you did?"

Ramon sank down on a bale of straw next to the fence, his long legs no longer steady. *"Dios mio,* what you are saying cannot be true."

"Your wife has proven her honor, Ramon, not once but again and again. She knows who you are and yet she says nothing. Perhaps she could even find the stronghold, if that was her wish." His veined hand reached for Ramon's broad shoulder, gave it a reassuring squeeze. "Can you not see your wife keeps her silence because she loves you? That she is Anglo is not reason enough to disregard her word."

"You must be wrong. It cannot be true."

"You have not seen your cousin in five long years, Ramon. Even if he was an honest man before—which I have come to doubt—you cannot know what so many years in prison might do to a man like him." Ramon said nothing. "Your loyalty to your cousin is commendable, my friend, but I do not believe he feels that same loyalty to you."

"What do you mean?"

"He is jealous of you, Ramon. It is there in his face whenever he speaks of you. If you had spent the least amount of time with him, you would have seen he is not the man you believe."

Ramon raked a hand through his sweat-damp hair. "You are telling me I am wrong. That my wife has not done this terrible thing. How can you expect me to believe that when I saw them with my own eyes?"

"Sometimes what you think you see is not what you see at all. Just like the trail leading into Llano Mirada. If your wife says she is innocent then I believe her. I would believe Caralee McConnell long before I would accept the word of a man like Angel de la Guerra."

Ramon ran his tongue over his suddenly dry lips. Inside his chest his heart throbbed dully. "What if you are wrong?"

"There is a way to know for sure."

"How? Tell me, I beg you."

"Look inside your heart, Ramon. The truth lies there. I believe you know what it is. I think you have known for some time. You are afraid to believe, that is all."

If you loved me, you would recognize the truth even when your eyes say it is a lie. "Are my prejudices really so strong, Pedro? Is it possible I have let my hatred of the Anglos blind me to what is real?"

"What do you think, Ramon? Only you can know for sure."

And suddenly he did know. So clearly the air around him rang with it. He stared out over the valley and the truth sweeping through him made the towering oaks seem taller, the golden grass more abundant, the sky a deeper blue.

"Por Dios," he whispered, Carly's beautiful tear-ravaged face rising up in the eye of his mind. *I love you, Ramon. I love you so much.* "She was fighting to save herself, not welcoming Angel to her bed."

"Si, that is what I believe."

"Santo de Christo, how could I not have seen?" In the back of his mind, he remembered Yolanda, the woman his cousin meant to marry. She had rejected Angel's suit because she had wanted Ramon. It was Ramon, not Angel, who had always attracted women. Beautiful, desirable women. Women his cousin must have wanted. Women like Caralee.

"He must have known she was my wife. If he saw me ride out, he could have waited, approached her in the dining room. He could have followed her up to our room and somehow broken in. He must have meant to rape her. He believed she would be too ashamed to tell me. He might even have believed I would take his word over hers."

When Ramon looked up, the world appeared blurred and something burned at the back of his eyes. "And I did, Pedro. I behaved exactly as Angel knew I would." Slowly he came to his feet. "I will kill him, I swear it."

Pedro gripped his shoulders. "Listen to me, Ramon. It is your wife you must think of now. You are certain about your beliefs? You must be, if you are to succeed. What you have done will not be easy to undo. There can be no doubts about her ever again."

Ramon swallowed against the tightness that had risen in his throat. "I cannot believe I did not see it before."

"For so many years you have hated the Anglos. But there is good and bad in all people. In your heart you know this. The loss of your brother has made you forget for a while."

Ramon just nodded. "I have made so many mistakes. Where my wife is concerned, I cannot seem to think clearly."

"You love her, my friend. Love can blind a man worse than the blackest night."

"I must go to her. Bring her home to Las Almas."

"It could be dangerous. You will not be welcome on del Robles land."

"I do not care. I will wait for darkness, then go in. Somehow I will convince her to forgive me." *Perhaps one day you will discover the truth . . . by then it will be too late.*

Ramon's stomach knotted. *Too late. Too late. Too late.*

As much as he prayed it wouldn't be so, if it was, he could not blame her. Never had he brought her anything but grief. Silently he vowed that if she would forgive him, he would spend the rest of his life making up for the pain she had suffered since the day that she had first met him.

Chapter Nineteen

Carly sat at her dressing table, absently drawing the silver-backed hairbrush through her long dark auburn hair. The whale-oil lamp burned low, casting her face in shadows, flickering on the whitewashed walls of the low-ceilinged room.

She was thinking of the past, of her days at Las Almas and the people she cared for. She was worried about Two Hawks, hoping the marks on his back had healed. She wondered if Ramon's mother and Tia Teresa had started making soap from the tallow they had rendered. She hoped the old women wouldn't work themselves too hard. She thought of Rey del Sol and little Bajito, of Pedro Sanchez and Florentia and the others in the stronghold.

She thought of Ramon and wondered if, now that Miranda had gone, he was once more sleeping with Isabel Montoya . . . or perhaps he had found someone new.

The image brought a swift shot of pain. Carly forced her thoughts in another direction, unfortunately one not so distant from those she'd just had of Ramon. Tomorrow her uncle and a dozen of his men would be leaving del Robles to join Captain Harry Love and his vigilantes—Hounds, they called them. This time, they believed, they would find the Spanish Dragon and finally bring him in.

Carly shivered to think of it. She shifted on the stool and glanced in the mirror just in time to see the curtains billow. A long, lean leg encased in snug black breeches thrust over the window sill and for several long moments, Carly's breathing ceased.

"Ramon," she whispered as his head ducked through the opening. She was on her feet in seconds, rushing to the night stand beside her bed, jerking open the drawer and grabbing the old single-shot cap-and-ball pistol her mother had given her after her father had died and they had been left all alone. The gun she'd brought with her around the Horn.

With shaking hands she aimed it in Ramon's direction, watched him straighten to his full imposing height, and a corner of his sensuous mouth kicked up.

"So, now you wish to shoot me."

"Believe it or not, I know how. I also know what you want and I'm not about to let you drag me off to Llano Mirada. You're not going to make me your whore."

The smile slid away. "That is what you think?"

"Th-that's what you said the last time. That Miranda was gone and you needed a w-whore."

His expression grew grim. "Miranda has returned, but it would not matter. You are my wife, not my whore."

"That isn't what you said before." The gun shook in her hands, her fingers suddenly damp and clammy, making it difficult to grip the handle.

He straightened even more. "Either pull the trigger, Cara, or put the gun away before one of us gets hurt."

She clamped her jaw. The pistol shook a moment more, then she sighed and let the hand holding it drop to her side. "All right, maybe I can't shoot you, but I still won't let you drag me out of here. I'll scream the house down if you take one step in my direction."

His mouth curved faintly. "I have missed you, *querida*. It has been far too dull at Las Almas without you."

"What do you want?" She glared at him, her body tense and ready to run if she had to. She wasn't about to let him abduct her again, to use her body and humiliate her with the desire she still felt for him, desire which already slid through her veins like melted butter just at the fact he was near.

"I came to talk, nothing more. There are things I wish to say . . . difficult things for a man like me. I only hope that you will listen." Why was he looking at her that way, his dark eyes searching and full of tenderness? It made her insides quiver, make a soft ache swell inside her heart.

He took a step closer, but Carly backed away. "I mean it, Ramon. I'll scream for my uncle. There'll be a dozen men in this room before you can get near me."

"Do it, then. Perhaps it is your wish to see me dead. If that is so, I would not blame you." He started moving closer, his long strides slow but determined.

"I'll scream, I swear it!"

He only kept walking until he stood right in front of her. "I do not think so." He eased the gun from her limp hand, set it on the dresser behind him.

"Damnit—I hate you! I loathe you with every ounce of my heart and soul." And in that moment she did. She hated him for making her love him. She hated him for making her blood pulse wildly at the sight of him standing there so tall and male.

"Perhaps you do. As I said, I would not blame you."

"What do you want? Why did you come here?"

His hand came up to her cheek. She noticed that it trembled. "So many reasons . . . so much I want. Yet I will have none of those things if I cannot make you see."

She eyed him warily, trying to unravel his words. "I asked you what you want."

He took a deep breath and released it slowly. "I came here to tell you I was wrong about what happened in Monterey."

Carly's stomach tightened and suddenly she felt dizzy. "It was just as you said—I doubted you because you are Anglo. My hatred of the *gringos* blinded me to the truth."

Carly swayed on her feet, felt Ramon's long fingers reach out and grip her arm to steady her.

"You are all right?" he asked, his expression taut with concern. She nodded and he slowly released her, with some reluctance, it seemed. "It was not just losing Rancho del Robles, or the death of my brother . . . there were things that happened in my past."

"Wh-what things?" Carly asked. Her stomach felt queasy and her mouth was dry. She dampened her lips with the tip of her tongue and saw Ramon's eyes suddenly darken. With a force of will, he smoothed his features and the hungry look faded away.

"There was a woman," he said, "a beautiful *gringa* woman. Her name was Lily. Perhaps I was in love with her. When I think of what I feel for you, I do not really believe it, but I cannot be sure. I was younger then, foolish. She meant everything to me, but I meant very little to her. One day I found her in bed with two young men from the university, friends I knew in school." His eyes turned distant, hard, as if he could still see them. "After Lily, there were other Anglo women, only this time I used them."

He shifted and glanced away, the subject obviously painful. "That night in Monterey . . . when I returned to our room . . . I saw what I had always believed one day I would see—my Anglo wife betraying me with another man."

Carly stared up at him, her heart aching, tears of frustration burning her eyes. "How could you think that, Ramon? There was no one I wanted but you. From the first moment I saw you, there was never anyone but you."

"I am sorry, Cara. I know that is not enough but that is what I came here to say. And to tell you that I love you. Perhaps that is hard to believe, but it is the truth."

Carly bit hard on her trembling bottom lip. How she had longed to hear those words. Now that Ramon had said them, she realized they couldn't erase the doubts that still burned inside her. "Sometimes loving someone isn't enough," she said softly.

Ramon's dark gaze scorched through her. "I do not believe that is true. If I did, I would not be here. I love you. You said that you loved me. You are my wife, Cara. I want you to come home."

She looked into his beautiful brown eyes, remembered the fiery nights she had spent in his arms, and a hard ache rose in her throat. Just days ago that was exactly what she wanted. Since then she'd had time to think things through, to see matters clearly for the first time in weeks. "I-I can't do that, Ramon."

A muscle tightened in his cheek. "Why not? Rancho Las Almas is where you belong."

She only shook her head. Inside, her stomach quivered and she fought to hold back tears. "We're too different, you and I. Time and again you have shown me that. You knew it from the start, but I was too much in love with you to see. What happened in Monterey could happen again. Your prejudice runs deep, Ramon. I don't think your loving me is enough to overcome the problems between us."

"You are wrong, Cara. Already I see things as I had not been able to before. You are the reason. You are the one who has made me see." The depths of his feelings blazed like a fire in his eyes. It made her want to touch him, to hold him and take away the pain. "Come back to Las Almas, Cara. Be my wife."

Her gaze ran over his beloved face, the strong bones and hollows, the straight nose and hard jaw. She reached out to him, slid her arms around his neck, and he crushed her against him.

"I love you, Ramon," she said, but as much as she did,

she knew she couldn't go with him. Something else might happen. She wasn't willing to chance this kind of pain again.

She felt his long dark fingers in her hair, tilting her head back, forcing her to look into his eyes. *"Te amo,"* he whispered. I love you. *"Te necesito."* I need you. He kissed her then, tenderly at first, then with building force. Carly trembled at the heat of his mouth over hers and the strength of his hard arms around her.

She blinked to keep from crying. "I love you, Ramon, so much I think sometimes my heart will break in two. But I can't go with you, no matter how much I might wish it. Something else might happen . . . and there are things about me you don't know."

She felt his arms stiffen around her. "Do not tell me there is another man. If there is I swear I will kill him."

She gave him a faint teary smile. "It's nothing like that. It's just . . ." *that I'm not what I seem. I'm not the daughter of some wealthy easterner, as my uncle led you to believe. I'm a poor ragamuffin from the mine patch.* But Carly didn't say it. She couldn't force herself to utter the words that would make him look at her the way he had that night in Monterey.

"Please, Ramon, my uncle has already started the annulment proceedings. Once it's final, you can marry a true Spanish woman—"

His kiss came swift and hard, bruising her lips with its force. Lifting her into his arms, he carried her over to the deep feather bed, rested her in the middle of the mattress, then followed her down, pinning her with his tall lean body.

"We can't, Ramon. It isn't safe for you here. If my uncle should hear us—"

"I do not care."

"I do." She struggled beneath him, determined to break

free. "I won't let you do this. I want you to go back where you'll be safe."

"You are my wife," he said. "I do not want another. When I am finished, you will beg me to take you home." He ravaged her mouth again, thrusting his tongue inside the hot moist cavern. His fingers worked the buttons on the front of her night rail, then he stripped it off over her head.

"I won't let you, Ramon. You have to leave."

Cursing softly, he left her, crossed to the dresser, jerked open the top drawer, rummaged inside then returned to the bed.

"What are you doing?"

"I do not wish to fight you. I wish only to give you pleasure, to show you the way I feel." He drew one of her silk stockings from among those he held in his hand, tied an end to the bed post and the other around her wrist. Carly only gaped as he did the same to the other wrist.

He smiled at her with a mixture of fierce desire and infinite tenderness. "I will have you, Cara. If you wish to stop me, cry out for your uncle. But I do not think you will."

He caught her ankle, wrapped a length of stocking around it and tied it to the post at the foot of the bed. The last stocking went into place and he secured it to the bed, spreading her wide for him. Carly's face went hot that he should see her thus, yet a fierce, wet heat slid into the place between her legs.

She watched him strip away his shirt, her eyes fastened on the ridges of muscle rippling across his broad dark back. Thick cords and taut sinews bunched on his shoulders as his breeches slid down his long, lean legs, leaving his narrow buttocks bare, and making little shivers dart into her stomach. When he turned to face her, his shaft rode high and hard against his flat, ridged belly.

"Ramon . . ." she whispered when he bent to kiss her

again, teasing her mouth with his tongue, sliding it across
her quivering bottom lip. Then he was nuzzling her throat,
nipping her ear, trailing hot, moist kisses along her shoulder. He stopped to suckle a breast, laved her nipple, licked
it, then bit the end. He drew the full mound deeply inside
his mouth, then moved to her opposite breast, showing it
the same fiery attention.

Ramon moved lower, his lips hot and damp against her
skin, and paused to ring her navel, raising goose-bumps
across her stomach and the flat plane beneath. Carly gasped
as she realized his intentions, started to strain against her
bonds at the feel of his warm breath on the damp folds of
her sex. Then he was parting her with his tongue, laving her
gently, determinedly, nudging the plump bud at her core
into aching arousal.

His tongue slid deeper, curled around her, then plunged
deeply again. He slid his hands beneath her buttocks to lift
her against his mouth then suckled the crown of her desire
and stroked her with his tongue again and again. Carly's
body trembled, tightened, her back arching upward until
her limbs went rigid and she shattered in mindless release,
biting her lip to keep from wildly crying his name. Bright
lights swirled as the pleasure swept through her, so powerful it made her dizzy. Ramon came up over her, his hard
shaft pulsing against her belly, his beautiful dark eyes on
her face as he watched her spiraling down from her peak.

"You liked that, *querida*. No?"

She blushed again, felt the hot embarrassment in her
cheeks.

"It is all right, Cara. I liked it too. Can you not tell?" He
filled her then, his shaft as thick and hard as she had ever
seen it. She struggled against her bonds, wanting to hold
him, desperate to draw him deeper inside, only to discover
she had already been released.

Moaning at the feel of his heavy length inside her, she

wrapped her legs around his lean hips and pulled him deeper, until his hardness touched the end of her womb. The sensation was incredible, yet in that moment, all of her doubts came crashing in, all of her terrible fears. With a man as virile as Ramon, sooner or later, there would be children. Half Anglo children. Would he love them as much as children of his own blood? What would happen if he discovered she was raised in a Pennsylvania mine patch? How would he feel about their children then?

Or perhaps some other question would arise, and he would not accept her word. If he didn't believe her, he might send her and their children away, or worse yet, keep the children and banish her as he had done before. If he did, she could not bear it.

Her throat clogged with tears. She wound her fingers in his thick black hair to draw him nearer, opening herself to him, taking him deeper still. She clutched his shoulders and kissed him, a passionate, yearning kiss full of all the love she felt inside but knew she would have to deny. The wetness burned her eyes and began to slide down her cheeks. When this night was ended, her life with Ramon must end as well. This time she would listen to her uncle, maybe even marry Vincent. She would guard her heart and protect herself from the pain she could not endure.

Ramon thrust deep and hard, pounding with such force he lifted her up off the bed. Love and passion swirled together, a heady mix that heightened her arousal to a fevered pitch. She was squirming beneath him, arching upward to meet each of his heavy strokes, matching his frenzied pace with a driving need of her own.

Tonight he was hers. Tomorrow he would be gone. "Ramon . . ." she whispered again, clinging to him, burying her face in his shoulder.

"Te adoro, mi amor." I adore you, my love.

She sobbed against his shoulder, clung to him as if she

would never let him go. They reached their peak together,
their bodies slick with perspiration as a rising tide of pleasure washed over them. For a time they did not stir. She
should make him go, she thought, the ache rising up, burning in her throat. She was afraid to imagine what might
happen if her uncle found him here. Instead when he began to kiss her, began once more to grow hard inside her,
she only moaned softly and gave herself over to his tender
embrace.

It was almost dawn when she awoke, saw Ramon at the
foot of the bed, dressed and ready to leave. For a moment
the terrible thought struck that he had used her again, had
only said he loved her so he could spend the night in her
bed. Then she gazed up at him, saw the ravaged hollows in
his cheeks.

"Do not look at me that way," he said. "I meant each of
the words I said and a hundred more I did not speak."

Carly bit her lip, relief so strong she sagged back against
the pillow.

"You were crying in your sleep. Do you remember?"

"No." Her heart squeezed, knotted up inside her.

"You begged me to leave. You said you could no longer
trust me. That is the way you feel?"

Her fingers knotted in the sheet. "In some ways I would
trust you with my life. In others . . ."

His jaw went hard. Dark turbulence gathered in his eyes.
"For weeks now, you have held my life in your hands, yet *I*
did not trust *you*. I tell you this now. From this day forward,
I will be the husband to you I should have been before. I give
you my solemn vow. No matter what happens, no matter
who would speak against you, I will not doubt you again."
He turned away from her and started across the room.

"Where are you going?"

He paused and his eyes fixed on her face. "When I came
here, I meant to take you with me, but you are not ready to

leave. You are more afraid of me now than you were that first night in the mountains. But I am no longer afraid of you, or of what I feel for you. I will win you, Cara. And the next time I claim you for my wife, I will never let you go."

A sheen of tears rose in her eyes as she watched him at the window. With a last soft glance in her direction, Ramon swung a long lean leg over the sill, ducked his head, and jumped to the ground below.

Carly watched him slip into the darkness, her heart aching inside her breast. But the words he'd said would not leave her. Was it possible to put her faith in him again? Did she dare to hope that things might work out between them? He had wanted her to come home, to return with him to Las Almas, the only real home she'd had in years.

It was what she wanted, she realized, more than anything else in the world. And yet she was afraid.

Exhausted, she lay back on the pillow, listening to the silence, then later the sounds of the awakening rancho. An hour passed. Her uncle rode out with his band of armed men, and her fears for Ramon overrode those for herself.

Had he gone to Llano Miranda? She prayed with all her heart that if he had, her uncle would not find him and that he and the others would be safe.

Two days later, Captain Harry Love, Fletcher Austin, Jeremy Layton, and at least thirty men stormed the pass at Llano Mirada.

Angel de la Guerra watched them come, riding like a windswept fire up through the wagon trail at the rear that was meant to be used for escape. They had taken out the guards, picking off some of them quietly before they started in, taking out the others with a well-placed gunshot as they thundered past on their lathered horses. The women screamed and raced inside their small cabins, hoping to shield their children from harm.

Tomasina Gutierrez stood at her husband's side, firing a long Sharp's rifle, while Santiago cocked and fired a Remington army pistol in each of his powerful hands. Pedro Sanchez, Ruiz Domingo, Ignacio Juarez, and a dozen others fought on horseback, aiming their rifles and firing, then riding to a different position and firing again. Miranda Aguilar crouched behind the watering trough, shooting the heavy Navy Colt's .36-caliber that Ramon had given her and taught her to use. Her fourth shot took out a beefy man astride a buckskin horse, who hit the dirt and rolled to a bloody stop just inches away from the hem of her red cotton skirt.

Amazingly, they fought back the first wave with the loss of only the rear guards and four of the men, forcing the vigilantes to retreat to the edge of the camp.

"They will not wait long before they return," Angel said, crouching beside Pedro Sanchez.

"No. And we cannot hold them long once they do." He turned to Ruiz Domingo. "Get the women and children into the forest. Tell them to scatter and hide as best they can. It is the men they are after. We will hold them as long as we can, then ride out. We will meet in the cave at Arroyo Aguaje." A plan they'd made at the start, should the stronghold ever be taken.

They wasted only a moment with silent farewells and looks that said they knew their chances were slim. Instead each man set to his task and when the vicious Hounds hit again, they were ready. They held them for longer than they had imagined, two solid hours of beating back wave after wave of riders and an endless hail of flying lead, their forces gradually thinning as men and horses slipped off quietly into the heavy brush and towering granite boulders that lined the canyon.

A moment of silence hung in the air between rounds of rifle fire as Pedro Sanchez, Ignacio Juarez, Carlos Martinez, and three other men, all that was left of the defenders, crouched in the rocks above the rear entrance to the stronghold.

Their circumstances were dire, yet Pedro amazed the others by grinning. "They will be surprised, no? When they finally break through, only to discover most of the men have escaped."

Ignacio smiled, too. "It is El Dragón they want most of all, and just like the rest, he is not here."

Pedro pondered that. The others were safe, but if he and his *compadres* continued to resist, in the next fiery wave they were sure to be killed. If they gave themselves up, there was a chance they might be arrested, taken back to San Juan Bautista—before they were hanged. If that was the case . . .

"Take off your shirt, amigo," Pedro said to Ignacio.

"What?"

"I wish to be ready. The minute the men begin to fire, we are going to surrender."

"Have you gone loco?" Ignacio started to argue, but Pedro quickly explained his thinking and soon the younger man was nodding his agreement.

"It is a chance, at least," Ignacio said. "Better than dying here. I will tell the others." Stripping off his dirty white shirt and handing it to Pedro, he crouched in the tall, thick grasses, carefully picking his way through the dense buck brush and sage to each of the men defending the stronghold.

When the shooting began, they answered fire only for a moment, then Pedro began to wave Ignacio's torn and bloody white shirt on the barrel of his rifle. Carlos Martinez fell to a lead ball in the chest before the final shots ended, as did one of the other men. Pedro, Ignacio, and two other vaqueros were captured by the crowd of angry men, one of which Pedro recognized as Fletcher Austin, another who was the sheriff of San Juan Bautista, Jeremy Layton.

It was the sheriff who approached him, his rifle casually aimed at the middle of Pedro's chest. "Where is he?"

"Who, Senor Sheriff?"

"You know who we want—that bastard who calls himself the Spanish Dragon."

Fletcher Austin pushed his way forward. "Let my men have a go at him, Sheriff. We'll make the greaser talk." Austin jerked Pedro up by the shirtfront and punched him hard in the stomach, doubling him over making him gasp for breath.

"Hold it, gentlemen." That from the man named Harry Love, the leader of the vigilantes. "There is no need for further violence," he said with his thick Texas drawl. He smiled wolfishly. "The others may have escaped, but not the man we came for. Gentlemen, may I present the infamous El Dragón."

Pedro's stomach knotted. He scanned the crowd of angry men, then turned toward the sound of voices and the scuffling of stout leather boots. Powdery dust rose up as a man in black was dragged forward, his hands and feet bound, and tossed into the dirt at Pedro's feet.

The man was Angel de la Guerra.

*C*hapter *T*wenty

*H*is beautiful wife lay sleeping, her pretty face framed by the burnished cloud of her hair. Her cheeks looked pale and her eyes were slightly puffed, as if she had been crying. A small hand was fisted beneath her chin and her petite figure curled into itself, making her look like a helpless child.

He moved closer to the bed, watching the way her chest rose and fell with each of her shallow breaths. Leaning forward, his hands framed her face, his long fingers soaking up the warmth in her cheeks. A heavy knot gathered in his chest as he bent his head and kissed her, a soft, gentle kiss that made her lips curve slightly upward. His tongue brushed the corner of her mouth in a gentle caress, then swept over her bottom lip, and she began to awaken. He smiled as her eyes slowly opened.

"Ramon . . ." she whispered sluggishly, "what are you . . . ?" Then she sat bolt upright in the bed. "Ramon! My God, how did you escape? Uncle Fletcher said they were going to hang you!" She glanced frantically toward the door. "Dear Lord, you shouldn't be here. If he finds you here, he'll kill you. You have to get away!" She swung her legs to the side of the bed and stood up, but Ramon simply caught her against him.

"Easy, Cara, give me a chance to explain." Big twin pools of green stared into his face, and her cheeks looked even paler than they had when he had first come into the room. She made a soft little sound in her throat and her arms went around his neck. Ramon crushed her tightly against him.

"I was so worried," she said, trembling in his embrace. "When my uncle rode in this afternoon, he said they had finally found the stronghold. He said they had captured El Dragón and four of his men, and that Captain Harry Love and Sheriff Layton were taking them to jail in San Juan. He said they were going to hang them three days from now in the square in front of the church."

"You did not mention my name?"

"No, of course not. I didn't want them to know I knew who you were."

He relaxed a little. He hadn't considered that Carly might inadvertently tell them who he was. Inwardly he scoffed. Angel still had plenty of time for that.

"Tell me what happened," she said.

Ramon sighed wearily. "The Indian trackers the vigilantes hired discovered the back way into Llano Mirada."

"Dear God. What happened to the others, to Pedro and Florentia, the women and the children?"

A muscle bunched in his jaw. "Nearly a dozen men were killed. Many of the others were wounded, I am not sure which ones. All of the women and children got safely away. They arrested Pedro and three of the vaqueros from Llano Mirada."

"What about you? How did you escape?"

"I was not there. By the time I arrived, the fighting was ended. I uncovered the story in bits and pieces from the men I found hiding in the woods. My cousin Angel is the man the *gringos* believe is El Dragón."

"Y-your cousin?"

"*Si*. So far he has let them continue to believe it. Why, I am not sure. I suppose it is fortunate for me that things happened as they did. After I left you that night, I was headed for Llano Mirada. I had some . . . unfinished business . . . with my cousin I wished to attend."

"You were going after Angel because of me?"

"You thought that once I knew the truth I would let him live?"

"Dear God, Ramon, you can't just kill him."

"I could kill him with my bare hands for what he tried to do to you. And for what losing you has done to me."

She searched his face for long, breathless moments, then she came up on tiptoe, tightening her hold on his neck, and he dragged her fiercely against him, burying his face in her hair. It smelled of cinnamon and roses.

"I had to see you," he said. "I will be riding out tonight, meeting the men at a place called Arroyo Aguaje. In three days time, the night before the hanging, we will ride into San Juan and set the vaqueros free."

She drew away from him, stared worriedly into his face. "You can't do that. Surely they'll be waiting."

"I do not think so. They believe the men have scattered, that their leader is in jail. Besides, it does not matter. Pedro and the others are going to hang. I cannot let that happen. With the help of my men, I believe I can free them."

Carly bit her lip, her eyes wide and searching. "I don't want you to go. I'm afraid for you, Ramon."

A corner of his mouth curved up. "Does that mean that you are ready to come home?"

Carly let go of him, took a step away. "How . . . how are your mother and aunt?" she evaded, uncertainty clear on her face.

He sighed with frustration. "My mother has been ill, but she is fine now. Tia is as she always is, a steady rock for all of us to cling to. Both of them have nagged me without end to stop acting foolish and bring my wife home. In the end, as usual, they were right."

Her eyes searched his face. "What if I came back and they discovered what happened the night Andreas was killed, that I was the one who sounded the alarm by ringing the bell? Can you imagine the pain it would cause them? How do you think they would feel about me then?"

"They would feel as I do. That what you did was no different from what Two Hawks had to do when he fought the men who attacked his village. You did only what any of us would have done if our home had been threatened. And they do know, Cara. Tia told me they have known since the night of the *fandango.*"

"They knew?"

"Si. Even I did not know they had heard the story though perhaps I should have guessed. Tia worried in some way that was part of the reason you did not return with me from Monterey. I did not tell her it was my cruelty, my prejudice that was keeping you away."

Her head came up, golden lamplight shining on her fiery auburn hair. His body stirred at the shapely curves outlined beneath her thin white nightgown.

"You speak of the past so lightly," she said. "But it is more important than that. Have you considered that if I came back, sooner or later, there would be children? Mixed blood children, Ramon, part Anglo, part Spanish. How would you feel about that? Would you love them less because their mother was a *gringa?*"

He moved toward her, gently gripped her shoulders. *"Madre de Dios,* I cannot believe I have done this to you—made you doubt the very heart of me. Do you really believe I would not love our children? *Santo de Christo,* I cannot imagine a sweeter, more beautiful child than a little girl like her mother. Or a son with your courage and strength."

A sheen of tears appeared in her eyes. She blinked and pushed them away. "I'm not courageous, I'm a coward. I'm frightened that if I come back I might lose you again, and if I did, I wouldn't be able to bear it."

He pulled her back into his arms, kissed her eyes, her nose, pressed a soft kiss on her mouth. "You will not lose me. I have made mistakes, but I am not a stupid man. I will not make those same mistakes again. I love you. If you will come home, I will prove how much every day for the rest of our lives."

The wetness reappeared. A single tear slid down her cheek. "I need time, Ramon. I keep hearing those things you said, those terrible names you called me. I keep thinking—"

"Do not say it. I know the kind of man I am. I know that I can be ruthless, at times I can even be cruel. I have learned to be as I am, but it is not truly my way." He raked his hands through his hair, his muscles taut with frustration mixed with rising desire. "I am not saying I am an easy man to live with. I know I have a very bad temper and I can be arrogant at times."

A corner of her mouth curved faintly. "Yes, you can be quite arrogant at times."

"Am I really so bad, Cara?"

She looked into his eyes, seemed to probe deeply inside him. "You're obstinate and overbearing. You're demanding and nearly insatiable in bed. And you're the most wonderful man I've ever known."

"Cara . . ." His heart expanded with love for her. He wanted to carry her over to the bed, to take her as he had the last time he had been there. He wanted to bury himself in her tight, damp heat, to feel her trembling beneath him. He wanted to claim her, possess her, make her admit that she was his. Instead he ignored the pulsing in his loins and forced his mind to think of the reason he had come.

"I will be back for you as soon as I have freed the men.

When I do, I will not let you refuse me, even if I have to
carry you away."

She cupped his cheek in her palm and he felt the trembling of her hand. "Be careful, Ramon. I wouldn't want to
live if you were killed."

He drew her against him and kissed her with savage
force, thrusting his tongue into her mouth, claiming her as
his. She belonged to him and he wanted her to know it. "I
will come back for you," he said in a voice gone rough, "I
swear it."

He wished he could stay, but his men were depending
on him. He shouldn't even have come, but he'd had to see
her one last time. The plan he intended was bold and dangerous. The odds were greatly against him. Yet his friends'
lives depended upon him, and he meant to save them if he
could. He kissed her again, quick and hard, then crossed
the room, went over the sill, and slipped quietly to the
ground. In minutes he had disappeared into the darkness.

If he rode hard, he would reach the cave at Arroyo
Aguajes by midday tomorrow. The others were there, he
knew, word had come through one of his vaqueros. Just as
a message had arrived from Alejandro de Estrada, telling
him his efforts in finding the old church records had all
been in vain.

After examining the documents, the Land Commission
refused to alter their findings. They would not reopen the
case. There was no legal way, Don Alejandro's missive
said, the de la Guerras could win back Rancho del Robles.

And illegal methods had not worked. The raiding they
had done had not begun to weaken Fletcher Austin's power
or that of the other Anglos in the area. Though Andreas
had believed they had a chance, Ramon had known from
the start they could never defeat their enemies that way.

The past was over. One way or another, El Dragón's
days were at an end. Just one last foray into the night, one

last raid to free his men, and his outlaw days were finished. If he could survive one more night—and if Angel had not betrayed him again—he had a chance to put all of this behind him. He could fetch his wife home and make a life for them at Las Almas. It wasn't the life they would have had at del Robles, but Carly didn't seem to mind and if she could be happy, then so could he. Together they would build a future, have children, be content.

One more raid, he told himself as he swung up on the saddle of the big blood bay that would carry him to Arroyo Aguajes where his tall black stallion stood waiting.

Just one more raid.

If he could somehow manage to stay alive.

Carly barely slept that night. She was too worried about Ramon. He would be riding into San Juan Bautista, confronting the sheriff, risking his life to save his men. She had not tried to stop him. She knew him too well for that. He loved Pedro Sanchez like a father, and the other men were his responsibility as well. At least that was how he would see it.

She dressed in the sapphire blue riding habit that came with the things Two Hawks had returned, but much of her clothing and personal items remained at Las Almas. Why Ramon kept them she wasn't sure. For herself, she had left them there on purpose, unable to sever her ties with him completely. It was a small thing, yet it gave her some connection with the place she still thought of as home.

Thinking of the people she missed at Las Almas, Carly left the house and made her way to the stables. She needed some time to herself and riding had become the means to that end.

"Jose, are you in here?" she called out, and the tall vaquero who worked with the horses stuck his head out of one of the stalls.

"*Si,* senora. I am here."

"I wish to go riding. Would you saddle me a horse?"

He grinned so wide, she could see the white of his teeth even in the shadows of the barn. "*Si,* senora, I have just the one."

She eyed him with some speculation, following him back toward the stall he'd just come from. Carly's breath caught as he opened the door and led out the most beautiful palomino mare she had ever seen.

"For you, senora, from your husband, Don Ramon. Mariano brought her here only this morning."

A hard ache swelled in her throat. Ramon had done this for her. Ramon. "She's beautiful, Jose. The most beautiful horse I've ever seen."

"She is Andalusian," he said. "Don Diego, Don Ramon's father, used to raise them by the hundreds when he lived at Rancho del Robles. They were sold when the rancho went to sale. Don Ramon bought back a few. His stallion, Rey del Sol, was among them."

'I knew about Rey, but not the mare. I've never seen her before."

"It was to be a surprise. A wedding present, Mariano said. The don has been raising her somewhere in the mountains. One of the vaqueros has been training her for you."

Pedro Sanchez, most likely. Perhaps at Llano Mirada. "She's beautiful," Carly said again, stroking the mare's velvet nose. "What's her name?"

"Sunflower."

Carly blinked hard. Still, the tears collected behind her eyes and several spilled over onto her cheeks.

"Mariano said the don meant to give her to you himself, but yesterday he changed his mind. He said this way, no matter what happened, you would always remember him."

Carly bit hard on her lip. Dear God, he wanted her to have the mare in case he was killed in San Juan. She had to get out of there before she started crying in earnest. "Saddle her for me, will you, Jose?"

He smiled, "*Si,* senora."

Carly brushed the wetness from her cheeks and waited outside while her sidesaddle was placed on the prancing golden mare with the snowy mane and tail. She looked exactly like Rey del Sol, only smaller, more petite. It occurred to her suddenly that she *had* seen the horse before, that this was the mare she had seen in the meadow, mating with Rey del Sol. Even now, the little mare must be carrying the stallion's colt.

It was a gift without measure, a gift that could come only from love.

Thinking of Ramon, of how much she loved him and how worried she was for his safety, Carly climbed up on the mounting block and settled herself in her sidesaddle atop the little mare. She rode all morning, appreciating the horse's perfect gait, the way the animal obeyed her commands without question. Unconsciously, she made her way deeper into the hills and eventually wound up at the pool where she and Ramon had made love.

As worried for him as she was, she found herself smiling. When he came for her again, she would go with him and gladly. She loved him and he loved her. She had never really been a coward—only for just a short time. And she would risk anything for the love of a man like Ramon.

She dismounted from the mare and let the horse drink from the mirror-smooth surface of the pool, nostrils flaring, muzzle sinking deeply. Stroking the horse's sleek golden neck, she ignored the terrible barb of fear that Ramon would be killed in San Juan and never return to take her home.

* * *

Miranda Aguilar knocked on the door to the *cocina* at
Rancho del Robles, and buxom Rita Salazar pulled it open.

"Dios mio!" Rita's black eyes misted with tears. *"Mi
hija,* where have you been?"

Miranda hugged the mother she hadn't seen in the last
three years. "Many places, Mama. I did not know that you
were here."

Rita slid a stout arm around her daughter's slender
waist, urging her into the kitchen, and they sat down on a
bench in front of a roughhewn table.

"I only came to del Robles a few months ago," Rita
said. "Before that I was in San Miguel. Your father is dead.
That is why I left Monterey, where we had been working."

"I am sorry, Mama, I did not know." Miranda swallowed and glanced away. "I tried to find you, but Inocente
was never in one place long enough. You were right about
him, Mama. I never should have married him. He was a
hard man, often he was cruel. Sometimes he even beat me.
I was not sorry when he was killed."

"Pobrecita," her mother crooned, smoothing the thick
black hair away from her daughter's pretty face.

"His family was nice, though. I went to visit them at a
rancho called El Tejon at the end of the great central valley. They wanted me to stay, but I decided not to. I learned
you were here from one of the vaqueros. That is why I returned to Llano Mirada, the place where Inocente took me
before he was killed. That is where I met El Dragón." Miranda didn't mention she had slept with Ramon de la
Guerra, or with Ruiz Dominguez, after Ramon had gone.

Rita crossed herself. "Senor Austin and the others, they
have finally captured the outlaws."

"Si, I was there. I am lucky I escaped."

"Por Dios, how did you get away?"

Miranda sighed heavily. The journey from Arroyo

Aguajes was along one, but she'd felt she had to come. She wasn't sure when she would see her mother again.

"When the shooting started, one of the vaqueros, a man named Ruiz Dominguez, led the women and children deeper into the mountains. Always we had planned that if anything should happen, we would meet at a cave in the hills. The men are gathered there now. They plan to ride into San Juan the night before the hanging and free those who were captured. I heard them talking."

"*Por Dios*—they will all be killed!"

"I do not think so. They will go in quietly, break into the jail, then ride out to the south through an old dry arroyo that circles the town. The plan is a good one, I think."

Rita hugged her daughter, her pendulous breasts in contrast to Miranda's slender form. "You must say nothing more of this. Senor Austin would be angry."

"I told you only because I cannot stay. I am returning to the mountains." Beneath her dark skin, her cheeks grew slightly flushed. "I am going away with Ruiz. He is a fine vaquero, Mama, and I have come to care for him."

Rita's plump hands cradled her daughter's face. "I am glad you came. Once you are settled, you can visit me again, no?"

"*Si*, Mama. That is what I am hoping."

"You must eat before you leave. You are too skinny." Rita squeezed her daughter's hand. "I have just made tamales and a batch of fresh tortillas. You will have time for that, no?"

Miranda smiled. "*Si*, but I must hurry. I am told Senor Austin's niece is here. If she discovers I am also here, I will no longer be welcome."

Rita frowned but said nothing more. She was worried about her daughter. She wished her child could stay for a visit, but for now it was not safe. She was only glad Senor

Fletcher would not hear of these things. If he did, he would be waiting the night of the raid. Her daughter's *novio* might not live to return to the hills.

Angel de la Guerra sat alone in his cell in the small uncomfortable jail in San Juan Bautista. In another cell at the opposite end, Pedro Sanchez and three of El Dragón's vaqueros curled up on the thin corn husk mattress or sprawled on the hard wooden floor. Sheriff Jeremy Layton sat in his office in a separate building a dozen yards away.

In the square across from the mission, a makeshift gallows held four lengths of rope, each of them looped with a thirteen-coil knot. A hangman's noose. And one of them was waiting for Angel de la Guerra.

Sitting on the floor of his cell, a corner of his mouth twisted up. Always he had known it would end like this. He'd been lucky to escape the gallows after the first man he had killed. Even telling them he wasn't El Dragón would not save him. He had been in hiding at Llano Mirada. He had been firing at the vigilantes, had wounded at least four of their men.

And he was wanted for murdering one of the guards at the prison during his escape.

He almost smiled. Andreas was El Dragón but Andreas was dead. Ramon de la Guerra had used the name as well. Angel was also a de la Guerra. Why shouldn't he have a little of the glory? In fact if he was going to die, why shouldn't he have it all?

His chest rumbled with humorless mirth at the thought. Ramon would never admit the truth and neither would any of his men. Angel would go down as a legend. An outlaw almost as renowned as Joaquin Murieta.

Yes, if he was going to hang, this was the way he wanted to go. His head fell back against the cold hard wall of the cell. A cockroach skittered across the floor at his feet, and the smell of dampness and urine assaulted his nose. If the choice was death or more years in a place like this, he would choose death for sure.

He squashed the cockroach with the heel of his boot, the crunch of its shell echoing off the walls of the cell. Perhaps it was poetic justice. Ramon had always bested him, always come out on top. Now Angel was gaining a place in history—a fair exchange for the night he should have spent in his cousin's pretty wife's bed.

"I hope you're sure about this." Fletcher Austin threw a hard look at his tall rangy foreman, Cleve Sanders, who stood next to him outside the barn while they finished saddling there horses. Dusk had fallen, a dark purple glow that hovered on the horizon.

Sanders merely smiled. "Sure as I can be, considering my sources. I told you what I heard, but you can always ask the woman yourself."

Fletcher frowned. Rita wouldn't utter a word against her Spanish friends. He'd have to beat it out of her and he wasn't about to do that. Not unless he had to. "I think we know as much as much as we need to. We'll let them go in, then be waiting for them when they come out. That way no one in town will get hurt when the lead starts flying, and we'll have the bastards dead to rights."

"Makes sense to me," Sanders said with a satisfied smile. "We know which way they'll be heading out. All we gotta do is sit and wait."

"Exactly." Fletcher pulled the cinch tight on his saddle, bridled the horse, drew the reins up, and swung up on the animal's back. Impatiently, he sat waiting for the others to finish and join him. He was gazing back toward the house, eager to be away, when he saw the curtains flutter and his niece's face appear at the window.

The next thing he knew she was opening the door,

running toward him across the yard, her plum silk skirts rucked high above her ankles. Damn, would the girl never learn to behave like a lady?

"Where are you going, Uncle Fletcher?" She stopped beside the horse, a little breathless and obviously unnerved. "I didn't know you and the men were riding out tonight."

"It's nothing to worry yourself about, my dear. The men and I have some business in town."

"Y-you're going into San Juan?"

"That's right. You needn't wait up. Odds are we won't be back until some time tomorrow."

Carly wet her lips. "You're wearing your gun. Are you expecting some kind of trouble?"

"As I said, it's nothing to worry about. Go back inside. It's time for us to leave."

"But—"

"Do as I say, Caralee. I don't want to tell you again."

Carly said nothing, just backed away into the shadows, then turned and walked off toward the house. Her uncle had barely spoken in the last two days. He was angry at her for accepting Ramon's gift of the mare. He'd demanded she return the horse to Las Almas, but Carly had staunchly refused.

Now she wished she had placated him somehow. Perhaps he would have told her his plans for tonight. Instead, she had only just chanced to see the men outside and now her heart pounded with fierce trepidation. She waited inside the house till the men rode out of sight, her legs feeling wobbly and her hands shaking with fear. There wasn't time to change her clothes. Instead, as soon as the riders dropped over the rise, she raced to the barn, opened the door to Sunflower's stall, and led the little mare outside.

In minutes, she had the horse saddled, bridled, and ready. Climbing up on the mounting block, she hoisted herself up into the sidesaddle, bunching her plum silk skirts around her, gathered up the reins, and set off into the darkness.

How in God's name had her uncle discovered the plan to free Pedro and the men? Or perhaps he didn't know for sure, just suspected they might make the attempt since the hanging was set for tomorrow.

She tossed that notion away. If that was the case, the men would have been watching the jail for the past two nights. They wouldn't have known for certain for which night the raid was set. But they did know, Carly was sure. Someone had told them.

Who could have known?

Who would have betrayed them?

Who—besides herself?

Carly's insides clenched so hard she swayed and nearly lost her seat atop the mare. God in heaven, Ramon would believe she was the one who had told them. He had told her his plans. He would believe she had told her uncle. Ramon would be killed and even as the shots slammed into his body, he would believe she had betrayed him again.

Dear God, she couldn't bear to think of it.

Carly kicked the mare into a gallop, her chest so tight she could barely drag in a breath. She had to catch up with the men, but she couldn't let them see her. She had to discover what her uncle intended and somehow warn Ramon.

The mare stumbled over a rock and nearly went down. Carly eased up on the reins, let the animal regain its feet, then rode on, her heartbeat more rapid with every passing mile. No moon shone, just a thin sliver of white and a faint silver trail to light the way. Dark swirling clouds rolled past, obscuring even that small source of comfort for long, ink-black minutes at a time.

She topped a ridge above the low, rolling, oak-covered hills and caught a glimpse of the men below. They were moving rapidly, covering much of the way at a gallop. She followed behind them, keeping up a steady pace yet always careful not to get too near.

As the night grew more chill, she untied the blanket she carried behind her saddle and drew it around her bare shoulders and the generous portion of her breasts the expensive silk gown exposed. Her stiffly starched muslin petticoats chafed against her legs and her whalebone corset pressed into the underside of her breasts. The pins in her hair came loose as the horse's hooves pounded against the earth, and her long, dark copper hair flew wildly around her shoulders. Still she rode on.

She was nearly exhausted by the time she reached the outskirts of San Juan Bautista, slowing the mare when the lights came into view and silently picking her way along the dry arroyo the men had ridden into ahead of her. She drew rein when she heard them speaking and realized they had all dismounted.

Tying the mare some distance away, she crept over the rocky surface of the old dry streambed, ignoring the jab of a sharp stone in her shoe, until she got close enough to see what they were doing. They were settling in, she saw, finding places to lie in wait where they wouldn't be discovered. Crouching behind downed trees, granite boulders, and out of sight around a bend in the arroyo, they prepared themselves to ambush Ramon and his men.

The trap was deadly. None of the men would escape.

A sharp stab of fear gouged through her as she made her way back to where her little mare waited.

*C*hapter *T*wenty-one

*R*amon sat astride his big black stallion, Viento Prieto. Dark Wind had carried its master as if he were the wind in truth, moving like a zephyr through the night. Beside him, Ruiz Dominguez, Ignacio Juarez, and a dozen of his vaqueros, all that remained after the raid on Llano Mirada, surveyed the village of San Juan Bautista, nestled at the base of the foothills in the fertile valley below.

"Each of you remembers what he is to do?"

"*Si*, Don Ramon," muttered the men. The tension among them was so palpable even the horses could sense it. They snorted and blew, their nostrils flaring, hooves shifting nervously, and there was a wildness in their eyes that matched that of the men.

"Ruiz and Ignacio will come into the jail with me," Ramon reminded them. "Emilio and Esteban will guard the door, while the rest of you take up the positions you were assigned. You are ready?"

Another muttered agreement.

"Fan out and move in quietly. Do not spare your horses once the men are freed and we are ready to ride out of town." Grim-faced they set off down the hill, each of them knowing the price they would pay if they failed. Their friends would hang. And they would all be dead.

As they had planned, they spread out and rode in, traveling quietly along the narrow lanes and alleys till they reached the sheriff's office across the street and down from the mission. Ramon's jaw tightened at the sight of the makeshift gallows in the square, its four swinging nooses a grisly reminder of what might await them. Moving with stealth, he eased closer to the stoutly constructed, thick-timbered jail with its two small windows, and nodded to one of his men, who took out the guard at the rear.

The butt of a pistol silenced a second guard, this one leaning against the building that housed the sheriff's office. The sign above the door fluttered briefly in the turbulence stirred up by the men below, and Ramon held his breath that the sound of squeaking hinges would not be noticed. The noise finally faded and no one inside appeared at the door. Another guard fell soundlessly as a big, beefy vaquero wrapped a thick forearm around the man's throat and squeezed off his air supply.

None of the men were killed. Ramon had warned them to use only as much force as necessary. The fury of their pursuit would be lessened, and murdering men in the name of justice seemed at odds with his beliefs.

He stepped closer to the guard who stood beside the door to the jail holding a scatter gun in his hands, a fat cigar clamped between his teeth.

"Pleasant evening for a smoke, no?"

The big man whirled toward the sound of the voice. "Who the hell are you?" he said around the cigar.

Ramon's long-barreled Colt swung up in answer, the smooth wooden stock clipping the man on the chin. He went down with a muted groan, his long body crumpling into the dirt, the cigar broken in two, one end still glowing, a wisp of smoke drifting up.

Ignacio stepped from the shadows. "The sheriff and two

more men are inside his office. There is only one guard inside the jail."

Ramon nodded and rapped twice on the thick jail door.

"That you, Wilkins?" sifted through the heavy oak planking.

"Let me in," Ramon said, working to hide his accent. He must have done it because the door swung open, and the minute it did, the barrel of his rifle cracked hard against the man's balding head. "Get the keys," he commanded Ignacio, who wrested them from the pocket of the guard lying on the floor, a thin stream of blood running down his forehead, along his nose, and onto his cheek before it pooled on the floor.

"Don Ramon!" Pedro Sanchez rushed forward, gripping the bars of his cell along with Santiago Gutierrez and the other two vaqueros.

Ramon smiled, glad they appeared to be in good health. "It is good to see you, *compadres*."

"Far better seeing you, my friend," Pedro said. Ignacio worked the key, the heavy iron lock grating, and the minute the door swung wide, the men stumbled out of the cell and into the small airless room.

"What about Angel?" Pedro asked, reading a moment of indecision in Ramon's hard face.

"I ought to let him hang."

Pedro smiled, crinkling the lines at the corners of his eyes. "*Si*, but I do not think you will."

Ramon shook his head. "No, I do not suppose I will." Striding to the end of the corridor, he unlocked the door to Angel's cell, then wordlessly turned and walked back toward the other three men.

"*Vamanos, amigos.* We have spent too much time here already." He didn't look to see if Angel followed, just strode out the door and swung up on his night-black horse.

"We ride out through the old arroyo that circles the town. Once you are safely away, cut back and head into the hills."

"*Si* . . . El Dragón," one of the freed vaqueros said with a grin. Four saddled horses waited for the men, who swung hurriedly up on their backs. Ramon whirled Viento, made a high sign to the men, touched the horse with his spurs, and galloped off down the street toward the dry wash leading out of town.

I'm not going to make it! The frantic thought tore through Carly's mind as she raced her horse across the grassy square in front of the mission. A little to the right of the huge carved doors into the church, she reined the mare to a sliding stop and leapt down from the sidesaddle, losing her balance, landing hard, and twisting her ankle.

Muttering an unladylike curse, she jerked her plum silk skirts to mid-calf and started limping as fast as she could through the heavy wooden door and up the stairs leading to the choir loft and the ropes that rang the bells in the *campanario,* the towering bell wall beside the church. By the time she had spotted Ramon, he was already riding into the town and it had been too late to stop him. Her only chance now was to warn him.

She knew the risk she was taking. Her daring plan put him in even more danger, yet it was the only chance he had.

She prayed he would know what her frantic warning meant.

Wincing with every step, she made her way up the stairs and looked up at the bells mounted with rawhide thongs in each of the three arched openings. She grabbed the long dangling length of hemp tied to the one at the top, pulled with all her might, and began to ring the huge iron bell.

The loud clang of metal sent a vibration down the rope, up her arm, and rang out over the big church plaza. It carried past Segundo Street, down Castro, and started to rouse the town. Curtains flew open, heads ducked through windows, people came out of their houses to see what was going on. Nothing was scheduled at the church this time of night, no weddings, no socials, no funerals. Something had to be wrong.

At the edge of the city, Ramon cursed the sound. In seconds the entire town would know about the breakout. The sheriff and his men would be behind them in hot pursuit. He wondered who the hell was sounding the alarm, then frowned at the irony that whoever it was had chosen to ring the big bell. First Andreas had fallen to the sound, now it appeared to be his turn.

Ramon's stomach tightened as a cold fissure of warning sliced through him, a feeling so strong he could not shake it. They had almost reached the arroyo, were just seconds from disappearing out of sight in the dry old wash that would carry them to safety.

Or would it?

"Hold up!" he commanded, raising an arm to the men who thundered along in his wake. "We will take the alternate route, ride through the plaza, down the hill to the river. Go! Do it now!"

They did not wait for an explanation. Too many times in the past El Dragón's instincts had been right—the only thing that had saved them. And now that instinct was telling him the way to safety lay not in the way they had planned but in the opposite direction.

The men whirled their horses, dug in their spurs, and urged their mounts into a flat-out run. A rifle shot rang out, then another and another, the shots not coming from town, but from somewhere behind them. Over his shoulder, Ramon saw a wave of men, mounted and riding full tilt, surge out of the arroyo and thunder toward the town. His own men answered fire, but didn't slow down. One man fell, another took a lead ball in the shoulder but kept on riding.

Ramon jerked his pistol from the bandolero across his chest and fired over his shoulder, bringing one man down, while Ignacio wounded another. They rode past the front of the church and the men, now riding ahead of him, dropped over the ridge off toward the river. Ramon didn't follow. Instead, the moment he dropped out of sight, he wheeled his horse, leaned low over Viento's neck, circled around to the left, and came up at the back of the mission.

Making his way toward the high bell wall, he saw what he knew he would see. Caralee's palomino mare, his wife limping frantically toward her.

"Ramon!" she cried out when she saw him. He was down from his horse, running toward her, catching her up, and tossing her into the saddle before she could say any more.

"Ride, Cara—back through the arroyo. The men are no longer there and I will be right behind you."

She spun the little mare and the horse leapt forward. Shots still rang out but they were coming from the riverbed below them, more sporadic now and echoing from different directions. The men had split up, their pursuers would have to do the same.

Ramon smiled grimly. His vaqueros were the finest horsemen in the world. In a life and death contest like this one, he did not doubt the Californios would win.

He glanced ahead, saw his wife leaning over her horse's neck, riding hard through the arroyo ahead of him. Her plum silk skirts rode well above her knees, her petticoats white in the sliver of moon, her seat on the horse sure and steady. If he hadn't been so worried for her safety, he might have smiled at how much she had learned. Instead, he closed the distance between them, shielding her from whoever might follow, then they settled into a steady lope over the rocky terrain.

They had just rounded the corner leading out of town to

safety when hoofbeats sounded behind them. A rifle shot rang out, cutting the air beside his head, then another and another.

"Keep riding!" he shouted to Caralee, drawing his pistol once more. He fired at their pursuer, once, twice, saw the man stiffen as the lead ball slammed into his shoulder then snap off a return shot before he careened off his horse.

Ramon grunted in pain, the hot lead hitting him like the blow of a hammer, burning into his back and tearing out through his chest. The scorching pain nearly knocked him out of the saddle.

Unconsciously, his hold grew tighter on the reins and Viento began to slow.

"Ramon!" Carly shouted, her voice high-pitched with fear as she whirled her mare and rode up beside him.

"We have to keep going," he said through teeth clenched hard against the pain. "We will not be safe until we are far from here."

"But you're wounded!"

"We will stop as soon as it is safe."

"You need a doctor. We have to—"

"We must ride, *querida*. There is no other way."

"A-are you sure you can make it?"

He smiled grimly, fighting the dizziness, trying not to succumb to the beckoning lure of unconsciousness. "Do not fear, Cara. I have much to live for. I will make it."

They rode without stopping till they were well into the mountains south of town, then looped back toward Las Almas. By now, the others would have scattered. The safest place Ramon could be was at home.

Fighting his dizziness and the pain knifing into his back and chest, he glanced at the woman riding close beside him, her face tense with worry. Austin and his men had been waiting in ambush. Just a few seconds more and the trap would have been sprung. He and his men would be dead if it hadn't been for Carly and the ringing of the bell.

He thought of it with an odd sense of rightness, just before he slid from his horse.

"Ramon!" Carly jerked rein on the mare, her heart leaping hard against her ribs. Scrambling down from the saddle, she limped back to where Ramon lay in the dirt. He was conscious, she saw, but only barely, groaning softly as he tried to sit up.

"Dear God . . ." Biting back a sob, she eased him down on the ground. "Don't try to move," she instructed, trying not to sound as frightened as she was "just stay where you are until I can find some way to slow the bleeding."

He settled heavily onto his back and lay still for a moment, his breathing harsh and labored. Carly tore open his shirt with shaking hands. Dear Lord, there was so much blood! A jagged hole yawned from a place just above his heart, the skin badly torn and already turning purple. The bloody entrance hole wept a stream down his back. It was a vicious, painful wound, one he could die from, yet she could not—would not—entertain the thought. They had come too far, suffered too much. The God she loved would not be so cruel.

"Rest easy, my love," she said softly. "Everything's going to be fine." She bit hard on her lip to stifle the trembling in her limbs. Instead of giving into her fear, she yanked her silk faille skirt out of the way and hurriedly began to tear strips from her white ruffled petticoat. Folding the lengths into a pad, she pressed them against the exit wound in his chest, ignoring Ramon's hiss of pain.

"The shot went all . . . all the way through," she said, blinking back tears at the agony etched into his features. "I-I suppose that's good, if we can get the bleeding to stop." *If.* Such a frightening word when someone you loved might be dying.

Dear Lord, she prayed, I'll do anything you ask—if you'll only just let him live.

"I-I need to move you a little. I'll try not to hurt you." With gentle care, she rolled him onto his side and placed a second thick cotton pad over the entrance wound in his back. By the time she finished binding the makeshift bandages in place, using a strip of petticoat wrapped around his broad chest, her hands were shaking so badly she could barely tie the knot.

Ramon's long fingers gently tightened around her wrist. "Do not be frightened, *querida*. We have made it this far, we will make it the rest of the way. We can do anything . . . as long as we are together."

A painful lump rose in her throat. "I didn't tell them, Ramon. I don't know who did, but it wasn't me—I swear it."

His eyes came to rest on her face. "Never once did I think that. You have never betrayed me. If one of us has failed the other, it is I who have failed you. Mine is the only betrayal."

She glanced away from him, her heart aching, unwilling to meet his gaze. "There's something I have to tell you. Something I should have told you long before this." She turned to look at him, uncertainty making the words come out soft and a little too strained. "I-I'm not who you think I am. My family wasn't wealthy . . . the way my uncle made everyone believe. I was born in a Pennsylvania mine patch. I'm nothing but a poor miner's daughter. Compared to your family's lineage, I'm not fit to carry a de la Guerra's shoes."

"I wondered how much time it would take before you told me."

A mist of tears touched her eyes. "You knew? How could you possibly have known?"

"You talked about it when you were ill, those days at Llano Mirada. It made no difference then. It does not matter now."

"But surely—"

He pressed a long dark finger against her lips. His hand smoothed her hair, slid under the thick dark auburn strands at the nape of her neck. Urging her toward him, he brought her mouth down to his for a soft, gentle kiss.

"*Te amo, mi corazon,*" he whispered. "*Te amo como jamas he amado.*" I love you, my heart. I love you as I have never loved before.

She started crying then. Big, salty tears that scalded her cheeks and splattered onto his bandaged chest. She loved him so much. She couldn't bear it if she lost him.

Ramon smiled with tenderness, lifted her chin with his hand. "Now is not the time for crying. You can cry along with my mother once we are safely back home."

Carly sniffed and her head came up. "You're going to ride?"

"*Si,* that is the only way we will get there."

"But you've lost so much blood, and—" Carly stiffened her spine. The thick cotton bandages were helping. The blood pumping out of the wound had begun to slow. If they could make it back to Las Almas, his mother and Tia could help her take care of him. They could make him well again—she would make sure of that herself. "Can you make it to your horse?"

"*Si.* For you, *querida,* I can do anything."

Leaning heavily against her, he climbed unsteadily to his feet and together they limped over to the horses. She helped him shove a boot into his stirrup. Ramon swayed forward and Carly heaved him up in the saddle. After tying her mare's reins so they wouldn't trail on the ground, she let the little horse roam free, knowing it would follow, then led the black stallion to a rock and climbed up behind Ramon. Wrapping her arms around him, she turned the stallion toward Las Almas, and they set off in that direction, the mare jogging along a few feet away, Carly praying she could handle the fiery black horse.

A hundred times, she thought they wouldn't make it. Or that even if they did, that it would be too late. The rough ground they crossed had his wound bleeding badly again, leaving him barely conscious from loss of blood, groaning with pain at each agonizing jolt of the horse's hooves. Several times, he slipped into blackness and only the hold she kept tightly around him kept him from falling off the horse.

All the while she kept praying, calling on God and the Blessed Virgin to help them get back home.

The night seemed endless. Darkness stretched like a curtain in front of them, the tiny sliver of moon all that lighted their way. The screech of an owl erupted from the shadows, followed by the howl of a wolf, and later the low-pitched growl of a bear somewhere ahead of them in the darkness.

Carly shivered to think what might happen if one of the prowling beasts attacked, or even frightened the stallion enough that she would lose her tenuous grip on the saddle. And the trail itself was a problem. They had taken a lesser-used path that was heavily overgrown and sometimes disappeared completely.

Just when she was certain she had somehow lost their way and would never get home, she crested the rise above the rancho and spotted the small adobe hacienda in the valley below.

"Thank God," she whispered, never meaning it more. Relief slid through her while renewed hope lifted her spirits. Nudging the big stallion forward, she headed down into the valley, and a worried Mariano rushed out to meet them. Two Hawks appeared, little Bajito yapping at his heels, followed by Tia and Mother de la Guerra.

"Santa Maria," Tia Teresa whispered, hurrying toward them on her long, spindly legs.

"Ramon's been shot, Tia. I'm afraid he's injured very badly." Even as Carly said the words, the ache returned to her throat. On the trail, she'd been able to keep her fears under control—there wasn't time for hysterics. Now that his family was there, it was all she could do not to crumble into a fit of tears.

Mariano and Two Hawks carried Ramon into the house.

"Don Ramon is strong," the boy said. "He will be all right, senora . . . now that you are home." He gave her an encouraging smile, then went out to rub down the lathered horses, grain them, and put them away. Tia helped Carly limp into the bedroom, then Carly and Ramon's mother began to strip off his bloody clothes while Tia Teresa went outside to help Blue Blanket boil water to cleanse the wound.

"It is not so bad as you think." Ramon's soft voice drifted up from the middle of the bed. "I have survived far worse." Now that he was home, some of his strength had returned. Though his face looked pale beneath his dark skin, his features drawn and tight, he smiled at Carly with warmth, and she reached out to clasp his hand.

"I am not going to die," he said, "though perhaps I should pretend to such a thing. I am not above doing so, if I thought it would bring you back home."

Her heart wrenched, tilted inside her. "I am home, Ramon. I'm never going to leave you again."

Tia and his mother exchanged silent glances, turned and slipped quietly out of the room.

Ramon squeezed her hand. "You cannot stay here, Cara, not tonight. Your uncle must not guess your involvement in this—nor mine. If he does, everything we have worked for will be lost."

Her eyes dimmed at his words. "But—but I can't just leave you—you're wounded! I have to stay here and take care of you."

He smiled at her with tenderness. "You know that I am right."

"My uncle won't be back until tomorrow. Surely I can stay until then."

Ramon watched her with such longing it made her heart turn over. "Do you think I wish for you to go? What I want is for you to stay here. If there was any way I could survive it, I would drag you into this bed and pull you beneath me. I would show you in a hundred different ways exactly how much I love you. Instead I must send you away."

Carly clutched his hand. "Let me stay."

"It is too dangerous for you to remain. The women will see to my wounds—you must not worry about that. I told you before, I have suffered far worse . . . and I have much to live for." He pressed a gentle kiss into the palm of her hand. "Two Hawks will bring fresh horses. Mariano will ride with you back to the ranch. When it is safe for you to return, I will be waiting."

The ache in her throat returned. Her eyes glazed with tears and a tight knot formed in her chest. She glanced at Ramon and even as he watched her, his eyes drifted closed, the loss of blood and fatigue dragging him once more into unconsciousness.

He might die tonight and she would not be with him.

He might die and she would never see him again.

He might live and her absence from del Robles would alert her uncle and surely get him hanged.

Her heart thudding dully, Carly bent over him and pressed a soft kiss on his lips, then she turned to see Tia and Mother de la Guerra standing in the doorway.

"We will care for him well," Tia promised, her own rheumy eyes clouded with tears.

"*Si*," said his mother, "but the best medicine for my son is that his wife will soon be home."

Carly blinked back a fresh round of wetness. "I don't want to go, but I must. I have to keep him safe."

The older woman nodded.

"I'll be back just as soon as I can." She hugged them as she made her way past, and they helped her outside. Standing in the yard, Two Hawks and Mariano waited with fresh horses. The stout vaquero lifted her up on a tall bay gelding, swung into the saddle of his own bay horse, and tied Sunflower's reins to his saddle horn.

They rode in silence back toward del Robles, neither of them voicing their worry for Ramon, or that Fletcher Austin might have already returned to the rancho and discovered her gone. What would she tell him if he had? What lie could she make him believe?

At the top of the hill overlooking the rancho, she traded horses, letting Mariano help her up on Sunflower's weary back, then she rode off down the hill to the stable, careful to skirt the bunkhouse and praying no one would see her.

Inside the barn, she slipped tiredly down from the mare, wincing at the pain in her twisted ankle. In the thin light streaming in through the window, she began to unsaddle her horse.

"I will do it, senora."

Carly jumped at the sound of the voice. "Jose! Dear God, you nearly frightened me to death."

"I am sorry. I did not mean to." The tall vaquero stepped up beside her and began to loosen the cinch. "Go inside the house," he said, turning to face her, "and do not worry—I will tell no one that you were gone."

Carly nervously wet her lips. "Thank you, Jose." He merely nodded as she slipped outside into the shadows of the barn and made her way quietly back to the house. Candelaria was waiting in Carly's bedroom when she arrived and quickly began helping her out of her clothes.

So many people to keep silent, and yet she believed they would.

"Hurry, senora. Senor Austin will be home any minute."

"He said he wouldn't be back until tomorrow," Carly corrected, thinking of her uncle's parting words.

"He will be here and soon. One of the men rode on ahead. He said your uncle was wounded in the fighting in San Juan."

"What!"

"That is what he said. I am afraid I know nothing more."

"Does the man know I was gone?"

"No. I told him you were sleeping, that I would tell you Senor Austin had been injured and that they were bringing him home."

"Thank you, Candelaria."

The girl only shrugged. "We are friends . . . and you are Don Ramon's wife."

Carly said nothing else, just slipped into her night rail and pink satin wrapper then went into her uncle's bedroom to see that it was prepared.

"Wake Rita," she told Candelaria. "Have her boil some water and gather whatever supplies we'll need to tend my uncle's wounds."

"*Si,* senora."

But surely he wasn't hurt badly, she thought, trying to imagine her seemingly invincible uncle any other way but issuing orders and bellowing commands. It was Ramon who was critically injured. It was her husband who needed her—and she wasn't there.

*C*hapter *T*wenty-two

*S*he would have been pacing if her ankle hadn't throbbed. Instead she sat before the window in her bedroom, her leg propped up on a pillow, worrying about Ramon and concerned for her uncle when the thunder of hoofbeats rent the air.

Tightening the sash of her pale pink wrapper, she limped to the door to meet the group of mounted men who pounded into the yard, raising a cloud of dust.

Near the front of the group, slumped over and tied onto his horse, the sight of her uncle's bloody figure sent a shaft of terror slicing through her.

"Dear Lord," she whispered through lips that went suddenly dry. She gripped the door frame at Cleve Sanders's approach.

"It's real bad, Miss McConnell."

Numbly she nodded. "Hurry, bring him inside so we can tend him." Sanders and three other men eased him down from the horse then carried his blood-soaked body up the back stairs and into the house. His breeches were ragged and dirty from the fall he had taken from his horse, his shirt stained crimson from the massive wound in his stomach. Another bloody hole seeped fluid from his chest.

"Take him into the bedroom." Carly bit hard on her lip, fighting back the strangled sounds of fear that threatened to erupt from her throat. Suddenly all the heated words they'd said, all the disagreements, all her uncle's machinations meant nothing. Uncle Fletcher was dying. He was hurting and he was frightened. In his own way he had been good to her. He was family. Her mother's only brother. And she was all he had.

"Caralee?" He said her name so softly she almost didn't hear him. She moved closer as the men laid him down on the deep feather mattress and began to pull off his boots.

"I'm right here, Uncle Fletcher." She forced a smile and brushed the tears from her cheeks, then reached over and caught his hand. She sat down in the chair beside him, her legs no longer steady. On the opposite side of the bed, Cleve Sanders helped Rita strip away his torn and bloody shirt and begin to wash his wounds, but all of them knew the effort was futile.

A low sound of pain struggled up from his throat. He dragged in a breath and slowly released it. "Didn't mean for it to end like . . . this." He stared up at her, his cheeks sunken with pain, his skin as waxen as a candle. "Wanted . . . to be sure you'd be . . . taken care of. Your mother . . . would have wanted that."

Her throat ached. She felt as if she might strangle. "You did your best, Uncle Fletcher."

"Hoped . . . you and Vincent . . ."

"I know. Don't try to talk. You have to save your strength." Dear God, he was dying! Somehow she couldn't make herself believe it.

"No . . . time for that." His weak hold on her hand tightened faintly. "Want you to know . . . in my own way I . . . loved you. Never said that to anyone. Not . . . my way. Never told your mother either. Always . . . regretted that."

She swallowed past the ache. "I love you, too, Uncle

Fletcher. In the years after Mama died, I was so lonely. I came here and you took that loneliness away."

He grimaced as a ripple of pain speared through him. "Wanted you to be happy . . . have the things your mother never had." He started coughing and a trickle of blood seeped out from between his thin blue lips.

Carly pressed a clean white handkerchief against his mouth to blot the red liquid away, her hands shaking, tears flooding her cheeks. "I am happy, Uncle. And I have everything I want—I promise you that."

He gazed at her with a measure of his old wily shrewdness. "You're talking about . . . the Spaniard. You're still . . . in love with him. Saw it almost from the start."

"I know how you feel about him, Uncle Fletcher, but—"

"He'll take care of you . . . never doubted that. Good man to have as a friend . . . bad man for an enemy."

Carly said nothing, just gripped her uncle's white-knuckled hand. "I wish this hadn't happened. I'd give anything if—"

"Just the way life is, honey. Lots of things . . . I wish I hadn't done. Things I wish I could . . . change."

A sob welled up, but only a soft sound escaped.

"Where's Rita?" he asked.

"I am here, Senor Fletcher." She hurried forward, her face ashen, tears flowing freely down her cheeks.

Fletcher sucked in a wheezing breath of air. "I'll miss you, woman. Never said that before, either."

Rita began to speak to him in Spanish, intoning him not to leave her, but already he was slipping away. Carly could almost feel his life-force dimming in front of her eyes.

"Caralee?" he whispered.

"Yes, Uncle Fletcher?"

"Be happy," he said on a final breath of air and then he was gone.

Rita bent over him, sobbing unashamedly against his

thick chest, but Carly slipped quietly out of the room. Walking numbly, hardly aware of the pain in her ankle, she moved past the low-burning lamps in the hall and made her way into the darkened living room. Sitting down in front of the embers that had burned to ashes in the huge rock hearth, she leaned wearily against the back of the horsehair sofa.

In one night her whole life had changed. Ramon was gravely injured and her uncle was dead. The sheriff still prowled the hills for Pedro Sanchez and the rest of the men.

They all still searched for El Dragón.

She bent her head, laced her fingers together, and said a quiet prayer for her uncle. When she finished, she said one for Ramon and the rest of his men. A shuffling noise intruded, then voices sounded in the hall.

Cleve Sanders paused beside three of his men. "At least we got the filthy bastard who done it."

Carly stiffened on the sofa. "What—what did you say?"

"Sorry, Miss McConnell, I didn't know you were in there."

"That's all right. What were you saying?"

"I was just telling the boys we got the man who murdered your uncle. Riley Wilkins killed the Spanish Dragon."

Were they talking about Ramon? Had something happened at Las Almas after she had left there? Carly's heart constricted. Dear God, it couldn't be true! "Wh-what happened?"

"We were following them up a trail north of the river. The outlaws split up and we lost them in the hills, but the leader circled back. He climbed up in the rocks and ambushed your uncle."

"How did you know it was El Dragón?" she asked carefully.

"I seen him that day we took Llano Mirada. We were with Sheriff Layton when they carted him off to jail."

"And that was the same man who killed Uncle Fletcher?"

"That's right. Riley Wilkins shot him deader'n a slaughtered steer."

Carly said nothing more. Just got shakily up from her seat in front of the empty hearth and made her way unsteadily down the hallway toward her room. She wished she could go to Ramon, tell him her uncle was dead and so was his cousin, but now was not the time. She couldn't take the chance of leading them to Ramon. If they discovered he was wounded, they would know he'd been with the men at the jail that night.

She would have to send Jose to find out how he was. She was certain now that she could trust him. Tomorrow afternoon, perhaps she'd be able to go to him herself. Now that her uncle was dead, people wouldn't be surprised when she returned to the care of her husband.

Numb clear to her bones, more frightened and alone than she had felt since her mother died, Carly went inside and slowly closed the door to her room.

Ramon tossed restlessly in the deep feather mattress. He had slept off and on, weakened by loss of blood, his condition growing worse in the hours since his return to Las Almas. By mid-afternoon of the following day, a fever raged through his bloodstream and he passed in and out of consciousness, only dimly aware of his surroundings.

Jose brought word of his condition to Carly, who wrung her hands and fought back tears, who paced and fretted, but knew she dared not leave the rancho. Not with Sheriff Jeremy Layton waiting for her in a chair in her uncle's study.

He came to his feet when she walked in, frowned at the slight limp she tried to conceal, then gave her a polite nod of his head.

"Real sorry to hear about your uncle, ma'am."

"Thank you, Sheriff Layton."

"I know this isn't a very good time, but there's a couple of questions I need to ask."

She sat down in the chair next to him, straightening her full black bombazine skirts around her. "Of course. I'll be happy to help any way that I can." Adjusting the prim white lace on her cuffs, she tried not to look as nervous as she felt. "What is it you wish to know?"

The sheriff returned to his seat. "I'm gonna be real straight with you, ma'am. Your uncle had a mighty strong suspicion your husband was involved, some way or other, with the outlaw who killed him. He figured maybe the don was passing information, possibly even rode on some of his raids. I thought maybe that had something to do with the reason you left him and came back here."

"I'm afraid I don't know what you mean."

"What I'm saying is if the don was involved in something you didn't approve of, maybe that was the reason you wanted the marriage annulled."

So he knew about the proceedings her uncle had started. Then again Jeremy Layton seemed to know just about everything.

Carly forced her eyes to his face. "Actually, I had already decided to go back to my husband before my uncle was killed. The truth is I never should have left him in the first place."

"I know it ain't exactly my business, but it would surely set my mind to rest if you would tell me why you did."

She fumbled through her mind, groping for an answer he would believe—one that didn't involve Angel de la Guerra. "I—I, to be honest, Sheriff Layton, I was jealous. I discovered my husband had been keeping a mistress— before we were married, of course. My feelings were hurt, I suppose. Now, well, we've straightened the whole matter out. The woman no longer plays a part in my husband's life, and he has convinced me I'm the only woman he needs." She straightened in her chair. "I'm sorry to disappoint you, Sheriff, but my husband does not now, nor ever has had anything to do with the outlaw El Dragón."

The sheriff unwound his long lanky frame and stood up. "Well, then, I guess that puts this matter to an end . . . long as there ain't no more trouble."

"What about the others? Won't you and the vigilantes be going after them?"

He shook his blond head. "I figure they're miles from here by now. Without their leader, I don't think they'll be back." He smiled. "Glad to hear you and the don have worked things out. The truth is, I've always kinda liked him."

"I'll give him your best," she said, also standing up.

Jeremy Layton plucked his wide-brimmed felt hat from the back of the chair. "Guess . . . the way things turned out . . . we'll never know the fellow's real name."

"You mean the Spanish Dragon?"

He nodded. "Nobody round here seems to know him. Leastwise if they do, they ain't sayin'. Then again, maybe it's better that way." He gave her a probing look Carly didn't dare respond to, then twirled his hat in his hands as he headed for the door. "I suppose now that Fletcher's gone, you and the don will be livin' here at del Robles."

Carly's head came up. She stopped and stood stock still. "What did you say?"

"Seems only logical. Place is yours now."

"Rancho del Robles is mine?"

He nodded. "Sure is, ma'am. That was something Fletcher Austin made no bones about. He said anything ever happened to him, del Robles belonged to you. He told me more than once that you were his only kin."

"Yes . . . I suppose I am. Things happened so quickly, I hadn't even thought about it."

"I'm sure he took care of it nice and legal. Might be

something in his desk. You get a chance, you go through his papers. 'Course one of them fancy lawyer friends of his up in San Francisco will probably be handlin' the details. Whatever the case, I'd bet my last gold eagle, the place belongs to you."

Carly just stared at him, hardly able to absorb the words. "Thank you, Sheriff Layton. I'll make a point to do as you suggest."

Rancho del Robles was very likely hers. Good heavens, she could hardly believe it. And yet she wanted to—more with each second that passed.

They buried Fletcher Austin late that afternoon. He would have liked the pomp of a big funeral service. He would have liked his wealthy friends from San Francisco to have been in attendance. There wasn't time for them to get there, and as far as Carly was concerned, dead was dead. Her worry now was for the living.

While the cooper who worked at del Robles built a sturdy oak coffin, her uncle's body was washed and made ready, and he was dressed in his finest black broadcloth suit. Carly, Rita Salazar, Cleve Sanders, and the dozens of people who worked on the rancho stood at the top of a hill beneath an ancient oak overlooking the hacienda. It was a glorious spot to face eternity. She knew at least she had pleased him in the choice of his final place of rest.

It was all the lovely valley owed him. More than what he should have had, she admitted—after the ugly truth she had discovered just that morning.

Still, he was her uncle. As ruthless a man as he was, she had cared about him. She cried as she stood at the grave and Riley Wilkins solemnly read verses from the Bible. If only things could have been different. When the service was ended, everyone walked back to the house, where a huge assortment of food had been set out: chicken en mole

and fresh cooked tortillas, platters of steamed corn, fried
potatoes, and stewed meats. A bullock roasted on a spit
over the coals. There was wine and sangria to drink and
homemade custards and chocolate rolled in tortillas.

As soon as she had received everyone's condolences,
Carly slipped off to her room to change into her riding
clothes. She had waited long enough. She was going to Las
Almas, she told the others, returning to her husband. She
needed him, now that her uncle was gone. And she loved
him.

All of which was the truth.

She didn't let them know how worried she was about
him, that with every step her little mare took in his direction, her heart ached for Ramon.

Ramon stirred on the bed and his eyes popped open. His
shoulder throbbed and the skin around the wound burned like
a fiery brand. But his head no longer pounded and his skin felt
cool to the touch, no longer hot and clammy. In the night he
had thrashed off the sheet and his naked body sprawled with
familiar abandon on the clean white muslin sheet.

For a moment he said nothing, just enjoyed the fact he
was going to live, the sight of a sky outside the window
brightening from yellow to blue, and the quiet breathing of
the woman who slept in a chair beside his bed.

He knew she had come, had sensed the very instant she
had walked into the room, yet he hadn't really seen her.
His skin had been so hot he was sure it would burst like a
cooked potato. His eyes wouldn't open and he didn't have
the strength to lift his head.

Then he'd felt something cool against his forehead,
heard his wife's sweet voice soothing his troubled sleep.
She wasn't going to leave him, he'd thought vaguely. Caralee was here to stay.

He'd rested easier after that. The fire in his body burned

itself out, allowing him to sleep, and even as he did, his strength had begun to return.

As quietly as he could, careful not to wake her, he pulled himself into a sitting position, propped his back against the headboard and reached for the water glass on the table beside the bed. He rinsed his mouth and drank the rest, then ran a hand through his tousled black hair. He glanced in his wife's direction, noticed her blouse had come unbuttoned, and caught a glimpse of rounded pale flesh. His body stirred. He pulled the sheet up over his growing arousal.

Yes, he was definitely feeling better.

Still, he didn't want to disturb her. She needed her rest, and he liked just sitting here beside her. He smiled at the way her dark copper hair gleamed in the early morning sunlight, itched to pull the pins that held it in a coil at the nape of her neck then stroke his fingers through it. He wondered how long she would make him suffer before she declared him well enough for a return to his bed.

He grinned at that. Not nearly as long as she would like, he vowed.

She stirred on the chair beside him and her eyes slowly opened. Bright leaf green orbs fixed on his face. "Ramon?"

"Buenos dias, querida."

"Ramon!" She was off the chair in an instant, stopped just short of hurling herself into his arms. Instead she frantically reached out to touch his forehead, testing the heat with her palm. "Your fever's broken!"

"Si, mi amor. I am well on my way to recovery." He looked at his wife's ruby lips and his shaft stirred again beneath the sheets. He grinned wickedly. "Already I am almost back to normal."

Carly eyed him from head to foot, noticing the wavy black hair curling over his forehead and the muscles rippling across his bare chest when he moved. "How can a man who's been injured as badly as you possibly look as good as you do?"

He laughed at that then winced at the pain that speared through his shoulder. "I am glad you think so, since already I am planning your seduction."

Carly grinned. "My, you are feeling better." The soft smile faded as she took his hand and sat down beside him on the bed. "I've been so worried. I'm sorry I couldn't come sooner."

"It was better that you waited. Everything is all right at Rancho del Robles?"

Carly shook her head. "There's so much I have to tell you."

"Tell me you will be staying at Las Almas. That is all I wish to hear."

Her grip on his hand grew tighter. "Are you sure you're feeling up to this? Maybe you should rest for a while. I don't want you to tire yourself out."

"Tell me, *chica*. I wish to hear what you have to say."

"My uncle's dead. He died in the fighting outside San Juan Bautista. Angel was killed as well."

"Angel is dead?"

She nodded. "They still believe he was you. It's over, Ramon. The sheriff says they aren't going after the others, so unless there's more trouble, all of this is ended."

His head fell back against the pillow, relief flooding through him, yet suddenly he felt fatigued.

"You were right about my uncle," Carly said softly. "The day of his funeral, the sheriff came. He suggested I go through my uncle's papers. I found a ring of keys in his desk to a set of locked drawers. In one of them, I found a file containing a record of his bank drafts as far back as 1851. There was one in particular, made out to a man named Henry Cheevers. The amount was two thousand dollars. I might have thought nothing of it, except for the month it was written—April of 1853—and the fact that Uncle Fletcher took title to Rancho del Robles less than thirty days later. In another file, I discovered Henry Cheevers was on the U.S. Board of Land Commissions."

He quietly absorbed the words, but a slight tension had settled around him.

"I think my uncle bribed Henry Cheevers to deny your family's claim to Rancho del Robles. Instead, the land was sold to Thomas Garrison for almost nothing. There was a draft to Garrison as well, then a separate one for the purchase of the rancho. Even with the bribes, Uncle Fletcher bought the land for a tenth of its worth." A mist of tears glazed her eyes. "My uncle stole your land, Ramon, exactly like you said."

I am bounden for to love thee,
And my constancy I'll show;
O the troubles of a fellow,
When he loves a woman so!

What hard knocks befall a fellow,
When he falls in love at sight!
Takes to wine and gets befuddled,
Goes to bed without a bite.

Do not kill me, do not kill me,
With a pistol or a knife!
Kill me, rather, with thine eyes, love,
With those red lips take my life.

Old Spanish Ballad
"El Capotin" ("The Rain Song")

*E*pilogue

*T*hey were having a *fandango*. It was a special evening
planned by Ramon, though he'd been strangely quiet about
it. He'd simply said there would be a grand fiesta to cele-
brate a grand occasion. Carly wasn't sure what that occasion was, but she didn't care. She had a surprise of her own
for Ramon.

The sounds of music drifted toward her. Outside the
window, musicians played Spanish guitar and violin, entertaining the guests that had already arrived while Carly
sat fidgeting on the tapestry stool in front of the mirror,
wishing Candelaria would hurry and finish her hair.

"Can you not sit still?" the Spanish girl scolded. "If you
wish me to hurry, you must not squirm so much."

"I can't help it. I should have been ready long before
this. Ramon will be wondering where I am."

"You should have let Rita oversee the preparations, as
the don suggested, instead of trying to do so much of it
yourself."

"I only helped with the food. I wanted to be sure there
was enough."

The little maid simply frowned till Carly stifled her nervous movements. Six months had passed since the death of
her uncle. Several weeks after, the will had been read,

leaving the ranch to her as the sheriff had said. But documents had to be drawn, there were business accounts to be transferred into her name, a dozen different papers to sign. Two months after Uncle Fletcher's death, she and Ramon moved back to Rancho del Robles, and Ramon took over the running of the rancho.

His mother and aunt decided to remain in the small adobe house at Las Almas. It was only a short ride away and the older women had come to think of the place as home.

"Rancho del Robles is no longer where I wish to live," his mother said. "There I see your father's hand in everything I do. The memories are too painful. I am more at peace here." Mariano remained as well, and Blue Blanket and some of the vaqueros. The rest of the men, including Pedro Sanchez, returned to Rancho del Robles.

Several times over the past few months, Carly had spoken to Ramon about ownership of the rancho, but he refused to discuss it. Legally, the rancho was hers, he said. It was enough for him that he and his people could return to their home.

It wasn't enough for Carly. She meant to rectify the wrong that had been done and tonight was the perfect opportunity.

"We are almost finished, senora." When Candelaria stepped back to survey her handiwork, Carly stood up and walked over to the cheval glass mirror.

Smoothing her full silk skirts, she surveyed her image, satisfied the décolletage of the ruffled bodice was low enough but not too low, glad that her waist looked so small, pleased with the long dark auburn ringlets Candelaria had so artfully arranged on one bare shoulder. "It's a lovely color, don't you think?"

"*Si,* senora. The same bright green as your eyes."

"I hope Ramon will be pleased."

Candelaria smiled. "Your husband is pleased by whatever it is that you do. I only wish I could find a man who would love me half as much as the don loves you."

Carly felt the heat rising into her cheeks. "I hope he knows how much I love him."

The dark-haired serving girl just smiled. Lifting a beautiful black lace mantilla that matched the trim on her dress, she helped Caralee drape it over the high combs inlaid with mother-of-pearl that Ramon had given her as a gift earlier that evening.

"I know it's silly, but I'm nervous. I can't imagine why."

"Perhaps it is because the don has planned this night especially for you."

Carly turned to face her friend. "Do you really think so?"

"You will find out soon enough. Go now. Do not keep your impatient husband waiting any longer."

Carly left the big master bedroom she and Ramon now shared, went down the hall and into the *sala*. Her handsome husband was pacing the floor in front of the window, the wide red-satin-lined bottoms of his tight black breeches flaring out over his polished black boots with each turn.

He smiled the moment he saw her. "Aye, *querida* . . ." His dark eyes shone with pleasure. "The sight of you steals my breath."

Carly smiled softly. "I'm glad you like the gown."

"Mostly I like the woman who is wearing it." He raked her with a too-bold glance that made the heat creep into her cheeks. "But come, there will be time for that later. For now we have guests. Tonight is *fandango!*"

Together they walked out of the house onto the patio. It was decorated with colorful paper lanterns and dozens of handmade paper flowers. Streamers hung from the branches of the trees, and the tables bore garlands of roses. Musicians dressed in black *calzonevas* and short *charro* jackets stood at the end of the wooden dance floor playing a Spanish serenade.

Already the party was well underway. The Herreras, the Juarezes, the Montoyas, and dozens of others already had arrived. Don Alejandro de Estrada and the Micheltorenas had come from Monterey. Vaqueros—Two Hawkes beaming with pride that he was accepted among them—had come from ranchos as far away as San Miguel. Many still sat their horses, as was the custom, others had dismounted and begun to join in the dancing.

Ramon's aunt and mother were there, laughing and happy as Carly had rarely seen them. It was Tia Teresa who spoke to her first.

"It is a wonderful wedding fiesta, no?"

"Wedding fiesta?" Carly flushed. "I don't think—"

"*Si*, Tia," Ramon said with a smile, "it is a fine celebration of our marriage."

Carly looked up at Ramon. "That's what this is? A wedding reception?"

"*Si*, that is what you would call it. I wanted my neighbors and friends to meet the woman I married. Like any new husband, I wished to show off my bride."

Carly's throat went tight. Suddenly she understood why he had planned the evening so carefully. It was his way of letting the people he cared about know how much she meant to him. He was telling them that she was the woman he wanted. That she was an Anglo did not matter. She was now a de la Guerra, and he was proud that she was his wife.

"Thank you." Tears rose in her eyes. Ramon must have seen them for he lifted her chin and gave her a feather-soft kiss.

"I am glad that you are pleased. I only wish I had done it long before this. Now come. There are people I wish you to meet and then I will teach you to dance La Jota."

And so they began to mingle with their guests. Ramon proudly introduced her to the people she didn't already know, reacquainted her with those she had already met, then they joined in the dancing.

Laughing with pleasure, they danced one song after another, Ramon patiently teaching her the steps until she was finally able to master them. Friends cracked colored *cascarones,* hollow eggs filled with gold and silver tinsel scented with cologne, over their heads as they would have a true bride and groom, and the bits of glittery paper scattered over their hair and clothes.

The vaqueros coaxed Ramon into drinking some of their fiery *aguardiente* and the potent alcohol had him laughing and joking, joining in the bawdy songs they'd begun to sing.

He wasn't really drunk, she saw as he came to take her hand and lead her back to the dance floor, just high on the goodness of life, the joy of being with old and dear friends in times that were sweeter than they had been in years.

Smiling at her softly, he motioned to the musicians and the tempo of the music changed. One by one, the other couples stopped dancing and turned toward Ramon, forming a circle around him.

He lifted Carly's hand, bent over and pressed his lips against her palm. "This I dance for you," he said, his voice suddenly husky, then he raised his elegant dark hands above his head.

Clapping once, twice, stomping a boot heel down on the wooden dance floor, he arched his back and gracefully began dancing to the beat of the music, his boot heels rapping hard again and again. Lantern light sparkled on the silver conchos down the side of tight black breeches, gleamed on the silver-embroidered lapels of the *charro* jacket that barely reached his narrow waist.

His dark eyes fixed on Carly, he held his head high, his

gaze as fierce as the night sky over their heads. It seemed to bore into her, hold her as captive as she had been those days in the mountains. His hands moved senuously, gracefully, and it was almost as if he touched her.

Her breathing quickened, making her breasts rise and fall above her low-cut gown. Her heart fluttered, started an uneven pounding inside her chest. Her eyes moved down his body, taking in the breadth of his shoulders, the flatness of his stomach, the sinews in his hard-muscled thighs that tightened with each of his graceful movements. His breeches were so snug they outlined the heavy bulge of his sex, leaving no doubt of his virility.

She wanted to reach out, to touch his powerful chest, to feel those elegant hands running over her flesh, stroking her, easing deeply inside her. She wanted to taste the heat of his mouth over hers, to know the scorching fire of his hard length thrusting into her core.

Her nipples peaked, began to ache beneath the edge of the ruffle flirting with the top of her bodice. His eyes fixed there the moment they crested and a corner of his sensuous mouth curved up. He knew the power of his dancing. He had used it before, she realized, a thread of jealousy sliding through her, and yet it also heated her blood to think what he meant to do.

The music peaked, increasing in tempo, building with a force that matched the heat blazing through her. Ramon twirled, stomped his feet, and clapped his hands. When he arched his back, his maleness thrust forward, and a surge of dampness gathered in the place between her legs. Unconsciously, her tongue touched the corner of her mouth, ran along her bottom lip, and Ramon's eyes darkened with hunger. There was no mistaking that look, not by anyone in the crowd. He wanted her. It was the hunger of a man for his bride, and no one there doubted that Ramon meant to have her.

She might have blushed if she hadn't been so caught up. Instead, as the song came to an end, as his boots came crashing down with greater and greater speed and the crowd began to clap and shout in frenzied rhythm, she simply moved closer, her eyes still locked with his. The final crescendo came, his heels came pounding down and his head snapped up, but his eyes never left her face. He never blinked, never wavered, just stood waiting, beckoning her to come to him.

The crowd stepped back as she walked toward him, stopping just inches from his lean hard frame. Raising on tiptoe, she slid her arms around his neck, felt a hand clamp around her waist, then he was crushing her against him, bending her backwards, taking her mouth in a fiery kiss that had all of them whooping and shouting.

She was breathless by the time he ended the kiss, barely aware that he was lifting her into his arms and striding away, carrying her off toward the house. She did blush then, the heat rising into her cheeks, but also rushing into the tips of her breasts.

"You were wonderful," she whispered, "beautiful . . ."

"It is you who are beautiful, *querida,* and I am the luckiest man in the world." He nudged open the door to the house with his boot and carried her into the entry. It was lit by low-burning lamps, and the soft glow of candles beckoned down the hall. He strode in that direction, entering their bedroom, which smelled of the fresh cut flowers sitting in the cut glass vase on the dresser. Petals were strewn on the bed.

Ramon pulled the pins from her hair, letting the heavy dark auburn mass cascade down her back. "Do you know how much I love you?"

Carly felt the sting of tears. "Yes, my beloved, I know. Tonight you have shown me how much."

A corner of his sensuous mouth curved up. "I have only ̇ st begun to show you. It will be morning before you finally know the true extent of my feelings." With that he began to undress her, but Carly eased gently away.

"First there is something I have to do." Moving toward the dresser, she opened the drawer and removed a folded piece of paper. She returned to his side and held it out to him,

"What is that?" he asked.

"Tonight you gave me something more precious than anything I've ever owned. You made me a true de la Guerra; you gave me a place in your life."

"I gave you only what you deserve. What I should have given you before."

"No, you gave me more than that. You gave me friends who care about me. You gave me a family to love. You made me feel that I belong. Now there's something I want to give you." She nudged the paper into his hands. "Go on, open it."

He carefully unfolded the stiff piece of parchment. GRANT DEED, it said in elegant ink blue script.

"This is the title to Rancho del Robles." He looked up at her, dark turbulence gathered in his eyes. "The deed says the rancho belongs to me."

"That's right. It belongs to its rightful owner. That man is you."

"I cannot—"

"Think of Andreas, Ramon. Think of your father." She reached out and touched him, rested a hand on his cheek. "I'm your wife. I'll be here to share it with you, and soon I'll give you sons. But the land belongs to you, as it should have from the start." Tears stung her eyes, began to slide down her cheeks. *"Te amo, mi corazon. Te amo como jamas he amado."* I love you, my heart. I love you as I never have loved before.

Ramon swept her into his arms, the muscles in his throat constricting, his heart near to bursting with love for her. Carly clung to him as he kissed the side of her neck, arched toward him when he slid his hands inside the ruffled emerald silk to cup and stroke her breast.

In minutes he had stripped off her clothes and his own, and carried her over to the bed. He meant to take her gently, cursed when instead he found himself plunging inside her with fiery abandon. Yet it seemed to be exactly what she wanted. She begged for his bold caress, his driving heat and passion. She demanded to be swept up in his hunger, that he satisfy her own.

When the fury of their lovemaking subsided, they lay quietly together, arms and legs entwined, listening to the sounds of laughter and music still throbbing outside their window. Then he took her again, gently this time, arousing her slowly, then filling her again and again until she reached her peak and softly cried out his name. Holding her into the circle of his arms, he watched the flush gradually fade from her cheeks.

"I love you," she said on a slow breath of air.

Ramon stroked her hair, kissed the silky strands at her temple. "As I love you, *mi vida.*" My life. "Never once did I believe I would be such a fortunate man." He smiled at her softly, awed by the incredible gift he had been given.

He had found a woman of strength and beauty to love throughout the years. The woman of his heart. She had seen his lands returned—Rancho del Robles would belong to his sons, and those of his sons after that.

He had found peace at last through the woman he held in his arms.

Ramon had finally come home.

Author's Note

The 1850s in California were known as the Decade of the Desperado. Joaquin Murieta and dozens of men like him, many of them displaced Californios who had been mistreated by the Anglos or robbed of their lands, raided and pillaged for years before they were stopped.

Harry Love was the man given credit for killing Murieta. I took the liberty of pitting him against Ramon de la Guerra as well. I also took some license with the town of San Juan Bautista in that some of the buildings I mentioned were not built for several more years. However, the place was then, and still is, the epitome of the early Spanish town.

The Indian words I used were Yocuts's, though in early California each small tribe had its own separate language. It was an exciting place to be in the fifties, a time of growth and tremendous opportunity. I hope you enjoyed Ramon and Carly's story and that I'll have the chance to write another novel set in this fascinating period.